ara Colter shares her life in beautiful British Columbia, anada, with her husband, nine horses and one small omeranian with a large attitude. She loves to hear from aders, and you can learn more about her and contact er through Facebook.

ichelle Major grew up in Ohio but dreamed of living he mountains. Soon after graduating with a degree in rnalism, she pointed her car west and settled in olorado. Her life and house are filled with one great isband, two beautiful kids, a few furry pets and several ell-behaved reptiles. She's grateful to have found her ssion writing stories with happy endings. Michelle ves to hear from her readers at michellemajor.com

Also by Cara Colter

Interview with a Tycoon
Meet Me Under the Mistletoe
The Pregnancy Secret
Soldier, Hero...Husband?
Housekeeper Under the Mistletoe
The Wedding Planner's Big Day
Swept into the Tycoon's World
Snowbound with the Single Dad
His Convenient Royal Bride
Cinderella's Prince Under the Mistletoe

Also by Michelle Major

Falling for the Wrong Brother
Second Chance in Stonecreek
A Stonecreek Christmas Reunion
Anything for His Baby
A Baby and a Betrothal
Always the Best Man
Christmas on Crimson Mountain
Romancing the Wallflower
Sleigh Bells in Crimson
Coming Home to Crimson

TEMPTED BY THE SINGLE DAD

CARA COLTER

FORTUNE'S FRESH START

MICHELLE MAJOR

MILLS & BOON

First Published in Great Britain 2020
by Mills & Boon, an imprint of HarperCollinsPublishers,
1 London Bridge Street, London, SE1 9GF

Special thanks and acknowledgement are given to Michelle Major for her contribution to *The Fortunes of Texas: Rambling Rose* continuity.

ISBN: 978-0-263-27862-0

0120

FSC
www.fsc.org

MIX
Paper from
responsible sources
FSC™ C007454

This book is produced from independently certified FSC™ paper to ensure responsible forest management.

For more information visit: www.harpercollins.co.uk/green

Printed and bound in Spain
by CPI, Barcelona

TEMPTED BY THE SINGLE DAD

CARA COLTER

To the brother I found in my place of endless summer,
Jeffrey Byron Werle.

CHAPTER ONE

It was a perfect moment. Of course, if there was one thing Alicia Cook had a right to distrust, that was it. Perfect moments.

Still, with a sigh, and a sip of her lime-infused club soda, Allie gave herself over to it. The setting sun was gilding the foam on the ocean waves, and turning the beach sand to pure, luminous gold. From the hanging porch swing in the shadows of her covered veranda, she observed as the daytime crowds dissipated.

Now, one last family remained, the father deflating a humungous ride-on dragon water toy, the mother shaking out a picnic blanket and calling the children back from the water's edge as she packed the remains of their day into an oversize basket.

A pang of pure longing hovered at the edges of Allie's perfect moment, so she shifted her focus. Farther down the beach a couple strolled, hand in hand.

The sense of longing intensified.

"Don't believe a word he says," Allie muttered, watching through narrowed eyes as they stopped, leaned into each other and he nuzzled her ear and said something to her that made her laughter carry up the beach.

Allie's muttered words were a defense, of course, against all that weakness that was still there, even though she, of all people, should know better than to long for dangerous things.

Perfect moments. To not be alone. To share life. To be deeply connected…there, her perfect moment was gone. She looked away from the couple, ignored the family and took a determined sip of her drink, concentrating furiously on the beauty of the setting sun, hoping to get it back.

No, the moment had been as iridescent—and as fragile—as a soap bubble blown from a child's wand. It was gone.

She set down her drink, leaned over and drew her guitar from a shadowed corner.

"Perfect moments do not pay bills, anyway," Allie told herself sternly. The contract to produce a jingle was the practical approach to solving her financial difficulties.

The guitar, however, was unmoved by the urgency she felt. She ran her thumb coaxingly down the six strings—E, B, G, D, A, E—but the guitar refused to be seduced. The instrument was acting like a friend who was mad at her, silent, refusing to speak.

It was almost a relief—a reprieve—when Allie heard a muffled noise through the patio door that opened into the cottage behind her. What was that? Was someone at her front door? She strained her ears. That had to be her imagination.

The very same imagination that would not give her a song, was quite happy to indulge her fears, she noticed.

But as she strained to hear, she could have sworn the sound she was hearing was very real. She was hearing the creaky front door handle being tried!

A recent newspaper article had been pinned to the community bulletin board in front of the post office. Mimi Roberts's villa—located just down the beach—had experienced a break-in. An audacious thief had come in the front door while Mimi was home, but fortunately for the well-known celebrity, she was out back enjoying her deck. A Sugar Cone Beach police spokesman said there had been several similar break-ins in the neighborhoods surrounding the beach community and urged people to lock those front doors, even while they were at home.

Honestly, Allie had had trouble sleeping ever since, awaking to every sound, too hot because she was keeping the doors and windows firmly locked. No wonder she couldn't write a simple jingle. Sleep deprived.

A muffled *bang* made her jump. Okay. It was definitely her front door. Being kicked in? No, probably something way less threatening, like a newspaper being thrown up against it.

You don't get the paper, a little voice insisted on reminding her.

Still Allie tried to reason with herself. It would take an extraordinarily unambitious thief to choose her little cottage for break-and-enter purposes. The end of Sugar Cone Beach that was farthest away from her had long since gone to developers. High-end hotels and condos, with their main floor restaurants and shops, vied for every inch of space along that baby-powder-fine stretch of sand.

But the beachfront properties at this end of Sugar Cone Beach—a sheltered bay—were largely single-family homes that had become the enclave of the very wealthy, like Mimi Roberts. For the past twenty years extravagant beach houses had been popping up here. The glass, concrete and steel behemoths rose out of the sand on either side of Allie.

And there she sat, in the middle of them all, in a sagging and tiny gray-shingled cottage, that had been her grandmother's for as long as she could remember.

Gram. Allie felt the ache in her throat that momentarily overrode the adrenaline that was beginning to pump through her. Her Gram was the one person who had stuck by her, believed in her and never given up on her.

Gram was gone now but the cottage that was so beloved to them both had been her final gift to Allie.

If Allie could hold on to it. The taxes alone took her breath away. And every day, someone came, ignored the unfriendly sign that said No Soliciting and knocked on her front door. They were developers and real estate agents, and people just passing by, putting temptation in front of her, offering her ridiculous sums of money to sell the one place in the world where Allie felt safe and hidden from prying eyes.

And where the love of her grandmother remained, as comforting as a hug.

There was definitely somebody at the door but Allie calmed herself with the rationale it was probably not a thief, though it was unlikely to be a real estate agent at this time of day, either. Whoever it was, they weren't ringing the bell.

The bell hasn't worked for three weeks, Allie told herself. *It's not a thief.*

But whoever it was, they weren't giving up, either.

Allie put down her guitar, not unaware that she felt relieved for a distraction, no matter how unpleasant that distraction might be. She got up, and went through the back into the cottage, not sure of the proper protocol for a would-be break-in.

Should she make lots of noise and throw on all the lights so it was apparent someone was home? Or should she tiptoe up to the door and peek out the front window?

Coming from the brightness outside into the cottage was like being plunged into a mine shaft. It had originally been a fisherman's place—the only one that remained on this stretch of beachfront. Back in the 1920s, when it was built, no thought at all was given to such frivolous concerns as where to place windows to take most advantage of the view. Windows would have been regarded as a luxury in those days.

And so the kitchen was in the back of the house, cramped and dark. Faucets dripped and cabinet doors hung crookedly, and the painted wooden floor was chipping. Despite all that, there was a determined cheeriness to the space, a laid-back beach vibe that Allie adored.

One summer she and her grandmother, in an attempt to brighten things up, had painted all the cabinets sunshine yellow, and they had liked the color so much they had done the kitchen table, too. They had installed a backsplash of handmade sea-themed tile, and hung homemade curtains with a pink flamingo motif.

Off the kitchen, there was a narrow hall, painted turquoise, with Allie's childhood art hung gallery style. There were three tiny bedrooms on one side of the hall, each holding little more than a bed, a bureau and a nightstand. Her grandmother, a quilter, had loved fabric and every closet in the whole cottage was stuffed with it. Allie could not bring herself to throw a single remnant away. Each bed was adorned with a handmade quilt. Allie's favorite, the double wedding ring pattern, was on her own small bed.

Still tiptoeing, Allie followed the hallway to the front door, and the arched opening to the living room, where a paned picture window looked onto the street. The furniture and the wooden floors, worn to gray, sagged equally with age and good use.

In the heyday of her career—imagine being twenty-three years old and the heyday of your career was already over—Allie had been in many houses that looked like the ones on either side of her. Houses that were open plan, with light spilling in huge windows, and stainless steel appliances bigger than most restaurants required. They had miles of granite countertops, gorgeous beams and sleek furniture. Not one of them had ever made her feel this way.

Home.

That's what she needed to remember about the career that had soared like a shooting star, and then fizzled even more quickly, and that's what she needed to remember when another million-dollar offer was made. Neither success nor money could make you feel at home. She steeled herself to the possibility of temptation as she moved past the door to have a peek out the window.

But before she made it past, there was another thump. Someone *had* kicked the door! Her heart flew into double time. Then, to Allie's horror, the door creaked open an inch. Allie stopped and stared, her heart in her throat. Her first instinct, the one she had reasoned herself out of, had been correct.

Home invader.

She was sure she had locked the front door since seeing the news report.

Not that it mattered. Locked or not, her space was being invaded! Her safe place was being threatened.

In one motion, she reached out and grabbed the nearest thing she could lay hands on—a heavy statue, one of her grandmother's favorites. It was a bronze of a donkey, looking forlorn and unkempt. Weapon firmly in hand, Allie threw her weight against the opening door, trying to force it closed again.

Sam Walker was beyond exhaustion. He'd been late getting away. The traffic heading to the beaches of Southern California, in anticipation of the upcoming Fourth of July holiday, had been horrendous. And his traveling companions were cantankerous.

The key had been sticky, but finally worked. But despite trying to persuade it with his foot—twice—the door remained stuck.

He was used to the cottage being a touch temperamental, but his patience was at a breaking point. Sam had had quite enough of cantankerous *anything* for one day. The floorboard beneath the door was probably swollen with moisture or age. He'd put it—and the lock—on his list of things to fix while he was here. Not even in the door yet, and he had a list of things that needed doing. *Normal, mature man things. What a relief.*

The door had finally opened a miserly inch and then jammed stubbornly. Sam's patience broke. He put his shoulder against it and shoved, hard, two years on the college football offensive line finally put to good use.

The door flew open, and his momentum catapulted him through the opening. He was rendered blind by the sudden entrance into cool darkness, in sharp contrast to the outside, where the world was being washed with end-of-day light.

The hair on the back of his neck rose when he heard a startled grunt somewhere in the dark space in front of him. He squinted, his muscles bunching. Hadn't he seen on the news there had been break-ins along this stretch of beach?

Sure enough, there was the intruder. The force of the door opening had slammed him to the floor, where he lay, stunned, catching his breath. He didn't look immediately threatening—small, probably a teenager up to no good.

Casting one quick look at his cantankerous companions—thankfully, stuck in the yard—Sam thrust himself forward. He realized the kid, burglar, intruder, whatever, was starting to sit up. It appeared he had something in his hand to use as a weapon.

"What the hell do you think you're doing?" Sam asked, his voice a growl of pure threat. And then he lunged forward, easily won a tug-of-war for the object and tossed it aside. He pressed down on the kid's shoulder, hard, forcing him to sit, not rise.

The squeak of pain was sharp and, he registered slowly, *not* masculine. At all. A light, clean fragrance tickled his nostrils.

The momentum that had been propelling Sam forward came to a screeching halt.

His eyes adjusted to the lack of light. It wasn't a kid. And it wasn't a boy, either. Eyes as big as cornflowers, and nearly the same color, flashed up at him, filled with fury and indignation.

He let go of her shoulder instantly, but still, held up his hand, warning her not to get up.

It was the perfect ending, he thought wearily, to a perfectly awful day.

CHAPTER TWO

ALLIE PULLED HERSELF to sitting, feeling stunned and winded. She glared up at her attacker, filled with impotent fury mixed with panic. A stranger was in her house! Asking *her* what the hell she was doing! Ordering her, with imperious hand signals, to sit here, as if she was a prisoner!

Was she a prisoner? Her shoulder tingled oddly where he had touched it, and she resisted the urge to rub it, as if that would betray weakness.

As he folded his arms over the rather impressive contours of his chest, and planted his long legs, she felt, weirdly, as though her panic was put on pause. She had a sense of being caught in a luxurious place of slow time suspension as she studied him.

Surely home invaders did not look like this? She could see the man was very tall. The last bits of sun creeping over his extraordinarily broad shoulders spun his dark hair to milky chocolate. He looked strong and fit, and carried his body with that casual confidence she assigned to athletes, not to someone up to no good.

Allie saw the man was well dressed in pressed khaki shorts that made his bare legs look very long, and a sports shirt that hugged the enticing muscle of very masculine arms.

There could be worse people to take you prisoner.

She was appalled at this traitorous thought.

Of course he would look well dressed. That was exactly how a thief would try to blend in, as he was out trying door handles and breaking down doors in an upscale neighborhood like this one.

The intruder backed up from her, slowly, keeping his eyes on her, until his hand was on the doorknob.

Leaving, she deduced with relief.

But then he took his eyes off her for a moment, and glanced outside. It occurred to her he had a partner in crime, an accomplice.

Then she noticed keys dangling from the lock. How could she have been so stupid? She had locked the door, yes, but left the keys in it. The pressure to produce the jingle was making her absent-minded, obviously.

Allie weighed her options and saw two. He was distracted right now. She could get up and race back down that hallway, and out onto the beach before he knew what had happened.

She was rather shocked to discover her unwillingness to retreat. This was her *home*, her safe place. This was the one thing she had left that she was willing to make a stand for.

"Get out while you can," she ordered him. She staggered to her feet. She hoped her voice wasn't as wobbly as her legs were. Thankfully, she had lots of experience overcoming nerves, especially with her voice. She slipped her hand into her shorts pocket. "I have a weapon."

The part about a new weapon was a complete fib. Still, you would think he would have the decency to be startled at this latest threat to his diabolical plan, whatever it was.

But no, the man turned back to her, ever so slowly, and regarded her through narrowed eyes. With the last light spilling in the front door, she could see her home invader was one long, tall drink of handsome!

"I think we've already dispensed with the weapon," he said, something dry in his tone, almost as if he found her laughable.

"I have another one," she insisted, pressing her finger up against the shorts pocket in what she thought was probably a fair approximation of a pistol barrel.

He had chiseled, perfect features and eyes as dark brown as new-brewed coffee. His cheeks and chin were ever so faintly whisker-shadowed, but in a way that made him look roguish and sexy, not at all like the home invader that he was.

Allie was hoping, given her warning, he would bolt back out the way he came, but he didn't. He *frowned* at her, any amusement he felt at her efforts to defend herself completely gone.

He moved across the space that separated them in less time than it took her to take a single breath. He caught both her arms, tugged them out of her pockets, and pinned them to her sides. Her squirming to release herself only served to tighten his grip, so she stopped.

To her relief, it was apparent his hold on her arms was not intended to hurt, but to control. His touch was warm and made her pulse with a strange, electrical awareness of him.

It seemed to be an entirely inappropriate time to notice he smelled good, like a deep forest afternoon on a hot summer day.

Why hadn't she run when she had a chance?

"Who are you?" he asked, his voice an unsettling growl of something between menace and seduction. "And what have you done with Mavis?"

Shock shivered along Allie's spine. He knew her grandmother? He could have read her name on the mailbox.

No, he couldn't have. It had faded a long time ago. So, yes, he knew her grandmother. So what? Did that give him the right to barge into her house?

"What have *I* done with Mavis?" Allie stammered. She tried, again, to wiggle away from his grip, but he held her fast.

"Where is she?" He managed to say that as if Allie was barging into his home, and not the other way around.

"You think *I'm* the home invader?"

"You're the one with the pistol in your pocket."

She managed to wiggle her fingers just enough to reach into her pockets and turn them inside out. He looked unsurprised, and not impressed, at all. It was all too much. She had gone from panic to fury to this. Her life wasn't in danger. This was all some kind of misunderstanding.

Allie began to giggle. Okay, it might have had a tiny bit of a hysterical edge to it.

"I fail to see the humor," he said tightly. "It's been on the news. There have been break-ins in this neighborhood. Mavis would be very vulnerable."

She giggled harder. "I'm not the intruder. You're the intruder."

He let go of her shoulders completely, and looked down at her, his brow knit in consternation. "Who are you?"

"Who am I?" she sputtered. "I live here. I think the question is, who are you? And how dare you just walk into my home?"

"Your home?" The frown deepened around the exquisite corners of a wide mouth.

"I've rented this cottage from Mavis, in this time period, every year for the past ten years. My mom and dad rented it before that. That's why I have my own key."

What? Allie thought, completely taken off guard. She

noted his voice was a masculine and sexy rasp. She could still feel her upper arms tingling from where he had held her fast.

Now that there was, obviously, no threat, her thoughts wandered. She despised herself for the wish that flitted through her mind: that her hair was not rumpled, towel-dried from her last swim, the tips still a shockingly different color than the rest of her blond hair. She wished she was not standing there, barefoot, in a too-large T-shirt that ended just past the shorts she had pulled on over a still-damp bathing suit.

Allie actually wished she had makeup on, which was totally against the cottage rules.

She snapped her mouth shut, since it had fallen open as she struggled to make the leap from home invader to well, home invader. Suddenly, it didn't seem very funny at all, and the giggle, hysterical or otherwise, died within her. He didn't know, and she hated being the one to break it to him.

"Mavis is my grandmother." Somehow, she couldn't bring herself to say *was* as if that would erase something too completely from her world. "She's gone."

"Your grandmother," he said, cocking his head at her, as if trying to discern truth.

"Yes, my grandmother."

Did he see some resemblance? People had always said she had her grandmother's eyes. They certainly shared a diminutive size. His shoulders suddenly relaxed. "Mavis goes every year. To visit her sister. But when I saw you here, it just shocked me. I wondered if she had come to harm."

"Do I look like the type of person who would harm an old lady?"

He looked at her carefully, as if he was weighing this. "You claimed you had a weapon in your pocket."

"When I thought I needed one for self-defense."

"You came at me with a lamp…or something."

"It's a statue, and I didn't exactly come at you."

"But you would have, if I hadn't knocked you over with the door."

Well, she couldn't deny that.

"That was an accident, by the way," he said, his voice both rough and soothing, "I thought the door was stuck so I threw my shoulder behind it. Are you okay? I didn't hurt you, did I?"

He must have decided she did not look like a mugger of old ladies, if he was interested, albeit reluctantly, in her well-being.

"I'll live."

He gazed at her steadily, as if trying to make up his mind, then rolled his shoulders, ran a hand through his hair.

"I apologize for acting as though you were an intruder. It's just that I was shocked to find you here. You're Allie, then. Allie of the artwork on the hallway walls. I guess I pictured Mavis's granddaughter as much younger. To match the artwork."

There was something vaguely unsettling about this stranger being familiar with the artwork of her younger self. Better to nip any familiarity in the bud.

"I'm sorry. I have some other shocking news. Mavis hasn't gone to visit my great-aunt Mildred. She—" But somehow, when she went to say the actual words, her lips quivered, and she could feel tears welling.

Talk about an emotional roller coaster! But maybe that is what shocks did to people? Put them through their whole range of emotions?

Understanding dawned in his face. “Mavis died?”

“Yes.”

“I’m terribly sorry to hear that.” He looked genuinely taken aback. He raked a hand through the dark silk of his hair again, and then glanced back outside.

Sorry. What an inadequate word. She made herself swallow back the tears that were forming and assume a businesslike tone. “I inherited the cottage. I wasn’t aware of any rental arrangement.”

“That explains being met at the door with—” he squinted over her shoulder “—a bludgeoning device.”

“My grandmother called him Harold. The bludgeoning device.”

“Is the fact that the bludgeoning device bears a name supposed to make it more or less threatening?” he asked.

There was something about the faint smile that tickled the edges of that extraordinary mouth that made her feel just a little more off-kilter.

“As you said, there have been break-ins. I saw it on the news, too. Defense by Harold seemed like a good idea at the time.”

“Look, you are about the size of a garden gnome…”

A garden gnome?

“…I don’t think tackling an intruder head-on is the best idea. Harold or no Harold. The fake pistol in your pocket was really dumb.”

Ouch. Not just a garden gnome, but a dumb garden gnome.

Allie had to get rid of him. She made her tone deliberately unfriendly. “I hardly need lectures from strangers.”

“Not even a stranger you tried to bean with a sculpture?”

“Unsuccessfully,” she muttered.

"I make my case." More softly, he said, "I don't feel as if we are exactly strangers."

The fact that he had seen her artwork did not make them friends.

"I liked your grandmother a great deal," he said softly. "I think she would have wanted me to warn you against tackling intruders."

Allie did not like how his expression had softened with concern, as if she was a silly child who was in *need* of his supervision. Still, no point being churlish about it, especially since he was right: her grandmother would have approved of his well-meaning words.

"Well," Allie said, "thanks for your sage advice." Maybe the tiniest hint of sarcasm had gotten into her tone, because he was looking at her with his brows lowered in a most formidable way.

She would not be intimidated. "So, our mutual caring for my grandmother notwithstanding, I think our business here is concluded. Let me show you the door, Mr.…er…"

"Walker. Sam Walker."

"Mr. Walker, then. My apologies for the mix-up. It will have left you in a bit of a pickle, but—"

"The pickle may be yours, I'm afraid. I have a contract."

CHAPTER THREE

ALLIE STARED AT Sam Walker, entirely flabbergasted by his arrogance.

The concern, along with his sympathy, had evaporated. His tone suggested he felt that the existence of a contract resolved everything. He did, unfortunately, radiate a certain power, a man very accustomed to obstacles melting before his considerable presence.

"I'm not sure what you think that means," Allie said, "that you have a contract. Or that the pickle may be mine."

"It means, legally, I have possession of these premises for the next two weeks."

"Are you a lawyer, then?" she asked, folding her arms over her chest.

"No. But I have access to some pretty good ones."

"Are you threatening me?"

"Not really."

But he was threatening her. Somehow this threat felt more like a clear and present danger than him barging into her house.

"And what am I supposed to do?"

He lifted a shoulder, but seemed preoccupied with something he was looking at outside. "Vacate, I guess."

She didn't like this one bit: that in the blink of an eye

she had gone from the one throwing him out, to the one being thrown! He was the kind of man who was like that: life-altering storms practically brewed in the air around him.

Vacate? Her own home? "You expect me to leave to accommodate you?" Her tone was properly indignant. And she hoped imperious.

He turned back to her. She got the impression that her indignation barely registered with him and that her leaving was exactly his expectation.

"I don't have anywhere to go," she sputtered. She sounded defensive. And faintly pathetic. Who didn't have anywhere to go? Plus, worst of all, she sounded as if she had already given up, as if she would defer to him and his stupid contract.

She had been so right not to trust that perfect moment of just minutes ago. Why did calamity lay in wait for her?

He lifted a shoulder and glanced back at her. "I don't, either. It's been a long day, and I'm not about to start searching for alternate accommodations now."

She could see, suddenly, that all that handsomeness had hidden a truth from her. His face was lined with weariness. And something else was in those devil-dark suede eyes…hurt? Loneliness?

Allie, she scolded herself, *you are in the middle of a crisis here.* She did not need to be exploring the damage to the dark stranger who had appeared on her doorstep.

And he did not want her to know, either, what painful secrets he held, because the window that weariness had opened briefly in his eyes slammed shut.

His voice had an edge of hardness to it when he spoke. "I couldn't find anything on such short notice, regardless."

That was true. It was the beginning of July. Sugar

Cone Beach was one of the most sought-after holiday locations in California. People booked, particularly the July the Fourth holiday, well in advance. Sometimes, years in advance. People who had yearly arrangements—like him apparently—clung to them. She had heard of rental agreements being passed down, generation to generation, and that might be the case with him. He'd said his parents had it before him.

Still, it was even more reason she was not abandoning her house to him. She would not be able to find anything else, either. Though the contract thing was a little worrisome. The last thing she needed was a legal battle. The truth was, after the shock of the tax bill, she was barely squeaking by.

Allie cast Sam a glance. He looked like he had a lot more money than her if it came to that.

Still, she couldn't act intimidated, and she couldn't take it on. It was his problem, not her problem.

"Who doesn't at least make a phone call before heading out on their holiday?" she asked, her tone querulous. "It's not as if my grandmother was young. Did it not occur to you things can change?"

He looked her over with narrowed eyes. His voice was cold when he spoke. "I happen to be one of the people most aware of how things can change, without warning, how an entire life can be thrown off course in a single second."

She was suddenly dangerously aware they were not talking about a rental agreement gone wrong. He looked stunned that he had revealed that much of himself, and covered his tracks quickly.

"We're going to have to reach an agreement," he said.

His tone was reasonable, but Allie could feel herself bristling. Despite that lapse where he said a life could be thrown off course without warning—his life presumably—he was the kind of man who wouldn't like that. Who wouldn't like that one little bit. Who would move heaven and earth to make sure it didn't happen to him again. He practically oozed the kind of irritating confidence bordering on arrogance of a man who expected everything to go his way. Who would *make* everything go his way.

He was in for a surprise this time. He was going to have to go, and that was that. She was in creative mode—or trying desperately to be in creative mode—and she knew how easily the muse could be derailed. She had a deadline to meet. She had to stand as strong as him. This cottage was hers, and she was not leaving it!

"I doubt an agreement that is satisfactory to both of us is possible," she said.

"Thus the invention of contracts."

With his contracts and his annoying confidence, Allie decided she didn't like him at all. And that was a good thing. So much easier to make him go.

Wasn't possession nine-tenths of the law?

She opened her mouth to tell him—*Allie, show no weakness, particularly to a man like this*—but before she could say a single word, he was back out the door. The screen slapped shut behind him, and she went to see what had caught his attention so suddenly.

His keys still hung there. Maybe she could pull them out, slam the door and lock him out? She could imagine, with some satisfaction, the astonished look of disbelief that would bring to his unfairly handsome features.

Childish, she told herself, but in the face of his arrogance, his absolute certainty that he was right and she was wrong, she could not help but feel a certain glee at the prospect.

But when she moved to the front door fully intending to remove his keys, she saw what had pulled him out of her house with such urgency.

Allie's mouth fell open, her resolve evaporated and her heart dropped. Now what?

Just as Allie had first suspected, when she had seen Sam glance back out that door and hold it open, Allie's home invader had not arrived alone. No wonder, even as he spoke to her, he had been keeping a sharp eye on the front yard.

He was now crouched beside a small boy, who was trying to unstick a red wagon that had gone off the concrete pathway, and had its two side wheels imbedded in the soft dirt of the somewhat neglected flower bed that ran beside it.

The child was adorable: he looked to be maybe three, with a head full of tangled blond curls and the sturdy build of a tiny wrestler. Dimpled legs poked out of denim overall shorts. The chubby legs ended in tiny hiking boots. He had on a red T-shirt, and a faded superhero cape, one hem drooping, was draped over his shoulders and tied under his chin.

The wagon contained a small suitcase and a stuffed toy of some sort. The child was determined to free it himself.

He furiously waved off Sam, who could have freed the wagon in less than a second. Sam stood back, hands up, in the universal sign of surrender.

Allie realized it might be just a wee bit petty to take delight in seeing the self-assured Mr. Walker taking his orders from a child.

The little boy grunted and pulled, but the wagon did not move. But the stuffy did. It lifted its head, gazed with a combination of adoration and long-suffering at the child—

an expression nearly identical to the man's, actually—then sighed, and put its head back down. Not a stuffy, then, but a dog. It looked like a cross between a cocker spaniel and a red feather duster.

Allie considered all of this. Finding accommodations would be hard enough in Sugar Cone in July. The complication of the dog and the child would make it impossible.

Which meant what?

She could harden her heart to Sam Walker. It would take effort, of course, he was one of those men who effortlessly caused softening in the region of the female heart. However, she thought she'd become rather good at hardening her heart to men, and particularly one like him, who seemed altogether too sure of himself.

But the little boy? And that moppet of a dog?

What was she going to say? *Go sleep in your car? Go home where you came from? I don't care about you, or your excitement about a holiday on the beach?*

For all that she had been through, had she really become that person? Was she going to allow herself to be callous and hard?

It was a sensible approach to life, she tried to convince herself. She touched the ink-dark tips of her hair, as if to remind herself which way she needed to go if she did not want to be hurt any more.

But an attitude of complete cynicism did not feel as if it fit her, as much as she might have wanted it to. And her grandmother would not have approved.

Her grandmother had *known* this man. Possibly she had known him since he was a child. She had never mentioned a rental arrangement, but Allie had never visited her at this particular time of the summer, either.

It occurred to Allie there might be a Mommy somewhere, but a quick glance at the curb showed no one else coming from the car that was parked there.

She couldn't identify the silver car, low-slung and sporty, beyond the fact that it was clearly *expensive.* The kind of car that a man who could afford a team of lawyers drove.

But then she thought of what she had glimpsed in the man's face, beyond the travel weariness, and it came to her. Not hurt, so much, and not loneliness.

It was a subject she was something of an expert on, enough that she could spot it in others. Loss. That is what was in the sharpness of his tone when he had told her that he, of all people, knew that life could turn on a hair.

Sam Walker knew some incredible, heartbreaking loss. That is what she had seen, naked in his eyes, before the veil had slammed down.

Of course, she probably had it all wrong. A divorce, plain and simple. In this day and age that would hardly cause a flicker. It was probably more the norm than not: marriage broken, daddy inheriting his kid for a week or two in the summer. What better plan than to head to the beach?

Allie sighed, and recognized it as a surrender. For tonight, anyway. She had two extra bedrooms. It was unlikely that a longtime tenant of her grandmother's had morphed into some kind of ax murderer. And also unlikely that an ax murderer came with a child and a puppy in tow.

Plus, there was the unhappy existence of a contract to consider.

Maybe there was a bright spot in all this. Maybe she needed to suck it up and consider going beyond tonight. Maybe, particularly since her guitar was locked into an unfathomable silence, Allie needed to consider giving up two weeks of her precious privacy in trade for something she needed more desperately than solitude right now.

Money.

Sam Walker sensed the girl had come outside behind him before he actually saw her. Awareness of her tingled along his spine, as she pressed by him, somehow not touching him, though the walkway was narrow. She paused at where the wagon was stuck.

"Hi," she said to Cody, who glanced at her, then ignored her.

She ignored him, too, none of that gushing over his curls that Cody and Sam were equally allergic to. Casually, barely seeming to move at all, she tucked her toe under the wagon, and lifted the stuck wheels back onto the walk. Sam noticed there was nary a protest from Cody, who trundled by her without acknowledging her help.

"I guess we can work something out," she said. Her voice was reluctant, but her eyes on the child had softened with a sympathy that turned them a shade of violet that Sam felt he could look at—or get lost in—for a long, long time.

He shook the feeling off, but still could not seem to stop looking at her. His initial reaction, in the poor light of the hallway, after he'd realized she was not a boy, had been that she was barely more than a child.

She had tufts of very short blond, sun-streaked hair—really sun-streaked, not from a bottle—in a rumple around her head. While the rest of her hair looked natural, there was an odd half inch, right at the tips, that was a disconcerting shade of black, as if it had been dipped in an inkwell.

She was wearing a too-long T-shirt, damp in the front,

suggesting a swimming suit underneath it. She had very long, sun-browned legs, but otherwise was tiny, the kind of person who would be chosen for the part of Peter Pan in a play. Or maybe Tinkerbell. Despite being Cody's guardian for nearly eight months—all of them excruciating—Sam still wasn't really up on his children's stories.

Outside, the light dying, but better than it had been in the cottage, he could see she was not a child. At all. Maybe in her early twenties.

He could see, too, that she was the antithesis of the kind of women who populated his world. They fell into two categories: the very glamorous, with perfect makeup and salon hair, with manicured fingers and toes, and everything in between manicured, too. Those women wore designer clothes with casual flair, and tossed two-thousand-dollar handbags over gym-toned shoulders.

The other kind were his colleagues, professionals, as driven as he was, but as perfectly turned out as their glamourous counter parts, with a wardrobe of designer power suits and stylish eyeglasses.

Sam dated—occasionally—women from both those categories. Women sophisticated enough to understand that if they were looking for picket fences and happily-ever-after, he was not their guy.

But if they were looking for the kind of good time—travel, posh restaurants, good wine, galas, charity balls, premieres—that money could buy, they could hang out with him. For a while. As long as there were no demands and they didn't get in the way of business.

This woman, with her blown-in-off-the-beach look, would not fit into either of those two convenient categories. He thought he had known women who were bold, but this woman who grabbed a statue named Harold and headed toward danger, instead of away from it, could redefine that word.

Next to any other woman he could think of she seemed, what? Distressingly real, somehow.

Not that categories for any kind of woman existed in his life anymore, Sam reminded himself.

No, his old life, that guy who worked hard and played harder, who was carefree and unfettered, was a distant memory, eight months behind him.

"Is there something wrong?" Ally asked.

On the other hand, maybe he would be getting his old life back soon. It was what he had wanted and wished for, almost on a daily basis.

And yet now that it was a possibility…his heart did a sickening fall.

CHAPTER FOUR

"IS SOMETHING WRONG?" she asked again.

He gave Allie of the hallway art—and possibly his landlady—a look. This was the second time he'd gotten the unsettling feeling that she might see things about him that others didn't. No one but his sister had ever seen past what he was prepared to show them, and he didn't like it.

But then he saw she wasn't even looking at him. She was looking at the dog, Popsy, lying in the wagon, one paw trailing, looking as boneless as a pile of rags.

"With the dog?" she clarified.

Sam felt huge relief that she was talking about the dog, not him.

Cody was now facing the challenge of the steps leading up to the cottage. With huge effort, he lifted the limp Popsy off the wagon. The dog reluctantly found its legs.

"Not permanently," he said and hoped that was true. The dog was unusually attached to Cody. The two were inseparable. He did not think his sudden cosmically ordained family unit of uncle and nephew and dog could sustain another loss. And yet he didn't feel quite ready to tell her what the vet had said.

The dog is depressed.

Who knew that dogs got depressed? Or that little

kids gave up speaking when the unspeakable happened to them?

"I thought I caught a whiff of something as they went by," she said, trying to word it delicately.

"The dog got carsick."

"Oh, no!"

Her sympathy was so genuine that he couldn't resist sharing the full horror. "You have no idea. At sixty-five miles per hour, with wall-to-wall traffic and not a rest stop for thirty miles. Then, when I finally could pull over, I had to unpack the suitcase to find new clothes. Not the Superman cape, though. I don't have an extra one of those.

"And guess how long the new clothes lasted before Popsy got sick on Cody again? I may never get the smell out of my car. Sheesh. I may never get the smell out of Popsy."

He stopped himself, embarrassed. He sounded just like those moms at the playgroup the counselor had recommended for Cody. Sam had tried to drop Cody off there several times.

Nobody warned me it was going to be this hard.

Cody, to Sam's consternation—he was trying to do the right thing, after all—and his guilty and secret relief, had used his limited communication skills to make it known he *hated* the play group.

"Cody is your son and the dog is Popsy?"

"Cody is my nephew, but yeah, that's the whole cast of characters."

Sam really hated sympathy, which made his recounting of the horrible trip down here even more mystifying. Still, right now, that sympathy—the soft look on her face as her gaze followed Cody and Popsy as they went up the stairs—served Sam well. He was seeing a whole shift in attitude.

"You must all be exhausted. I'll show you which rooms to take, and put out some towels. I'm sorry for the welcome I gave you earlier."

"Not your fault," he said gruffly.

"Well, let's start again. I'm Alicia Cook. Welcome to Soul's Retreat."

She held out her hand. Maybe it was a mistake to take it, because any sense he had left of her being a child disappeared in her grip. Her touch made him look at her differently. She was extraordinarily feminine, and her hand held the unconscious sensuality of the sea in it.

She was very pretty, her bone structure exquisite, her eyes a shade of blue bordering on violet that he would not have been able to name if asked. He was aware of a scent tickling his nostrils, and realized she smelled of the sea and something else. Lemons? Whatever it was, it was faintly ordinary and faintly exotic and faintly enticing.

It occurred to him that she had welcomed them as if she planned to be their hostess. Maybe that's why sympathy was not a workable strategy. Shared accommodations weren't going to work, and he needed to let her know right away. It looked like when she got an idea in that head of hers it was hard to displace it!

"I hope you won't have too much difficulty finding a place to stay," he said, and heard the cool, no-nonsense tone he used when closing a deal for his computer systems company.

All of it—especially the *enticing* part—made getting rid of her seem imperative.

That tone he had just used could—and had—intimidated business tycoons with global reputations. But her mouth—plump and pink—set in a very unflattering line, and her brows lowered.

"I'm not going to find a place to stay," she said firmly. "Your arrival has taken me completely by surprise, but I'll accommodate you and Cody to the best of my ability tonight. Tomorrow we'll look at options. Maybe it will be workable for you to stay. With me."

"You want to share accommodations?" he asked her slowly. "With someone you don't know?"

"*Want to* seems to be overstating it a bit. None of you looks dangerous. The dog doesn't even look like it has the energy to bite."

Sam felt this odd little niggle, for the second time, of wanting to be protective of her.

Just as when she said she had a weapon when it was so pathetically obvious not only that she didn't, but that she wouldn't use it if she did.

Are you crazy? You don't invite strangers to stay with you.

But he managed to bite his tongue. He looked at the set of her jaw and felt a sudden exhaustion. It had been a horrible day. That *look* on her face felt as if it would take a lot more energy than he had to sort this out right now.

He needed to get Cody into the bathtub and into a bed. He had dealt with three of Cody's legendary meltdowns today. For a kid who didn't talk he was an absolute master at making his displeasure known to all. Sam was not up to another one any more than he was up to dealing with whatever the stubborn set of Alicia Cook's little mouth meant.

She was right. Tomorrow, they would look at options. Tomorrow, he'd deal with it. His team of lawyers could let her know he had an ironclad contract and she could find someplace else to stay for two weeks.

He knew, despite a team of people working for him, that another place on Sugar Cone was out of the question for either himself and Cody or Mavis's granddaughter. They'd had a devil of a time finding a condo on the busier side of the beach for Cody's Australian auntie and uncle and their kids, arriving later in the week.

We need to know him better. He's all we have left of Adam.

Sam had met them, of course. At the wedding, the christening, Christmas two years ago. At the funeral. Good people. Decent. Hardworking. Real, somehow, in the same category that the woman in front of him was real.

And yet, when he thought of meeting them this time, he could feel his heart sinking to the bottom of his feet.

Despite the fact he was pretty sure he was botching nearly every single thing about raising a three-year-old, just like Cody was what they had left of Adam, he was what Sam had left of his sister, Sue, too.

And Sam had a history with this little cottage. He had been coming here for a long time. He had memories of endless days of him and Sue running on that beach as children. He desperately wanted Cody to feel the kind of unfettered joy that they had felt here.

Sam's parents had let the lease lapse when he and Sue were teenagers, but when they died, he had approached Mavis and asked about the possibility of leasing again. She, he remembered, had been delighted, almost as if she was waiting for him to come back. Since then, the cottage had always provided exactly what the sign, swinging at the gate with letters so faded you could barely read them, promised.

Soul's Retreat. Sam Walker was counting on this place

to give him something that was in very short supply in his life right now.

Serenity.

Wisdom.

Wasn't there a prayer about those things? Not that he was a praying kind of man, though given the desperation of the decision he had come here to make, he wasn't going to rule out the possibility of becoming one.

What he didn't need were any further complications to a life that was seriously complicated right now.

And this woman, Alicia—Allie—with her black-tipped hair, and a tiny bit self-conscious in her wet, too-large T-shirt, and trying hard not to let it show, had *complication* written all over her.

He was sympathetic about her grandmother. Of course he was. But, after tonight, she couldn't stay here with him under the same roof.

She looked like she was still the artsy type that her hallway art indicated. She'd probably love to go to Paris for two weeks. There. Problem solved. He would offer her a round-trip, all-expenses-paid to Paris so he and Cody could have the cottage to themselves.

If only all of life's problems were so easy to solve.

His more immediate problem was this: he had a very stinky dog and a very stinky kid on his hands. Neither of them liked baths.

"You've eaten, right?" Alicia asked, as she watched the shocking change in her life unfold before her very eyes.

Sam Walker stood in the bedroom she had suggested for Cody. The bedroom was not large, at the best of times, but now it looked positively tiny. Sam's shoulders seemed to be taking up all the space. He was rummaging through the small suitcase Cody had dragged up the walk on his wagon.

Cody and the dog peeked out at her from under the bed. The man and the boy had identical eyes, large, dark brown and soft as suede. There was something in them that could weave a spell around the unwary.

Which she was not.

"Yeah, we stopped at Pizza Palooza," Sam said, his voice a growl of unconscious sensuality. "Perfect Pal Happy Deals all the way around. Did they make me happy? No. I'm pretty sure that's what the dog threw up. I wonder if I can sue for misleading advertising?"

Allie felt a jab of sympathy for him. She reminded herself to be wary of spells, and overrode the sympathy. Much more sensible to see this as a reminder that he had a team of lawyers at his fingertips, and presumably, he was not afraid to use them.

Still, she had to venture, "I don't think the Perfect Pal Happy Deals are dog-designated."

"Did you hear that, Cody? The Happy Deal is not dog-designated. No more feeding Perfect Pal to Popsy. So, how about a bath, buddy?"

Sam had extracted a pair of pajamas from the suitcase. They looked as if they would fit a good-size teddy bear, and they had fire engines on them. Allie was finding this level of adorable invading her home doing very odd things to her heart, wary as it was.

The dog and the little boy shrank back a little farther under the bed. The man shot her a look, then got on his knees, rear in the air—and a very nice rear, at that—and looked under the bed.

"Come on," he said, his tone soothing, despite the exasperation Allie had so clearly seen on his features.

The boy scooted right out of sight. The dog made

a sound that wasn't quite a growl, more like a hum of dismay.

Allie backed out of the room to leave Sam to his challenges, which seemed substantial. She reluctantly closed the open patio door—a precaution against the possibility of a burglar in the neighborhood. She was aware she felt a little safer with Sam in the house, though this reliance on a man to feel safe made her annoyed with herself.

Allie retreated to her bedroom, taking her tablet and her guitar with her. The bedroom proved not to be any kind of retreat at all.

For one thing, the cottage, with the closed patio door, was hot, her tiny bedroom window open a tiny burglar-proof crack, was not providing much of a breeze. She would normally leave her bedroom door open, but with guests in the house, that wasn't possible, especially since, as a defense against the suffocating heat, she stripped down to the bathing suit that was under her clothes. She appreciated its tininess, as much of her skin as possible exposed to the stingy breeze coming in her window.

She picked up her guitar and strummed it hopefully with her thumb, but it told her, with a certain sullen stubbornness, *no.* Which was too bad, because it might have covered the other sounds coming through the paper-thin walls of the cottage.

While she listened, the child was snared, a bath was run, the little boy splashing while his uncle made motor boat sounds.

There was something about Sam—so confident and so handsome—making motorboat sounds that made him all too human. He was a man way out of his element. And yet trying, valiantly, to do the right thing.

At some point Allie realized the little boy was not speaking, and it distressed her and made her realize she had not asked enough questions before allowing this pair, plus a dog, to share her home.

Why was she assuming Sam was doing the right thing? How did an uncle and nephew end up together on holidays? Why wasn't the little boy speaking? Where were the mommy and daddy? Was Sam Walker really the child's uncle? What if she had inadvertently embroiled herself in a parental kidnapping of some sort?

Though honestly, Sam didn't look like he was enjoying the exercise in child-rearing enough to have used illegal means to experience it.

Sam Walker did not look like a kidnapper any more than he looked like a home invader. In fact, he looked the furthest thing from a man capable of any kind of subterfuge. There was something in his eyes, in the set of his mouth, in the way he carried himself—in the way he handled the child and dog—that made him seem like a man you could trust, even if you didn't particularly like him.

Her grandmother had known him, she reminded herself. Had not just known him, but liked him enough to share an ongoing rental relationship with him for many years.

Still, Allie was aware that not only was she not sure what the *type* who became involved in a parental abduction would look like, but that she had an unfortunate history of placing her trust in people who had not earned it. While other people could trust their instincts, she had ample and quite recent proof that she could not.

Determined to not be naive, she put on her headphones to block out the noises coming from the bathroom and typed Sam Walker into the search engine on her tablet. Not too surprisingly, there were thousands of Sam Walkers. She changed tack and put in "recent abductions." Also, sadly, way too many of them, though no photos of a curly-headed little boy who looked like Cody. No abducted children *with* dogs.

Giving up, Allie Googled the legal ramifications of rental contracts, only to find out lawyers were quite cagey about dispensing free information over the internet.

After that, she went through her grandmother's documents, stored in a box under Allie's bed, hoping for the rental contract, but found nothing.

Through the headphones, she heard the muffled sounds of the bath ending. She took them off and listened.

The bed in the room next to her creaked, a small creak, and then a larger one. Too easy to picture.

"Get off, Popsy, you stink. And you're next for the bath. Don't even think of hiding. Okay, where is *Woozer, Wizzle, Wobble*? Here it is."

One bedtime story, read three times.

Again, that deep, sure voice, sliding over those silly words was all too endearing: "'And then the witch said, woozer, wizzle, wobble and turned the toad into a donkey.'"

Ashamed to realize that she was acting like an eavesdropper and that the little scene playing out in the bedroom made her ache with that same weak longing the family on the beach had caused in her earlier, Allie put the headphones back on. She turned the music up.

She pointed her finger at her silent guitar. *You are not my only source of music.*

Then, she stretched out on her bed, and let the faint breeze play over her skin. Without any warning, the three nights of not sleeping suddenly caught up with her.

CHAPTER FIVE

CODY FELL ASLEEP before Sam had finished the third reading of *Woozer, Wizzle, Wobble*. He knew better than to stop. His nephew could rise out of a deep sleep, his neck swiveling like he was trying out for a part on an exorcism film, if he thought he'd been cheated of the entire third reading of his favorite book. For a kid who had given up on talking, Cody was remarkably adept at making his thoughts—particularly displeasure—more than apparent.

Sam finished the book, then slid out of the bed. Carefully, he undid the string that fastened the superhero cape around Cody's neck. A tender protectiveness for his nephew rose up in him, but it was followed with brutal swiftness by his awareness that when it had mattered, he had not been able to protect Cody at all.

As happened sometimes, the memory hit him without warning. His brother-in-law, Adam, laughing, as he and Sam chased after a shrieking Cody trying to get the cape off him for Sue to put in the laundry. Cody, fresh out of the bath, had been naked, save for the cape.

The dog had been there, racing joyously beside them, as they went in circles around the house, out into the yard, back into the house. Popsy had no idea what the game was, but loved it, nonetheless. They all had. Sue had pretended disapproval, but snickered anyway, when he and

Adam had finally captured Cody and dubbed his garb "the Pooperman cape," a name that stuck.

What Sam hated the most was at the time he'd had no idea—none—how precious those moments were.

What he hated the most? Was that he had no idea if it—spontaneous joy—ever would come back. For any of them left living.

He was exhausted—which was probably why the uninvited memory had snuck in—but the dog was going to stink up the whole house if he didn't look after it.

He peered under the bed.

Popsy stared back at him, the picture of innocence. His face clearly said *What smell?* Sam made a swipe for him, and missed, which made Popsy retreat farther under the bed. Naturally, the dog made him crawl all the way under. At least he didn't growl—he saved that for when he was protecting Cody from the horrors of bath time. When Sam finally did manage to get him out and had him pinned in his arms, the dog trembled. Then he whimpered, a high, squeaking sound akin to the wire on a barb wire fence being tightened.

"Shhh," Sam told him, nudging open the bedroom door with his foot, "you'll wake Cody up." But what he was really thinking was *She's going to think I torture you.*

He stepped out into the hall. The house was dark and silent. Her bedroom door was firmly shut and no light came out from under it.

He tiptoed down to the bathroom. He had kept Cody's bathwater, and he slid the dog in. The dog yelped and squirmed, so with a deft motion, still hanging on to the dog, Sam managed to get his shirt off before he ended up completely soaked.

"This isn't my first rodeo," he informed the dog, who

scrabbled to get out of the tub and, as he had predicted, totally soaked him within seconds.

He managed to keep hold of Popsy. The smell intensified—wet dog and vomit—as the water saturated the dog's fur. Sam reached for Cody's baby shampoo, somehow managing to hold the dog and dispense shampoo at the same time.

He lathered up the dog. Popsy resigned himself, giving a good demonstration of where the expression "hangdog" came from. Soon, the sweet smell of the baby shampoo began to smother the more noxious odors.

Sam splashed up water to get the lather off, and realized he was going to have to let the old water out of the tub to do a proper rinse. His guard went down ever so slightly and in a flash, the dog leaped out of the tub, nudged open the bathroom door and flew down the hallway, leaving a trail of water and soap in his wake.

Popsy burst through Allie's closed bedroom door, with Sam hot on his heels. In the murky darkness, Sam watched as the dog leaped onto the bed, landing with a squish on a rather delectable female body, lying on top of the covers. Even in the bad light Sam could tell she was wearing, well, next to nothing.

A pair of headphones and red bikini underwear.

Allie woke up flailing, her eyes wild with fear.

"Get away from me!" she screamed, throwing off the headphones, sitting up and swatting at the air. Popsy stayed on the bed but backed into the corner behind her, cowering.

Given the possibility she had a Harold nearby, or a suitable substitute, there was no explaining what Sam did next.

He moved slowly into the room, and sat down on the bed beside her. "I'm so sorry," he said in a low, soothing voice. “I was giving the dog a bath, and he broke away from me. I don’t know how he got in your room. Maybe the door doesn’t latch properly?”

She went very still, the screeching stopped, and she drew in a long, shaky breath. “Sam?”

“Yes.” The fact she was glad it was him shouldn’t be having the effect on him that it was.

“Oh, God, I thought you were the burglar.”

And then she snuggled against him, tears chasing down his bare, already wet, chest. It was his turn to go very still.

He was nearly naked, and she was nearly naked.

And not at all in the way a man and a woman were usually nearly naked together. It shouldn’t have felt as good as it did, and yet somehow, he could feel himself leaning into the warmth and suppleness of her skin. He recognized the closeness, the human contact, was pushing away some of the despair his memory had caused him just moments ago.

Thankfully, the romantic picture was completely interrupted by the sopping, soapy dog deciding to insert itself between them.

She laughed, a little of that shakiness still in her.

Against his better judgment, ignoring the wet puddle of dog, he stroked the short, spiky tufts of Allie’s hair, and found them surprisingly silky. Allie softened more against him. The smell of her hair and the wet dog mingled, and somehow was not as unpleasant as it should have been.

This, he realized, was going badly off the rails. Very badly.

“How would you like to go to Paris?” he asked.

“Okay, if I wasn’t certain I was dreaming before, now I am.”

"No, I'm serious. Two weeks, all expenses paid. Paris." He moved an inch away from her. It took all his strength. Should it have taken so much strength? She was his landlady. He barely knew her.

"Paris," she said, her tone bemused, maybe even irritated.

He stood up, turned back, and faced her. "You could leave in the morning."

"I'm not following," she said. She didn't sound the way he had hoped she would sound. Which was happy. Who wasn't happy when they got an all-expense-paid trip to an exotic location?

"Obviously, this can't work," Sam informed her with elaborate patience.

She folded her arms around the wet dog, thankfully hiding most of herself, and looked at him with those eyes that could make a strong man weak. "What can't work?"

"You and me together under the same roof. I mean…" He waved a hand at her. "You can't wander around in your underwear."

"It's not my underwear," she said dangerously. "It's a bathing suit."

"Dear God," he muttered under his breath, trying not to be a complete pervert. That meant overriding his desire to look and see what the differences were between the underwear he thought it was and the bathing suit she proclaimed it to be.

"And I was not *wandering* around in it. You barged into my bedroom."

"Popsy," he corrected, weakly. "And the latch. Not working."

She went on as if he hadn't made those important clarifications. "Though it's a *bathing suit* and I live on a beach so it would be perfectly okay if I was wandering around in it."

Yes, indeed it would. It would be perfectly okay. For her to be prancing—wandering—around her own beachside cottage in a bathing suit. The fact that it was perfectly okay made it more of a problem, not less of one.

For him. A normal hot-blooded male.

That thought gave him pause. He had not thought of himself as normal for a long time. And hot-blooded had not been part of his equation since the accident had taken the lives of his sister and brother-in-law and plunged him into the familiar land of grief and the foreign one of parenting.

Is this how it would happen? Little normal moments would just insert themselves in his life when he was least expecting them? Not that this was a normal moment. Of course it wasn't. And yet, still, for one heady second, he had been dealing with a very normal, hot-blooded reaction to a woman.

Was he ready for that?

He didn't think so. She was the type of woman who would probably bring all kinds of unexpected surprises with her for a man foolish enough to tangle his life with hers.

Even ever so briefly.

Even for two weeks.

Besides, he had Adam's family arriving soon. What would they think about him cohabitating with a young lady given to skimpy red bathing suits? Surely they wouldn't think that was good for Cody?

No, he had to convince her to go to Paris. It felt as if his life—or what was left of it—might depend on that.

Allie glared at Adam. Paris, indeed!

Of all the places he could mention, did it have to be

that one? Her ex-beau, Ryan, had whispered in her ear once, *We will explore the world together, and I will kiss you in Paris and my kisses will taste sweeter than wine...*

She shook away the memory, focused on something else. She was not in her underwear!

"Come on, Popsy," she said, getting up off the bed, and taking the dog firmly by the collar. "Let's get that soap off you."

The truth was, she was quite self-conscious in her red bikini. And a little bit pleased with the effect it was having on Sam, too!

He looked pretty stunning himself: his chest bare and wet, his shorts, also soaked, hanging low off slender hips. He was making her bedroom feel claustrophobic, just as he had Cody's.

Just moments ago, she had been cuddled up to him. Her skin was still tingling from it. How was she going to cleanse that memory from the room?

She could throw on a robe, but it felt as if that would be an admission he might be right about the wisdom of them sharing close quarters. It felt imperative not to let Sam win, somehow. Plus, she was going to be spraying off a dog. How much sense did it make to get dressed for that activity? She pushed by Sam.

"But you haven't given me an answer about Paris."

When her day had started this morning, Allie could not have predicted any of its events, and certainly not for it to end with this kind of surprise: finding herself in the arms of a gorgeous man...who apparently would prefer her in Paris!

In fact, in her wildest dreams she could not have pictured any of this. There was something oddly invigorating about it all. In her attempts to make her life stable, and predictable, had it somehow teetered over an edge into boring?

On the other hand, she had to remember that playing with fire might also be considered invigorating. She had to remind herself where *excitement* could lead, and that she had already visited that place, with disastrous results.

"I'm *never* going to Paris," she told Sam firmly. "You are being ridiculous."

She glanced back at him. His brow was furrowed. People did not tell him he was being ridiculous, apparently.

Leaving Sam standing there, clearly stunned by her refusal, she took the dog out the patio doors, and down into a small fenced yard, where a hose was hooked up. It had a spray nozzle on the end. Popsy twisted her wrist trying to squirm out of her grasp.

"I thought cocker spaniels were water dogs?" she scolded him.

"Here. I'll hold him, you spray."

Sam had followed her outside and came down the stairs. He had put a shirt on. It felt like a reprimand.

He took the dog firmly in grasp while she hosed him off. The first time she squirted Sam instead of the dog, it was an accident. But the second time, it wasn't. Really? Who put on a shirt to wash a dog? And the third time it was pure devilment.

Of course, it was all fun and games until he grabbed the hose from her!

Given the heat of the night, the cold water hitting her did not have the effect she suspected he had hoped for. There was no cowering, no pleading for him to stop. The water felt delicious. She opened her arms to it, and tilted back her head and closed her eyes. The water stopped hitting her. She opened her eyes to see the stars studding an ink-black sky.

She lowered her gaze to earth. The hose had been set down. Sam was retreating, Popsy's collar firmly in his grasp. He stood, for one moment, at the sliding door, looking down from the deck at her.

From here, his eyes looked darker than the night sky.

And then Allie was in the empty yard alone, soaked, her very skin tingling with an awareness of life that she had not allowed herself to feel for a very, very long time.

She was aware she did not feel afraid of a burglar. For the first time in forever, she didn't feel afraid of anything, at all.

When she went in the house, she left the patio door wide open, so the breeze could cool off everything that had overheated this night.

Sometime during the night, her bedroom door creaked open, and she woke up, not to see the burglar the open door might have invited, but Popsy. The dog shuffled in, sniffed her hand and whined. The smell of baby shampoo barely masked the wet fur smell.

"What do you want?" Allie whispered.

The dog took that as an invitation. He put both front paws on her bed, hefted himself up and then snuggled his still-damp and somewhat smelly self into her side. He licked her cheek once, burrowed deep under her armpit and fell fast asleep.

She lay there for a moment, contemplating the rise and fall of his breath, and his uncomplicated affection for her. Maybe she needed a dog.

In the morning when Allie woke up, the dog was gone, but his scent lingered. She felt a bit cranky, almost like she'd had too much to drink the night before. The moment when she had felt so free and alive—in her drenched bathing suit under a star-studded night—now felt overlaid with embarrassment.

Allie forced herself to go for her normal early morning run along the beach.

If the trials of the past few years had taught her anything, it was that there was value in discipline and routine.

In a moment of weakness—thinking of the child, not the other set of deep brown eyes—she went as far as Mrs. Jacobs's Beachfront Bakery and bought half a dozen world-famous—according to Mrs. Jacobs—Sugar Cone muffins. They were hideously expensive.

Worth it, a half hour later, seeing the little boy, adorable in those pajamas with red fire engines all over them, and his hair an untamed tangle, chomping enthusiastically on his muffin, dropping crumbs to the dog. Popsy looked shiny and alert this morning. There were even signs of enthusiasm in the way he was noisily vacuuming Cody's offerings from the floor.

"Let's talk about Paris," Sam said.

He hadn't even said good morning. Or thanked her for providing breakfast.

CHAPTER SIX

"PARIS," ALLIE REPEATED, and slid Sam an incredulous look. "I thought I made it pretty clear last night how I felt about that idea."

"But that was before you had a chance to sleep on it." He smiled at her.

That smile made the sun, already drenching the kitchen, seem to shine more brightly. Sam Walker looked rather amazing in the morning. His teeth were straight and white and perfect, and when he smiled one side of his mouth lifted up more than the other.

He was also totally sure of himself in the tight confines of the kitchen, as if he wore pajama bottoms and bare feet in front of women all the time. Which seemed likely.

The plaid pajama bottoms hung low on slender hips, and his T-shirt hinted he might have participated in an Ironman or some other equally challenging display of masculine agility and strength.

She, on the other hand, had made a choice to cover herself up this morning, and was wearing ugly sweatpants and a shapeless T-shirt. Her hair was sweat-slicked.

His dark hair was also slicked, but in a much more attractive way.

Obviously he had showered. He had not shaved and

his whiskers were even darker on his chin and cheeks this morning. It was a criminally sexy look.

She could tell he was used to being both charming and criminally sexy.

But something about all that charm was not reaching his eyes and it grated on her that he was used to getting his way because he had become adept at turning on the charm and throwing around some money.

"I am never going to Paris," she said, trying not to clench her teeth.

"Now *you* are being ridiculous. Everyone wants to go to Paris, someday. I can recommend a little café—"

Of course he could recommend a little café. He was obviously a citizen of the world, unlike her, a gauche girl from a small town who would fall for anything. Who had fallen and fallen hard. *We will explore the world together, and I will kiss you in Paris and my kisses will taste sweeter than wine...*

It made her stronger in the face of his considerable charm. "Mr. Walker—"

"I think we're well past that kind of formality," he insisted charmingly. She actually blushed, thinking of cuddling against him, and then doing her version of *Flashdance* under the stars.

She couldn't let that memory make her weak when she needed to be strong.

"I am not going anywhere," Allie said with all the firmness and sternness she could muster. She sounded like a schoolmarm speaking to an unruly boy. "I am not making a choice."

"But—"

"No! You obviously have a great deal of money you don't mind throwing around, so you go. I ran by a place for sale this morning. Go buy it."

He squinted at her with patent disbelief. The smile faded.

"I have the contract," he said.

"I don't care. I looked on the internet last night. It's debatable whether I have to honor a contract you signed with a deceased person." It hurt, more than she expected, to think of her Gram as a deceased person.

Thankfully, Sam didn't pick up on her sudden feeling of weakness. "You're taking legal advice off the internet?"

She folded her arms over her chest. Under normal circumstances, she might consider what he was offering.

After all, Paris! Maybe it would be exactly the right recipe to get over the lies and duplicity of Ryan once and for all, to put the "kisses like wine" promises behind her. But now was just not the time to be distracted. She had an unfortunate history of throwing away golden opportunities, and Paris was a temptation, *not* an opportunity.

Plus, she had seen a video of how airlines treated guitars. Her guitar was sulky enough at the moment.

Naturally, Sam would think she was crazy if she shared the fact that the needs of her temperamental guitar were part of what she needed to consider.

Was she crazy? Who thought their guitar talked to them? Or didn't, as the case might be.

"Have you heard the expression *no means no*?" Allie asked him.

"I've heard *of* it," he said. "Have I heard it personally? As in addressed to me? No. Of course not."

Of course not.

"I don't think you are using it in context," he told her. "I'm not propositioning you. The exact opposite, in fact."

"Oh!"

"It seems faintly inappropriate for you and I to consider staying under the same roof for any length of time, when we don't know each other. Red underwear notwithstanding."

"I told you it wasn't underwear," she protested, but knew he would be satisfied by the blush she could not control making her face feel hot.

"I'm not sure if you have a boyfriend," he continued persuasively, "or a mother, but I'm pretty sure neither of them would approve."

"I don't have a boyfriend, anymore," she snapped.

Sam tilted his head at her, pouncing on the one thing she did not want him to pounce on. "Anymore?"

She regretted adding that *anymore* instantly, as if her whole pathetic history was now on display. She wanted her lack of boyfriend to make her sound like an independent woman and not like a loser.

She diverted the talk—she hoped skillfully—away from the boyfriend. "Of course I have a mother. I'm quite used to her disapproval."

Used to it did not mean that she did not long for its opposite, had in fact spent most of her life longing for it, not that she would let that show on her face.

He looked surprised by that, as if she did not look like the kind of girl who earned her mother's disapproval. She felt a ridiculous desire to defend herself: *It's not my fault.* Instead, she stuck out her chin at him, and said, "I am not going anywhere."

"You need to think about that."

"No, I don't."

"Yes, you do."

She suddenly became aware of the stillness at the table and cast her gaze toward Cody. He had lost interest in his muffin, and his wide eyes were going from her to his uncle anxiously.

His uncle looked at Cody at the same time. He glared at her as if this was her fault, and then he smiled reassuringly at his nephew. "How's that muffin, big guy?"

Cody did not look the least reassured. Or like he thought the argument was her fault. He frowned at his uncle. At least one person seemed completely immune to Sam Walker's considerable charm.

Why did it make her feel a little sad that it was his nephew? If the child was, indeed, his nephew.

"Let's step outside for a moment," Sam suggested.

"Good idea." All the better to grill him about parental abduction!

"Why can't you leave?" he asked her in a low voice once they were on the deck.

"I have a deadline."

"For what?"

None of your business would be the appropriate answer, but she cast Cody another glance through the patio door, and knew she had to be civil for the child's sake. There was something very fragile about the boy. Plus, if she gave a little information, maybe Sam would be lulled into reciprocating with a little information of his own. "I write. Songs."

Not that her deadline was a song, exactly. In fact, once upon a time, she might have found her contract a bit humiliating. Apparently her guitar still disapproved, as if writing jingles for money was tawdry and superficial and would turn her into some kind of character from a sitcom.

But she had *finally* landed a contract for writing jingles. Paul's Steakhouse was due next week. It could lead to other things. It *would* lead to other things. Charlie Harper's success was nothing to sneeze at. If she delivered. If she showed she could be creative and commercial, plus disciplined enough to meet impossible deadlines.

"I knew it," he said. "Artsy. Paris would be perfect for songwriting."

"No, it would not," she said firmly. She would not allow herself to be distracted by Paris, and he would never understand about the guitar liking it here. "Every single thing I've ever written that was any good has been written here."

He looked like he got that, however reluctantly. "So, what do you suggest?"

"Couldn't you go to Paris?"

"No. There's nothing there for a three-year-old."

Here was her opportunity. "What is you and Cody's relationship?" she asked.

"I told you, he's my nephew."

"That's not what I meant."

"I'm his guardian." His voice was low. "My sister was his mom."

"Was?"

There was a long pause. For a moment the pain in Sam's eyes was so white hot, Allie felt as if she could be burned to ash by it.

"She died," he said, his voice low. "Her and her husband, in a car accident."

This was as unexpected as a slap. Allie felt her indignation dying in the light of this much larger revelation. She could barely speak for the emotion that clawed at her throat.

"That's why Cody doesn't talk," she whispered.

Something sagged in Sam's magnificent shoulders, as if the weight of what he carried suddenly became too much for him to carry alone.

"His pediatrician says to give it time."

"How long has it been?"

"Eight months." He turned from her abruptly, looked

out at the sea. "I don't know about this time thing. I don't know if it heals all wounds. My parents died in an accident, too, when I was just eighteen."

He looked as if he regretted saying that as soon as the words came out of his mouth. But she was left with an almost stunning awareness, not just that he was alone, but that he would have a terrible time trusting life. Worse than her.

In fact, her own wounds suddenly seemed to pale into insignificance. She missed Gram every day, but Mavis had known she was sick and her attitude and acceptance had helped Allie deal with the loss.

I'm old, she had said, patting Allie's hand. *This is the way of it—the old ones go, and the new ones come.*

But Sam's losses were completely different. They were unnatural and unexpected and he'd been blindsided by them. It felt as if Allie should know what to say—Gram would have known what to say—but she didn't and her silence coaxed more words from him.

"In some misguided moment," he continued, his voice a rasp of pure pain, "where Sue and Adam thought nothing bad could ever happen to them—despite the fact our family already had had terrible things happen—they named me as Cody's guardian in their will. They were probably having a glass of wine when they decided. I bet they laughed. I bet Sue said to Adam, 'Let's name Sam as guardian. That would be hilarious. He can't even keep a plant alive.'"

Allie moved beside him. Where words failed her, an instinct made her put her hand on his arm. In that place where there were no words, she needed to touch him.

He looked away from the water, and glared down at her hand, and she withdrew it rapidly, remembering her instincts were often so wrong.

"We're meeting some family here," Sam said, his voice gruff. "They've rented a place down the beach. They're coming from a great distance, and the arrangements have been in place for some time. That's why we can't go anywhere else."

There was something about the formality of all this, and the way he said *family*, with just a touch of hesitation, that told her what the answer to her next question was going to be. Still, she had to ask.

"And you can't move in with them?"

He shook his head, firmly, no.

"Well, then, we'll have to share."

"Share?"

Share—that concept five-year-olds learn in kindergarten. But somehow the sarcasm died within her before she spoke it.

"I'll stay out of your way," she promised. That was a vow she would keep, because looking at him she was suddenly aware there were distractions much bigger than Paris. "And you stay out of mine."

He looked annoyed. "This house is probably less than nine hundred square feet. Pretty hard to stay out of anyone's way."

"You could consider the beach an extension of the house."

"I don't want the family to get the wrong impression," he said, his voice a growl.

"The wrong impression?"

"Like you and I are cohabitating. Obviously, they would think that was bad for Cody."

Suddenly, she understood something far more than what he was saying was going on here. He did not look like the kind of man who gave two figs what anyone thought.

"What's the family connection of the people visiting?"

"It's my brother-in-law Adam's family. From Australia."

Something shivered along her spine. She could not take her eyes off his face. "Are they seeking custody of Cody?"

CHAPTER SEVEN

SAM DELIBERATELY LOOKED away from her. He did not like how astute she was, how she read him so easily, how she voiced a fear he had not even articulated inside himself.

He focused on the beach. There was a beachcomber out there this morning using a metal detector to look for treasure. One person's loss could be another person's gain. Beyond him, the waves lapped at the shore. He made himself look at Allie.

She had obviously made a huge effort to cover up this morning. She looked like an "after" picture for a weight-loss spa. She was dressed in too-large sweatpants and a shapeless T-shirt. It looked as if she could hold open the waistband of those pants and stick three more of her in there.

But no matter what Allie did, or what she wore, he could not un-see what he had seen last night. Or un-feel what he had felt when she was pressed against him on that bed.

Add that physical awareness of her—sharp in the air between them—to her kind of spooky intuition, and you had an equation that equaled trouble.

Still, had Sam actually ever put that question into words? Though the feeling of unease had gnawed at him, there was the question, point-blank. Did Adam's family, his brother, Bill, and his sister-in-law, Kathy, want custody?

"They haven't said those words," Sam admitted.

They hadn't said those words, and he hadn't said those words, but everyone would want what was best for Cody. And that was the million-dollar question, wasn't it? What was best for Cody? A single guy? Or a family?

One person's loss could be another person's gain.

He could feel her thoughtful eyes on him, scanning, picking up the things he was not saying. He felt as if she could see, or sense, the sinking in his stomach and the tightening in his heart.

"We'll make sure there are no wrong impressions," she promised.

We. As if they were a team.

"I'll stay out of your way," she promised again. "If they happen to meet me, we'll just have to explain the mix-up over the contract. There will be no doubt in their minds that we are not involved in some casual fling. Besides, I think it would be pretty obvious to them, or anyone really, that a guy like you wouldn't be involved with someone like me."

Now she had his full attention. He could feel a frown pulling down his brows.

"Why would you say that?" he asked cautiously. That was certainly not what he had felt when he held her last night.

And not what he had felt at all when she had thrown her arms open to the spray of water from the garden hose, transforming her into a goddess of the night and sea.

He had felt the very real danger of some chemistry building between them.

"Oh, you know," she said breezily, "corporate king, beach-dwelling, barely-making-it musician."

"Corporate king?" he sputtered, vaguely insulted. "That's a weird conclusion to arrive at. It can't be the way I dress. You've seen me in shorts and sandals, and my pajamas, for Pete's sake."

"Ha. *GQ* on vacation. I bet you have a corner office, in a glass building with a stunning view. You probably built some kind of empire, from the ground up. Computer tech of some sort."

He could feel his brows knitting closer together, and made a conscious effort to relax them. "Did you do an internet search on me?"

"Aha! I'm right, then. I might have tried to do an internet search. Just to make sure there was no abduction afoot. Do you know how many Sam Walkers there are?"

"I have no idea."

"Thousands. No, it's the flashy car in the driveway, legal beagles ready to defend your contracts…everything about you radiates wealth and power. You send out the unmistakable tycoon vibe—"

"*Tycoon*? Me? I get a picture of a bunch of people stranded on a tropical island, and the tycoon being the snotty one who won't get his hands dirty."

"I was thinking something more current. Like the tech wizard, Mitch Jones. He's the guy who invented that app—"

"I know who he is," he said drily.

"Or that guy who created the company that morphed into the big search engine—"

"Henrich Pfitzer," he said.

"See? You know him. I knew it. Computer tech billionaires. They're your tribe."

"I don't know him! They are *not* my tribe. I don't have a tribe."

"Yes, you do."

He thought of telling her his "tribe" had shrunk quite a bit in the past eight months. Popsy and Cody. He was barely at the office anymore, running things remotely, putting good, good people in charge. But she didn't know that, and what's more, she didn't need to know that.

"It's the *I have arrived* tribe," Allie told him, "whereas, I, on the other hand…"

She lifted a slender shoulder in wry self-deprecation that was somehow heart-wrenching.

Or would be if you had a heart, which he reminded himself, sternly, he no longer did.

"Anyway, it would be more than obvious to the casual observer, that you and I would be a terrible combination. Unworkable."

He should have found that conclusion a relief. Instead he found it somewhat distressing and found himself studying her. Sam became aware some hurt practically shimmered in the air around her.

Something—or more likely someone—had stolen her confidence from her.

He *hated* that. But he acknowledged he would be the worst possible choice to try to fix it. He had failed spectacularly at marriage. After the demise of his marriage, Sam had embraced a play-hard lifestyle. His sister had been fond of telling him that he had the emotional depth of a one-celled organism.

And all that was before more grief and a troubled nephew and a depressed dog had turned his life and his world upside down. It shocked him that he still projected the old him: wealthy and powerful, self-assured with the world at his feet. That's not what he was anymore.

He was a man who woke up every morning with a new sense of drowning in his own inadequacy.

You didn't grab onto someone else when you were drowning.

He knew that from a brief stint as a lifeguard when he was a teenager. A drowning person just pulled others down, too.

And two drowning people? Catastrophe.

"I don't see that we have a choice," she continued when he was silent. "We'll have to share the accommodation."

As if it was that simple: as if there was no history. No her coming at him with Harold, and no red bathing suit.

Last night, after the house had gone quiet, he had heard a door squeak open. And then another.

He'd gotten up and looked.

Popsy had always only been loyal to two people. Cody and Sam's sister.

Last night, the dog had managed to open the door of Cody's room and Sam had peered through the partially open door of Allie's to see the dog snuggled up with her on her bed.

Both door latches were worn out.

"You needn't worry," she assured him brightly, as if his worry at the brief but compelling history between them was written all over his face. "At all. Even if I was your type—so obvious I'm not—I'm not in the market for a relationship. Been there, done that."

She rolled her eyes as if her *been there, done that* meant nothing, but if he was not mistaken, that was a badly bruised heart she was wearing on her sleeve.

He shouldn't ask. But he did. "How old are you?"

"Why do you want to know?"

"Because you seem awfully young to have given up on happily-ever-after already."

"I'm twenty-three," she said, as if that was plenty old to have given up on romantic dreams.

"To be frank, you look like a poster child for picket fences and baby carriages, like those are the things that would make you happy."

"What a terribly old-fashioned thing to say." Bright spots rose up in her cheeks that told him he had hit a nerve.

"Ah, me and Thurston Howell are like that," he said. "Old-fashioned tycoon types."

"So, we both have some misperceptions we have to give up. How old are you?"

"Twenty-eight."

"And where are you at with *happily-ever-after*?"

He was annoyed by the question, but in fairness, he *had* started it.

"I gave it a try," he admitted, reluctantly. "I was married. I'm pretty good at math, so I should have realized, statistically, a fairy-tale ending was a long shot."

Why had he felt compelled to reveal that? For a frightening moment, he thought she was going to probe that, delve into his very private life. He could tell she was tempted. But, in the end, she didn't.

"My point exactly," Allie said. "I gave it a try, too. So, if we've dispensed with the personal part of the roommate arrangement, maybe we could move on?"

"To?"

"I can't seem to find the actual contract that you signed with my grandmother. Do you have a copy of it?"

"Not with me. It will be at my office. I can have someone send it, if you want. Is there something in particular you need clarified?"

"I was wondering if you already paid my grandmother or if I can look forward to some funds?"

He suspected this was still about the relationship she was not planning on having with him. She wanted him to be aware of all the chasms that separated them, finances probably being the biggest one.

And she wanted it to look as if all she really cared about was the money, as if that was why she was agreeing to sharing her cottage with him. She wanted it to look as if she was capable of keeping this relationship strictly business.

"So Paris is completely off the table?"

"Completely," she said firmly. "I can't go anywhere else. Not right now."

He saw it. For one second, he saw something flash through those clear eyes. For all her brave front and businesslike tone, it was apparent Allie was terrified of going out into the larger world.

"My grandmother used to say the cure for anything is salt water," she said, though he was not sure which of them she thought needed curing, her or him.

"Salt water?" he asked, softly.

She looked at him. "It's a quote, she found in an old *Reader's Digest* from the thirties. Along with her fabric collection, my grandmother's closets are stuffed with those. The quote is, 'The cure for anything is salt water—sweat, tears or the sea.'"

It confirmed what he had glimpsed: something in her was afraid, hurt, broken. Seeking a cure, even in the brittle yellowed pages of old magazines. He should have known how deep the fear was in her when she tried to clobber him with Harold!

He didn't know the why of it—why such a beautiful young woman was hiding out here. He didn't actually *want* to know the why of it. He was shocked to find out there were enough pieces of his heart left intact to break some more. For her. Someone who was practically a stranger to him.

Suddenly, he saw the truth of it: if he insisted on her moving out, if he followed the letter of the law and enforced his contract, she was not going to see how sensible it was, how it would protect them both.

She was going to see it as more proof that the world was out of her control, that bad things could happen to her without warning, that this place where she felt safe was not safe, either.

He was not the man to fix whatever had gone wrong for her. He knew that. But he knew, as a person who had found out exactly that hard truth about the world—that there was no safe place—he could not make it any worse for her, either.

Sam took a deep breath and looked out over her shoulder again, at the perfect stretch of beach. The beachcomber had paused and was digging through the sand. He held something up to the sun, and it glittered gold.

Sam had been holding on to this place, in his mind, thinking long, summery days of sand and water could help Cody. Help *them* create the bond he felt was absent. Help them become a family, of sorts, or let go of that notion altogether. He had counted on this place, so special in his world, to help him know what to do.

The complication to his plan, Allie, turned and looked at the stretches of golden sand and gently lapping waves, too.

If she was prepared to keep it all business, so was he. That was his specialty, after all, business. It was apparent she needed the money.

But it was her words, not her need of money, that he was thinking of. *Sweat, tears or the sea.*

Her words held a promise of something. Hope.

Which, of course, was the most dangerous thing of all.

So, maybe not the wisest thing to share a space with

her but, as she had pointed out, they could avoid each other.

They could use the beach as an extension of the house. Though Sam did not consider himself intuitive—at all—he had a deep sense of Cody *needing* the beach, that carefree place of sandcastles and kites and leaping waves.

Besides, he didn't have any choice, really.

Life had been showing him that lately. He didn't always have choices. He hated that. He hated feeling powerless, as if the most important things in life could be wrested from his control in an instant.

"Okay," he heard himself saying. "I thought these days were well behind me, but let's be roommates."

She held out her hand to shake on it.

He hesitated, and then took it. The full danger of what he was letting himself in for was in the delicate strength and vulnerability of her touch.

And yet, somehow in that touch, too, was a sense of having, impossibly, found something gold in a vast expanse of sand.

He sighed. One more complication in a life that was already way too complicated.

CHAPTER EIGHT

THERE, ALLIE THOUGHT, it was official. They were roommates.

She felt something when they shook hands. A jolt. A tingle. She couldn't deny that. But she had spoken the absolute truth to him: she was done with chasing happily-ever-after. She hated it that he saw picket fences and baby carriages in her, as if wisps of her unrealistic dreams clung to her like a mist.

But he was done with dreams, too. He'd been married. And it hadn't worked. For some reason that surprised her, maybe because of what she'd seen in his interactions with Cody in just this short time.

He didn't look like a man who gave up on love. He didn't look like a man who would take a vow and then break it.

But whatever, life had made him cynical and her cynical and what could be more perfect for both of them?

Except there was something about Sam Walker's desperate I'll-never-give-up-on-you love for his nephew that had just cracked open some barrier around her heart that she would have sworn was made of stone.

And that jolt she had felt when their hands touched? That was a power she might be very foolish to feel she could control. So, yes, the best plan was avoidance.

Easy for two weeks.

Strictly business.

"So do you owe me anything?" she asked, crisply.

He told her how much he owed her and her mouth fell open. It was everything she could do to prevent herself from dancing a little jig. She didn't care how much she had to suffer for the next two weeks. It was worth it.

Three full days later, Allie realized she might have been a little overconfident in assessing her own ability to suffer the inconveniences of having two roommates thrust into her world, one totally adorable, and the other totally sexy.

Oh, they had managed to work out the small details of living together. Sam was startled that the television was gone, but adjusted quickly, and played morning cartoons for Cody on his tablet. They provided their own groceries and the top two shelves of the fridge were his, the bathroom was set aside at seven each night for Cody's bath, she surrendered the porch and went for a walk and swim every afternoon so that Sam could have it to read during Cody's nap time.

But still, sharing quarters with an absolutely gorgeous man, a sweet small child and a dog who could melt the heart of Attila the Hun, all the while maintaining a suitably aloof distance, was difficult.

The house took on their presence.

When Sam noticed things that needed repair, he just did it, casually, without fanfare, and with a certain enviable male confidence, as if wielding a hammer and a screwdriver so naturally was just what real men did, as if it was nothing to get things ship-shape.

The evidence of the men in her life was suddenly everywhere: a shirt left on the swing, large flip-flops beside small ones at the back door, a small truck on the table, a partially completed Lego structure on the back deck, a load of underwear left in the dryer.

A radio was left on. She had long since stopped listening to the radio, but thankfully it was on a classical station, no gossipy chit-chat. A book, a memoir of surviving the Second World War, not a suspense thriller, was left open on its spine on the table on the back deck. She told herself she hated people who left books open on their spines, even while she looked at his reading material with way more interest than she should. She overheard him having conversations with his office that underscored that he was as confident and powerful in that world as he was adorably inept in his “daddy” role.

She felt like a detective collecting clues to who he was.

And who Sam was, was in his voice as he read stories to Cody. It was in the kitchen, where she saw that his culinary skills were clumsy, and ran to peanut butter on crackers, frozen fish sticks and fries, order-in pizzas.

It was watching from the porch as the two of them, Sam and Cody, headed across the beach, in the morning. Cody’s little chest and face glistening white with generously applied sunscreen, his shoulders covered by his Superman cape. As far as she could tell, Sam wore no sunscreen at all.

It was feeling her heart squeeze at the sight of the small hand in a large one, towels tucked under Sam’s arm, sand toys and buckets held firmly in his free hand. It was feeling something sigh within her when they returned, sleeping pale boy over Sam’s broad, sun-kissed shoulder, as he juggled all their other items, the sand-encrusted Superman cape tied around his own shoulders.

But Sam Walker, not just as a daddy, but as a man, also emerged. The scent of him. The encounters. His hand accidentally brushing hers as they both reached into the fridge. The shared laughter when Popsy licked a spill off the floor.

She had practically smacked into him this morning when he had come out of the shower dressed only in a towel.

It had done things to her pulse that were not in the Roommates Rules of Order.

Now, within hours, she had nearly smacked into him again in the same hallway. This time he was wearing only shorts. "Thought you were out," he said, by way of apology.

She had been out.

"I thought you were out," she said. She had come back in that red bikini they had a shared history with.

"Cody needed the bathroom."

There they were, nearly naked together again. It seemed criminal that he was so perfectly made, his skin turning golden from the beach days. She wanted to touch it.

Some unmistakable heat sizzled in the air between them.

"Thanks for fixing things," she said, trying to find safe ground. "The front door bell, the kitchen faucet, the cupboard doors."

"It's nothing. I used to do it for Mavis, too."

"I noticed you fixed the latch on my bedroom door."

"I didn't think you'd appreciate the nocturnal visits from Popsy."

"I actually kind of like them," she admitted. Then blushed, as if she had said she didn't like sleeping alone. "Now that I know it's not a burglar, that is."

"I noticed you haven't been locking the patio doors at night."

"Should I?" She had felt totally safe since that night they had stood outside together rinsing off the dog.

He smiled. "I sleep pretty light. I'll look after you."

That was what had been creeping into her house without her being aware of it. A sense of being looked after. Protected. She could see how ferocious he would be if she and Cody needed protecting.

It made something warm unfurl in her stomach.

She could argue she didn't need his protection. Or his fixes. But she didn't feel like arguing about it.

In fact, she felt deeply and dangerously aware of what he had brought to her house. She lifted her hand. Was she going to touch him? Why?

Just some gratitude bubbling within her that needed to find expression…the bathroom door burst open and Cody raced out.

Sam stood, frozen.

Just for a second, until they heard small footsteps pounding across the back deck. It broke the spell between them.

"Hey," Sam yelled, racing after him. "Did you wash your hands?"

The cottage was suddenly too quiet, and Allie stood there, feeling as if they had had a near miss of some sort. Had she been about to touch him?

She brushed her fringe out of her eyes, as if she could convince herself *that* had been her intention all along.

It felt more imperative than ever to put distance between them, but Cody went for his nap early that day, and their paths crossed again as Sam settled on the deck.

"See you later," she said breezily, coming out the back door, a very proper swim cover-up in place.

"Yeah, have a good afternoon."

Something in his voice stopped her. She noticed he

wasn't reading his book, but gazing out at the beach. The afternoon crowds had begun to arrive. The scent of coconut oil drifted up to her, and bright umbrellas dotted the sand. An inflated ball blew out to sea as a little girl shrieked her outrage at its loss.

There was something in the quietness around him that made her stop partway down the stairs and come back up them.

"Sam?"

He pulled his attention away from the beach.

"Are you okay?" she asked.

"Sure. Yeah."

Something made her wait instead of taking his words at face value.

"It's just that they're arriving tomorrow. My in-laws. I guess they're my in-laws. What do you call the relatives of your in-laws? Are they in-laws, too?"

She was seeing what she suspected was a very rare flagging in his confidence. Her need to preserve her own sanity fled. She pulled out a chair at the table.

"Cody's aunt and uncle and cousins are arriving tomorrow," he clarified.

"What are their names?" she asked him softly.

"Bill. That's my brother-in-law, Adam's brother. His wife is Kathy. Their kids are Nicole and Bryan."

"Then that's what you call them."

He nodded. "Of course. Simple." But his voice sounded strained. "It's not as if they're strangers. I've met them. Half a dozen times. We video chat. *I* video chat. Try to think of things to say, because Cody can't."

"They'll see how good you are with Cody," she assured him. "I have."

Sheesh! She might as well admit she had been spying on him.

But he didn't seem to notice. "Will they? Don't you think they'll look at him not talking, after all this time, and wonder what the hell I'm doing? I haven't actually told them he doesn't talk. Maybe I should have sent a memo, I don't know."

"They must have figured it out from the video chats," she told him gently.

"His cousin, Nicole, is six. She fills all the silences. She sings to him, sometimes she'll read a story. But surely they've noticed he doesn't speak, surely they've wondered about it every time we've done the video thing. Maybe that's why they're coming."

"I think they'll look at you and see a man doing the best that he can."

His voice was very low. "I'm afraid it's not good enough. That's my fear. That my best is not good enough. For Cody. And that that will be immediately obvious to anyone looking."

She felt his pain and his desperation. "It's not obvious to me," she said softly.

She did what she had wanted to do since she had found herself cuddled up to him that first night. She touched him. Only not in the same way she had wanted to touch him then.

She reached across the space that separated them, and touched his cheek. She could feel the rough, sensuous scrape of his whiskers beneath her fingertips, beneath that, the sharp and glorious contrast that was the silk of his skin.

But more than the physical sensation of touching him, Allie felt what he was feeling. His tremendous insecurity. His desire to do the right thing by his nephew, even at personal cost to himself.

She could feel the depth and strength of his love, and she was tremendously moved by it.

"It's going to be okay," she said.

His eyes met hers, and she could see he longed to believe her. He looked like a drowning man who had been thrown a life preserver.

He covered her hand with his own. It seemed like the most natural thing in the world when he slid her hand toward his mouth, and kissed it.

"Thank you," he said, his voice a soft growl of pure emotion. "Thank you, Allie."

She looked at where her hand rested against his lips. She *felt* the exquisiteness of his lips touching her skin. She felt it as intensely as she had ever felt anything: as if the crowds on the beach and the slap of the waves, the dog at their feet, Cody snoozing away in his bedroom, all faded.

This became her whole world.

His lips.

Her skin.

Part of her was amazed that her hand was not smoking, pre-ignition. The awareness of him that had been building in her for days felt as if it exploded.

She grabbed her hand away from him.

Suddenly protecting herself felt imperative again. Sam as *vulnerable* and strong and loving was just too potent a combination. It made her heart hurt.

"Well," she said, standing up, straightening her swim cover, "off I go."

She tried to act casual as she went off the porch and walked through the sand, dodging umbrellas and people to find herself at the water's edge. She tried to act as if her whole world had not just shifted on its axis.

Allie shucked her swim cover, and hurled herself into

the waves, certain that she could hear a sizzle as her overheated self hit the cold water.

And she was sure she could feel his gaze as it followed her. And it was overheated, too.

CHAPTER NINE

BEYOND THE UMBRELLAS and the people, Sam could still see Allie. He watched as she arrived at the ocean's edge and dropped her swim cover.

She was wearing a one-piece bathing suit today, turquoise and navy shades swirling together. The back was an open U, dipping just below her hipbones, leaving the tenderness of her neck exposed, and her naked back. Her skin was golden and flawless. The bathing suit was every bit as sexy as the bikini had been. He felt mesmerized by her, and was relieved when she flung herself into the ocean with a kind of reckless abandon.

He contemplated the gift she had just given him. He didn't know which was more dangerous: the physical allure of her or the emotional sanctuary.

She believed in him.

He hadn't known he had needed that. He was a man who had always believed in himself. He did not know why it meant so much to him.

She barely knew him, or Cody, for that matter. And yet, they shared a space. She probably, at this point, knew more about his and Cody's relationship than any other living being, aside from Popsy, who hardly counted.

Popsy, who crept out of Cody's room every night, pushed open Allie's door and climbed into her bed. Now that Sam had fixed the latch, Allie must be letting the dog in, because Sam still woke in the morning to Popsy slinking out of Allie's room, as if he had been caught in an indiscretion.

The indiscretion being that Popsy had never once slept with Sam.

"And that is going to be the only indiscretion in this house," Sam muttered, as he watched Allie swim out past the wave break, and begin a strong crawl across the mouth of the bay. He decided, when Cody woke up, they would go out for dinner.

A good strategy, because when they came back, the house was empty. It was only after Cody's bath that Sam realized he had forgotten to get milk while they were out.

Cody was already in his pajamas, but sometimes he was upset by small changes to his routines. With that one notable exception, when he'd had the muffin Allie brought him for breakfast, he ate cereal for breakfast. Bits O' Goodness, nothing else.

The counselor had told Sam that Cody's rigidity about his routines, and what he ate, were a way of trying to make his world safe and predictable.

Since tomorrow they were meeting his aunt and uncle and his cousins, it didn't seem like it would be a good morning to test the waters with a new breakfast, say of toast, or waffles.

Sam wanted the day to be perfect, not to start with friction between him and Cody, or with one of Cody's meltdowns.

There had been no meltdowns, he realized, since they'd arrived. The long days of sunshine, water, sand, were doing everything he hoped.

"Come on, buddy, let's get dressed and go get some milk."

Cody shook his head, vehemently, *no.*

Which would be safer? A small disruption to the bedtime routine now, or trying out something new for breakfast tomorrow?

"You can pick some things. It will be fun. You like the grocery store. You can pick cookies."

Cody shook his head, no, again, then dashed by his uncle at lightning speed. He went out the back door and, thankfully, skidded to a halt when he saw Allie out there, her guitar across her lap, a blank piece of paper beside her and a pencil behind her ear.

Sam came out. She'd been so quiet he hadn't realized she was home. He certainly hadn't heard a guitar.

"Come on," he wheedled. "Chocolate chip."

"What's up?" Allie said.

"Uh, we're out of milk. I thought I'd make a quick run to the store. I'm bribing Cody to come with me. Please don't tell me bribing is not part of good parenting."

She smiled at him. "I'm no expert on good parenting. You can go for milk if you want, me and Cody can hang for a bit."

"I don't remember that being part of our arrangement."

"Well, sometimes life requires flexibility." She ran her thumb over the strings of her guitar. The notes were rich and full. Definitely a sound Sam would have noticed if it had happened before.

She didn't even look at Cody, but ran her thumb over the strings again. "You want to hang with me while your uncle goes and gets groceries?"

Sam could feel himself holding his breath. Cody didn't like letting his uncle out of his sight.

But Cody looked at her, then nodded with a certain insulting vehemence.

"Sheesh," Sam said.

"Before I got sidetracked, I took two years of early childhood education at university, so I'm imminently qualified for half an hour of child care." Allie strummed at her guitar, took the pencil from behind her ear, wrote something down, frowned and crossed it out.

"My guitar hates Paul's Steakhouse," she muttered.

"I ate there once. I hated it, too."

She groaned. "Don't tell me that. I'm supposed to be writing a jingle for their radio ad."

"Like a character on a sitcom?"

She shot him an annoyed look. "Kind of like that," she said. "Only without the sleazy part. Or the fabulously wealthy part."

Cody settled on the floor of the porch in front of her. He raised his arms in the air and made fluttering movements with his fingers.

Allie glanced up from her guitar, shot Sam a puzzled look. He frowned.

"I think maybe he's requesting a song," Allie said.

Sam looked from her to his nephew, and then recognized exactly what Cody was doing. "You're right! His Aussie cousin Nicole sings him that one. On the video conferences. 'Inky-dinky Spider.'"

"Oh!" Excited, Allie began strumming her guitar. "It's 'itsy-bitsy,' not 'inky-dinky.'"

"Thank you," he said drily. "I consider myself edified."

She ignored him, strummed the guitar, fiddled with the frets and then began to sing.

"The itsy-bitsy spider," she sang, playing simple, accompanying notes on the guitar, *"went up the water spout."*

Sam felt a quiver go up and down his spine. The guitar made a sound he had never heard an instrument make before: as if it had its own voice.

"Down came the rain and washed the spider out."

And Allie's voice was beyond incredible. Nothing in the way she spoke could have prepared him for the tone of it, rich, deep, sensuous.

"Out came the sun and dried up all the rain."

It seemed suddenly as if the world was infused with that very sun she was singing about, as if light had come out from behind a rain cloud and made the world sparkling and new. Cody was sweeping his arms from side to side, forming a semi-circle for the sun. For a suspended moment, Sam was aware of the corn silk color of Cody's hair, the roundness of his cheeks, the thickness of his lashes.

The light extended to Allie. Sam felt as if he was nearly vibrating with awareness of her, of the unconscious sensuality of her fingers as she strummed, of the light playing with the black tips of her sun-streaked hair, of the golden tone of her skin and of the plumpness of her lower lip. He was aware of the way her too-large light blue button-up shirt had slid off the slenderness of her shoulder, revealing a bra strap as white as snow. He was aware of the snugness of her shorts, and sun-browned legs, and bare toes tapping the rough wood of the porch.

"And the itsy-bitsy spider climbed up the spout again."

Her voice was rich, it was stunning, it was magical, the kind of voice that could weave a web of enchantment around the unwary, that could wake a man who had been sleeping, that could make him so acutely aware of everything around him, and of his own heartbeat and the summer heat coming off his skin, that it felt almost painful to be alive, to be breathing.

Was that silly song really about life? Climbing up,

being washed down, the sun coming out and giving you the courage to try again?

The enchantment seemed to have oozed over Cody like warmed honey. He clapped with delight. He smiled! Not that secretive little smile that sometimes Sam caught sight of, as Cody moved into his imaginary world of superheroes and cars, but an open, engaged smile of pure delight.

"You're really good at this," she encouraged Cody. He puffed up under her approval. She began the song again at the beginning.

Cody swayed happily, and acted out the sequence.

First the dog, and now Cody, Sam thought, watching, trying to hide the fact that this small event was making him feel alive, his nephew's obvious pleasure was making him extraordinarily emotional.

"What?" Allie asked, glancing at him.

"Nothing," Sam mumbled. But it wasn't nothing.

He thought of asking her if she was an enchantress. That's how he felt, with her music, her beautiful voice washing over him, as if he could follow the dog and his nephew and fall, fall, fall under her spell.

The worst possible thing he could do was give himself over to it. She'd agreed to hold down the fort. He needed to go get milk. But instead, in the grip of something larger than him, and larger than all of them, Sam found himself sinking onto the deck, cross-legged, beside Cody.

"Can you do 'Do Your Ears Hang Low?'" Sam asked her.

"Of course."

Allie sang every rollicking, motion-based children's song that she knew. And then she slowed it down and sang quieter songs, until finally she was singing lullabies.

At some point, Cody climbed onto Sam's lap, inserted his thumb in his mouth, and despite his fighting it, his eyes finally closed and stayed that way. His warmth puddled against Sam and made him feel the glorious and terrifying pull of pure love.

Sam got up, his nephew in his arms, and went into the house. He tucked Cody in and stared down at the sleeping child, so aware of the gravity of his responsibility, so aware love complicated decisions—it didn't make them easier.

He untied the cape string, and tiptoed out and shut the door. He told himself not to go back out on that deck, but how could he not thank her for the look he had seen on Cody's face?

"He didn't even wake up for bedtime stories," he said. "It's the second time today I feel like I owe you a big thank-you."

"Not at all. That was really fun for me, too."

He came and sank down on the swing beside her. It felt as if it was the most natural thing in the world.

"I saw something tonight that I wasn't sure I'd ever see again," Sam confided in her. "While you were singing, Cody was the way he used to be. I mean, not talking. But happy. Especially with his aunt and uncle coming tomorrow, that means so much to me."

His hand found hers, again as if it was the most natural thing in the world. He squeezed it. Some part of him wanted to hang on. Forever.

Despite the itsy-bitsy spider encouraging him to try again and again, Sam knew the saddest lesson of all. There was no forever.

He slid his hand from the warmth of hers.

Allie loved the weight of Sam on the swing beside her, the gentle creak as he shoved it back and forth with the balls of his feet.

"It made me happy, too," she admitted, "in a way I haven't been for a long time."

He stopped pushing the swing back and forth with his feet. He looked at her, ran his hand through his hair, looked toward the darkened beach, the moonlight capping the waves in snow-white froth. He was making a decision, Allie thought, whether to go or whether to stay here with her.

"Allie, how come you haven't been happy?" His voice was a rasp.

She was aware they were standing at a crossroads, of sorts. Life had taught her it was dangerous to trust people. Just like Sam, she had a decision to make right now, too.

So did she protect herself? Or did she throw caution to the wind?

CHAPTER TEN

WAS ALLIE READY to open up, to anyone, let alone Sam Walker? She could feel herself leaning away from what he was offering.

But then it was as if she heard her grandmother's voice. *A burden is made lighter for sharing it.* She knew she would feel lighter if the secret she carried was revealed.

"Tell me about how your life got side-tracked," he invited softly. "It seems to me you would have made the best teacher ever."

She contemplated that, that he had listened to her. Why not tell him what had happened to her? The stars were winking out, he was a solid presence beside her, she had seen his gentle, firm way with Cody.

Why not trust him?

Because the world has taught you the danger of trusting, a voice inside her said, and this time it was not her grandmother's voice.

To her surprise, she chose to ignore that voice. She chose to throw caution to the wind.

"I had just completed my sophomore year at university. It was a small campus, so everyone was shocked, and really excited, that the show *American Singing Star* chose us as a location to hold tryouts. People knew I sang, and everyone wanted me to try out. There was quite a lucrative financial prize, so there I found myself in front of a panel of judges."

"*American Singing Star*? The television show?" he asked.

She had the horrifying thought he might have seen her spectacular fall from grace. "Yes, have you seen it?"

"No, I have to say television isn't my thing. Until Cody. Now it's *SpongeBob SquarePants*, *Rugrats*, *Doug*. But I know what it is. Kind of an offshoot of that really famous reality singing show, right?"

"Yes, that's the one. Anyway, I did fairly well. I got to the finals. And then I failed. It was quite a ride, from soaring successes to utter humiliation, all conducted under the unforgiving lens of the public eye."

"That seems like the short version," Sam said. "Why didn't you go back to school after it didn't pan out?"

"The whole thing was so public. For a while everyone knew who I was." *And hated me.* "It's dying down now, a bit."

"So, you *are* hiding here," he said softly.

She shot him a look. "A conclusion you had already arrived at?"

He lifted a shoulder and looked at her, his eyes on her face making her feel there was no keeping secrets from him. "You're a lovely young woman who told me you don't believe in happily-ever-after. Why don't you tell me about that part?"

"Maybe another time," she said, thinking it would be way too easy to tell him everything.

"I can go look online," he said. "You already told me whatever happened played out publicly."

She sighed. The stars were winking on above them, and the waves were picking up. She could hear their gentle lapping turning into crashing. What would Gram tell her to do?

The temptation of being relieved in some way of this burden was too much to resist. To have someone, anyone, know the truth.

"At first," she said, "everything about that show was exciting. They gave me a different name, one of those one-name things like Cher. They redid the original audition tape, with me coming out and introducing myself as Tempest.

"Of course it was obvious I was the furthest thing from a tempest you could imagine. I was a small-town college kid in pigtails and jeans. One of the judges—the same one who suggested the change to one name—rolled his eyes. I should have realized how scripted everything was, right then, that it was really live theater. And maybe I did, but it was all so exciting.

"I kept getting put forward to the next round. I was like this instant celebrity—singers I'd admired were inviting me to their homes. There was talk of record deals and guest spots at concerts and collaborations. It was all very heady stuff."

"But?" he asked.

"They were telling me how to dress, and doing my hair and doing my makeup. They gave us a place to live—all the finalists in this fancy-fancy mansion built into the hills, with a pool. At the time it felt right. It felt as if this glossy, beautiful, beloved by-the-public creature, *Tempest*, was who I was always meant to be.

"There was a guy in the same competition. We were under the same strains. Ryan was cute. He was friendly. I started leaning on him, and he on me. It became more and more romantic. I didn't realize how much of our relationship was being orchestrated. Looking back, there was probably a subplot in play from the first audition.

"The script probably read something like this—wholesome, small-town geek, whose music style is folksy, will fall for big-city super-suave rock star type. As the competition moves along, the geek will become more and more glamourous and superficial, and he will become more and more down-to-earth, with his heart on his sleeve.

"A romance among the two most popular contestants was great for the show. Imagine what that did for ratings! But I was oblivious to all that. Ryan was part of this exciting new future that was going to be mine. I was head over heels for him and I thought he was for me. He was always doing these crazy little things—presenting me with bouquets of dandelions, drawing hearts in lipstick on my dressing room mirror, sneaking kisses, making promises and plans.

"Gone was the studious girl whose greatest ambition had been to teach kindergarten, meet a nice guy someday, get married, have a few kids. Ryan insisted we were going to be as famous as other megastar couples and that our music and our love was our ticket to the whole world.

"The night before the final competition, Ryan told me it was all fake. He'd been put up to the whole thing by the show's producers. He didn't love me. He didn't even think of the dandelion bouquets or the lipstick hearts himself.

"I was devastated. Did they know how devastated I would be? I don't know, but I think they did. I think I was played like a fiddle. I couldn't pull myself together for the final show. I didn't even want to win anymore. I didn't care enough.

"But he did. Oh, Ryan went on that final show, live, and talked about how I had broken him in two. He sang a heart-wrenching ballad about treachery and lost love. He even squeezed out a tear with his final note."

Sam said a word under his breath that he could not say around Cody, but that summed up how she felt *exactly.*

"This adoring public, this mega fan base, turned on me in a blink. I went from being America's sweetheart to the most hated person on the planet. I couldn't turn on a television set without some entertainment guru weighing in on it.

"Social media lit up with everyone commenting on how despicable I was. I cut my hair, and people still recognized me, though most weren't quite as nasty in person, thank goodness, as when they were hiding behind their keyboards. Still, I had to wear a disguise to go get groceries, oversize sunglasses and a ball cap. Going back to school, where everyone had been so proud of me, seemed out of the question.

"And so I retreated to here. To my grandmother, who never lost sight of who I really was, even when I did, and to this place. She got rid of the television. She was sick, but she seemed to rally to help me. We played cards, and cooked and sewed together, and talked and talked and talked. Looking back it was the worst of times, because she was sick and I was hurting, but also the best of times, because we were together in such an intense, loving way.

"But I can't seem to write songs anymore, not even the jingle I've been hired to write. Tonight is the first time, in a long time, I've actually played my guitar and sang. And you know what was great about it? It wasn't about me. It was about the music bringing joy. Somehow, that's part of what I've lost."

She didn't realize she had started crying until he placed a finger on her cheeks and caught a tear.

And then he gathered her in his arms, and held her

with such exquisite tenderness that she thought it was possible to die from it.

"My turn to thank you," she managed to choke out.

"That's a lot to carry by yourself," he said. "Where's your family in all this? Especially since Mavis died?"

"Humph," she said, against his chest.

"I remember you saying once, in passing, your mother disapproved of you. Because of this?"

She was stunned by how carefully he had listened and by how intuitive he was. Somehow, that was not what she would have expected from him.

"When people think of mothers they think of PTA and cookies, but my mom wasn't like that. She was a single mom, and darned proud of it, a career woman who made her own way. She referred to my father as *the donor.* I actually thought I was a product of a sperm bank.

"She was a professor of economics at that same small-town college I ended up going to. She was a nontraditional person in a very traditional town. I craved every single thing she eschewed about that town—neat little houses behind trimmed hedges, churches with Sunday services, marriage, families with mommies and daddies, babies. I wanted to celebrate normal Christmases, she wanted to shop and go to plays in New York. I wanted to spend summers here at the beach with my grandmother, but I only got a few weeks. The rest of the time I was dragged off to Europe with her.

"When I went to college to study early childhood education, my mother was appalled. She saw that choice as reflecting a shocking lack of ambition. She wasn't totally behind the whole *American Singing Star* thing, but she applauded the ambition. She actually let it slip that maybe I took after my father. I wheedled it out of her that he'd been a college music teacher by day, and a guitar player in a band at night.

"She disliked Ryan, and saw our great romance for what it was—a sham. She saw right through him. But if I expected sympathy after the big public humiliation, what I got instead was a kind of self-satisfied *I told you so*, as if being right was far more important to her than my feelings."

Sam said that word he couldn't say around Cody again. His fury on her behalf made her sniffle again.

"Anyway, she took a position as a visiting fellow at Oxford shortly after it all happened, and I came here."

"Aw, Allie…"

It was the genuine tenderness in his voice that undid her. The tears came, hard, soaking his chest.

"I'm sorry," she said. "This is the second time I've fallen apart on you, and gotten your shirt all wet. You'll think I'm such a crybaby. And nothing could be further from the truth."

"Liar," he said, and that same tender note in his voice kept it from stinging. At all.

Still, she felt honor bound to correct him. "No, really. It's not a lie. I'm very strong. Independent. Resilient."

"Uh-huh."

It was pretty hard to make a case for strength, when she'd already admitted she was hiding from the world. Suddenly, it did not feel like such a bad thing to be *seen*.

Allie just wanted to know what he saw. She pulled back from him, and studied his face. When had it become so familiar to her that she felt she knew every plane of it, and every nuance of expression?

"What do you see?" she asked, wondering if she was ready for his answer.

Without even a moment's hesitation, Sam said, "I see you as compassionate, sensitive, creative."

He lifted her chin with his finger and scanned her face. Her arguments caught in her throat.

"But not strong," she said.

"The world has quite enough strong people. The world needs you."

"Ha," she said.

"No, I'm not kidding. It's people like you," he told her softly, "who have the hardest job. You have to try and make the world more beautiful. Paint the pictures. Tell the stories. Sing the songs."

"I don't sing anymore. Not publicly, anyway."

He seemed to consider that, and then, as if words could not be enough to express what he was feeling, Sam lowered his head and touched his lips to her lips.

Not in a sexual way.

In a far more powerful way. In a way that said he saw her. And approved of what he saw.

But the kiss was like a tiny spark held to the dry tinder of her soul. Allie felt something white-hot blaze through her. She might have deepened that kiss into something quite different, but Sam stood up abruptly.

"Shoot. I forgot the milk," he said, his voice pure gravel, as he stared down at her. "I better go grab it before the store closes."

Sam drove away from the cottage feeling two things: a kind of helpless tenderness toward Allie, and a kind of impotent fury at the world and how it had treated her.

And maybe he reserved a touch of that impotent fury for himself. What was he thinking kissing his landlady?

But this went deeper, and he was aware he had felt such fury only once before, when Sue and Adam had been killed.

The events, he knew, were not on the same scale, but

the feeling was so similar: a kind of helplessness in the face of life's unfairness, in the face of cruelty to people who did not deserve it. Allie had been manipulated and betrayed and it made him so angry he wanted to punch someone.

Still, no matter what he was feeling, surely kissing her had not been a proper response to that?

And yet, what other way, to let her know, *he saw her.* In the past few days, he felt as if he had seen who she really was.

He knew he shouldn't do it, but he did it anyway. He pulled over to the side of the road and yanked out his phone.

He searched Tempest, *American Singing Star*. He only watched half of one of her performances.

It was not that she wasn't talented. It was not that she couldn't sing.

It was that he could barely recognize her with the long, jet-black hair, the false eyelashes, the form-fitting black leather outfit.

Watching her performance only intensified the helpless rage he felt at all of them: the show, Ryan, her mother.

He turned off the phone. He put the car back in Drive. He went to the store and got milk. It was on his way out the door of the store that he stopped, stunned by his realization.

For the first time since the accident had taken Adam and Sue, he genuinely cared about someone outside of the walls of his little world.

He wasn't ready.

And life hadn't asked him if he was.

CHAPTER ELEVEN

ALLIE MADE A point of not being up when Sam got back from the store. He'd made it clear he wished that brush of lips between them had not happened.

And it was humiliating that she felt the opposite. As if she would like it to happen and happen some more.

Embarrassing! In the morning, anxious to avoid more embarrassment, and the longing being in the same room as his lips was going to cause her, she was up and out the door before Sam and Cody were even out of bed. She took her guitar and some peanut butter sandwiches, and headed away from the beach—way too crowded in light of tomorrow's Fourth of July celebrations—and toward the hills that overlooked Sugar Cone.

It wasn't that she hadn't liked what Sam said to her but that she had liked it way, way too much. She needed to start crossing days off her calendar, a countdown to how many days before Sam and Cody would be gone.

Her life would be back to the way it was before.

Yawningly empty, a little voice informed her. And worse, all about her.

She found a favorite overlook with a bench and set up. By late afternoon, she had eaten her sandwiches, watched butterflies, listened to birds, talked with six strangers, petted several dogs and done a few yoga stretches.

What she hadn't done was made any progress on her jingle. Last night, she'd thought the creative block was over. Her guitar had been speaking to her again, humming like a living thing under her flying fingers as she sang to Cody and Sam.

Today the instrument was stubbornly and silently back on mute. The lyric part of the exercise was no better. Every time she thought of Paul's Steakhouse, the only thing she could think of that even remotely rhymed was *make-out.*

Which led her right back to the feel of Sam's lips on hers.

She couldn't concentrate. It had nothing to do with the taste of his lips. Or those words, those tender, beautiful words: *The world needs you.*

Oh, who was she kidding? It had everything to do with that kiss, and especially those words.

It felt to Allie as if those words were in some way pivotal. They were the words she had needed to hear her entire life. That there was not just a place in the world for her, but that it needed her.

And how was she repaying the kindness of those powerful words? Hiding. Just as he had accused her of doing.

Hiding from the world.

Hadn't she been hiding, even when she was in the competition? Hadn't she denied that, with each level that she moved forward in *American Singing Star*, she'd moved further and further from herself, willingly trading her identity for fame and accolades? Hadn't she hidden who she really was in order to gain approval? In order to fit in? In order to be loved?

Today, Sam was meeting Cody's aunt and uncle and cousins. They were probably doing it right now.

How was it going? Was he going to be okay? What if he needed someone to talk to about it?

Who was she *really*?

The safest thing was to run away from him, to hide in these hills, possibly right up until his departure date. To go back to making the world all about herself: her pain, and her betrayals and her challenges, how unfair the world had been to her.

But had that preoccupation brought her one single thing to like about her life? Had it moved her any closer to a satisfying existence?

Her grandmother had always known who she was. And her Gram would tell her, in no uncertain terms, to go home to the beach cottage, and be strong enough to offer Sam exactly what he had seen in her.

Her compassion, her creativity, her sensitivity.

As she packed up her things and headed back to her car she felt as if this might be the bravest thing she had ever done. It felt as if she was honoring the person her grandmother had always known she was.

This was her lesson, her legacy from Gram. Bravery was not stepping out in front of a live audience of thousands and a TV audience of millions.

But bringing the gift of herself to another human being. Believing that she had a gift to offer. She missed her grandmother so much in that moment, and felt so grateful for her that Allie thought she might weep.

Cody and Sam had already returned from meeting the Australian relatives when she got back. Popsy greeted her as though she had been gone for years instead of hours. Was it her imagination or was Popsy more lively?

Even with Cody having his nap, and Sam with his feet up on the back deck, her house felt *full* in ways it had not felt before they had arrived in her life. Taking a deep breath, ordering herself to be brave, Allie grabbed a water and joined him on the deck.

"Hey." She suddenly felt shy, and wondered if she was intruding.

Do not look at his lips.

She looked. Good grief, he was gorgeous.

But he nudged a chair with his foot, an invitation, a confirmation she had done the right thing. She took it.

"How did the family reunion go?" she asked.

"Actually, really well. The whole family has this kind of laid-back vibe. We built sandcastles on the beach. I took verbal orders from two pint-size people, and hand signals from another. Tears from all as the tide came in and swept it all away. Nap time."

"Are you okay?"

"Oh, sure. Why wouldn't I be?"

"I don't know. You look…pensive."

Actually, *sad* would have said it much, much better.

"The little girl, Nicole, just took Cody under her wing as if she was a mother hen. Bossing him around, playing with him, teasing him, teaching him little songs, ignoring the fact he didn't sing one word back to her. There was a kind of instant connection between him and both those kids."

"Cousins," she said. "They often have those bonds."

"Do they? Is this from your expertise file on early childhood development?" There was an edge to his voice.

"Did Cody seem happy with them in a way he isn't with you?" Allie asked with soft caution.

"I *want* his happiness," he snapped.

"Tell me what happened, Sam." She realized that he was trying to hide the sadness from her, that he didn't know it was so apparent in the lines of his face.

He looked at her as if he was going to tell her to go to

hell, and then he ran his fingers through the dark waves of his hair, looked out to sea and looked back at her. Debating.

When he spoke, his voice low and pained, she realized she had stopped breathing, recognizing this as another pivotal moment.

He would trust her with his deeper self, or he wouldn't.

"Bill is so much like my brother-in-law, Adam, that it hurts. You think the ragged edge has come off grieving and then, there it is."

"They look alike?"

"It's that, but it's more. So much more. The accent, the humor, the way of *being.* Adam was my best friend. I met him when I was just starting my company. He came to work for me. I introduced him to my sister."

He smiled, possibly the saddest smile Allie had ever seen. "I used to call him a dumb Aussie. He was the greatest guy I ever knew. Losing one of them would have been more than I could bear, but both? If it wasn't for Cody, I don't know how I would have continued to get up every day.

"But I look at that poor kid, and I think, if it's doing this to me, a full-grown man, supposedly with a few coping skills for life, what's it doing to him?"

He took in a long, ragged breath. "Cody took to Bill immediately. And the cousins. And you are probably very right. Seeing him with a family—a real family—made me aware of all the things I haven't been able to give him. I do want his happiness. I want it with all my heart. I just wish more of it came from being with me."

She contemplated that. And then she said, "You know what I see when he is with you? You are his rock. In a world that has shown him it is not always safe, you are his safe place. The place where it's okay for him to grieve in whatever way his three-year-old self needs to grieve. He doesn't feel pressured to be happy around you, to talk, to meet your needs. He knows you are the adult and it's your job to meet his needs. He trusts you completely. He knows you are in this together. And you are so sure that he saw his father in his father's brother, Bill. Of course he did.

"But don't you think he sees his mother in you? Every single day?"

"I doubt that. We looked like we came from different parents. She's the one Cody got all those blond curls from."

But I bet he got those soulful liquid-brown eyes straight from your family line, Allie thought.

"It's not so much about looks," Allie said, slowly. "Though I'm sure you have resemblances to your family you are not aware of. And mannerisms. Like Bill has some of the same quirks as Adam, I bet you, unknowingly, have some of your sister's. Maybe the way you tilt your head when you listen, or the way you throw back your head to laugh."

Oops, letting him know she was observing him way too closely, but getting Sam to hear this seemed far more important than protecting herself.

"I'd be willing to bet," she continued, "that you shared a value system with your sister, a kind of bone-deep decency, a courage for facing life, a determination that Cody sees in you every day, and is reassured by."

"Stop it," Sam growled, "you are going to make me choke up. Very unmanly."

Allie was gratified by the spark being back in his voice, gratified that somehow she had stumbled on just the right words. "Go ahead. Cry. As if there could be enough tears."

"To be honest? I don't think I have any left."

This was exactly why she had come back from her hike, some instinct—or perhaps all that was best about Gram alive in her—drawing her here, to where she was needed. She didn't say anything. She just sat with him, the silence comfortable between them as they watched the waves in the distance, and the crowds on the beach.

Children playing in the sand, teenagers shoving each other near the water's edge, women who had undone the back strap of their bathing suit tops, shirtless guys throwing footballs and posturing for those women who pretended not to see them. There were sounds, waves crashing, and birds cawing and shouts and laughter, mommies calling after their children.

Life, really. Ordinary life, unfolding before them on the beach. A simple scene that was so reminiscent of the kind of happy, carefree days of lighthearted spirit that summer brings.

"They've got a full day planned tomorrow," Sam said, breaking the comfortable silence between them. "They're quite excited about being here in the States for the Fourth of July celebrations. There's a parade on Main Street in the morning, some kind of festival after, and then fireworks on the beach tomorrow night."

"I always wanted to be here for Fourth of July," she said. "But that was always the week my grandmother went away to visit my great-aunt Mildred. I usually came toward the end of the summer, when my mother needed to get ready for the fall semester. I can't even tell you what coming here meant. Such a sense of being accepted, of being home, of being loved."

Allie sighed. "I miss her so much."

He looked at her. "You should come with us."

"Me? Why?"

"Because you'll be missing your grandmother. It feels

like one of those family celebration kind of days that you should share with someone."

"Do you feel sorry for me?" she asked, appalled she had let her wistfulness for those days with her grandmother be so apparent. "Because of what I told you about missing Gram?"

"I don't think I would have said I felt sorry for you. It's just that I know what it's like to miss people."

He actually ducked his head, looking faintly embarrassed. She realized, stunned, he felt *connected* to her. He *wanted* to share the day with her.

"I thought you weren't anxious to have them meet me," she reminded him, worried he would regret acting on this momentary connection brought on by shared confidences. "Your roommate."

"Okay. Maybe you should forego the red bikini."

She realized he was teasing her. It felt strangely and gloriously intimate. She gave him a little punch on the arm.

He pretended to be hurt. "Just for the parade part!"

"Okay. I'll wear my black one instead."

He threw back his head and laughed. The sun hit the column of his throat, and his laughter rang down the beach.

That felt strangely and gloriously intimate, also.

"No, seriously, come," Sam said. "After spending the day with them, they just don't seem like the type to jump to judgment. Plus, anybody who knew you for more than ten minutes would know how decent you are."

She snorted. "At last count about two point four million people would disagree with you."

He was silent for a moment, and then his voice low, he admitted, "I watched one of the *American Singing Star* videos last night. Part of it."

She froze and stared at him.

"After you told me about it, I wanted to see for myself. You didn't even look like you." His eyes went to her hair.

She touched it self-consciously. Sometimes she was still shocked by how short it was. "This is my natural color. But they already had a blonde. So, they suggested one of us dye our hair so the audience would have no problem differentiating us. I'd like to say we picked straws, but eager-to-please me just wagged my hand in the air."

"It was so long."

"It was long, but not that long. Extensions," she said. "They had stylists who did it all. Hair, makeup, outfit selection."

"I'm somehow reassured that you didn't pick that outfit for yourself. I just don't see you as a black leather kind of girl."

His simple statement made her feel validated in some way. While she had been growing increasingly uncomfortable with her talent show transformation, every single person she knew had gushed about it.

"I didn't pick the song, either. *Everything* was choreographed. Even—" she heard the faint bitterness in her voice "—a romance."

"I'm glad you weren't seduced by it. I'm glad it ended in a way that made it so you would never want to go back. All that phoniness would have killed you."

His words washed over her. For a blinding moment Allie stood in the truth. She had seen that show as the triggering event in a landslide of losses: her career, her love, her dignity.

But in Sam's simple words, for the first time, she understood what the real loss had been.

She had lost herself.

"You in black leather," Sam said with a dismayed shake of his head. "So wrong."

It felt as if she needed to keep the enormity of her discovery to herself. She kept her tone light. "You haven't seen the black bikini yet!"

He laughed again, but then grew serious. "Those people? All two point four million of them? They didn't know *you* at all."

She realized, looking back on that period of her life, she didn't know who she was, either. So eager to please, so eager to gain the prize they held out for her, so sure somehow the *real* her could not accomplish that, a belief they had underscored with every request: change this, wear that, try this song.

She saw now that it wasn't necessarily money.

Or fame.

It was approval they had held out to her.

And then snatched away.

"You should come tomorrow," he said softly. "Bill and Kathy seem to know a whole lot about having wholesome family fun. When's the last time you did that?"

"Wouldn't that involve having a wholesome family?"

He laughed. "Come. Have fun."

Quit hiding.

But hiding was oh, so safe. The last time she'd gone way out of her comfort zone, she'd auditioned for the show. With disastrous consequences, she reminded herself. It had been the end of her "wholesome" family dream, the one he had so clearly seen in the mist around her, the picture of picket fences and baby carriages.

What if a day spent like this triggered all those longings she had set aside?

But suddenly the appeal of spending a fun-filled day with him and his makeshift family was too much to resist.

Suddenly she saw herself as way too introspective, too serious, too safe. He wasn't asking her to marry him and help him raise Cody. He wasn't asking her to adopt his Australian family as her own.

He was suggesting she get out and have some good old Fourth of July fun: parades, ice cream, hot dogs, flags, fireworks.

What could be more wholesome—and harmless—than that? Besides, what would her grandmother tell her to do? She could almost feel Mavis giving her a little push toward Sam.

"Okay," she said.

It felt as if she was closing her eyes and stepping off a high diving board.

But it felt as if *she* was doing it: the real Allie, not some imposter whose whole life had been created to gain ratings on a television show.

CHAPTER TWELVE

"You're touching Pooperman's cape," Sam said the next morning, aghast. He had come into the kitchen to find Allie hunched over the table.

"Pooperman's cape?" She glanced up at him, a needle in her hands.

He was pretty sure she was in her pajamas. The outfit was not what you would call sexy—it looked like she was wearing a man's shirt, that was rolled up bulkily around her arms, and ended above her knees.

But the shirt had fallen off one shoulder, and her legs were totally exposed and undeniably gorgeous.

Somehow the shirt was more sexy than the damned bathing suit.

Or maybe sexy was the way she was looking at him, her tongue caught between her teeth, her eyes luminous.

The cape in question was spread across her lap, a needle and thread in her hands. There was a pair of scissors there.

Sam had to fight an itch to pick up the scissors, and cut those black tips out of her hair—what remained of *Tempest*.

"That's what Adam and I called his cape. You can't touch it. I have to sneak it into the laundry when Cody is sleeping."

"I just added an American flag lining to it, for the parade. We can take it out again after."

"You can't add things to Pooperman's cape!"

"It loses its magical powers?" she said drily.

"You have no idea what you are playing with," Sam said. But looking at her, sitting there, so adorable in her men's shirt and messy hair and bare feet, he wondered which of them had no idea what they were playing with. Had he really invited her to spend the day with them?

"I can take the lining out in a jiffy if it upsets Cody."

There was a neat stack of flag-patterned squares beside her.

"And what's this?" he asked, picking up the top square. The square unfolded into another cape. He frowned. "You're not expecting me to wear one, are you?"

She gave him a disparaging look, as if she had already figured out he was too much of a poor sport to play along. Why would he feel vaguely insulted by that?

"I made one for each of the kids." She looked away, and said, softly, as if she didn't want him to think she was an idiot, "And one for Popsy, too."

He stared at her. "Were you up all night?" he finally asked.

"Just half of it."

"Who has this kind of stuff on hand?" he asked, incredulously. "Like what? Fifty yards of American flag material?"

"My grandmother was a quilter. There's tons of fabric here. She taught me how to sew when I was just little. It reminds me of her, in the nicest way, when I sew."

Sam looked at the perfect little stack of capes, and at the look on her face. It was that luminescent look again, her eyes shining, a contented little smile drifting across the plumpness of her bottom lip.

It occurred to him that Allie was excited for the day. Isn't that what he'd wanted when he convinced her to come? To get her to reengage in life, instead of hiding? He wanted her to let go of the notion she was the one who had something to be ashamed of over the whole *American Singing Star* fiasco.

Still, there was something about the enthusiasm in her that was a little dangerous.

"You can't just add stuff to Pooperman's cape," Sam said again, just to make sure she knew there were rules that couldn't be ignored.

"Sorry, I didn't know." She didn't sound very sorry. Well, she hadn't seen one of the famous meltdowns.

Come to think of it, there still hadn't been any famous meltdowns. Not since they'd arrived. That had to be a record. That would probably all change when Cody awoke to find his cape was not only not within reach, but had been altered.

On cue, Cody came out of his bedroom, rubbing sleep from his eyes. Astonishingly, he seemed not to notice his cape had not been on the floor beside his bed this morning. He stopped when he saw them at the kitchen table with the cape in between them.

Allie flipped the cape off the table and went and sank down on her heels in front of him. "Look," she said, "I added something to your cape just for today. And I made Popsy a matching one!"

With a flourish she put the cape around his shoulders. And then she called the dog and put the matching cape on him.

The two of them—make that all three of them—stood frozen, looking at her in disbelief.

"You look amazing," she declared.

Cody looked to Sam for reaction.

"Like you could vanquish evil with a simple wave of your hand. And paw," Sam said solemnly.

Cody obviously had no idea what *vanquish* meant, and probably not *evil*, either, but he fingered the shiny new lining of the cape, deciding. Then he smiled. It looked as though he was pretty sure he had been bestowed with a superpower he had not possessed before.

"Allie made Nicole and Bryan capes, too," Sam said, and that was the final reassurance Cody needed. He smile deepened to a happy boyish grin, and he spread his arms like a plane and flew out the back door onto the deck, with Popsy on his heels. Their rambunctious running around the deck made the whole house vibrate.

"Did we just dodge a bullet?" Allie asked.

"We did, but that's nothing for a family of superheroes."

A light went on in her face, at the word *family.* That was a bit of a mistake to make it sound as if they—him and her and Cody and Popsy—were family. But still, Sam faced the truth about his invitation. It wasn't just about getting her out of hiding, assuaging some pain that had stolen her dreams from her.

Somehow, he wanted her to know that those dreams, the ones she had sworn she had given up on, were attainable.

Staying up all night to make the capes was a perfect example of the kind of life she yearned for and was suited for: dogs and kids and costumes. Family. Fun. Laughter.

Sam, of course, knew he was the worst possible person to be letting anyone know their dreams were attainable.

Especially wholesome, garden-variety kinds of dreams.

But Kathy and Bill, with their somehow perfectly imperfect little family, could show Allie how it could be. They could give her hope. He was certain of that.

He practically herded them all out the door and down the beach, as if he could reassign some of the responsibility he had taken on to others.

And from the moment they all met, Sam felt the relief of a plan going well. Nicole and Bryan made a fuss over Cody in his flag cape, and then threw themselves on Popsy, squealing even more about the almost unbearable cuteness of the dog in a cape. Popsy lapped it all up, while Cody looked pleased as punch to be the owner of such a marvel of a beast.

With a certain endearing shyness, Allie gave Nicole and Bryan their capes, too. Their eyes went round with the wonder of it. Soon the excitement had reached such levels that Kathy kicked them all—children and dog—out on the deck and shut the door firmly behind them.

"What a wonderful gift," Kathy said, and looked askance at Sam. He realized in all the hoopla of the cape presentations, he had not made introductions.

"This is Allie," Sam said. "She's my—"

He hesitated. Only a few days had gone by. How had she come to be so much? His roommate. Confidante.

"Landlady," he said, taking the safest route.

"You can't be a landlady," Kathy said, eyeing Allie after introductions. "You are much too young for that."

"Accidental landlady," Allie said, and explained briefly about the mix-up.

"Did you make those precious capes for everyone?" Kathy asked, apparently not finding their living arrangement worthy of any more attention.

"You don't think I made them?" Sam asked.

They all laughed at that.

"Yes," Allie said shyly.

"They are so adorable," Kathy said.

"Not too loud," Sam warned her. "Cody does not want

to be adorable. I don't think Popsy does, either. Superheroes are not adorable."

And then all the adults were laughing again, with a kind of ease, and Sam felt as if they had all known each other for a long time.

It soon became evident Bill and Kathy *loved* Allie. As they walked to the parade, Kathy and Allie talked easily. And Nicole, Bryan and Cody took turns squabbling over who got to hold the dog's leash and who got to hold Allie's hand. Well, what wasn't to love about someone who arrived with a child and a dog and all-American superhero capes?

Allie's initial shyness dissipated rapidly and she fit seamlessly into the lovely dynamic of this family. It was evident to him that Allie was a girl who needed to be loved. Who would thrive on it. Who would come into herself.

He wondered if he was playing with fire encouraging this transformation of Allie.

But as he stood beside her at the parade, looking at her shining face, he decided it was worth the risk.

This was what he was aware of since arriving at the beach. Basically, he'd been alone with the enormity of his grief, with the enormity of leaving his carefree bachelor days behind and becoming a parent.

That was not to say people had not been around him and that sympathy had not been plentiful. His coworkers, his staff in particular, shared his grief. Adam had belonged to all of them, after all.

And yet, the huge emptiness of his new world Sam carried alone.

The insecurity he felt about Cody, he carried alone.

Allie made him feel not alone with it, as if the touch of

her hand, and the look in her eyes, the way she listened, took some burden from it, made it lighter.

He made Cody surrender Popsy's leash to his cousins, then lifted him up on his shoulders so that he could see the parade better.

And felt the shine of the moment as the parade started and the children squealed with delight and excitement as the clowns danced out in front of them, passing out candy to the crowds.

They were followed by a band and cheerleaders doing amazing gymnastics. Then a wagon pulled by a pair of donkeys, who appeared indifferent to the local fire engine that followed them, sirens blaring.

The floats came next, from wonderful, like Fun Florist, to almost embarrassingly bad, Phil's Steakhouse. That float was blaring some awful song about *so delicious you can't miss us*, and had a man dressed as a large steak waving at the crowd.

"Did *miss* really become *mish*? You can't *mish* us?" Allie groaned and buried her face in her hands.

"Look at it this way," he said, "you can't do worse."

"My fear is maybe I can."

He put his hand around her shoulder, reassuringly. He squeezed. He should have let go. But somehow, one hand stayed holding Cody steady on his shoulder, and one stayed around Allie. She beamed up at him.

There had been so little happiness. What could it hurt to give himself and his nephew over to the day? To the days they had left here at Sugar Cone Beach?

Before he had to make a terrible decision about what was best for everyone involved, even if it left him more alone than he had ever been in his entire life.

Sam pushed that thought from his mind. Just for

today he would be carefree in a way that he thought would never be possible again.

Allie was not sure when—if ever—she had experienced such a perfect day. When the parade ended, they joined the crowds that went to the street fair. People stopped them to admire the kids' American flag Superman capes and to pet the dog. They had their faces painted, and they ate hot dogs. The kids all had red, white and blue candy floss.

Bill and Sam became quite competitive throwing baseballs at a target. Bill won a huge stuffed bear which he gave not to Nicole who wanted it, but to Kathy. There was something about the way they looked at each other in that brief moment that made Allie feel all squishy inside.

And then Sam won the same bear, and gave it not to Cody, but to Allie.

Of course, she told herself, it was probably because Cody already had his hands full with the dog's leash, and the bear was too big for him to carry anyway.

Still, there was something about a man winning a stuffed animal for you at the fair that was part of a perfect all-American dream and all-American day. And she felt even squishier inside.

The children turned the corner from happy to cranky in the blink of an eye, and they walked back through the July heat and the packed streets to Bill and Kathy's rental.

The beachfront rental could have been intimidatingly posh and a reminder of the life Allie had so briefly glimpsed with lots of glass and steel and marble, but somehow the glamour of it was overridden by flip-flops in various sizes at the door, toys out, colorful beach towels, children's books in leaning stacks.

Somehow, Bill and Kathy had, without trying, given

the place a sense of *home.* Anticipating a struggle to separate children, Kathy just put mats on the living room floor, and the kids all flopped down together. Nicole and Bryan protested, crabbily, they weren't at all tired.

They were given the stuffed bears to sleep with, and then, still muttering protests, Cody tucked under one of Nicole's protective arms, one bear tucked under the other, and Popsy tucked under his.

As if it was second nature to him, Allie watched as Sam leaned into the heap of sleeping children, the dog and the huge stuffed bears, and gently loosened all the cape strings from around sweaty little necks.

"I should go," Allie said, feeling suddenly as if she had overstayed her welcome, as if they were all family, and she was not. An interloper somehow. The adults would want to relax, they would want to read books or snooze in the sun. Her perfect day was over.

"Nonsense," Kathy said. "The monsters are sleeping." *Monsters* was said with an abundance of affection. "It's our turn. The guys can have a beer, and you and I will have a glass of wine and put up our feet. I've bought shrimp to put on the barbie tonight, and I've heard this is a great place to watch the fireworks from. There's a fire pit built into the deck. Let's make a day of it, shall we?"

Really, she should have insisted on going home.

But Allie was not strong enough to pull away from the circle of warmth she found herself in.

And so she sat on a lounger, with a crisp glass of white wine in her hand, watching as Sam and Bill, now shirtless and shoeless, threw a football back and forth on the beach.

Their voices floated up to the women: masculine, laced with laughter. Were they showing off just a bit, just as they had been when they won the teddy bears?

"Ah," Kathy said, watching them, "I can't tell you how good this moment is for my heart. I wondered if either of them would ever let themselves have moments like this again."

"It's been a terrible blow to all of you," Allie said. She looked over at Kathy. She saw a tear sliding down her face as Bill leaped high in the air to catch a ball Sam had deliberately made nearly impossible to catch.

"Life is beautiful, isn't it?" Kathy asked softly. "And sad, and hard and heartbreaking. And then, beautiful all over again."

Allie suddenly saw her own life in a different light, and realized how true Kathy's words were.

The talk between them turned lighter, a universal language between women. They discussed the latest book of an Australian author they both liked, and movies they had enjoyed, which actors made them swoon.

The children woke up, and the guys took them swimming, and Kathy and Allie got salads ready, and finally, as it got dark, put shrimp on the barbecue.

After a fabulous grilled dinner, they took lawn chairs onto the beach, joining the crowds of people there. Somehow, Sam was beside Allie, and they oohed and ahhed as much as the children. She could feel him there, a scent coming off his sun-warmed skin, his presence making the warm evening and the explosions of light, the effect doubled as they reflected in black water, absolutely and utterly enchanting.

At the first explosion, Popsy came out from under Sam's chair and leaped on Allie's lap. She watched Sam's hand play in the dog's fur, and felt a tickle of desire, completely inappropriate for such a family-friendly event.

After, they retreated to the deck of the rental, with its

built-in fire pit. Allie felt as if everything was fading, save Sam and her awareness of him.

The way he looked, the way he laughed, the way he was in the world. He teased the kids, talked to his brother-in-law, tickled the dog's ears, looked after the fire, supervised Cody, who had discovered the delight of swirling a red-tipped stick, fresh from the fire, against the night sky.

Each of those small things spoke to who he was: so strong, so sure of himself, so able to be himself in the world, whether he was aware of that or not.

She watched as he knelt beside Cody, whispered in his ear, hugged him briefly and tightly against his chest.

This is a good man, Allie found herself thinking. The feeling she had for him was so strong, she felt that desire, once again, to leave, to run away, to hide.

To protect herself from something that had hurt her before and could hurt her again. Looking back on the whole day, it filled her with a sense of longing.

Yearning.

She had a little war going on with herself. She needed to leave. She needed to stay. She needed to be cautious. She needed to be bold.

Kathy brought out a guitar. "This was in the unit," she said. "Does anybody play?"

CHAPTER THIRTEEN

"ALLIE DOES," SAM said softly.

For a moment Allie felt a sense of betrayal. She had told Sam she didn't sing publicly anymore. Still, this wasn't *really* publicly. Just a small family gathering.

Hesitantly, Allie took the instrument Kathy held out to her. It was a cheap guitar and badly out of tune, but she fiddled with the frets, and then finally, she strummed a few tentative notes.

The strange thing was she barely knew these people, and yet the fear of judgment that had filled her since *American Singing Star* was absent. In fact, having the guitar in her hands, people around her, the fire glowing, made her feel as at home as she had ever felt with a guitar.

She suddenly realized she was not in a war with herself, at all. The decision wasn't whether to leave or stay, to be cautious or bold.

The decision was whether or not to be herself. Whether or not to come home to herself.

"Okay," she said to the children. "I'm going to teach you how to sing in the round. You, too," she said to the adults. She went around the circle and numbered everyone, including Cody so he wouldn't feel left out, though obviously he would not be singing the rounds.

"One, two, one, two," she sang out. "All the ones, over here, all the twos over there."

"I forget which number I am," Sam said devilishly, and Nicole and Bryan yelled at him he was a two.

"This is the song," Allie said, "I'll sing it, and then we'll sing it all together. 'Flames are climbing, flames are climbing, come closer, come closer, In the glowing, in the glowing, Come sing with us and be joyous.' Is everybody ready?"

No one answered.

"What?" she asked.

"I think you may have the most beautiful voice I've ever heard," Kathy said. "Ever."

Allie blushed and dropped her head, but not before she saw that Sam was looking at her, and he was smiling.

As if he was proud of her. As if he had deliberately put an obstacle in front of her that he knew she could overcome. As if he saw the truth of her, and knew she had allowed her true self to come out.

Reading too much into it, she scolded herself. But she nodded at him.

"Sing," she said, and their voices rose together, riding the sparks into the night until it felt as though they were touching the stars.

As she played the guitar and sang, some of the neighboring families wandered over and were invited to stay. A sense of community leaped up.

They sang everything: children's songs and ballads. They sang rock and roll and theme songs from television shows. Sometimes the singing was good, and mostly it was terrible. Sometimes they could remember all the words and all the verses of each song but mostly they could not.

And as the night wore on, the songs became quieter

and quieter. One by one the children nodded off to sleep, Bryan in his mother's arms, Nicole in her father's, Cody in Sam's.

Her awareness of Sam, of his basic goodness and strength, his willingness to do the right thing, intensified every time she looked over at him and saw that child nestled so trustingly into his chest, fast asleep.

Allie was not sure she had ever enjoyed using her voice as much as she did leading a singalong, long into the night, on the Fourth of July at Sugar Cone Beach.

Finally, though, her voice was nearly gone, and she set the guitar down.

"One more?" Sam asked. "Please?

She realized she could refuse him nothing. They had known each other such a short time. How could she feel so strongly toward him? She reached for the guitar.

"Could we finish with this?" Sam asked. "It's a song my brother-in-law insisted I learn every word to."

His voice, a beautiful, rich, natural tenor rose, alone, into the night, as he sang the opening bars of "Waltzing Matilda."

One by one other voices joined Sam's. Allie picked up the song easily and accompanied on the guitar, but found herself so choked up she could barely sing.

Their voices rose and became one, until they were all Australians, and all Americans, and all part of that amazing beauty and sadness and heartbreak and then beauty again that is to be human.

The impromptu party broke up shortly after, neighbors—new friends—gathering their sleepy children and calling their goodbyes.

"What a splendid evening," Kathy said, as Allie and Sam organized Cody and Popsy for a walk up the darkened beach to their own place.

"You really have an incredible voice," Bill said. "I have a friend, in Australia, who is a record producer. Do you think—"

"No," Allie said quickly.

She couldn't follow that dream again. She just couldn't.

Sam seemed to understand. He nestled the sleeping Cody up on his shoulder and took her hand.

Together they walked out into the sand and the night. He didn't let go of her hand, presumably because it was dark, the silence companionable between them.

At the cottage, they stood outside for a minute before going in. The night was velvety warm, an embrace of stars and sea-scented water.

"Thank you for a beautiful day," Allie said huskily.

"No, thank you."

They stood there for a moment, as if both of them knew the perfect way to end a perfect day.

His eyes dark with yearning, Sam leaned toward her.

Wanting something from him that she had never wanted so much from another human being—more than a kiss, but connection—Allie leaned toward him.

But then Popsy pulled on his leash, wanting his bed, and Cody woke suddenly, and the moment was gone.

In her empty bedroom, by herself, listening to the sounds of Sam getting an uncooperative sleepyhead into his pajamas, she wasn't sure if it was a good thing or a bad thing that they had pulled back.

She did know she had experienced a near miss of a kiss. And she ached for the thing that had not happened.

Sam awoke in the morning, aware of three things: one, it was raining, a steady drum on the tin roof. Two, somewhere—probably in the kitchen—Allie was singing about how rare rain was in California. And three, that feeling he had woken with for eight solid months, that feeling of being in a black hole of despair, was gone.

Replaced, not quite with lightness, but with a cautious sense that maybe, just maybe, everything would be okay.

Did you fight a feeling like that? Or surrender to it?

Somehow, he had intended the day, yesterday, to be a gift to Allie. A message. *See? Life can be good. You can believe dreams come true. You can miss your grandmother, but still live life.*

But maybe it was the nature of gifts that the giver received as much as the recipient. Whether they were ready or not.

From the nest of his bed, Sam heard a knock on the back door.

"Is it too early?"

He recognized Nicole's voice, looked at the clock beside his bed, and was surprised by how late he had slept.

"We've brought breakfast," Kathy sang out. "And rainy day things. Board games. A movie."

Allie said something about the rain spoiling their vacation.

"We *love* rain," Nicole pronounced.

"Why do you love rain?" Allie asked.

"Well, first," Nicole answered, "because we don't get very much where we live, but second, it makes me like the sunny days even better!"

Rain makes you like the sunny days.

Way too deep, Sam chastised himself, when he started contemplating that. He got up out of bed, pulled on a T-shirt and some shorts and padded to the kitchen. He stood in the doorway for a moment, looking at them.

He hadn't realized Cody was up. He and Allie had been drawing pictures with crayons on a huge piece of newsprint spread out on the kitchen table.

Now the tiny kitchen was crowded, and yet somehow there was room for everyone around that table.

"Uncle Sam," Nicole said, "do you know how to draw a unicorn?" She was holding out a green crayon to him.

When had he become "uncle"? He hadn't really noticed. *His family,* he thought, stunned that he had a family again.

Stunned, and a tiny bit frightened. What had more potential to hurt than this?

He scowled at Nicole. "Don't be ridiculous," he said, scorning the crayon she held out. "Everyone knows unicorns are purple."

"Are they, Auntie Allie?" Nicole asked.

Sam looked at her. Allie was wearing one of her many I-lost-a-ton-of-weight-at-the-spa outfits. Faded blue T-shirt and sweatpants in the very same horrible shade.

She hadn't combed her hair yet, and it was sticking up all over.

She was so cute it took his breath away.

So, Allie was family, too. How could that possibly feel so right after such a short length of time?

As the rain pattered on the tin roof of the cottage, he pulled up a chair and searched through the crayons.

He added a purple unicorn to the unfolding mural.

Allie came over, and put her hand on his shoulder as she leaned over it to look. She leaned over him harder as she took the crayon from his hand, and made an adjustment to the horn.

Everything else in the room seemed to fade. Just her, touching him, filling his senses with her smell.

Somehow, everything felt so right. After that, the day unfolded with a delicious sense of endlessness.

They drew pictures and played games. They ate peanut butter sandwiches for lunch, and then defied the rain and went outside and jumped in puddles and swam in the ocean.

After, they came in soaked, and the whole house soon reeked of wet dog. Kathy went home and got a change of clothes for them all, and Nicole had a hot shower and the boys shared a hot bath together. They watched a movie. They built extravagant blanket forts in the living room. They ordered pizzas for dinner.

Sam noticed that, like him, Cody seemed to have turned a page. There was a lightness about him that had not been there when they had arrived at the beach. He had a willingness to engage.

And Allie! Ever since she had leaned over him this morning, it was as if everything else was just a backdrop to her: to her shining eyes, to her ocean-slicked hair, to her laughter, to her willingness to get down on the floor and play.

Nobody wanted the day to end.

He felt Nicole tugging on his sleeve.

"Can Cody come for a sleepover at our house tonight?"

It felt as if his world went strangely still. His world had been he and Cody for so long. They had not been apart for one hour since it had happened, let alone a whole night.

What if something happened?

What if he let Cody out of his sight, and something bad happened? What if they didn't watch him closely enough and he wandered onto the beach? What if a fire started? Or that burglar broke into their house while he wasn't there to protect Cody?

He knew these doubts were ridiculous. Kathy and Bill had managed not just to keep their children from harm, but to shape them into wonderful people. Creative, moving toward independence, sure of themselves.

Their children were speaking, a mean-spirited voice inside him pointed out.

He understood he was grappling with a bigger question.

What if he lost Cody, too?

"Please, Uncle, please, please, please?" Bryan joined the chorus.

CHAPTER FOURTEEN

ALLIE FELT SAM stiffen at Nicole's innocent question.

Kathy must have felt something, too. "Sleepovers!" she exclaimed. "I'm afraid they are all the rage among the six-year-old set."

"What exactly is a sleepover?" Sam asked.

"Oh, they're *soooo* good," Nicole said. "You watch movies, and dance to music, and talk *soooo* much. We might make popcorn or have another fire. Cody would love it!"

Cody looked up from his pizza.

"Wouldn't you love it, Cody?" Nicole asked.

Cody nodded, uncertainly at first, and then with enthusiasm.

"It's really Sam's decision," Kathy said firmly. "Nicole, it's been a long day."

"You want to go, buddy?" Sam asked.

Cody nodded. Though the truth was he seemed in shock as his things were packed up and he headed out the door.

At the last minute, he sat down furiously, shaking his head. He'd changed his mind. Allie shot Sam a look.

Did he look relieved?

"He wants the doggie," Nicole decided, and sure enough as soon as Popsy was included in the invitation,

Cody got up off the floor, put his hand in Nicole's and trundled out the door.

"I'll call you," Kathy told Sam quietly, laying her hand on his shoulder. "If he changes his mind, or there are any kinds of problems, I'll call."

She obviously knew something momentous was happening. Then they were gone, and the house fell into sudden silence.

Allie knew, after a day like today, and a day like yesterday, there was a kind of danger in being alone together.

And yet how could you possibly leave a man with that look on his face to struggle through his challenges alone?

"What is it with Nicole?" he asked. "How does she know what Cody wants?"

"I'm afraid my early childhood education program didn't cover psychic abilities between children. Should we go sit on the deck for a bit?" she asked.

He looked as if he was going to say no, as if he knew she had detected a weakness in him, and as if his very survival depended on denying that weakness.

But he surrendered.

"Sure," he said, "let's go sit on the deck for a bit."

They sat, and then said, almost together, "It's so quiet."

"Quiet," Allie said, "but not empty somehow. It's as if the day, the laughter, has soaked into the walls and floorboards."

She had a sudden sense that when it was all over, when her life had gone back to normal, she was going to feel bereft.

"These were the kind of days you were made for," he proclaimed softly. "I knew it as soon as I saw you."

"After you got over thinking I was a wacko who killed old ladies, that is."

He rewarded her by laughing.

"And what about you?" she asked. "What about you and rainy days, and houses that are full of noise, and smell of wet dogs?"

"I don't know about *made* for it," he said. "Thrust into it."

"Nonsense. A man pushed into something against his own will would never build a fort that enthusiastically. Or draw such a stupendous purple unicorn."

"Is he going to be okay over there?" he asked softly.

She knew she could pull out her early childhood information and tell him how important it was for Cody to *differentiate*, to begin to see himself as separate from others, and that was probably particularly true in light of his loss, but that wasn't the real question. Not at all.

The real question was, was Sam going to be okay?

Somehow, even with the danger sizzling in the air between them, she needed to know the answer to that.

Or maybe, she had to be part of the answer to that.

The thought that was forming in her mind was terrifying. She sought refuge in her guitar. The notes flew out of it, snapping, floating, dancing like those sparks from the fire finding the night air.

"I should be working on Phil's Steakhouse," she said.

"That tune could sell a lot of steak," he said.

"Unfortunately, this tune is not Phil's Steakhouse. My guitar appears to be on strike when it comes to Phil."

"What is it then?"

She sang a rollicking little tune about mud puddles and blanket forts and the sound of rainy days on the roof.

"You've found yourself, haven't you?" he asked quietly.

Had she? If she'd really found herself, didn't that have to extend to others? To him? Didn't she have to help him find himself, too? She could tell that the idea of Cody being away from him had left him feeling uneasy. He had given her this amazing gift of inviting her to experience family. What could she give him?

She set down the guitar. "We have the whole evening to ourselves. Let's be grown-ups," she suggested.

His eyes widened and he lifted an eyebrow wickedly at her.

She was not sure when she had become quite so comfortable with him, with his teasing, but she gave his arm a light punch.

"I mean, we're free. We don't even have the dog."

"Aren't you always free?" he asked her.

"I guess," she admitted, "though after that period where everyone recognized me, I got into a bit of a hermit habit. And I don't think I ever got back out." She could see the suggestion they do some grown-up things appealed to him much more once he determined it was also about her.

"Let's go to a movie," she said. "And maybe go for dinner after. We could be really wild. We could finish off the night with a drink."

Allie was aware she was holding her breath. It felt as if something important was being decided here. Earth-shattering. Because, really, no matter what she cloaked it in, her helping him, or him helping her, wasn't she asking him to go on a date?

"What movie?" he said, after a moment.

She felt the relief of his answer. "Anything but *Rugrats*."

"You don't even have a television. How can you be sick of *Rugrats*?"

"I can hear it when you play it on the computer. You know the walls in that cottage." In fact, she could hear *everything*, even the sound of him breathing.

He threw back his head and laughed, that beautiful, beautiful sound. “Agreed,” he said.

Several minutes later, as she tried to decide what to wear, her nerve faltered. But then she threw on a sleeveless white top that showed off her tan and the arms toned from daily swimming, and a short, colorful, summery skirt that swished around her legs. She put on a light dusting of makeup, even though it was strictly against the cottage rules. She hadn’t put on makeup since *American Singing Star.* She put a straw fedora on. It covered the worst of her hair.

She looked in the mirror for a moment. She looked *cute.* There were little pink spots on her cheeks. Her eyes were shining.

What was she getting herself into? Too late. She was already in.

She deliberately brushed the thoughts away. It had been such a perfect few days. She was making new friends and moving out into the world again. She didn’t need to analyze that endlessly. Wasn’t there a whole philosophy about being in the moment? Couldn’t she just do that?

There was no need to project into the future. Sam and Cody were here for a limited time, and it was counting down fast. There was no future.

Couldn’t she just have fun? Couldn’t she just be carefree, like those people who poured onto the beach in front of her house every day?

When she saw Sam’s eyes widen with a certain male appreciation, Allie was glad for both the choice of makeup and the fun, flirty skirt. She might have even given it a little extra swish as they walked downtown to the theater together.

Still, it wasn't a date! It felt as if they scrupulously avoided it becoming a date, by avoiding holding hands.

Sugar Cone only had one theater, and it was playing an action thriller. There was a brief verbal scuffle at the wicket, when she talked about paying and Sam gave her an incredulous look. Then there was something lovely—and normal—about sitting in a darkened theater together. They didn't hold hands, but they shared a bucket of popcorn. Who knew fingers brushing over buttered popcorn could be so sexy?

"I'm starving," Sam said as they came out of the theater. They stood on the sidewalk together.

Allie was aware of an admiring glance he got from a woman passing by walking her dog. The woman smiled at him. Why did it melt something in Allie that Sam didn't even seem to notice?

"How can you be starving?" she teased him. "You ate a whole bucket of popcorn."

"I didn't eat a whole bucket. I wanted to, but you suggested sharing."

It was a tiny thing, really, going back and forth like this. And yet it felt unreasonably good to be with him. Maybe she had taken the whole hermit-hiding-out thing just a little too far.

"Phil's Steakhouse?" he deadpanned.

And then they were laughing together.

"I think a hamburger at Marty's Milkshakes is more in my price range."

"Your price range? You aren't paying."

"Well, I suggested this outing. So—"

"Is this why you suggested sharing popcorn? Because you were being frugal?"

"Why else?" she asked.

"I thought you were being romantic."

He was obviously teasing. She blushed.

"I'm your landlady. I think it's against the rules to be romantic with you."

He rocked back on his heels, and looked very much like a rebel who wanted to challenge the rules, but instead, he sighed. "Okay, now that you've established the rules, could we eat?"

"Someplace cheap," she said. "Dutch treat."

"Oh, be quiet," he said, and put his arm around her shoulder. "That place across the street looks good."

"That's the swankiest restaurant in town," she sputtered. She touched the brim of her fedora self-consciously. "I'm not dressed to go in there."

"It's a beach town," he said, unperturbed. "The dress code everywhere is casual. You impose a lot of rules on yourself, don't you?"

It occurred to her she did, her legacy from her mother. She decided, just for a little while, to leave the rules behind. Her Gram would approve of that!

"Just own it," Sam whispered in her ear, and gave the brim of her hat a little tug that made it feel like just possibly it could be seen as jaunty and stylish instead of a quick cover for a bad hair day.

The maître d' did not act as if there was anything wrong, at all, with what they were wearing. In fact, he gave them the best table in the house: a beautiful corner table on the patio, overlooking the sea.

"See?" Sam said. "I told you to own it. Look where it got us."

"That wasn't me. You're sending out the tycoon vibe," she whispered to him. "That's why we got the good table."

"Ha. Let me tell you how men think." He pretended his fingers were a meter. "Tycoon vibe, gorgeous legs, tycoon vibe, gorgeous legs." His finger meter went off the scale every time he said "gorgeous legs."

He thought she had gorgeous legs! That meant he'd looked. She could feel her confidence growing by the second.

That's what being with a man like him did. His confidence just rubbed off.

"Let's start with some calamari."

She looked at the price of it, and hid a gulp.

When the waiter came he ordered a grotesquely expensive imported beer, and steak and lobster, the most expensive thing on the menu.

Was he showing off?

She cast him a look, and saw that he had not given his order a second thought. He'd simply ordered what he wanted.

"What are you having?" he asked her.

Old habits died hard. She could feel herself looking through the appetizers trying to find something inexpensive. He was paying, he'd already made that clear, but she couldn't make it feel as if she was taking advantage of him.

"Oh, for God's sake," he said as the waiter hovered. He took her menu from her and gave it back to the waiter. "Bring her the same."

"That's very controlling of you," she said, glaring at him.

"Think of it as masterful," he said with a wink.

"I can't eat that much," she protested. "And I think I've had enough butter for one evening."

He grinned at her. "There's no such thing as enough butter. And I'm hoping you can't finish, because then I'll get more."

His grin was so open and so mischievous—unconsciously charming—and she remembered her original goal. It was to keep his mind off Cody.

And it seemed to be working! What an unexpected bonus to see him looking happy and at ease.

And just like that, the moment of self-consciousness, of feeling somehow like she wasn't good enough for a place like this—or a guy like him—evaporated.

And they were just two people, doing what two people did. Getting to know each other.

What two people on their first date do, her mind insisted on telling her.

She took a sip of the beer that had arrived. "I had no idea beer could taste this good."

"Stick with the tycoons," he told her and lifted his glass to her. He came away with a deliberate foam moustache over his upper lip. It made her laugh.

She was not sure if anything had ever felt quite so wonderful as laughing with Sam Walker.

CHAPTER FIFTEEN

ALLIE BURIED HER upper lip in the foam, too, and made her own moustache. Then they were both laughing.

The food came.

"This is easily the most delicious thing I've ever eaten," she decided. She ate every bite, including all the butter.

"I saw crème brûlée on the menu. My favorite. I'm not sharing."

So two servings of crème brûlée arrived and the top was fired to golden, crunchy perfection right at their table.

"Am I in an episode of *Lifestyles of the Rich and Famous*?" she asked him, when the waiter had gone.

After dessert they sipped coffee, and she coaxed him to tell her about his business. He did, but then he turned pensive.

"I'm pretty driven. I like my work, a lot. Until Cody, it pretty much crowded out everything else."

"Maybe you just didn't find anything else you liked as much," she said.

"There really has been no room for anything else. My marriage was the first casualty."

"In what way?" She knew this hadn't just "come up." There was a warning in here. Enjoy everything he had to offer. Get attached to the stuff. But not him.

"I worked too much. She looked elsewhere."

His wife had had an affair? On Sam Walker? Looking at him, realizing how much he had come to mean to her, Allie found it difficult to believe. Worse, he seemed to think it was all his fault.

"That sounds like two people contributing equally to the demise of your marriage," she weighed in.

She actually felt she wanted to hit this woman she didn't know. How could anyone be so stupid? To be married to this man and step out on him?

"No, I take full responsibility."

He would, she thought, and yet he had made it pretty clear his wife had stepped out on him.

"She found someone new, and you are somehow responsible for that choice?" Allie pressed him.

"I got married, way too young, shortly after my parents died. It wouldn't take a genius to figure out I was trying to replace the sense of family I'd always had. But because I was so young, I felt I had to prove I could look after my wife. Not just look after her, but be the best at looking after her, the way my dad had been the best at looking after my mom. To me that meant being successful. Not just a little successful, a lot successful. Obsessed with successful, actually.

"Ironically, of course, since I thought I was doing everything for *us*, I pretty much neglected her. Long hours. Lots of traveling. She found someone who liked spending time with her. Who made her feel special. She stepped out. After we split up, she married him and got the life she always dreamed of, which, as it turned out, had nothing to do with having a great car or the best house on the block."

Allie hated her. "Sam, I'm sorry."

"I learned from it. Moved on."

Allie knew he was telling her exactly what he had learned from it. He was telling her not to pin any hopes on him. That steak and lobster and crème brûlée was all he was offering.

He was warning her he had priorities that did not involve a family.

"Cody has changed everything now, though, hasn't he?"

Something darkened in his eyes. It was not just Cody that had changed everything, but the awareness of loss lurking around the corner, waiting to pounce.

"I've had to pull back, because of Cody, but thankfully, I've been developing a team of really good people for years. They've stepped up. The business is thriving despite the challenges of the last few months."

Sam realized it was getting late. He had lost track of the number of times the coffee cups had been filled.

Allie made him laugh. And talk about things he had not talked about before. He loved how she frowned at the menu, and felt uncomfortable, and then came into herself, and then felt uncomfortable again, and couldn't even begin to hide how the prices on the menu made her feel.

He liked spoiling her.

And he liked being a grown-up, too. But he thought he'd be glad when Cody was back, acting as a buffer between them.

His phone rang. Its ring tone was a very distinctive *boing, boing, boing.*

"Normally, I'd ignore," he said, "but it's Kathy and Bill." She nodded her understanding and he saw his own sudden concern mirrored in her eyes.

"Hello?"

"Uncle Sam?"

Again, he was not quite sure how he'd become Nicole's uncle, but he realized he had no objection to it.

"Is everything all right?"

"Yes."

"Then what are you doing up? It's very late."

"I have jet lag."

"Are you whispering?"

"I took my mum's phone and found your number in it. She told me I wasn't to bother you."

"It's no bother."

"We're going to the San Diego Zoo tomorrow. Cody really wants to come. Mum said I wasn't to ask you, though."

"Why's that?"

"She wouldn't say, but I think she thinks you're sad without Cody."

Sam closed his eyes. Is that how people perceived him? Leaning heavily on a three-year-old to meet his emotional needs?

"I do miss him," he said carefully, "but I'm not sad. Allie is taking care of me."

He looked across the table at her. She looked like that was news to her.

"So could he come with us tomorrow?"

"How do you know he wants to go with you?" Did he really think a six-year-old was going to help him unlock the mystery of communicating with his three-year-old charge? If so, he was about to be disappointed.

"It's the *zoo.*"

This was said as if he was an idiot.

"Okay. I agree. Cody would like the zoo."

"Could you make it seem like it was your idea?"

"How am I going to do that?" he asked. "I didn't even know you were going to the zoo."

"You'll think of something," Nicole proclaimed confidentially. "I'm so happy. I love Cody so much."

Those words, spoken by a child, made him feel choked up.

He hung up the phone. Allie could obviously piece together most of the conversation from hearing one side of it.

"It's good for him to be around other kids," Sam said when the look on Allie's face suggested that, like Kathy, she wondered if he was sad without Cody.

"Well, it looks like I'm in charge of looking after you," she said.

He needed to set her straight on that. He'd only said that because it seemed like a simple thing to say to assuage Nicole's fears for his well-being. He didn't need looking after because Cody had other plans. He had a million things he could do. Should do. He could drive into the office, for one.

Or drive, period. Drive down the road the way that car was meant to be driven when there was no three-year-old in his car seat. And no dog throwing up. It had been eight months since he'd had a drive like that.

So, he needed to set Allie straight.

That he didn't need her or anyone else looking after him. He never had.

Instead, he found himself smiling at her.

"More grown-up things?" he said hopefully.

She smiled back at him so angelically it filled him with suspicion. "Yes, but on my terms."

"What does that mean?"

"Free," she informed him.

"What have you got in mind?"

"There's free yoga on the beach every morning."

"I don't know about that."

"You'll love it," Allie told him.

"Women in stretch pants doing incredible things with their bodies," he said, conceding to her way too easily. "What's not to love?"

In the morning, he called Kathy, and asked, ever so casually, what their plans were for the day.

She told him they were planning an overnight trip to the San Diego Zoo and he suggested Cody might like to go.

"Are you sure?"

"It's the *zoo*," he assured her.

"You could come with us. And bring Allie."

Sometime during the night, he realized he had become quite attached to the idea of having some more time with Allie to himself.

"We've made some plans," he said, still ever so casual. "But I'll drop by with some stuff for Cody and make sure he's up for it."

"How about if we come your way? Popsy can't come to the zoo. He'll have to stay home. And we'll need to get a car seat from you."

The family arrived at the cottage in a flurry of activity, energy and superhero capes. Poor Popsy looked more than ready for a day without children, and crept off to Allie's bedroom.

Cody leaped into Sam's arms, took both cheeks in his pudgy hands, and regarded his uncle solemnly. Another one making sure *he* was all right.

"You want to go to the zoo, buddy?"

Cody nodded vigorously and squirmed down out of Sam's arms. He and Bryan spread their arms and zoomed around the kitchen while Nicole yelled instructions at them.

Kathy placed her hands over her ears, gave him one long searching look, just like the one Cody had just given him. Her gaze drifted to Allie, and she gave a small nod, apparently satisfied Sam would be well looked after.

He fetched the car seat out of his vehicle and an overnight bag was organized for Cody. Then he and Allie were alone in the house. It seemed very quiet.

He was acutely aware of how great she looked in yoga pants. If somebody would have told him, a few days ago, that he would be looking forward to yoga on the beach, he would have scoffed.

In fact, if they had told him he would be looking forward to anything, he would have scoffed.

And yet, here he was, walking through the sand, carrying a yoga mat, with a beautiful woman at his side, feeling as if spring had come after a long, cold winter of darkness.

As it turned out, there was quite a lot not to love about yoga on the beach. Allie had failed to mention to him that the free, midmorning class was attended mostly by middle-aged and senior ladies who, whilst wearing yoga pants, were not exactly filling them out the way he had imagined.

Allie, who looked fantastic in the multicolored stretch pants and large T-shirt she was wearing, had placed herself where he couldn't see her.

Unless he really stretched—which, come to think of it, was the whole idea of yoga.

The teacher, a tyrant who seemed as if she had recently been released from her duties as prison guard or as a drill instructor for the marines, didn't approve of him stretching to try to catch a glimpse of Allie's downward facing dog. Or maybe she just didn't approve of him, specifically, or the entire male species, generally.

"She was mean," he told Allie after the class. They were sitting on their yoga mats, in the sand, in a shady area. He had his back braced against a tree, and his legs straight out in front of him. He took a tentative sip of some kind of green slime drink that Allie, in the spirit of keeping things free, had packed with her.

Allie's legs were still crossed in a serene lotus position. He felt like every muscle in his whole body was screaming.

"I've never thought she was mean," Allie said.

"Mr. Walker, press the perimeters of pain," he said, imitating her voice. "You're mean, too. A workout like that calls for a milkshake at the very least, and what are we drinking? Sludge."

"It's called Green Goddess. It's spinach and kale and celery. It's good for you."

"Nothing called Green Goddess is good for a man."

"Okay, yours is called Green Guy, then. And it's good for you."

"Why do those words always go hand in hand with something that tastes terrible? Like broccoli. Is there broccoli in this?"

He was making her laugh. He loved making her laugh.

After they finished their sludge, they walked back to the cottage. Allie was taking her job of keeping him entertained during Cody's absence very seriously. She dug old bikes from under the porch.

He eyed the one she offered to him suspiciously. "This seems rusty in all the wrong places."

"Don't be a chicken," she said. "I'll race you to the beginning of the bike path."

"I'm not fully recovered from yoga yet. And I'm lacking proper nourishment. And—"

She was on her bike and gone like a bolt of lightning. He wasn't just going to let her win!

He'd been right about the rust. The gears didn't work properly and he had to drag one foot on the ground to aid the mostly seized handbrake.

All of which turned out to be good. She beat him in the race. And he got the view he'd been vying for through an entire yoga class.

"I won," she crowed.

"I'm learning to be less competitive," he said.

Partway through the day, racing down a hill behind her, hearing her laughter, and feeling the thrill in his stomach from the speed, and her, and not knowing if he could stop, Sam was aware of something.

Despite the possible danger of crashing, he felt carefree.

Happiness had slipped in on him.

She stopped her bike. They were at a rocky outcrop that overlooked the ocean.

"Look," she breathed, "a whale."

But he didn't look at the whale. He looked at her face, radiating joy, and Sam Walker was filled with a sense of well-being.

"Race you home," she called as she took off again.

"You haven't got a hope," he yelled after her, knowing he didn't have the least bit of desire to wreck his view by getting in front of her. It was fun, though, to see her going as hard as she could, rising up on those pedals and casting anxious looks back at him.

Every time she did, he pretended he was working really hard to catch her.

Back at the cottage, she told him she had a wiener roast planned for dinner.

"Uh-uh," he said. "It's my turn. I'm planning dinner.

And I'll give you a hint. I've had about all I can handle of budget-friendly for one day."

"But didn't you have fun?" she asked, a bit anxiously.

"I did have fun. Now it's my turn to show you some fun. And I just want to see you wear the nicest thing you own."

Her mouth moved. She was going to protest. But in the end, he could see intrigue won out.

Somewhere along the way they had thrown caution to the wind. They were exploring each other's worlds, trading places, and they were doing it with all the fascination and openness of exploring a foreign country.

A voice inside him tried to be heard.

It said, *Slow down. Be careful.* But it seemed the brakes on the bike weren't the only ones not working today.

CHAPTER SIXTEEN

ALLIE STOOD IN front of her mirror. The nicest thing she owned was a dress she had tried on only once, and thought she would never wear again.

It was the one she was supposed to wear for the *American Singing Star* finale. Almost every single outfit she had worn for that show had made her uncomfortable. At first the outfits had been too geeky: buttoned-to-the-top blouses and calf-length skirts. Then the metamorphosis had begun, but again Allie had been dressed as a character, not as herself.

And so she had worn too-tight black leather pantsuits, form-fitting tube dresses, one-piece short suits that lived up to the word *short*.

But when she had been presented with this dress and tried it on, it felt as if her heart had stopped.

It wasn't like anything she had ever worn, on the show or off. And it didn't really speak to who she was or to who the show had made her into.

The dress spoke to who Allie could be.

The famous designer Iggy had made it, and adjusted it just for her. The dress was two things: it was the sea and it was flame. The top of it was the color of fire, reds and oranges and yellows licking together. Those colors poured down the dress like the slow ooze of lava, and then exploded into the turquoises and navy blues of molten rock hitting the sea.

It had a low V in the front, another at the back, a belt at the tininess of her waist. And then the dress swept down, past her knees, her calves exposed in a swirl of gauzy sea foam fabric.

When Allie had missed the finale, nobody had asked her for the dress back. They hadn't asked her for the shoes, or even the jewelry that came with it. She wasn't sure if it was an oversight, a payment or an apology.

Naturally, given the disastrous circumstances her claim to fame had ended with, she had sworn she would never wear the dress.

Now she was glad for that. She was glad the public had never seen her in it. And she was glad Ryan had never seen her in it.

She contemplated how she could think his name with absolutely no emotional charge. If she felt anything at all, it was a strange pity, as if every single contestant on that ridiculous show had been caught in webs woven out of their own dreams.

The dress was not the dress of someone who had given up on dreams. It was the dress of someone who *owned* them, who knew exactly who they were, and were not the least bit afraid to show it.

When had she become that person?

Almost the instant she had let an intruder into her house, almost the instant she had said yes to the adventure of letting the strangers who knocked on her door—or broke it down, as the case may be—into her world.

She was seeing herself differently.

She was seeing herself like this. She had promised Sam they would do grown-up things, and she had somehow transformed, maybe for the first time in her life, into a complete grown-up.

Allie liked it. She looked sensual rather than sexy, mysterious rather than an open book. She looked like a woman who was passionate and complicated and confident. She twirled in the mirror. She flicked her hair. She wished for just one change to those horrid black tips… but tonight, she did not cover it.

She strapped on the tiny shoes with their impossible heels. She felt grateful for all the hours practicing moves on heels for the show. Thanks to dozens of rehearsals, she could practically turn a cartwheel in high heels.

She took the necklace that had come with the ensemble. The necklace flashed and reflected the flames of the dress. It looked like diamonds though, of course, it was fake, like everything on that show had been fake.

They had tried to make her into a fake.

She gave the exhausted Popsy, stretched out full length on her bed, a pat on the head and a scratch on the tummy. Then she took a deep breath and stepped out her bedroom door. She went down the hall and into the kitchen.

Sam sat at the table. He was looking at his phone, and so engrossed in whatever he was seeing that he didn't look up.

It gave Allie a moment to study him. He wasn't as dressed up as her. Obviously his best suit had not come on beach holiday with him. Still, Sam was looking pretty glorious himself.

Dressed in jeans, the dark navy of brand-new denim and a pressed shirt, he looked strong and lean and confident. He was freshly shaven, his hair combed, but his clothes and his grooming only added to his allure, because what he was, he carried inside himself.

For a moment, she felt almost intimidated by the aura

of power and control around him, but then he noticed her and, with a grin that made him *her* Sam again, he turned the screen toward her. A video was playing, Cody in the foreground dancing happily in front of the tiger enclosure.

His grin faded as he took her in. The phone dropped from his hand. His mouth opened and then closed again.

In his eyes, she saw the reflection of what she was.

And for the first time, Allie stood in the full glory and gratitude of the fact that *American Singing Star* had not succeeded in making her into what they wanted her to be.

He got up from the table and came and took her shoulders in his hands.

"How can you look so dressed up without a suit?" she asked, looking up into his face, into the desire-darkened color of his familiar brown eyes.

He was a man comfortable in T-shirts and shorts and pajama bottoms and flip-flops. But he was also powerful and successful, rich beyond anything she had ever dreamed.

But she knew she had the confidence to explore this side of him, too. She was aware *her* Sam, the one who tossed Cody in the air, and left books open on their spines, and built sandcastles, and dove into the sea, and fixed things that needed to be fixed, was right here, co-existing with this man.

She was aware she wanted to know all of him.

She slipped her arm though his proffered elbow and he escorted her out to the car. The car was gorgeous, all deep leather and luxury.

But a faint smell clung to it, that made her laugh out loud.

They didn't drive very far. He went to the other side of Sugar Cone and pulled into the marina.

"You rented a boat?" she said. She felt her first moment of uncertainty. She wasn't dressed for a boat. What if his idea of showing her his world involved baiting hooks? No, Sam simply wasn't the kind of guy who would get something like that so wrong. You did not tell a woman to wear her best and take her fishing.

"Not exactly a boat," he said. "Not like a rubber dingy or a fishing boat. Actually, not even like a motor boat." He pulled up at a slip.

Her mouth fell open.

Behind an arch and beyond a gangplank, a boat bobbed graciously. Or would this be called a boat?

A yacht was probably the correct term.

While she sat there, stunned, a uniformed man came and opened her door, saluted them both as Sam took her arm and they made their way up the slightly swaying gangplank. Another uniformed man waited at the top.

"Mr. Walker, Ms. Cook, welcome abroad the *Queen of Love.*"

Allie gasped at the name.

"I'm Clark and I'll be your steward for your time with us. We're about to set sail, so I'll get you settled with a drink and then if you want a tour of the yacht I'd be happy to give it to you *or* I can take you straight to the dining area."

"A drink would be nice," Sam decided for them, thank goodness, since it felt as if the cat had her tongue.

They were brought to a fabulous area in the bow of the boat, a semi-circle of deep white leather furniture.

Champagne was presented in flutes, and a plate of hors d'oeuvres was set out.

Clark went to attend to whatever yacht people attended to while a boat set sail, and then returned.

"May I show you the boat?" he asked. He took them

through a main door and Allie stopped. It was a beautiful living room, more white leather, with a white grand piano to one side and a completely stocked bar on the other.

"We're supposed to have clear sailing for your dinner cruise tonight, however, if you are more comfortable in here, please just let me know."

They followed him through the yacht, being introduced to any crew they came across and finally ending in the wheel house where they met the captain. Allie noticed Sam was watching her with a smile as one experience after another unfolded in front of her.

"Just own it," he told her quietly.

"But what does—"

She stopped herself. Did it matter what it cost? He could obviously afford it, and he wanted to give it to her. And so she surrendered to it, she just gave herself over to the complete enjoyment of this exquisite experience Sam was giving her.

Was it a date? If the movie, yoga on the beach and getting sweaty riding bicycles had left any doubt, this did not.

They went out to sea, and anchored off a lovely little island. It had a cottage on it that reminded her of her house. They were given the choice of the outdoor or indoor dining room. Sam wanted her to choose, and she chose the outdoor dining room.

On the port side, the cottage lights came on and splashed across the sea, and on the starboard side, way in the distance, they could see as the lights of Sugar Cone Beach winked on, and the ones in the hills above it. The sea became like a dark piece of velvet studded with the jewels of reflected light.

Dinner was served.

"And I thought the restaurant last night was swanky,"

Allie managed, as dish after dish of exquisite food was presented to them under inky dark skies, by staff who were so graceful and quiet, it was almost as though they were alone.

The meal finished and coffee came.

And then the lights were lowered, and music poured through speakers.

"Would you care to dance?" Sam asked her.

She closed her eyes, as the dreamlike quality of the evening intensified. Then she opened them, looked at him and nodded. She put her hand in his. In a moment, her forehead resting on his chest, his chin on the top of her heard, they swayed together, letting all the magic they were experiencing outside of themselves come in.

Was it just days ago, Allie wondered dreamily, that she had thought she knew what a perfect moment was?

The truth was she had no idea.

And for the first time in a long, long time, she trusted it.

She looked up into his face. His eyes were closed and he was without a doubt the most beautiful human being she had ever seen. She nestled deeper into his chest, and put her arms around him, pressing into the small of his back to bring him closer to her.

She thought back over their days together.

He wasn't just beautiful outside. He was beautiful inside, too.

"I'll remember this moment forever," she whispered to him. And for an instant, it pierced the perfection of the moment, a reminder that all good things ended.

They could not dance on this deck forever.

Sam and Cody would be leaving soon. And they had never once discussed what happened next.

But in this perfect moment, it felt as if Allie knew exactly what happened next.

What they had experienced between them over the past few days was too strong to just walk away from.

This was the beginning of the courtship. Not the end.

She reached up, and took his lips with hers.

Sam tasted of champagne and the night stars. He tasted of the sea and of every great mystery humans had ever explored together. He tasted of gentleness and he tasted of strength. He tasted of simplicity and he tasted of complexity.

Allie shivered under the taste of his lips, the red-hot touch of his hand on the nakedness of her back, the way he pulled her into him, both savage and sensitive.

The kiss validated all she knew and all she was feeling.

And she tasted the beauty of him so fully that something in her that had been unfinished was suddenly completed.

Until he pulled away from her, stepped back, raked a hand through the dark crispness of his hair.

"I'm not sure we should go there," he whispered huskily. "I'm not sure."

How was that possible? How could he be not sure, when she had never been more certain of anything in her whole life?

That's what you get, a little voice inside chided her, *for having faith in perfect moments. Again.*

CHAPTER SEVENTEEN

THEY DROVE HOME in silence, some tension in the air between them that he wanted to move away from, and that Allie wanted to move toward.

"I'm not ready to go to bed," Allie said when they arrived at the cottage and went in the door.

"You're exhausting me," Sam informed her. "Don't you ever sleep?"

But she glanced at Sam from under her eyelashes, and he did not look exhausted.

They were home from their magical evening, at that awkward moment when it was time to say good-night, go to their separate rooms and shut the doors.

Lie awake and listen to each other breathing.

"I'm not ready for bed," she said, again.

He sighed. "Me, either. You know what I want?"

Oh, yeah, she knew what he wanted. She had seen it in his eyes tonight when they had danced, felt it in the heat of his body when the music had turned slow.

"What do you want?" Allie whispered.

He leaned forward. She thought he was going to kiss her. But he didn't. He touched her hair.

"I want to cut this."

"What?"

"I want to get rid of those little black tips. I want to banish Tempest forever."

Hmm…interesting…just when she wanted to let Tempest out.

Without waiting for her answer, he led her out onto the deck. He placed a stool in the center of it, and beckoned for her to sit down.

He went back into the house and got a towel and a clothespin, and secured them around her neck.

"It feels like Superman's cape," she said softly.

"Maybe that's what it is when you become yourself."

And then with exquisite tenderness he began to cut her hair. Deliberately, his hands brushed the soft nape of her neck. Deliberately, he placed his lips where his fingertips had been. The black hair fell around her, bit by bit, and his lips and hands took the place of everything that hair had represented.

"It's kind of like Sampson and Delilah," she told him softly, "only in reverse. My strength is coming back to me with every snip. I am becoming more who I am, not less."

Finally, he was finished. He took off the towel and stood back regarding her. He took his fingers and ran them through her hair. He fluffed it. He acted as though he could not get enough of staring at her.

"And who are you?" he asked.

"It's my turn to pick what we do. I want to swim with you," she said, and heard the huskiness in her voice. "I want to skinny-dip with you in the ocean."

"That's not a good idea," he said.

"I think it is," she decided. "I'm all done with letting other people decide what the good ideas are, even you."

Even you.

As if he mattered to her, but not as much as she mattered to herself. Allie had been beautiful before. As she interacted with him, and Cody and her guitar. But Allie stepping out of that pile of dark hair and fully into herself was more than beautiful.

It was irresistible.

She went into the house, and came back out with a towel wrapped around her.

Sam could feel his mouth going dry. She was naked under that towel.

He tried to reason with himself: she was *always* naked under something, her clothes, her bathing suit.

She walked by him, and helplessly he followed her to the water's edge.

She dropped the towel, and stood there. The night was dark and yet her skin glowed white, luminescent. She gave him one look, one seductive smile, and dove into the waves.

He dropped his shorts and followed her into the water.

She was swimming out beyond the break, treading water and tilting her head to the stars.

"You're going to get us arrested," he told her huskily.

She turned her face away from the stars and looked at him. He saw her bravery. He saw what she was asking.

He did what he had wanted to do since they had danced together, since he had cut her hair.

Since the first time he had tasted her lips, probably since the first time he had seen her, lying on the floor, those huge eyes taking him in.

Even then, the bravery had been there.

He closed the small distance of dark water between them. He growled her name. She answered by twining her arms around his neck, by pressing herself against him. Her skin was hot in contrast to the cool of the water. Her body was substance, something you could hang onto, something solid in a liquid world.

He took her lips.

Her answer was tentative. A tasting. A nibble.

And then less tentative. Her hands twined more tightly around him, and her mouth invited him deeper.

He could not refuse the invitation. He was a man who had been dying of hunger and thirst, and this moment offered him what he had turned his back on.

Life.

Her lips tasted of seawater and hope. Her lips tasted of the wine she had sipped earlier and of dreams. Her lips tasted of laughter.

Her lips tasted of a future.

He groaned, and pulled her to him. He carried her out of the water.

She nestled into him. "Warrior," she said, the maiden being carried off.

But nothing could be further from the truth. He was not a warrior—he was the conquered. This was the very thing he was sworn to fight.

But his weakness was such that he could not remember why he needed to fight. He set her down slowly, pulled on his shorts, watched out of the corner of his eye as she pulled the towel around herself.

And then he scooped her back up. He carried her through the darkness, through the sand, aware she felt featherlight. How could someone so powerful be so light?

He slid open the patio screen with his foot, carried her through the darkened house and to his bedroom. He tossed her on the bed, and stood drinking her in, the unearthly beauty of her.

He laid down on the bed beside her. He traced the sacred places of her. He made her quiver with wanting him.

He made her sigh and cry. He made her play out each of the things going on inside of him.

Far away, something was trying to pierce his awareness.

"Leave it," she whispered, a plea.

But he pushed up on his elbows and listened. It was his phone, in some faraway room.

Boing. Boing. Boing.

Allie's brow furrowed as she recognized the tone. "That's Kathy and Bill's ring tone," she said, sudden panic, that mirrored his own, in her voice.

"What time is it?" she asked.

He looked at the clock beside her bed. It was nearly three in the morning. Nothing good had ever come from a three-in-the-morning phone call.

He got up and raced through the house, following the sound of the phone. Allie, the towel pulled around her, was right behind him. The phone had been abandoned out on the deck.

He found it, and stabbed at the keypad in the darkness.

"Hello?" he cried desperately.

He could hear a sound, but not a voice. He was pretty sure it was Kathy, but she wasn't speaking.

She was crying.

It was a terrifying reminder of what happened when you let go of control, what happened when you let your guard down.

"What's happened?" Sam demanded. "What's happened to Cody?"

"Nothing," Kathy managed to stammer. "Sam, he's fine. I'm sorry I frightened you. No, he's more than fine. He's already gone back to sleep. But I wanted you to know.

"He spoke."

Sam knew he should ask questions. A good person would ask questions. A good person would not make it all about him. A good person would at least ask what Cody said.

He was silent, because he could not trust his voice if he spoke.

Kathy laughed, a little nervously. "I'm sorry. It's the middle of the night. I probably shouldn't have woken you. But Cody woke up, and he spoke, and I just wanted you to know so badly."

"Thank you," he said, forcing the words out past the lump in his throat. He could not trust himself to say more.

"I'll let you go." She was crying again. "I just wanted you to know. We're going to leave really early. We'll be back at the beach house in the morning. Come for breakfast. You and Allie. I'll tell you all about it then."

Allie was at his side as he ended the call, looking at him with those huge eyes.

"Is everything okay? Is Cody okay?"

"Yeah," he said, "everything is fine."

"Sam?"

Allie was touching him. Her hand on his naked skin felt scorching, like a brand. She was gazing at him with a look that could steal whatever was left of his strength.

But life had just reminded him of the danger of the kind of moments—minutes, hours, days—that he had let himself share with her.

Just as he relaxed, just as he began to allow himself to have hope, life let you know.

You are a failure.

Not at business. When it came to business, he had the proverbial Midas touch. But where it really mattered? With people?

He had failed his nephew. A few days with other

people—normal people, wholesome people—and Cody had spoken.

But his failures had begun long before that. He had failed his sister and brother-in-law. He had failed at marriage.

And he would fail Allie, too.

He knew what he needed to do. And he knew it was going to be the hardest thing he had ever done.

"What is going on?" Allie demanded. "What's happened to Cody?"

He forced his mouth into a smile. He forced himself not to look at her mouth, or her hair still wet from the sea, with no black left in it. He forced himself not to look at the long stretches of her not covered in the towel.

"Cody spoke," he said. "Kathy wanted to let me know."

"What did he say?" she asked. Her eyes filled with tears, joyous tears. "Sam! This is incredible."

She didn't get it. At all.

He had come here looking for an answer, looking for a sure direction, needing to know what was best for Cody.

He had come here begging to know what was right.

And now he knew.

"You," he said, "should not be luring men you barely know into middle-of-the-night naked swims with you."

"Barely know?" she whispered.

"No pun intended," he said coldly, and was satisfied to see her flinch and pull that towel a little tighter around her body.

It would make it easier for her if the cut was cruel. Oh, who was he kidding? It would make it easier for him if she didn't know the truth.

If she knew the truth—how hard it was to walk away from the light and back into darkness—she might wrap her arms around him again. She might soothe the demons in him with the sound of her voice. She might sing him back to *this* world.

He couldn't drag her down with him. He despised himself for how badly he wanted to go back into the circle of her arms, the comfort she was promising him.

He'd almost taken advantage of this fragile, broken girl.

Oh, sure he had cut her hair, he had led her part way back to who he could see she was. But would there be a worse choice than him to restore her?

No, he would be the worst choice.

He went into his bedroom. He shut the door, not with a slam, that might have revealed way too much, but with a click that said nothing at all.

He laid down in the bed they had shared. He could taste her on the air, and smell her in his sheets.

He waited until he heard her go to bed. And then he waited an hour beyond that. The dawn was coming up when he tiptoed out the door, a carelessly packed bag over his shoulder, and left.

He left Popsy with her. Even the dog knew the truth about him.

Allie woke up in the morning, with Popsy licking her face frantically. She realized it was very late. Well, it had been very late when she had finally slept.

At first the dog's attention made her feel happy, but then memories of the night before crept in. She remembered the terrible coldness in Sam's face after that phone call, and how nasty he had been to her. Then she became aware of a silence in the cottage, a feeling of utter emptiness.

She got up and raced to Sam's room. The bed was

neatly made. The closet was empty. She ran to the front room and looked out the window. His car was gone.

She went to Cody's room. His things were still there, his books, his suitcase. Sam would not abandon Cody.

Or Popsy.

With panic rising in her, she ran all the way down the beach to Kathy and Bill's. It looked as if they had just gotten back. Kathy opened the door, and let her in.

"Is Sam here?"

"Here? No. Why would he—"

"I woke up this morning, and he was gone." She tried to keep the panic out of her voice. She couldn't let Cody hear. "Something happened last night when you called. I don't know what—"

Kathy's phone rang. She looked at it, and then nodded at Allie. "Sam? Allie's here. Where are you?"

She listened and then said, "Sam, you've got this all wrong. When Cody woke up he said—"

She frowned and stared at her phone. "He's hung up on me."

"What did he say?" Allie breathed.

"Cody said *Need Unca.*"

As important as it was for Allie to hear that, that wasn't what she meant. "What did Sam say?"

Kathy shot a look toward the hallway to make sure no little ears listened. "Something about meeting with his lawyers. Something about us, Bill and I, taking custody of Cody."

Allie felt as if she was breaking apart inside. "He was worried from the moment he arrived that that's what you wanted."

"What? We never wanted that. Of course we love Cody. Of course we are aware that Cody is how Adam goes on. We have been exploring how to spend more time with him. Bill has been looking at a transfer to his company's American office. That's part of the reason for this trip. We feel Sam is as much a part of our family as Cody is. It's so apparent how they have gotten each other through this. We can see the bond. Anyone could see the bond. How could he think we would want to break that bond?"

"He thought Adam and Sue probably named him guardian as a lark, back when they thought nothing bad could ever happen to them."

"You know, nobody liked a lark as much as Adam. And Sue, too. But when it came to their child? That's the most ridiculous thing I ever heard. They would have made that decision with all the weight it needed. And they made the right one. It's so obvious when you see Sam with Cody, don't you think?"

"Cody talked for you, not him. Sam will see that as a failure, as proof that he's not the best person for Cody."

Kathy was watching her intently. Somehow, as she looked at Allie, the worry lines faded from her face.

"Oh, my," she said. "It's all way more complicated than Sam and Cody, isn't it?"

"In what way?" Allie stammered.

"You love him. And I wonder how he feels about you."

CHAPTER EIGHTEEN

"L-LOVE HIM?" ALLIE STAMMERED. "That's impossible."

She thought of Sam's final words to her, about luring men she barely knew into naked middle-of-the-night swims with her.

"And he doesn't have feelings for me. Or at least not positive ones."

But even as she told herself it was impossible, even as she told herself Sam did not have feelings for her, her heart was singing a different tune entirely. Kathy was smiling at her.

"I barely know him," Allie said, and then realized she had parroted the hurtful words he had said to her last night.

"You know, the very first time I laid eyes on Bill, something in me sighed, and said, *That's him*."

"Well, I had that experience, too, only it wasn't with Sam, and the guy I had it with definitely wasn't *him*. I don't believe in fairy tales."

"Don't you? Don't you ever ask yourself what fairy tales are based on, and why they have survived the test of time? Other stories come and they go. But those ones—those stories of love winning out over all the obstacles put in its way—they stay, don't they? Generation after generation, drawn to them, finding comfort in them."

"I don't know what to do," Allie whispered.

"Of course you do," Kathy said. "Your heart knows exactly what to do."

And Allie realized Kathy was right.

On two counts. Allie had fallen in love with Sam. And she knew you did not love someone and allow them to carry that enormous burden of pain by themselves. She saw his hurtful words last night for what they were, an attempt to keep what was going on between them at bay, a fear of hope.

"I don't even know where he lives," she whispered.

"I do," Kathy said. "I do."

He lived a long way away. Far enough away that some of the confidence and certainty that Kathy had made her feel, that she had felt as she looked in the mirror at her freshly snipped hair, had abandoned her.

The confidence faded yet again when she parked in front of Sam Walker's apartment building. The building reminded her what the past days had helped her forget. They were from totally different worlds.

She had known that from the beginning. She had told him that, for Pete's sake. That they were an impossible match.

The building was gorgeous: stone and glass and steel. There was going to be a guard at the door, and he was not going to let her in.

But for some reason Kathy's words gave her courage.

There was a reason fairy tales survived. Obstacles could be overcome. There could be happily ever after.

This, she reminded herself sternly, was not about her. It wasn't just Kathy giving her courage. It was the legacy of Allie's grandmother. Nobody had championed love more than her grandmother.

She had a sudden thought: all those beautiful weeks

with Gram, after Ryan's betrayal and the collapse of her dreams, before her grandmother had died. They had discussed the cottage going to Allie, but her grandmother had never once mentioned Sam's contract or his family, even though they had obviously been a part of her life for a long time. Was it possible her Gram had hoped a chance meeting between Allie and Sam could bring this outcome? Love?

It made Allie feel both happy and strong to think of her grandmother sweetly, and a little sneakily, trying to engineer her happiness as her last gift to her.

Now she felt tuned in to love and she listened. Love told Allie not to make it about herself. It was about him. It was about going in after him, when he thought he knew what was best for everyone.

She got out of her car. It seemed like the wrong kind of car to be parked in front of a building like this.

The doorman seemed to think so, too. He actually frowned as he held open the door for her.

While she'd been on *American Singing Star* she'd been exposed to many places like this: oozing the wealth of people who had arrived. Water trickled down a stone wall behind the desk and into a pond. The lobby had two deep leather couches facing each other in front of a fireplace. One of them looked as if it could be worth quite a bit more than her car.

Being in this kind of place when she was on the show had always made her feel *less than*, always made her feel like an imposter. It made her feel as if it was just a matter of time before they discovered who she really was and tossed her out.

But she didn't feel any of those things this time.

She found herself thinking: *This beautiful glass box is where he thinks he belongs?*

She could feel her resolve returning as she marched up to the desk. The security person looked intimidating, military bearing, probably a former Navy SEAL or something equally immovable. He was wearing a name tag that said *Benson.*

"I'm going up to see Sam Walker," she said. "I don't want to be announced."

His jaw dropped. "Uh, that's not exactly how it works."

"It's life-or-death," she said firmly.

The guy cocked his head at her, skeptically, and then his brows lifted. "Hey, aren't you Tempest?"

She waited for the look that followed, the judgment, the scorn.

It didn't come. Instead, the man's expression softened. "They sure threw you under the bus, didn't they?"

She knew she had stumbled upon a true fan. She knew if she said she was Tempest, the door would be opened for her. But she didn't want the door—especially not this door to Sam—opened for that reason.

Allie realized just a short time ago, she would have whole-heartedly agreed with him.

"Mr. Benson," she said, and heard the strength in her words, "I am not Tempest, and I never was. I was not thrown under the bus, I walked in front of it, with my eyes wide open. It was extraordinarily painful, but if it took a few obstacles for me to arrive at the conclusion that each of my choices has led me to exactly where I am today, every one of those obstacles was worth it."

His whole face opened up, a man who knew a few things—didn't everyone in the human family?—about obstacles.

"I'm Allie," she said. "Allie Cook. And I'm here to see Sam Walker on a matter of the heart."

"Just Benson," he said. "No Mister. I'll take you up, you need an elevator key to open at his floor."

His floor? Now was not the time to be weak. "Thank you," she said. When Benson got up from behind his desk, she noticed he really did know a thing or two about obstacles. He only had one leg.

"He got what he deserved, anyway, our boy Ryan."

"What do you mean?"

He squinted at her. "You don't know?"

"I turned my back on all of it when it ended." Turned her back wasn't exactly accurate. She had dug a hole. And she would still be in it, if it weren't for Sam.

"Smart to not look back. I saw it about Ryan in the tabloids. It wasn't even a headline. That's the thing about those talent shows, isn't it? You never hear what happens to any of those people next. Even the winners seem to fade away like cheap ink on advertising flyers. His record deal fell through. He's singing on cruise ships."

Strangely, that was the exact moment Allie knew just how much she had come to love Sam Walker.

Because a heart that held love could have no room for any malice toward another human being.

She didn't know she had been hanging on to anything, until that moment before the elevator doors whispered open, and she forgave Ryan.

And it made her feel strong, and absolutely ready for what she had to do next.

The feeling of strength lasted two seconds. The absolute opulence of the apartment beyond the opened elevator door hit her like a brick.

She considered telling Benson to close the door and take her back down. But he was looking at her, like a man who knew a thing or two about courage, and as if he had an expectation of her.

And then Allie realized that *this* was the perfect moment she had always longed for. It was the moment love called her, and asked her to be bigger than herself, and more courageous than she had ever been. Hadn't she started to recognize what love required that day she had come down from the hills to be with Sam, instead of hiding?

In this moment, she recognized exactly what love did. It was a kind of suspension of self, that asked not *what do* I *need*? but *what does* he *need*?

She stepped out of the elevator, and the door whispered shut behind her, taking away her escape route.

The far wall of the apartment was probably all windows, though you couldn't tell that at the moment, because the curtains were all drawn and it had the ambience of a cave.

She heard a growl.

And a bear's cave at that.

"Sam?" Her eyes adjusted to the dark. He was sitting up on a sofa, glaring at her, but he was rumpled looking, and she knew he had slept there.

In the course of just a few hours, he had changed completely. His hair was sticking up all over the place, his face was shadowed with whiskers, his T-shirt had a stain on the front. He was in boxer shorts. He looked haggard. And he looked tormented.

"What do you want?" he snapped.

"I want to know why you left."

He snorted. "I think that's obvious."

"It's not to me. You'll have to explain it."

She held her breath. He looked like he was in a dangerous and foul mood, the kind of mood that told nosy people to get lost, to leave him alone.

But, instead of telling her to get lost, to go away, Sam

took a shaky breath, and Allie felt herself start breathing again.

"I'm a failure, Allie. Do you get that?"

"I'm afraid I don't. Looking around it seems as if you are the furthest thing from a failure."

He snorted. "You, of all people, know that none of this matters."

"That's true."

"What matters is being there for people when they need you. Knowing the right thing to do. Cody needs a family, not some bumbling uncle. That's why he finally talked. You know it is. Because they knew how to make him happy. And I didn't."

"You never asked what he said," she told him softly. "When he spoke."

"It doesn't matter. He spoke. He spoke when he was with them and he never did it for me."

"The words he said were *Need Unca.*"

Sam went very still. He rubbed his eyes. She thought she saw a tremble in his shoulders.

"A three-year-old doesn't know what he needs. I just had a video chat with him. He was fine. Happy. Learning to make blueberry pancakes. Not that *he* chatted. Nope. Silence for me. I've failed him. I told you about my first wife, I failed her, too.

"This is the part you don't know, Allie, that you really, really need to know. I failed Adam and Sue. After my parents died, I promised myself I would look after her, that I would never let anything bad happen to her again."

The pain was quivering in the air around him. His voice was a croak of pure, unadulterated feeling.

"I was supposed to be with them that night. I begged off. You know why? Because some woman, named

Bambi or Bobbi or Barbie, called and made me an offer I couldn't refuse. It was more important to me than them.

"If I had gone with them, maybe I would have been driving. Maybe we would have taken a different route, or left at a different time. Maybe it could have been me, instead of them."

He put his head in his hands.

Allie could not bear to not be with him. She went and sank on the couch beside him and put her hands on his shoulders.

She could feel the strength he could not feel.

She could see the bravery he was blind to.

She could sense the torment that he was carrying alone, that he could not control the fates of those he loved, and she could not let him be alone with it anymore.

"At the very least, I could have had those moments with them," Sam said hoarsely. "One last night. To cherish them. To hold on to. Maybe I could have told Sue I loved her. I never said that to her. Thought it was sappy. Unmanly. Even after Mom and Dad died, I never said it. I never said it to him, either. I never told Adam I loved him like he was my brother.

"Love," he snorted. "I don't know anything about love. It's a relief that Cody is going to go with them, with Bill and Kathy. I have a life. I need my life back. My old life. Parties. Good times. Racking up successes like billiard balls before the break."

"Liar," she said, oh, so tenderly, just as he had called her a liar when she had claimed her independence and strength and resilience.

Now she could see the lie he was telling himself.

"The lie you are telling yourself," she said softly, "is that you are terrified of failure."

"That's not a lie."

"What you're really terrified of is love. You're so afraid of it wounding you again. So afraid that all your strength will not be enough. Not just to save yourself. I don't even think you care about yourself. You're afraid all your strength won't be enough to save others."

He was silent, so silent.

"You are," she said softly, "sacrificing your own happiness to do what you think is right. For me. For Cody. For Bill. For Kathy. Ironically, isn't that love itself? The ability to put the needs of others ahead of your own?"

Silent.

"I need you," she whispered.

"No! You are better off without me. Don't you get it? Both of you. Cody and you—"

She stopped him with a raised hand. "Unfortunately for you, Sam, you've hit me at a point in my life where I'm not letting anyone else decide for me what I need. I need you. And you need me. Desperately."

"I don't need you," he said scornfully, "especially not desperately."

She smiled at him. She touched his cheek. She looked deep into his eyes. "Especially desperately," she told him.

And then, tenderly, she claimed his lips, and kissed him.

Desperately.

And he answered her with equal desperation.

A long time later, Sam broke away from her kiss. How was it that something rooted in complete desperation could make him feel as if he had been pulled back from the brink?

He was aware that everything he had learned as a lifeguard was wrong. Completely and totally wrong.

Because he was not pulling her down with him.

She had the lifesaving ring. It was called love.

And it was strong enough to hold them both. It was strong enough to save them both.

CHAPTER NINETEEN

ALLIE SAT ON her back porch and strummed her guitar. The beach in front of her was packed. This was the last day of the Labor Day long weekend. Tomorrow, the beach would be nearly empty and the children would all be back in school.

She gulped. One of the neighbors who had joined the impromptu Fourth of July party at Kathy and Bill's—that seemed a lifetime ago—was a teacher. She had found Allie and asked if she would consider singing a few songs at the first-day-back-to-school assembly.

We can pay you a little bit.

Tomorrow. How had it arrived so quickly?

Unlike trying to produce a jingle for Phil's Steakhouse, which she had finally given up on, her guitar *loved* this assignment. The songs flowed out of her and her guitar: beloved children's rhymes, traditional tunes, folk songs, melodies and lyrics she created herself.

Was it the assignment that the guitar was reacting to, or was her guitar absorbing the love that shimmered in the air around Allie's life? Everything, including the music, seemed infused with light.

It had been the most blissful summer she had ever known. She and Sam had given themselves over to exploring what had leaped up so suddenly and so unexpectedly between them.

They had spent the summer going back and forth between each other's houses. At her house, they did yoga on the beach, and learned to paddleboard. They tried beach volleyball. They hiked in the hills that surrounded Sugar Cone Beach. They bought kayaks, and rode bikes and had sunset picnics. They played music and tried out recipes and danced on the back porch as the stars came out and the waves lapped at the shore.

At his house, they experimented with his expensive coffee machine and his state-of-the-art kitchen. They enjoyed his home theater, and the condo complex swimming pool. They went to five-star restaurants and attended live theater. They went dancing at exclusive clubs. He took her to the first Major League ball game she had ever been at. They swooped over twisting highways on his motorbike, her arms wrapped around the solidness of his waist, the wind playing with the tufts of her hair.

Kathy and Bill bought the beach house that Allie had run by—again, it seemed a lifetime ago—that had been up for sale.

Bill went home to tie up loose ends in Australia before transferring to the United States, but Kathy and the kids stayed for the summer.

And so, as well as exploring the amazing energy that sizzled in the air between them, Allie and Sam learned what it was to become a family.

They took all the kids to every Sunday matinee at the local theater. They built sandcastles and baked cookies. They made blanket forts on rainy days. They worked their way through the menu of the local ice cream store. They introduced Popsy to the new puppy that Kathy brought home for the kids to help them adjust to their new life.

Cody, Nicole and Bryan were a willing and enthusiastic audience as Allie tested every song she played and every song she wrote on them. Soon, all the neighborhood kids, new friends to the gang, seemed to be showing up for the little impromptu concerts that sprang up.

Allie had a sense that she and Sam looked after Kathy and she looked after them. Cody happily stayed with his cousins as the romance unfolded between Allie and Sam. Kathy cheerfully accommodated, and encouraged, Allie and Sam's growing need for adult time, alone time.

Cody spoke a little more every day, blossoming under the love that had taken so many different forms around him, the love that filled his life until it spilled over.

As she strummed her guitar, and thought about the wonderful summer she had experienced, and the new adventure she was going to have tomorrow, Allie heard a noise at the front door.

She smiled at the full-circle feeling of the moment, set down the guitar, got up and greeted Sam just as he came through the door.

How could her heart still pound like this every single time she saw him? He kissed her, his lips warm and familiar and lovely, and then held her back and looked at her. "Are you ready for tomorrow?"

"As ready as I've ever been for anything."

He smiled at her, that now familiar smile that made her world feel right and complete and as if she could do anything. Climb mountains, jump from airplanes.

Sing to three hundred small children.

"I've got a little surprise for you," he said.

This was what he was like. He loved surprising her. He seemed to have a theme, his gifts seemed intent on filling her world with beauty. They almost always had something to do with painting pictures, telling stories, or singing songs.

And so he had made her gifts of exquisite paintings and pieces of art, wonderful books, both old and new, and beautiful instruments like an antique ukulele.

Which she was going to use in one of her new songs tomorrow.

He handed her an envelope, and watched her intently as she opened it. She looked at the pieces of paper without comprehension.

"What is this?"

"Kathy has already agreed to babysit."

"Tickets?"

He nodded. "Airline tickets."

"To Paris," she whispered. Once, she realized, she had been afraid to go. Afraid of broken promises and her own expectations. Afraid to leave the safe little world she had created for herself.

But loving Sam had removed her limitations. It had filled her with curiosity about the world and a bold desire to explore it and to embrace all the adventures it held. Love had made her brave.

"It's supposed to be beautiful in the fall," he said, as if she needed coaxing.

"Are these first-class tickets?" she asked, pretending disapproval. As she hoped, it got a rise out of him.

"Look, Allie, as much as every man wants to be loved for himself and not his money, I have long legs. I need to have more legroom. I know you'd be comfortable in one of the overhead bins, but, for once, can't you just go along?"

She gave up the charade of being disapproving, allowed herself a little shriek of pure delight and threw herself into his arms, covered his face with kisses. "Yes,

yes and yes. I think it was Audrey Hepburn who said, 'Paris is always a good idea.'"

"You didn't think it was such a hot idea the first time I suggested it," he reminded her.

"You've been a good influence on me," she said, and fluttered her eyelashes at him demurely. He roared with the laughter that she loved drawing out of him.

Sam was quite familiar with Paris, but they explored it as if it was brand-new to both of them. They strolled the misty banks of the Seine at dawn, and experienced the Louvre at dusk. They ate take-away crepes, and freshly roasted chestnuts from street stalls. They drank *chocolat chaud* at the Café de Flore, one of the oldest cafés in Paris. A favorite historical haunt of painters, writers and philosophers—"The people who make the world beautiful," Sam reminded her—it served the melted chocolate and the hot milk in separate jugs. Then they walked the streets of St. Germaine until their feet hurt.

They reveled in the sights of Luxembourg Palace and its gorgeous gardens, kicking through piles of leaves with the delight of children. They discovered the underground world of the catacombs. They found the graves of Oscar Wilde and Jim Morrison in the Père Lachaise Cemetery.

Now, they sat in a small café with steamy windows, sampling the most delicious coffee and croissants Allie had ever tasted.

"This is the café you were going to recommend, when you first tried to get rid of me by sending me to Paris," she said softly, when they were settled.

Sam looked distracted. Normally he would have taken her words as an invitation to tease her about *Look what had happened because you didn't listen to me.*

"Is something wrong?" she asked him.

Sam looked flustered.

If there was one thing she had come to know about him, it was that he was never flustered. He handled life with great confidence and courage and aplomb.

They had just had a wonderful day, but he did not seem to be filled with the kind of contentment or wonder such a day should bring.

Instead, Sam was patting his pockets and stammering.

"Have you lost your wallet?" she asked him.

"No, I—"

He found what he was looking for. He pulled back his chair and took a deep breath. He stood up.

And then he sank down on one knee if front of her. He held up a small box to her and snapped open the lid.

But it wasn't the light that shone from the ring that set her heart on fire. It was the light that shone from his eyes.

"Allie, I was wondering—"

He cleared his throat.

"Allie, I was thinking—"

She was crying so hard she couldn't help him out. The other patrons had stopped what they were doing. The waitstaff had stopped what they were doing.

The whole world stopped, even in this city that celebrated such things all the time, the whole world stopped in the absolute stillness of what was unfolding here.

The sacredness of it.

"Would you be my wife?" he whispered, hoarsely. "Would you walk through this world, and the days of my life with me?"

His voice was gaining strength now.

"Would you be the one who gives me courage when mine falters, and who shows me the way home when I have become lost?"

Though not everyone in the restaurant understood

English, everyone seemed to understand the universal language of the heart. There was not a sound: not a coffee cup rattled, not a teaspoon moved, not a throat was cleared.

"Would you allow me to be the one who helps you up when you stumble, and who shows you the way back to yourself when you forget who you are?

"Can I be the one who is there as you sing your songs to the world?"

Through the tears, she said yes. Through the tears she told him that every song was really for him.

That every song was really about love.

He came off his knee and stood above her. He held out his hand to her. She took it. And entered his embrace.

The café exploded into the sound of people cheering and clapping as Sam kissed Allie and Allie kissed Sam.

But neither of them could hear a single sound above the rapturous beating of their own hearts.

EPILOGUE

"LOOK," CODY CALLED. "All you have to do, Allie, is hold the kite. Throw it up in the air when I tell you. Unca, you run!"

Cody was six. His three-year-old sturdiness had given way to knobby knees and ribs that showed, no matter how much they fed him. Today, he was wearing a suit. It looked as if he had already lost the bow tie, and the shirt was rumpled where it was untucked from his pants. Sam felt just a little gleeful about a six-year-old's innate ability to thwart anyone's vision of perfection.

Sam did as he was told. He ran.

"Faster, Unca, faster."

Sam did not think he would ever stop marveling at Cody's voice: strong, sure, light-filled.

"Okay, Allie, throw it!"

Sam turned to see the kite lift, then nosedive toward the earth. When he turned to run again—hoping to make the kite catch the wind—he lost his footing and fell headlong in the sand. He twisted into a roll, hoping Allie would admire his graceful athleticism. He turned to look at her, and felt the breath whoosh out of him more than it had when he fell.

Honestly? The baby was due any day. She should have looked like a leprechaun explosion in that tent of a jade green dress she was wearing. Instead, she looked gorgeous.

"I think you may have ruined the kite. You're definitely ruining your clothes!" she called to him, as if she hadn't noticed his brilliant recovery from his tumble at all.

Sam felt annoyed—again—at his mother-in-law. A beachfront wedding. So close to Allie's due date that she could have the baby out there on the beach. But there was no talking any sense to Professor Cook, Priscilla. She was bossy and controlling and easily the world's most annoying person. Sam was only sucking it up for Allie's sake.

He stopped his thoughts from going too far down that route, and gave himself over to the pureness of this moment, the joy shimmering in the air between the three of them, his family.

Three years.

Sam contemplated that, in the context of the brilliant light he felt he was standing in, despite the grayness of the day, despite Pricilla's aggravating wedding plans. He stood up and brushed off his pants, found the handle for the kite string as Cody and Allie fussed over the kite.

Time, he had heard over and over, *healed all wounds.*

This, he had found to be false. It was love, not time, that healed all wounds. Love, like the love he had experienced from his sister, Sue, and his friend and brother-in-law, Adam, making him ready when he had been blissfully unaware he would ever need readiness.

It was their love that had made him ready to say and do whatever love asked him to do.

The healing came from the love Allie gave him every day. And Cody.

Cody declared the kite flight worthy and ran toward him. "You have to run a little faster, Unca. Then it will go."

Sam looked back at the kite Allie was clutching, nearly said something and then didn't. Instead, with Cody trying breathlessly to keep up, he raced down the sand again.

Despite the fact they could have bought a dozen kites, or a hundred, or a thousand, Allie had insisted they make the kite themselves, following instructions they had found on the internet. Sam had carefully inspected their finished efforts last night. The kite was a thing of beauty, but the rainbow of colors on the hand-painted brown paper did not make it any more air-worthy. He had broken the truth to them as gently as he could. It would never fly.

And yet here he was running his heart out for it.

It was spring, the kind of blustery day that kept people off the beaches. It was a poor day for a beachfront wedding, and he could see, down the beach, the way he had come, the pagoda was already looking a bit bedraggled. He couldn't help but feel just a little happy about that.

For heaven's sake, it was a beach wedding. Why all the formality?

Beyond the pagoda was their Soul's Retreat. They had added the second floor to the cottage last year when they'd found out their news. It just wasn't going to be big enough for four of them as it was.

They'd renovated the first floor, too, taking down walls and adding windows, but somehow remaining faithful to the simplicity of the place, the soul of it.

Which was the love that lived there.

Still, the miracle of that love wasn't in the love he'd *received* in such generous abundance, both before and after the accident that had taken Sue and Adam—it was the love he had learned to *give.*

It was learning to be selfless in that giving—to put the needs of others ahead of his own, not resentfully and not reluctantly, but fully and generously—that had restored his heart.

He would do anything to have his sister back. And Adam.

And yet, sometimes, just for a second, when Cody tilted his head a certain way, there was Sue. And when he laughed, there was Adam. Going on.

So there was the basic truth: from Sam's darkest time had come his greatest lessons, from his darkest hours had come the reliance within himself that made him worthy of what Allie and Cody gave him every day.

And what Bill and Kathy, and Nicole and Bryan gave him. They would be here, soon, for the wedding, part of this crazy thing called family that Sam found himself totally immersed in.

What he and Allie's new baby would give him.

"How does it feel?" he had asked her the other night, his hand resting gently on the barrel-tightness of her tummy, the baby kicking furiously within.

"Like a miracle," she'd said.

"How does it feel that it's your own child?" he had asked softly.

She had stared at him, then blinked, as if the question was absurd. "They're all my children," she had said.

All her children.

The first Christmas they were together, she had made the kids of their family—Cody, Nicole and Bryan—a disc of all their favorite songs. And she had put in some of her own originals, including the never-before-heard "Pooperman's Cape."

When Bill had heard her music, he had sent it to his friend in Australia, the one who was a record producer.

Within a year, "Pooperman's Cape" was the number-one-selling children's song in Australia.

And then in Canada, and then and then and then…last year, she had made more money than him.

And yet she remained hilariously cheap. She *wanted* to make her own kites, and sew the new quilts for the beds.

Because she understood, perhaps better than most, it wasn't about the money.

Allie had found the part of herself that had been lost in that crazy world she had entered a long time ago. A world that had promised fame and fortune and acceptance, on the condition she sell her soul for it, on the condition she pretend to be someone and something that she was not.

They had all loved her—including her own mother—for someone she was not.

Some part of her had known the price was too high. Some part of her had retreated instead of moving forward.

But when she found herself, she was never letting go again of what she had found. That somehow the secret of life was not in having stuff—in fact, maybe all that stuff could overwhelm what was important—but in having moments. Experiences. Connections.

And she had connections. Now, they were *all* her children. The ones she visited in hospitals, the ones whose letters she always answered, the one out there flying the kite with her, the one she carried under her heart.

They were all her children.

And he had been given the amazing privilege of being there to watch her love unfold, of being the one who had helped her be brave enough. To see herself. To be herself.

Once, it seemed a long, long time ago, he had called her a liar when she had said she was strong. Independent. Self-reliant.

But then she had waded into the fire to get him. Was

there really any strength, compared to that one? The absolute bravery of saying yes to what love asked of you?

She constantly taught him new things about love. She had asked Ryan, whose star had plummeted as quickly as it had risen, to be on one of the albums with her.

Sam had disagreed—vehemently—with that decision.

But she had explained to him, so patiently, that she and Ryan had both been so young, so easily manipulated by the promises of *American Singing Star*.

"They found what we both wanted most, and played it," she said. "He wanted recognition."

"And you?"

"I wanted love."

And now, finally, she had found it. And love had made her this: full and forgiving, able to share the bounty of it with others, even those Sam would have found unworthy. Ryan, who had thrown her under the bus, and Priscilla, who was not exactly a candidate for Mother of the Year.

According to Allie, love made you more than you were before, not less.

Other truths had come to him over these years, truths he might not have seen if tragedy did not backlight them.

Time was a gift that could never be taken lightly.

Love was a gift that could never be taken lightly.

They had learned, together, he and Allie, to treat those things with the awed reverence they deserved.

And they had learned, together, the most important lesson of all.

When love beckoned you, followed it.

Soon, Priscilla would arrive. And Allie's father, Jim, a quiet, retired professor and lover of music, just like Allie. He and her mother had reunited on social media a few months ago.

And even Priscilla seemed to know, finally, after a

lifetime of the loneliness, of always being the one who was right, that when love beckoned, you followed it.

Priscilla and Jim were getting married on the beach today—rain or shine, Priscilla had proclaimed, and it looked like it would be rain—and settling here in California, so they could be near the grandkids.

Honestly, this messy thing called family gave Sam a headache sometimes. A headache, he realized, that he wouldn't trade for anything in the world.

"Now, Allie, throw it in the air now!"

Sam turned, breathless, just as Allie lifted that rainbow-colored kite high, and then tossed it in the air.

And that kite, the one Sam told them would never fly, defied all the odds. Just as his own life had defied all the odds, that kite suddenly found the wind, and lifted and lifted and lifted.

Until it danced with heaven.

Cody and Allie shrieked their delight, clapped their hands, lifted their faces to the sky. The wind blew her long hair around her face.

"Oh!" Allie cried. "Oh, what a perfect moment!"

It was, Sam thought, letting his gaze drift back to the kite, tugging, yanking, pulling, like a wild horse that wanted to be free, as close to a perfect moment as any person could ever expect on this earth.

* * * * *

Priscilla and Thomas were getting married on the beach today—one of the things Priscilla had proclaimed, and [illegible] would be [illegible] something here in Cale[illegible] so they could [illegible] grandchild.

Sam gripped the [illegible], just as Allie lifted the [illegible] the baby, and then tossed it in the air.

Cady and Allie watched their kite [illegible] clapped their hands [illegible] their faces to the sky. [illegible] laughter [illegible] her face.

* * * * *

FORTUNE'S FRESH START

MICHELLE MAJOR

To Jennie. Thanks for all the fun times
and morning chats. I treasure our friendship.

Chapter One

"You're going to be late to your own party."

Callum Fortune turned at the sound of his sister's teasing voice. "It's a ribbon-cutting ceremony, Squeak. Not a cocktail gala."

Stephanie Fortune, younger than Callum by three years but the oldest of David and Marci Fortune's four daughters, approached Callum's shiny silver truck. Her pale red hair was pulled back in a braid and she wore dark jeans and a gray sweater that could have benefited from a lint roller. As a vet tech and all-around animal lover, Stephanie was often covered in dog and cat fur. Or whatever breed of animal she was caring for that day. Her heart was as big as her personality and one of the things Callum loved most about her.

"It's past time you stop calling me that," she told him with an exaggerated eye roll. "What if someone in Rambling Rose hears you and the nickname catches on? I'd be mortified."

"It's our secret," he promised with a wink. "But you'll always be my Pipsqueak no matter where life takes either of us."

"I'm home," Stephanie said, her tone definitive. "There's no other place I'd rather be."

"Then I'm glad you came along on this adventure."

Callum agreed there was something special about Rambling Rose, Texas. The small town sat equidistant between the larger metropolitan areas of Houston and Austin. Callum had first learned about it through a documentary, *The Faded Rose*, he'd watched late one night when he'd had trouble sleeping. Shortly after, he'd traveled to Paseo, Texas, with his father for the wedding of David's brother, Gerald Robinson—or Jerome Fortune as he was once known. On a whim, Callum had driven to Rambling Rose and within a week he'd made offers on a ranch in a gated community outside town as well as a half-dozen commercial properties.

Real estate development was Callum's passion, and he'd made a name for himself in his home state of Florida and a good portion of the Southeast as someone who could revitalize small-town communities by working together with residents, local businesses and government agencies. He loved the challenge of breathing new life into spaces that had seen better days.

From that perspective, Rambling Rose was a perfect next step in Callum's career. The town had a long history in Texas but was sorely in need of a face-lift and someone to invest in the local economy. Callum's father, David, had his doubts. The entire Fortune family, both new and established members, had been shaken by the kidnapping that had almost ruined Gerald's wedding to his first love, Deborah, six months ago. David was a huge success in his own right thanks to his wildly profitable video game empire and had reservations about claiming his place in the extended Fortune brood even before that shocking turn of events. Even though the day had turned out happily in the end, David's protective instincts had kicked into high gear. He'd encouraged his eight children to stay far removed from any sort of involvement with the Texas Fortunes.

He and Marci, Callum's beloved stepmother, had been understandably concerned at Callum's rash decision to move to the small town, especially when his older stepbrother, Steven, younger brother, Dillon, and half sister, Stephanie, came with him. But Callum trusted his instincts when it came to real estate. He had no doubt Rambling Rose was the right decision, and his siblings' joining him was an added bonus.

He stood with Stephanie in the parking lot of the new Rambling Rose Pediatric Center, which was due to officially open its doors in two days. Callum was proud of everything his crew and the subcontractors he'd hired had accomplished in the past few months.

The building, which was situated about ten minutes north of Rambling Rose's quaint downtown area, had been almost completely gutted and rebuilt to house a state-of-the-art health facility where local children would receive primary medical, dental and behavioral health care at a facility designed just for them.

"We should go in," he said before Stephanie asked the inevitable question of whether he saw himself staying in Rambling Rose long-term. She wouldn't have wanted to hear his answer, but the thought of committing to the town longer than it would take to finish their projects made his skin itch.

Since he'd started his construction company, his modus operandi had always been to go with the work. He focused his efforts on small-town revitalizations but once he'd met his goals in a community, Callum moved on.

He wasn't a forever type of guy, at least not anymore.

"How are things at the vet clinic?" Stephanie asked as she fell into step next to him.

"On schedule to open next month," he answered, giving her a gentle nudge. "Don't worry, Squeak. We'll make sure you're still gainfully employed."

She gave him a playful nudge. "What do I have to do to get you to stop calling me that?"

"The dishes and my laundry for a week."

"Done."

He chuckled. "I should have held out for a month."

"Don't push your luck. I know how much you hate folding clothes."

"Been there, done that," he told her. He'd been three and his brother Dillon two when their father had married Marci. She'd had two boys of her own that she brought to the marriage: Steven, who was two years older than Callum, and Wiley, who was Callum's age. They'd had Stephanie right away and the triplets had followed five years after that. Marci was a great mother and treated all the kids with the same love and kindness. But the pregnancies had taken a toll on her health.

As a young boy, Callum had found himself responsible for the girls and running much of the household while his father focused on the explosive success of his first video game launch. The role had come naturally to Callum, but the added responsibility had robbed him of much of his childhood. He'd managed laundry for a household of ten from the time he was in elementary school until Marci's health had improved.

He didn't regret the time he'd dedicated to his siblings, but it definitely made him less inclined to take on more domestic tasks than were necessary to function as an adult.

"You still can't fold a fitted sheet the right way," Stephanie said in the flippant tone she'd perfected as an adorable but annoying little sister.

"No one can," he countered.

"Martha Stewart has a tutorial on it."

He shook his head as they approached the entrance of the pediatric center, where a small crowd had gathered. "I'm not watching Martha Stewart."

A flash of color caught his eye, and he noticed a woman pushing a double stroller toward the entrance. Two toddlers sat in the side-by-side seats, and one girl's blanket had slipped off her lap. The corner of the fabric was tangled in the wheel and the girls' frazzled-looking mother struggled to free it.

"There are Mom and Dad, with Steven and Dillon," Stephanie told him, taking a step toward their family, who stood near the swath of ceremonial ribbon that stretched in front of the center's entrance.

"Be there in a sec."

Without waiting for an answer, Callum jogged toward the woman and her two charges.

"Can I help?" he asked, offering a smile to the toddlers, who were mirror images of each other. Twins. No wonder their mom seemed stressed. He remembered what a handful his triplet sisters had been at that age.

The woman, who knelt on the pavement in a bright

blue dress, looked up at him. Callum promptly forgot his own name.

She was beyond beautiful…at least to him.

A lock of whiskey-hued hair fell across her cheek, and she tucked it behind her ear with a careless motion. Her features were conventional by most standards—a heart-shaped face, large brown eyes with thick lashes and creamy skin that turned an enchanting shade of pink as she met his gaze. Her mouth was full and her nose pert, but somehow everything came together to make her stunning. The sparkle in her gaze and the way her lips parted just a bit had him feeling like he'd been knocked in the head.

"It's caught in the wheel," she said, and it took him a moment to snap back to reality.

"Mama," one of the girls whined, tugging on the other end of the blanket.

"We'll get your blankie, Luna." The woman patted her daughter's leg. "This nice man is going to help."

Nice man. Callum wasn't sure he'd ever heard anyone describe him as "nice" but he'd take the compliment. He tried to remember the definition of the word while forcing himself to ignore the spark of attraction to a stranger who was probably some equally nice man's wife.

He crouched down next to the twins' mom and carefully extricated the fabric from the spokes of the wheel. It took only a minute and he heard an audible sigh of relief next to him once the blanket was free.

"Bankie," the girl shouted as she tugged the pink-and-yellow-checked blanket into her lap.

"Mama," her sister yelled like she wanted to be in on the action and then popped a pacifier into her mouth.

"Thank you," the woman said as they both straightened.

Callum was about to introduce himself when she stumbled a step. Without thinking, he reached out a hand to steady her.

"Are you okay?"

She flashed a sheepish smile. "Sorry. I stood up too fast. I didn't have time for breakfast today but managed two cups of coffee. Low blood sugar."

Callum had to bite back an invitation to go get breakfast with him even as he surreptitiously glanced at her left hand. No wedding ring, which didn't necessarily mean anything. Still, he could—

"Callum!"

He turned at the sound of his name. Steven waved at him from across the clusters of people gathered for the ceremony. Right. He was here for business, not to lose his head over a pretty woman.

His turn for an apologetic smile. "I have to go," he said.

She nodded. "Thanks again."

"You should eat something," he told her, then forced himself to wave at the girls and turn away after his brother called to him again.

Odd how difficult it was to walk away from a perfect stranger.

"The pediatric center would just be a dream for this community without the work of Callum, Steven and Dillon Fortune and everyone at Fortune Brothers Construction."

Becky Averill watched as Rambling Rose's effervescent mayor, Ellie Hernandez, motioned for the brothers to join her in front of the blue ribbon. How was it possible that Becky's stroller catastrophe hero was also the man she had to thank for her new job?

When the pediatric center officially opened a few days from now, she'd be the head nurse in the primary care department, reporting directly to Dr. Parker Green, who was heading up the entire center.

It was such a huge step up from her last position working part-time for an older family practice doctor who saw patients only a few days a week. In fact, it was Becky's dream job, one that would provide a livable wage, great health benefits for her and her girls as well as on-site day care. She couldn't believe how far she'd come from that horrible moment two years ago when a police officer had knocked on her door to relay the news that her husband had died in a car accident.

Becky had been only nine weeks pregnant when Rick died. They hadn't even learned she was expecting twins yet. Everything about her pregnancy had become a blur after that, as if she'd been living in some kind of hazy fog that never lifted.

Of course, things had become crystal clear the moment she heard her baby's first cry. Luna had been born two minutes before Sasha, but both babies filled Becky's heart with a new kind of hope for a future.

Her parents had wanted her to move back to the suburbs of Houston, but she refused. She and Rick had chosen Rambling Rose together, and despite being essentially alone in the small community, she never doubted that she belonged there.

Her girls were sixteen months old now, and life as a single mother hadn't exactly been a cakewalk. Rick's small life insurance policy had covered funeral expenses and allowed her to make her mortgage payments each month, but there hadn't been much left once she covered the essentials.

Not that she needed much for herself, but she wanted to give her daughters a good life. This job would go a long way toward her goal, but not if she messed it up by making a fool of herself before the center even opened.

Which was what she'd almost done with Callum Fortune. She hadn't been lying about missing breakfast, but her light-headedness had more to do with her reaction to the handsome stranger who'd come to her rescue.

Between work and caring for her girls, Becky hadn't even realized her heart could still flutter the way it did when Callum's dark gaze met hers. Butterflies had danced across her stomach and she'd had a difficult time pulling air into her lungs. Most women probably had the same inclination toward Callum. He would have been a standout in a big city like Dallas or Houston, but in the tiny town of Rambling Rose he was like a Greek god come to life.

Even now, her heart stuttered as she watched him smile at Ellie. Then his gaze tracked to hers, as if he could feel her eyes on him. His expression didn't change but there was something about the way he looked at her that made awareness prick along her skin. Dropping her gaze, she shoved a hand in the diaper bag that hung off the back of the stroller and pulled out a plastic container of dried cereal. The girls immediately perked up and she sprinkled a few oat bits into the stroller's tray before shoving a handful into her mouth. She really did need to remember breakfast.

Certainly an empty stomach was to blame for her dizziness, not the way Callum made her feel.

They cut the ribbon and the crowd, made up mostly of new employees of the center, cheered.

Luna clapped her hands at the noise while Sasha's chin trembled.

"It's okay, sweetie." Becky bent down and dropped a soothing kiss on her shy girl's cheek. "It's happy noise."

Sasha's big eyes widened farther as she looked around but after a moment she let out a sigh and settled back against the seat.

Meltdown averted. At least for now.

With twins, Becky rarely went for any long period without some sort of minor toddler crisis, but she wouldn't change a thing about either of her girls.

Callum and the rest of the pediatric center's VIPs had disappeared into the main lobby by the time Becky straightened.

"I hear they have cupcakes inside," a woman said as she passed Becky. "Your girls might like one."

"They're a little young for cupcakes," Becky answered with a laugh. "But I could use a treat."

"Those Fortune men are a treat for the eyes," the older woman said, giving Becky a quick wink. "If I were twenty years younger and not married..."

Becky was plenty young but also far too exhausted to consider dating. At least the fact that she could appreciate Callum's movie-star good looks proved motherhood hadn't destroyed her girlie parts completely.

As they approached the entrance, the woman asked, "You're the one who lost her husband a couple of years ago, right?"

She nodded, considering the joys and pitfalls of living in a small town.

"It's good you stayed in Rambling Rose. We take

care of our own. I'm Sarah. My husband, Grant, is the building manager for the pediatric center." The automatic doors whooshed open, and they walked into the lobby together. "Our kids are grown and moved away, so I've got more time on my hands than I can fill right now. If you ever need help—"

"Thank you," Becky said, forcing a smile. "I appreciate the offer, but I've got things under control."

Sarah gave her a funny look but nodded. "I understand. If you change your mind, Grant can get you my number."

Becky kept the smile fixed on her face until the woman walked away, then pressed two fingers to her forehead and drew in a steadying breath. She'd received at least a dozen similar offers since the twins' birth and had rejected every one. She hadn't really lied to Sarah. At this exact moment, she did have things under control. The girls were both sitting contentedly in the stroller watching the crowd.

Of course, things could go south at any moment. She'd handle that, too, on her own. She took the girls to a day care center when she worked, but otherwise didn't like to accept help. It had been her choice to stay in this town where she had no family. She didn't want people to think she was some kind of over-her-head charity case, even though most days she felt like she was treading water in the middle of the ocean.

But she didn't focus on that. She just kept her legs and arms moving so that she wouldn't go under. Her girls deserved the best she had to give, and she wouldn't settle for offering them anything less.

She was pushing the stroller toward the refreshment table when someone stepped in front of her path.

"Cupcake?" Callum Fortune asked.

Becky's mouth went suddenly dry, but she took the iced pastry from him. "Thanks," she whispered, then cleared her throat. "You did a great job with the building."

He shrugged but looked pleased by the compliment. "I love rehabbing old spaces, and this one is special."

"Ellie mentioned in her speech that the building used to house an orphanage." Becky took a small bite of cupcake and failed to smother a sigh of pleasure. It tasted so good.

Callum grinned. "Breakfast of champions," he told her with a wink. "And, yes. It was called Fortune's Foundling Hospital and dated back to the founding of Rambling Rose."

"Your family's ties to the town go back that far?"

"Apparently. I'll admit I'm still getting caught up on all the different branches of the Fortunes spread across Texas."

"You're royalty here," she told him, but he shook his head.

"Not me. I'm just a guy who loves construction."

"I think you're more than that." As soon as the words were out of her mouth, she regretted them. Somehow they sounded too familiar. People surrounded them, but for Becky the thread of connection pulsing between her and Callum gave the moment an air of intimacy that shocked and intrigued her.

His mouth quirked into a sexy half grin. "I appreciate—"

Suddenly, a woman burst into the lobby, clutching her very round belly. "Help me!" she cried. "I think I'm in labor."

"Get a gurney," Dr. Green shouted, elbowing his way through the crowd.

Becky took an instinctive step forward. Panic was clear on the woman's delicate features, and Becky understood that panic could accompany childbirth. But she couldn't leave her girls unattended.

Dr. Green straightened, his gaze searching the crowd until it alighted on her. "Becky, I need you," he called across the lobby.

She nodded and turned to Callum.

"I've got the girls," he told her without missing a beat. "Go."

She worked to calm her racing heart as adrenaline pumped through her. "Are you sure?"

She gave each of the girls a quick kiss and the assurance that Mommy would be back soon, then hurried toward the first patient in her new job.

"They're safe with me," he assured her, and although she'd just met Callum Fortune, she didn't doubt him for a moment.

Chapter Two

"Who knew Callum was such a spectacular nanny?" Steven asked an hour later, chuckling at his own joke.

Callum fought the urge to give his older stepbrother and business partner the one-fingered salute. Two adorable toddlers watched him from where they sat on a blanket he'd spread out in the pediatric center's lobby, so he wasn't about to model that kind of behavior.

The ribbon-cutting attendees had long since departed, the celebration cut short by the arrival of the pregnant stranger. Neither Parker Green nor the girls' mother had made an appearance again, and he wondered at the fate of the soon-to-be mom and her baby.

"We all know Callum is amazing with babies and children," Marci told Steven. "I'm not sure what I would have done without him when you all were little."

Steven was one of Marci's two sons from her first

marriage, but Callum's father had adopted both boys shortly after marrying his mother. The blended family had felt strange at first, but Stephanie's birth had solidified the bond they all shared. When Callum's construction business started to grow, Steven had joined him as a business partner, with Dillon coming on board soon after that. He'd changed the company name to more aptly describe their partnership, and Fortune Brothers Construction was still going strong.

"He'll be a great father one day," Callum's dad added with a knowing nod, prompting Steven and Callum to share an equally exasperated look. It was no secret their parents were intent on seeing both siblings happily married and starting families of their own.

Callum hadn't discussed future plans with his brother but got the impression Steven was as reluctant to settle down as Callum.

Stephanie walked through the doors that led to the center's small cafeteria. "I found plastic cups and spoons," she said. Callum had sent her in search of items to entertain the twins.

He took the makeshift toys and began stacking cups. The more confident of the girls, Luna, clapped her hands as if encouraging him to continue. He handed her a plastic spoon, which she waved in the air like a magic wand. One of the other nurses had told him the twins' names and that their mother was Becky Averill.

He'd asked about calling a husband and had been shocked to learn that Becky was a widow and single mom. It made him feel like even more of a heel for chastising her about breakfast. Becky was clearly an amazing woman, raising two children on her own while balancing a demanding career. No wonder she forgot to eat.

The shy twin, Sasha, scooted toward him. He held out a spoon to her, his chest tightening when her bottom lip trembled.

"Don't cry, darlin'," he told her softly and then scooped her into his arms. It had been an instinctual move. Callum had held plenty of babies when his sisters were younger. Sasha went rigid in his arms. Had he made a huge mistake? Then she relaxed against him with a quiet sigh, smelling like baby shampoo and oat cereal.

The front doors opened and two paramedics strode in. A moment later, Becky appeared from the medical clinic wing of the center. She and Dr. Green were wheeling out the pregnant stranger. The woman, a pretty brunette with big blue eyes, kept her worried gaze fixed on Becky, who appeared to be talking the patient through whatever was happening now.

There was no baby, and the woman seemed stable, so Callum could only assume things were good. Glancing over, Becky's expression softened as she caught sight of her twins. She said something to the pregnant patient, offered a quick hug and then walked toward Callum.

"How is she?" Stephanie asked immediately.

"We've given her something to slow her labor," Becky explained. "The baby's vitals are good, but Dr. Green thinks it will be better for her to give birth at a facility with a NICU. The paramedics are going to take her to San Antonio."

Callum's father nodded. "So she and the baby will be okay?"

"They should both come out of this healthy," Becky told them.

"Thank heavens," Marci added.

Callum stood, still holding Sasha in his arms. "It's a good thing you and Parker were here for the ribbon cutting."

"Dr. Green was essential," Becky clarified. "Anyone could have done what I did." She held out her hands, and Sasha reached for her, leaving Callum with an unfamiliar sense of emptiness.

"I doubt that's true," he answered. "You stepped in to help that woman without hesitation."

"I also foisted my kids off on you, and I appreciate you volunteering to watch them." She glanced down at Luna, who was still happily occupied with the spoon and cups, and then gave him a hesitant smile. "I'm Becky, by the way."

"One of the nurses told me," he said, that small smile doing funny things to his insides.

"You volunteered?" Marci stepped forward, patting Callum's shoulders. "I'm so proud."

"It wasn't a big deal," he mumbled.

"Your daughters are adorable," she said to Becky. "I'm Marci Fortune." She gestured to Callum's father and siblings. "My husband, David, and our daughter, Stephanie." Her smiled widened. "You know Callum, obviously. These are two of our other sons, Dillon and Steven."

Becky's caramel-colored eyes widened a fraction. "How many kids do you have?"

"Eight," Marci said proudly and without hesitation. Callum had always appreciated that his stepmother never differentiated between the children who were hers biologically and the two boys she'd taken on after marrying David.

"Wow," Becky murmured. "You must have been really busy."

"It's how we liked it," Marci assured her. She put a hand on Callum's arm. "Callum was such a help with his younger sisters. We also have triplets—Ashley, Megan and Nicole."

Dillon stepped forward. "Callum's nickname was Mary Poppins," he said in a not-so-quiet whisper.

Stephanie laughed while Becky tried to smother her smile.

"No one called me that," Callum told his brother with an eye roll. "Don't you all have somewhere to be?"

"You'd think with eight children," Marci said to Becky, ignoring Callum's question, "that we'd have a few grandchildren already."

"Gotta go," Dillon announced in response.

"Me, too," Steven added.

Stephanie grabbed her eldest brother's elbow. "I'll walk out with you."

Callum silently cursed his siblings as each of them gave Marci a peck on the cheek, told Becky it was nice to meet her and then quickly made their escape.

"You know how to clear a room, dear," David said, wrapping an arm around his wife's slim shoulders.

Marci only laughed. "I'd be an amazing grammy."

"Someday," her husband promised. "But we should go, too. We have a long drive to the airport."

Luna had lost interest in the makeshift toys and pulled herself up, then toddled over to Becky, who lifted her without missing a beat. "You aren't from Texas?" she asked Callum's parents.

David shook his head. "Fort Lauderdale, Florida. We flew in to see Callum's latest success. It's been quite an adjustment having four of our children move halfway across the country."

"The pediatric center is amazing," Becky said, glancing at Callum from beneath thick lashes. "It's lovely that you came all this way."

"Are you close to your parents?" Marci asked her.

Callum gave his father a look over the top of his stepmother's head. As much as he loved his big family, their friendly exuberance could be overwhelming. He didn't want to scare off Becky before he'd even had a chance for a proper conversation with her.

Before Becky could answer, David reiterated the need to get to the airport.

"I'll walk you out," Callum told them, then reached out and touched a hand to one of Luna's wispy curls. "Becky, I'll be right back."

She gave a quick nod, then seemed shocked when Marci leaned in and enveloped both her and the twins in a hug.

Marci turned to Callum at the entrance of the pediatric center. "She seems like a lovely girl," she said, her tone purposefully light.

"She's a single mother of twins," Callum felt obliged to point out. "And a widow."

"Tragic," Marci agreed as they walked into the cool January day. "I feel for those babies and for her. She deserves to find happiness again."

"It's not with me," Callum said. "I've committed to staying in Rambling Rose until the final project wraps up. Who knows what will happen beyond then?"

"I like this town more than I expected to," his father

interjected. "Of course, we'd love to see you back in Florida or somewhere closer, but if Texas makes you happy, that's most important."

"What about your mandate that we stay away from the Fortunes?"

David quirked a brow. "The only Fortunes in Rambling Rose are you and your siblings. I can live with that."

Callum walked them to the black sedan his father had rented. "Thank you both for coming to the opening." He hugged Marci first and then his father. "I'm proud of what we've accomplished here in such a short time."

"You should be," his father said.

"We're proud of you, as well," Marci added. "We always have been. But you work too much, Callum. Don't forget to take some time for yourself."

He didn't bother to argue. They wouldn't understand that his career fulfilled him in a way nothing else had. He knew people considered him a workaholic. Hell, that had been the main cause of his divorce. His ex-wife, Doralee, couldn't accept his hours or his dedication to the projects he managed.

But nothing made him happier than revitalizing older and historic commercial districts.

They said another round of goodbyes, and his parents climbed into their car and drove out of the parking lot.

As he walked back toward the entrance, Becky emerged, pushing the stroller.

"Thank you again," she said as he caught up to her. "I'd really like to repay you for your help today."

"No need." He held up his hands. "Thanks for stepping in with that woman. She seemed so terrified when she walked into the center."

A shadow seemed to darken Becky's delicate features. "She was scared and alone," she said, almost to herself. "And about to take on the greatest responsibility of her life."

"She didn't have a boyfriend or husband somewhere?" he couldn't help but ask. He fell in step next to Becky as she walked toward a nondescript minivan at the edge of the parking lot.

"Not that she'd tell us." She once again tucked her hair behind an ear and glanced over at him. "No family, either. I know how it feels to be alone, but there was something different about her. It was as if she was a speck of dandelion fluff floating in a breeze with no place to land." She let out a soft laugh. "I'm sure that sounds silly, but the woman—Laurel was her name—seemed like she really wanted to find a place to land."

"It sounds insightful," Callum murmured. In a single instant, his attraction to Becky Averill had gone from a physical spark to something more, something deeper.

"Sleep deprivation has robbed me of too many brain cells to be considered insightful." She pulled a key fob out of her bag and used it to open the minivan's side doors and cargo hold. "But I do feel for Laurel. I hope she and her baby flourish wherever she ends up."

Callum wanted to offer to do something to help with the twins and their stroller, but he felt like he needed to keep his distance. He'd been totally astounded by this woman today, but he had no place in her life and nothing to offer her. If his ex-wife had accused him of working too much, what would a single mother think of his crazy hours?

It didn't matter, he reminded himself as Becky turned to him with a tentative smile. "Are you sure there's no way I can thank you for today?" she asked. "I'm a pretty good cook and—"

"It's fine," he said, realizing how harsh he sounded only when her brows furrowed. "It was nice to meet you, Becky." He made his tone friendly but neutral. "You have cute kids." Without waiting for a response, he turned and walked away.

Becky finished with her final patient of the day, a three-year-old with double ear infections, and glanced at her watch as she walked toward the nursing station.

"Girl, you've been holding out on us." Sharla, one of the medical assistants in the primary care wing of the pediatric center, wagged a finger in Becky's direction. "We just heard Callum Fortune was your babysitter when that pregnant lady came in during the ribbon-cutting shindig."

Becky willed her face not to heat, but felt a blush rising to her cheeks anyway. This was her third shift at the center, and so far she'd loved every minute of it. Dr. Green, or Parker, as he insisted she call him when they weren't with patients, was an intelligent and caring physician. He had a rapport with both children and their parents, and Becky could see he took the utmost care with every patient.

Sharla and the other two nurses, Kristen and Samantha, were friendly and easy to talk to, and they all had good things to say about the doctors at the center. Becky had worked in enough different offices to appreciate the setup here.

"He offered to help," she said with what she hoped was a casual shrug. "It wasn't a big deal."

"Are you blind?" Kristen asked. "That man is ten kinds of a big deal."

"His brothers are just as hot," Samantha added.

"They aren't as handsome as Callum." Becky couldn't help the comment. Yes, the Fortune family had won the genetic lottery, but only Callum made her heart race. Every time she thought of the intensity of his dark gaze, her body seemed to heat from the inside out.

Sharla let out a peal of laughter. "I knew you had to notice."

"I'm a single mom," Becky muttered. "Not dead."

"So what are you going to do about it?" Kristen asked.

"There's nothing to be done." Becky placed the digital device she used for electronically entering patient data on the charging station. She wasn't going to admit to these three women that she'd offered to repay him for his kindness and he'd all but bolted from her.

Maybe it had been the minivan or her silly musings about the pregnant stranger or the reality of a woman with two toddlers in tow. Any one of those would have been a turnoff to a man. Add to that her reputation in town as the grieving widow and it was no wonder Callum had made a quick exit.

She'd obviously mistaken the intriguing thread of attraction between them or it had been all one-sided. No one would blame her for harboring a few harmless fantasies about a man like Callum, but that's all they were.

"My brother's insulation company is working on all of the Fortune Brothers Construction projects." Kristen tapped a finger to her chin, her green eyes sparkling. "I could get him to tell me when Callum is at one of the job sites and you could make an appearance there. He said all three Fortune brothers are really hands-on."

Sharla laughed again. "I'd like some Fortune hands on me."

Becky shook her head while the other two women joined in the joke. "I can't just show up at some construction site. What am I going to say? Remember me and will you hold one of my babies while I change the other one's dirty diaper?"

"Not the best pickup line I've heard," Samantha admitted.

Becky hadn't ever used a line on a man. Rick had been her first boyfriend. They'd met at freshmen orientation and dated through college, waiting to get married until after graduation because that's what her family wanted. He'd been an only child and not really close to his parents, who lived on the East Coast. Her mom and dad had expected her to hold off on marriage even longer, and their constant reminder that she and Rick had their whole lives to settle down had irritated Becky from the start. If she knew then what she did now, she would have married him right away so that they could have had more time together as a family.

No one could have predicted the car accident that had killed him, and Becky would always be grateful for the years he'd been a part of her life. But often she stayed busy, gave everything she had and more, because she was afraid if she ever stopped moving it might be too difficult to get up again.

"I'm not interested anyway," Becky lied. "I have too much going on to think about—"

"He's here," Sharla whispered.

All three of Becky's coworkers glanced at a place directly behind her, then quickly busied themselves.

As the fine hairs along the back of her neck stood on end, Becky turned around and came face-to-face with Callum Fortune.

"Hello," he said, running a hand through his thick mane of wavy dark hair. "I hope I'm not interrupting." He was dressed more casually today in a blue button-down shirt, dark jeans and cowboy boots. Callum looked perfect and she was painfully aware of her messy bun and the shapeless scrubs that were her work uniform. She glanced down to see some sort of crusty stain—probably baby spit-up—on her shoulder. Great. He looked like he owned the place, which he sort of did, and she was a scattered mess.

"Nope." Becky cleared her throat when the word came out a squeak. "I'm just finishing my shift and about to pick up the girls from day care."

She gave herself a mental head slap. Like he needed a reminder that she was a single mom with two young daughters.

"I'll walk with you," he offered.

"Oh." She stood there for a moment, trying to remember how to pull air in and out of her lungs.

"You remember where the day care's located, Becky?" Sharla asked from behind her. "Far end of the building and to the right."

She narrowed her eyes as she glanced at the other woman. "I remember. Thanks."

Callum offered a friendly smile as they started down the hall. "How's work going?"

"It's great," she said. "The facility is really great. The staff has been—"

"Great?" he asked with a wink.

"Sorry," she said automatically. "I'm always a little brain dead at the end of the day."

"Understandable. I can't imagine balancing everything you handle."

"It's not a big deal." She hated drawing attention to her situation. Becky found that the best way to stave off being overwhelmed was not to think about it. "I like to stay busy. What brings you to the center?"

She frowned as Callum seemed to stiffen next to her. Had she said the wrong thing again?

"Um… I needed to check on…some stuff."

"Sounds technical."

That drew a smile from him, and she felt inexorably proud that she'd amused him, even in a small way.

"I didn't mean to rush off the other day after the ribbon cutting," he told her as they approached the door that led to the child care center. "I think I interrupted a potential invitation for dinner, and I've been regretting it ever since."

Becky blinked. In truth, she would have never had the guts to invite Callum for dinner. She'd been planning to offer to cook or bake for him and drop it off to his office as a thank-you. The idea of having him to her small house did funny things to her insides.

"Oh," she said again.

"Maybe I misinterpreted," Callum said quickly, looking as flummoxed as she felt. "Or imagined the whole thing. You meant to thank me with a bottle of wine or some cookies or—"

"Dinner." She grinned at him. Somehow his discomposure gave her the confidence to say the word. He appeared so perfect and out of her league, but at the moment he simply seemed like a normal, nervous guy not sure what to say next.

She decided to make it easy for him. For both of them. "Would you come for dinner tomorrow night? The girls go to bed early so if you could be there around seven, we could have a more leisurely meal and a chance to talk."

His shoulders visibly relaxed. "I'd like that. Dinner with a friend. Can I bring anything?"

"Just yourself," she told him.

He pulled his cell phone from his pocket and handed it to her so she could enter her contact information. It took a few tries to get it right because her fingers trembled slightly.

He grinned at her as he took the phone again. "I'm looking forward to tomorrow, Becky."

"Me, too," she breathed, then gave a little wave as he said goodbye. She took a few steadying breaths before heading in to pick up the twins. *Don't turn it into something more than it is*, she cautioned herself.

It was a thank-you, not a date. Her babies would be asleep in the next room. Definitely not a date.

But her stammering heart didn't seem to get the message.

Chapter Three

Callum stood outside the soon-to-open veterinary clinic the following afternoon, frowning at the open back of the delivery truck.

"It's all pink," Stephanie reported.

"I see that," he answered, then turned to the driver. "We ordered modular cabinets in a pine finish."

"I just deliver what they give me," the man responded, scratching his belly. "Where do you want 'em?"

"Not here." Callum looked toward Steven, who was on his phone, pacing back and forth in front of the building's entrance.

His brother held up a finger and then returned to the phone call.

"This is a vet clinic." Stephanie gave a humorless laugh. "Not an ice cream parlor."

The cabinetry for the exam rooms and clinical areas had been ordered more than a month earlier. They needed it installed soon in order to keep the project on time and within budget. Callum and his brothers were sharing the responsibility of the vet clinic renovation, working with the staff of the local practice to design the space.

A moment later, Steven joined the group. "Take it back," he told the delivery driver before turning to Callum and Stephanie. "It was a clerical error. They typed in the wrong color code."

"Whatever you say, boss," the driver answered and pulled shut the overhead door of the delivery truck.

"It would have been my dream come true when I was eight," Stephanie said as the driver climbed into the vehicle and pulled away. "Working in a pink vet clinic."

"Where does that put us as far as the schedule?" Callum asked.

Steven's mouth tightened into a thin line. "I can get it done."

"I know that." Callum nodded, understanding that his older brother didn't appreciate being doubted. "I'm asking because if you need me to shift resources from other projects or change subcontractor timelines, we can make it work."

Steven's shoulders relaxed under his Western-style button-down shirt. "It's going to be tight. The supplier is putting a rush on the order so the cabinets should be here in two weeks. I can have the crew work on the flooring and finish the exterior. It's not ideal, but we'll make sure nothing falls behind."

"Let me know if we need to change our move-in date." Stephanie addressed them both. She not only worked at the current location of the vet center, but also acted as the liaison with the construction crew. "It's going to be all hands on deck at Paws and Claws to make it a smooth transition for our patients."

"Got it." Steven chuckled, then muttered, "Pink cabinets. We've had some strange setbacks, but that one might be the most colorful."

"If that's the worst unforeseen stumbling block in this whole process," Callum said, "I'll take it."

"The pediatric center opened without a hitch." Stephanie scrunched up her nose. "Other than a woman almost giving birth in the lobby."

Callum nodded. "I stopped by today, and the facility is already busy. Clearly there was a need for a children's health clinic in Rambling Rose."

"It feels like the town grows every day," Stephanie observed. "Have you noticed the new houses being built down the road from the ranch?"

Steven rubbed his thumb and fingers together. "Lots of money coming into the community. Hopefully that will mean plenty of business for each of our new ventures."

"Who needs a margarita?" Stephanie asked. "The pink cabinet fiasco made my head hurt, but it's nothing a salted rim along with a big plate of enchiladas won't cure."

"I'm in," Steven said.

Callum pulled out his phone and checked the time on the home screen. "I'll have to take a rain check. I have dinner plans tonight." He responded to a text from his foreman, then glanced up to find his brother and sister staring at him with equally curious expressions.

"Spill it," Stephanie said.

Callum feigned confusion. “What are you talking about?”

“He’s evading answering.” Steven elbowed their sister. “My money’s on the cute nurse from the other day.”

“He bombed out with her before he even got a chance,” Stephanie said. “Tell me it’s not that barista at the coffee shop in town who always flirts with you. She has crazy eyes.”

“Enough with the inquisition.” This was the issue with coming from such a close-knit family. Since they’d moved to Rambling Rose, he and his siblings had mostly hung out together. Sure, each of them had made a few casual friends. But they stuck together. The ranch they’d purchased just outside town had a sprawling main house as well as several guesthouses on the multiacre property.

He figured if his brothers and sister ever wanted more privacy in Rambling Rose, he’d buy out their portion of the ranch. But none of them seemed inclined to move out on their own anytime soon. It worked for Callum. He’d needed space after going to school at a local college in Florida. That was part of the reason he’d started looking for projects to take on in other areas of the Southeast. Coming from such a big family and growing up with so much responsibility for Stephanie and the triplets on his shoulders, he’d needed a break.

But after the wreck of his short marriage and subsequent divorce, life had become too quiet. Now he liked being close to his siblings. It had made the move to Texas not so daunting and gave him a sense of confidence, which was probably why he’d taken on a slate of so many ambitious projects.

“Then tell us,” Stephanie prodded. “Don’t think I

won't follow you. Remember when I was in eighth grade and crashed your date with Ava Martin after you snuck out to meet her?"

"How could I forget?" he replied, trying and failing to hide his smile. "I got grounded for a month."

"You were already grounded, which is why you got in even more trouble."

"No one is going to ground me now," he told her.

"Come on, Callum. Just spill it."

"I'm having dinner with Becky from the pediatric center."

"Called it." Steven did an enthusiastic fist pump. "You were so obvious the other day."

"I wasn't obvious," Callum said through clenched teeth. "I was helpful, and she's thanking me with dinner."

"How romantic," Stephanie said in a singsong voice.

"Her twins will be sleeping in their bedroom. It's hardly romantic."

"Mom and Dad had four boys under the age of five when they were first married," Steven reminded them. "They still managed to find some time for romance."

"This isn't anywhere near the same thing, and you both know it. You're just trying to get under my skin."

Stephanie wiggled her eyebrows. "It's working, too. I can tell." She leaned closer. "I can also tell you like her. You were pretty obvious at the ribbon cutting."

"Go back to Florida," he told her, deadpan.

"I'm like a rash," she countered. "You can't get rid of me."

Steven laughed. "You do realize you just compared yourself to a bad skin condition."

"Fitting," Callum said.

Stephanie only rolled her eyes at their gentle ribbing. "What are you bringing?"

Callum shrugged. "Nothing. She said she'd handle it all."

She groaned. "Don't be an idiot right out of the gate. What about flowers or wine or chocolate?"

"You sound like Marci," Callum told her. "Enough with the matchmaking."

"Li'l sis is right," Steven said. "Step up, Callum. Your pretty nurse has been through a lot. Even if it's just a thank-you, make her feel special."

"She's not 'my' anything," he protested, although his heart seemed to pinch at the thought of a woman like Becky belonging to him. He should listen to that subtle sharpening and not get any more involved with her when it could only end badly. "But she is special."

"Then show her," Steven urged, laughing when Stephanie gave him a playful slap. "Hey, what was that for? It's good advice."

"I'm just shocked it came from you."

"Remember, I'm the oldest." Steven pointed a finger at each of them. "That also means I'm the wisest."

"Hardly," Callum said on a half laugh, half cough. But his brother had a point. He didn't know much about Becky Averill, but it was obvious she worked hard, both at her job and taking care of her girls. She deserved to have someone treat her special. Despite knowing he could never be that man, he couldn't help wanting to ignore the truth—even for one night.

The doorbell rang at exactly seven o'clock that night.

Becky stifled a groan as she finished fastening the snaps on Luna's pajamas. "Of all the nights for things to go off the rails," she said to her girls as she lifted them into her arms and hurried toward the front of the small house.

She opened the door to Callum, who stood on the other side holding the most beautiful bouquet of colorful flowers she'd ever seen. "Am I early?" he asked, his dark gaze taking in the twins as well as Becky's bedraggled appearance.

"Bedtime is running late," she answered.

Luna babbled at him and swiped a chubby hand at the flowers while Sasha snuggled more deeply against Becky's shoulder.

"What can I do?"

Her heart did that melty thing she couldn't seem to stop around this man. "Give me five minutes," she told him as she backed into the house. "This night is to thank you for helping the first time, not to force you into another round of child care duties."

"I don't mind," he assured her, grinning at the girls.

"The flowers are beautiful," she said.

"They're for you." He looked down at the bouquet, then up at her again. "You probably guessed that."

Despite her nerves and the craziness of the evening, Becky grinned. "I have a bottle of wine on the counter. Would you open it while I put them down?"

"Sure."

It felt a bit strange to leave him alone in her house when he'd just arrived, but she didn't have a choice.

She began to sing softly to the girls as she made her way back to their bedroom. As if on cue, both Luna and Sasha yawned when Becky turned off the overhead light in the room, leaving the space bathed in only the soft glow from the butterfly night-light plugged in next to the rocking chair in the corner.

She placed them in their cribs, smiling as they babbled to each other in that secret language they seemed to share. She finished the song, gave each one a last kiss and said good-night. After checking the monitor that sat on the dresser, she quietly closed the door to their room.

Once in the hallway, she glanced down at herself and cringed. The twins were normally asleep by six thirty so Becky had thought she'd have a few minutes to freshen up before Callum arrived. She'd changed from her scrubs into a faded T-shirt and black leggings, both of which were wet thanks to the dual tantrums she'd dealt with during bath time.

Hurrying to her bedroom, she changed into a chunky sweater and dark jeans, cursing the fact that she hadn't been shopping for new clothes since before the girls were born. She hadn't done anything for herself in far too long, which was why this night felt so special.

She dabbed a bit of gloss on her lips, fluffed her hair and headed for the kitchen and Callum. Her heartbeat fluttered in her chest once again.

Her reaction to his presence felt silly. He'd helped with her daughters and agreed to come for dinner. Nothing more. He probably regretted it already and was counting the minutes until he could make his escape.

But the warmth in his gaze when he looked up from his phone as she walked into the kitchen told a different story. One that made sparks tingle along her spine.

"You arranged the flowers," she murmured, taking in the bouquet that had been placed in a vase on the table.

"I found a vase in the cabinet." He offered a sheepish smile. "I hope you don't mind. It was one less thing you'd have to deal with tonight."

"They're perfect," she told him, then breathed out a soft laugh. "You can manage multiple construction projects and excel at the art of floral arranging. Quite the Renaissance man, Callum."

Her silly comment seemed to relax them both. She could hardly believe he had nerves in the same way she did, but the thought made her feel more confident.

"Something smells really great," he told her.

"I almost forgot about dinner," she admitted, pulling a face. "It's not fancy, but I hope you like chicken potpie."

"I like everything."

And didn't those words just whisper across her skin like a promise? Becky gave herself a little head shake. He was talking about food and she stood there staring at him like he was the main course.

"My grandma used to make it when we went to her house for Sunday dinner. I make some modifications so the recipe doesn't take so long, but the crust is homemade."

"I'm impressed." He handed her a glass of wine. "To new friends and new beginnings."

She clinked her glass against his and took a drink of the bright pinot grigio. It was only a sip but she would have sworn the tangy liquid went right to her veins, making her feel almost drunk with pleasure.

More likely the man standing in her kitchen caused that. The first man who'd been there with her since her husband's death.

"New beginnings," she repeated softly, then busied herself with dinner preparations.

She'd done most of the work when she got home earlier. The pie was warm in the oven, and the scent of chicken and savory dough filled the air when she took it out and set it on the trivet she'd placed on the kitchen table.

She took a salad from the refrigerator, then frowned at the simple supper. Surely a man like Callum was used to fancier fare.

"I haven't cooked for ages," she admitted as she joined him at the table. "I'm out of practice at entertaining."

As if understanding there was an apology implicit in her words, Callum shook his head. "This looks amazing, and I appreciate you going to the trouble for me."

"It was no trouble." She dished out a huge helping of the classic comfort food onto his plate. "I hope you're hungry."

As he took a first bite, he closed his eyes and groaned in pleasure. "I could eat this every night."

"I used to make things that were more gourmet, but with the girls' bedtime routine I figured I'd have better luck with a recipe I know by heart."

"I'm not much for gourmet."

"That surprises me." She forked up a small piece of crust, pleased that it tasted as good as she remembered. "I figured anyone with the last name of Fortune would be accustomed to the finer things in life."

"Nothing finer than a home-cooked meal," he said, helping himself to another portion.

She chuckled. "Do you always eat so fast?"

"Only when it's this good." He shrugged. "My branch of the family is relatively new to the notoriety of the Texas Fortunes."

"Really? Is that why you moved here? To get your moment in the spotlight?" She mentally kicked herself when he grimaced. He'd helped her and now her nerves had her babbling so much she was going to offend him. "I'm sorry. That came out sounding rude."

"Rambling Rose appealed to me because I'm here in Texas, which gives me a sense of connection with the Fortune legacy, but it also feels like I'm blazing my own path."

"That's important to you?" She stabbed a few pieces of lettuce with her fork.

"Very important. You met my dad and stepmom and three of my siblings. Imagine four more added to the mix. There wasn't much time for individuality growing up. I could hardly do my own thing when I constantly had a brother or younger sister trailing me."

"Are you the oldest?"

He studied his plate for a long second, as if unsure how to answer. "No. Dillon, who was at the ribbon cutting ceremony, is a year younger than me. Our parents divorced when I was a toddler, and Dad met Marci shortly after. They married almost immediately. She also had two boys from her first marriage. Steven is two years older and Wiley is my age, although he has a couple of months on me. It felt like I went from being the oldest to the little brother overnight."

"That's a lot of blending," Becky murmured, not quite able to imagine how that would have felt for a young boy.

He nodded. "We were a handful, especially at the beginning. I think each of us had something to prove. Unfortunately that meant we pushed every one of Marci's buttons any chance we got."

"How did she handle it?"

"Like a champ," Callum confirmed. "I didn't see my real mom much after the divorce, but Marci always made Dillon and me feel like we were her sons as much as Steven and Wiley. If we were testing her, she passed with flying colors."

"And things got easier?"

"Stephanie was a turning point for the family. She was the most precious thing I'd ever seen. Suddenly, these four rowdy boys had something in common—our sister. She brought us together."

"It's obvious you're close with her."

"Yeah." The softening of his features gave her that fizzy feeling again. "Mom…" He cleared his throat. "Marci became mom to me pretty quickly. She loved having a big family, but had a couple of pregnancies that ended in miscarriage after that. It took a toll on her."

"I can imagine."

Fine lines bracketed his mouth, as if the thought of the woman who'd become a mother to him hurting caused him physical pain, as well.

"Then the triplets were born. They were miracle babies, really."

"Multiples are special," Becky couldn't help but add, thinking of her sweet girls.

"It took Marci some time to recover. There were complications and she wasn't herself for a while after."

"From how she made it sound, you were a huge help."

His big shoulders shifted and an adorable flush of color stained his cheeks. "I kind of had a way with the ladies, even back then."

Laughter burst from Becky's mouth, and the excitement bubbling up in her felt like she'd gulped down a flute of champagne. Was there anything more attractive to a mother than a man who was good with children?

"You certainly worked your charms on Luna and Sasha," she told him. "They aren't accustomed to having men in their lives."

"Someone told me your husband died while you were pregnant," Callum said quietly. "I'm sorry."

The pleasure rippling through her popped in an instant. Grief had been a sort of companion to her after Rick's death, and she knew the facets of it like the back of her hand.

"It was a car accident," she said. "I'd just taken a home pregnancy test but we didn't know I was carrying twins." She bit down on the inside of her cheek. "I wish I could have shared that with him. I wish I could have shared a lot of things."

She held up a hand when he would have said more because she knew another apology was coming. Not that he had any responsibility, obviously, but people didn't know how to talk to her about the loss she'd suffered. Some things were too unfathomable for words.

"We're okay," she said, which was her pat line even when it wasn't true. Sometimes she struggled, but she was dealing with it and making the best of things for her daughters. She blinked away the tears that stung the backs of her eyes.

"In some ways Rick is still with us," she told Callum. "There's a park outside of town where he and I used to go on walks after work. Now I take Luna and Sasha there when I want to feel close to him. I sit on the bench near the pond and talk to him, and I feel him with us. I know how much he would have loved his girls and he's their guardian angel. Some people don't get that or they think I'm just trying to see the silver lining in a tragedy that has none. But it's what I know."

His cleared his throat as if unsure how to respond. Becky mentally kicked herself. No guy wanted to spend an evening talking about a woman's dead husband, even for a homecooked meal. This was the reason she could never hope to date, especially not someone like Callum Fortune. She had enough emotional baggage to fill a freight train.

"Can I ask why you stayed in Rambling Rose?" Callum asked after several awkward moments.

She opened her mouth to give him a pat answer, but was somehow unable to tell this man anything but the complete truth. "This was the home Rick and I chose together." She glanced around the small kitchen. "And we picked this town because we wanted to be a part of a close-knit community. Neither of us was tight with our families growing up."

"Do you have brothers and sisters?"

She shook her head. "Only child. Rick was, too." She lifted the wineglass to her lips, watching Callum from beneath her lashes. Maybe it was inappropriate to talk about her late husband with a man she felt attracted to, but Callum's steady presence made her feel like she could share anything with him.

She appreciated that more than she could say. Yes, she'd loved her husband deeply and would give anything to change the tragedy that had stolen their future.

That loss was woven into the fiber of her being. It had formed her into the woman she was today, resilient and fiercely protective of her daughters. She understood the only way to celebrate Rick's life was by honoring what had brought her to this point.

Callum helped her clean up the dishes after they finished dinner, another point in his favor. They said goodbye, and Becky watched him drive away as she tried to tamp down the disappointment at the night ending so soon. Seriously, she needed to get out more. One simple thank-you dinner and she felt like a silly girl with a crush on the most popular boy at school.

Callum had called her a friend and that was how she should think of him, as well. Too bad her body wouldn't cooperate.

Chapter Four

"What's your next move?" Stephanie asked as she joined Callum in the main house's expansive kitchen later that week.

The morning had just begun to dawn, with the sky outside the window turning the Fame and Fortune Ranch a dozen shades of pink and orange.

"I don't have one," he said, keeping his gaze trained on his laptop. He took another drink of coffee as he perused the article on trends in the food and hospitality industry. "What would you think about an upscale restaurant in Rambling Rose?"

"I think it won't compete with the local Mexican food," she said, dropping into a chair across from him at the table.

"The idea isn't to compete," he explained. "I want to expand the options for folks around here. What if you wanted to go on a special date?"

"At this point," Stephanie said with a slightly sad smile that tugged at his heart, "my favorite men have four legs and fur."

Callum hated that his sister seemed to have given up on her chance at love. Unlike him, Stephanie had so much to give. "Hypothetically," he clarified.

"Are *you* looking for a setting for a special date?" Stephanie kicked his shin under the table. "You still haven't said anything about your dinner with Becky the other night. I'm tired of waiting for details."

"She's a great cook," he said.

"I don't care what you ate." Stephanie pushed his laptop closed. "You like her, right?"

"She's nice." Callum reached for his coffee, ignoring his sister's raised brow. Of course, *nice* was a wholly inadequate way to describe Becky. He'd never met anyone like her. She'd suffered a devastating tragedy yet still seemed to be filled with a bright light that wouldn't be dimmed.

He didn't understand the connection he felt with her and knew it could go nowhere even if he wanted it to. Which he didn't because he'd learned his lesson about commitment and getting hurt the hard way. Things were better all around when Callum focused on the parts of his life he could control. Matters of the heart definitely didn't fall into that category.

"What did you talk about?"

"Stuff."

"You know how persistent I can be," she said. "I'll follow you around all day until you spill it." Stephanie grinned when he narrowed his eyes. "Might as well just tell me now."

"We talked about a lot of things." He shrugged. "My family, her family. Her late husband."

She made a soft sound of distress. "Was that awkward?"

"No," he answered simply. Maybe it should have been. Although the way she'd described Rick made the man sound just about perfect. Callum knew he was bound to pale in comparison. There was no use pretending that he'd gone to dinner at Becky's just to be kind. He couldn't stop thinking about her.

He wasn't just attracted to her physically. He wanted to know as much as he could about her, which included her past. Losing a husband so young had obviously played a large part in shaping the person she was today.

"I haven't seen you like this since Doralee." Stephanie tapped a finger on the tabletop, and Callum focused his attention on that instead of meeting her insightful gaze.

"It isn't the same," he muttered.

"I can tell." She leaned forward until he lifted his gaze to hers. "Your divorce doesn't define you, Callum. At least it shouldn't."

"I know," he agreed, although the wreck of his marriage had changed him. All the things he'd thought he wanted from life shifted in the wake of his pain and the blame his ex-wife placed squarely on his shoulders.

He deserved every bit of it. Growing up in a large family had led him to assume the path of marriage and kids was the one that made the most sense for him. But he'd been dedicated to his business and not able to give Doralee the attention she'd wanted. They'd had a whirlwind courtship of only six weeks before getting married, both of them enamored by the heady feeling of new love.

Once the novelty wore off, it had become clear they weren't compatible in most of the ways that counted. She had unrealistic expectations and he seemed doomed to fail at meeting them. It was a blessing for both of them that she'd had the guts to end things. He hadn't wanted to hurt her but couldn't seem to do anything right. He'd believed he was building a future for the two of them, laying the groundwork for their life together. Turned out to be a foundation built on sand, shifting and crumbling under the pressures of life.

Of course his failings had shaped him, but in a different way from how Becky's had her. She'd had tragedy befall her and risen above it, while he'd been the cause of his own pain. He might be infatuated with her, but he wasn't about to open himself up to that kind of hurt again. Becky's life was complicated and he remained determined to keep his as simple as he could manage.

"You can find love again," Stephanie continued.

"I'm not looking for love." He pushed back from the table and walked toward the counter to refill his coffee. "It was one dinner. You're making too much of it."

"I know you, Callum. All I'm saying is don't shut the door on a possibility before you've given it a chance."

He paused with his hand on the coffeepot's handle. His sister was right, of course. He'd decided after his divorce that he valued his independence too much to make a committed relationship work. The decision hadn't been a problem because no one he'd met had made him question it.

Until Becky.

"When did you get too smart for your own good?" he asked.

Stephanie grinned. "I've always been brilliant. You're just realizing it."

"I'll keep that in mind," he said with a laugh. They talked some more about possibilities for an upscale restaurant in Rambling Rose, and then Callum headed out to start his morning.

He appreciated the pace of life in Texas. He could move quickly, but things also seemed to adjust to fit the wide-open spaces and the sense of community pride that felt uniquely Texan. This was a setting that made a man earn his place. The residents of Rambling Rose might be curious about his ties to the famous Fortune family, but people seemed more concerned with his dedication to the town.

Callum felt at home here in a way he hadn't during any of the other projects he'd taken on over the years. It made his desire to succeed burn even brighter and caused the future to beckon in ways he hadn't anticipated.

Later that week, Becky looked up from the lunch she'd packed to see Callum walking toward her across the pediatric center's sunny courtyard. A slow smile spread across her lips as awareness tingled along her spine. This was the third day Callum had appeared during her lunch break.

Maybe she shouldn't read too much into it. He'd explained he had business at the pediatric center. She had no reason not to believe him.

"What's on the menu today?" he asked as he slid into the seat across from her. Becky always took her lunch early since most mornings she didn't have time for breakfast.

"Turkey and cheese," she said, then pulled out the extra sandwich she'd made. "I have one for you if you're hungry."

He stared at the plastic baggie for so long she wasn't sure if he was going to take it or get up from the table and run the other direction. When he finally reached for the sandwich, it embarrassed her that she'd even made the effort to bring something extra for him. "Thank you," he said. "That's thoughtful."

Electricity zipped along her skin as his fingers brushed hers. Her reaction to Callum continued to surprise her. She couldn't remember a time when anticipation had played such a huge part in her life. Despite her busy work schedule and how much effort she put into mothering her girls, Becky felt like she had energy for days. Just the idea of seeing Callum at some point during the day had excitement zinging through her veins like a jolt of caffeine.

"Are you here checking on the mechanical systems again?" she asked.

"Um…yes."

"Will they have it fixed soon?" She pulled a container of apple slices from her lunch sack.

"Probably." He took a bite of sandwich. "Although I may need to stop by for a while longer to make sure it's all going well."

"That has to be frustrating. I'm sure you're ready to move on to your other projects."

"I like seeing how well things are going here," he told her, then leaned in close. "Talking with you is an added bonus."

"Oh." Heat bloomed in her cheeks. "That's nice."

She gave herself a mental head slap. A man said something sweet and her reply was completely boring. She imagined men like Callum came out of the womb knowing how to flirt, and Becky reminded herself that it didn't mean anything. That she didn't *want* it to mean anything.

"How are the girls?" he asked, grinning at her like she wasn't making an absolute hash of flirting with him.

"They're enjoying the new day care." She tugged her lower lip between her teeth. "I'd like to visit them during the day but the director told me it's too disruptive for their schedule."

"You're a dedicated mom," he murmured.

"Sasha and Luna are my whole world," she told him. That was probably the wrong thing to say, as well. What single man wanted to hear a woman gush over her children? But she couldn't deny it.

"Maybe I could take the three of you to dinner?" His smile turned almost bashful. "If you have a free night sometime?"

She clasped a hand over her mouth when a hysterical laugh bubbled up in her throat.

"What's so funny?"

"All of my nights with the girls are free. Unless you include dinner, bath time and reading board books as a busy schedule."

"So dinner would work?"

"Sure." She felt a frown crease her forehead. "Why would you want to subject yourself to a meal with two toddlers?"

He inclined his head as if pondering a response. "Um…we all need to eat and as great as my brothers and sister are, I sometimes need a little break from the family togetherness."

"I'm not sure dinner with the twins constitutes a break, but I won't say no to an evening out."

"How about tomorrow night?"

"Yes," she breathed, then cleared her throat. "Tomorrow would be great. I get off work at five, which I understand is early for dinner. But with the girls' bedtime..."

"Do you like the Mexican restaurant in town?"

"I haven't been there in ages," she told him with a smile, then gave a nervous laugh. "Not because I don't like it. I do. It's great. I haven't been anywhere, really." She covered her face with her hands, then spread her fingers to look at him. "I'm babbling."

"It's cute," he said, his tone soft like velvet. "You're cute, Becky."

"You're cute, too."

He chuckled. "No one has ever called me that."

She lowered her hands and arched a brow. "I bet you were an adorable baby. A handful, but adorable."

"Definitely a little terror," he agreed.

She sighed. "You have a way of making me jittery, then calming my nerves in the next instant."

"I'm glad."

"I'm glad you asked me to dinner," she said honestly.

"Me, too."

They sat in a charged silence for a long moment. His full lips quirked into a smile, and she wondered what it would be like to feel that mouth against hers. The desire zipping through her was a thrill. She longed to see where it might take her.

Nowhere fast, a voice inside her head warned. Not

with this man. She hushed that voice and offered Callum a wide smile. "I need to get back to work. I'll see you at the restaurant tomorrow?"

He stood as she did, leaning close to whisper in her ear. "I can't wait."

Her nerve endings buzzed with the pleasure of his breath tickling the fine hairs along her neck.

Not trusting herself to speak, she simply nodded, then grabbed her lunch sack and hurried toward the primary care wing.

She had a date with Callum Fortune.

Tomorrow couldn't come soon enough.

Later that evening, Callum stared at the familiar name on his cell phone's screen for a few seconds before accepting the call.

"Hey, Doralee," he said as he put the phone to his ear. "This is a surprise."

"Hello, Callum," his ex-wife said, her voice the same rasp he remembered. It seemed like a lifetime ago that they'd flown to Vegas and gotten married on a whim. He'd been young and in love, not exactly sure he was doing the right thing but willing to take a chance because he knew it would make her happy.

In the end, their rash decision had achieved the opposite effect. He'd always regret hurting her, even though it had never been his intention.

"It's good to hear from you," he lied, not sure how this conversation was supposed to go.

She laughed. "I don't believe you for a minute, but I still appreciate hearing it. How's Texas?"

"Big."

"Are the projects going well?"

"So far they are. There have been a few hiccups, but we're on schedule."

"No doubt thanks to your time and dedication."

He gripped the phone more tightly. "I can't tell if that's a compliment or a veiled criticism."

"You're the best at what you do," she answered without hesitation. "The rest of your life might take a hit because of it, but I'm sure you'll have as much success in that tiny town as you did back here."

"Thanks," he murmured. He didn't exactly appreciate her willingness to point out what he'd sacrificed for the sake of his career but he also couldn't deny it. "How are things?"

"Great." He heard her blow out a slow breath. "That's actually why I'm calling, Callum. I have some news that I wanted you to hear from me first."

His stomach pitched like he'd just raced down the first big drop on a roller coaster. "What news?" he asked, although he had a feeling he knew what she was going to say.

"I'm engaged."

"Congratulations," he said, forcing his tone to stay neutral. "I'm happy for you." That part wasn't a lie. He wanted the best for his ex-wife. Just because things hadn't worked out for the two of them didn't mean he'd stopped caring about her.

"I appreciate that," she said. "John is a great guy. He wants to start a family right away, and you know I wanted children."

"Yes," he managed before his throat constricted. Her desire to have children and his unwillingness to start a family had been one of their biggest ongoing arguments during their short marriage.

"It seems like we're both getting the lives we wanted," she continued. "You have a thriving business and I'm going to have a family."

When he didn't respond right away, she continued, "We're planning a spring wedding. Not that you care but like I said, I just wanted you to know."

He swallowed and tried to keep his regret over the past in check. "Please tell your fiancé I said congratulations."

"I will. Are you dating anyone?" she asked, but continued before he could answer. "Never mind. I already know the answer. Even if you're dating it isn't serious. The business is your first love and no one can compete with that."

He mumbled something about wishing her luck, and they ended the call. A thin sheen of sweat covered Callum's forehead.

Up until the moment of hearing Doralee's news, he would have also claimed his life was happy. But her comments about his devotion to his career, whether well-meaning observations or insidious slights, made his gut twist.

He didn't disagree with her assessment of his dedication to the company, but suddenly that seemed like a paltry excuse for the choices he'd made to avoid serious relationships since the divorce.

His ex-wife had moved on with someone who would probably make her far happier than Callum ever had. It was an unwanted but necessary reminder of what he was unwilling to give in a relationship, in large part due to the responsibilities he'd taken on as a child. He couldn't make that kind of commitment and the thought that he might be giving Becky the wrong signals made him doubt everything.

Should he cancel the date with Becky?

He couldn't play around with the emotions of a single mother, especially one who had survived the tragedy of losing her husband. In truth, it didn't feel like he was toying with her. Becky was like a Fourth of July sparkler come to life. Through everything she'd endured in life and how hard she worked to support her daughters, she practically sparkled with energy. She made him feel alive in a way that even his work hadn't for a long time.

Doralee had reminded him of how little he had to give, but thoughts of Becky inspired him to be more. To give more. To want more. If only he could be that man.

Chapter Five

Becky parked the minivan around the corner from Las Delicias, the Mexican restaurant situated on Rambling Rose's quaint main street. She remembered the first time she and Rick had made the trip to visit the town. She'd been charmed by the rustic beauty of the town, a little worn down and in need of some love but with so much potential and the feeling of home.

Now the man she'd agreed to meet for dinner was the one breathing new life into the community. It wasn't just the pediatric center. She knew Callum was working on a new vet clinic, an upscale shopping mall, a spa and even had plans for a boutique hotel. Up until his investment in the town, most of the money had been limited to the outskirts of the community. He lived in a wealthy enclave, but many of those residents kept to themselves, as if they didn't want to tarnish their fancy image by rubbing shoulders with the true locals.

Becky wasn't exactly a local, but she was raising two daughters who'd been born in the town. She appreciated that Callum didn't seem to care about the differences between them and that he wasn't intimidated by her situation.

Part of why she hadn't thought about dating in the past two years was her fear that a man would assume her twins were simply complications. Becky wasn't sure her heart could stand that.

She quickly checked her makeup in the visor's small mirror. Normally she didn't bother, but tonight she'd actually put some effort into her appearance. It had felt good, like she was some kind of single mom butterfly emerging from her chrysalis. With the help of a dab of concealer and a few subtle swipes of shadow, she looked more like the Becky she remembered and less like an exhausted, overworked mom.

The change made her smile.

"Mama," Luna shouted from the back seat. "Go."

"Go," Sasha repeated softly.

Her girls were learning new words every day, and Becky loved this time in their development. They were little sponges, soaking up everything and making even the most mundane parts of life an adventure.

But she couldn't deny that kids complicated dating, especially two squirming toddlers. Becky unstrapped the girls from their car seats, scooped them up and then slung the diaper bag over her shoulder. She hit the fob to close and lock the car just as Luna dived for her ring of keys. They fell from Becky's grasp and landed on the pavement, skittering underneath the vehicle.

"Uh-oh," Sasha said, her voice grave.

"Mommy will get them," Becky promised, cursing the pale yellow jeans she'd chosen for the evening. They'd seemed so fresh at her house, but this latest small catastrophe was the exact reason she normally didn't wear anything but jeans, scrubs or sweatpants.

"I've got it," Callum said, appearing at her side like some kind of superhero. He deftly crouched down to retrieve the keys, the fabric of his striped shirt stretching across the lean muscles of his back.

"Thanks," Becky said when he straightened again, wishing she could control the blush that seemed to appear every time he looked at her.

"My pleasure," he answered. "You ladies look lovely this evening." He held out his hands, and to Becky's surprise, Sasha reached for him.

"She usually doesn't let other people hold her." Becky's mouth went slack as Callum grinned at her shy daughter, then tucked an arm around her like it was the most natural thing in the world.

"Sasha and I have an understanding." He winked at Becky. "She's helping me win points with her mom."

"Very true." Becky returned his smile. "You have a way with babies." They started toward the restaurant. The evening was particularly mild for this time of year, and the fresh air helped to cool her heated cheeks.

"I had way too much experience in my own family."

The words were spoken lightly, but somehow she could sense that they meant more to him than he was letting on. If that was how he felt about children, what was he doing there with her and the twins?

"There were four brothers all around the same age, right?"

Callum nodded.

"I'm wondering why you were designated your stepmother's helper."

"It started with Stephanie," he said. "I had a connection with her from the start. I didn't even realize what I was taking on until it happened. There were things that Marci needed done with the baby, so I did them. Even if Stephanie was crying like crazy, she'd settle down once I played with her."

"I bet your parents appreciated that." Becky knew she would love that kind of baby whisperer.

"Yeah," he agreed. "They also came to rely on it in a way that none of us realized was too much for a kid my age to handle. The same thing happened when the triplets were born."

They'd reached the restaurant and he held open the door for her. The interior was a homey homage to south-of-the-border decor. Strands of lights hung against warm yellow walls, with colorful flags and sombreros rounding out the decorations. The place was more than half-full, which Becky thought was good for so early on a weeknight.

A stocky man with a pencil-thin mustache strode forward to greet them. "Mr. Fortune," he said, pumping Callum's free hand. "We have your table ready. What a beautiful group of women you have with you tonight."

"I'm a lucky man," Callum answered easily.

Becky felt the eyes of a pretty hostess behind the podium assessing her. Like Becky, the young woman probably wondered what Callum was doing out with a mom and two toddlers. Rambling Rose was a quiet town, but there were enough available women that he could have enjoyed an evening without a baby's sticky hands patting his cheeks, the way Sasha did to him now.

The man, who introduced himself as the restaurant's owner, led them to a table in a quiet corner, already set up with two high chairs. The girls, unaccustomed to dining out, looked around at their new surroundings with wide-eyed curiosity. She and Callum strapped each of them into a high chair, and she took out the travel toys she'd brought to entertain them. A waitress quickly brought water and took their drink orders before hurrying off again.

Becky smothered a giggle as she took a seat next to Luna. "I've never been treated like this at a restaurant," she admitted, glancing around to make sure no one could hear. "Even before I had the twins. Now on the few occasions I've tried to go out to eat with them it feels like the waitstaff resents every moment I'm taking up space. Must be nice to be a true VIP."

Callum blinked as if he'd never considered his elevated status or the perks that came with it. "Why would anyone mind if you had the girls with you?"

As if on cue, Luna chucked a wooden block across the table. Callum reached up and caught it without missing a beat.

"You just intercepted the first reason," Becky told him with another laugh. "There's also the distinct possibility of a meltdown by one or both of them. Not to mention more food falls on the ground than makes it into their mouths."

"People go out to eat with kids all the time," he countered. "It's no big deal."

She shrugged and glanced down at the menu. "Maybe I feel it more because I'm on my own. I don't get to tag out or divide the responsibility. I wouldn't change having twins, but it can be a lot. I'm sure that's why your stepmom ended up depending on you so much with the triplets."

The waitress returned to the table with a beer for Callum and a margarita for Becky. They ordered, and then Callum lifted his glass in a toast when they were on their own again.

"Tonight's toast is to you being the VIP for the night," he told her, the warmth in his gaze setting off an answering heat low in her belly. Luna lifted her sippy cup, and Callum gamely clinked his beer against her plastic cup and then Sasha's. "And a toast to me being with three very important ladies tonight," he said, making funny faces that had the girls squealing in delight.

Becky tried to shush them, but he seemed to enjoy the noise. She couldn't figure out Callum's contradictions. Although he clearly loved his family, it was just as obvious that he still harbored some resentment over the position he'd been put in as caregiver to his younger sisters. Why would he willingly get involved with her when he knew her situation?

She took a breath and put those thoughts aside.

It didn't matter why. She needed to just enjoy the evening.

They talked and laughed, and Callum continued to entertain her girls. When Sasha began to fuss, Becky pulled out a binky and the girl popped it in her mouth and sucked contentedly. Luna wasn't so easy to pacify, so Becky was grateful that the toddler appeared completely enamored of Callum.

Like mother like daughter.

Just as their food arrived, Luna decided she'd had enough of the high chair. Becky lifted the girl into her arms, a pro at eating one-handed.

"I forgot how good food tastes when you don't have to cook," she told Callum around a bite of chicken enchilada. "It's the closest I've had to gourmet in ages."

"What would you think of going out sometime, just the two of us?" he asked as he deftly caught the pacifier Sasha tossed at him. The girl offered a wide grin and put it back in her mouth when he returned it to her.

Becky tried not to react, but the words turned the yummy food she'd eaten into a lead balloon in her stomach.

"I'm sorry," she said automatically, still bouncing Luna on her knee. "This was a terrible idea." She pushed away her half-eaten plate of food and began gathering the girls' things into the diaper bag. "If you see the waitress, I'll take care of the check… It's the least I can do."

Callum covered her hand with his. "What's wrong? Did I say something?"

She shook her head as she stared at the back of his tanned hand and the smattering of fine hair covering it. His body was so different from hers, and just the thought of it made her heart swoop and dance.

But it didn't matter if he couldn't accept the reality of her life. "It's not you. It's me." She made a face. "That sounds like a line, but I mean it. This is why I haven't dated. The girls and I are a package deal. I get we're a lot, and I don't expect you to be okay with it. I just thought—"

"I know how dedicated you are to your daughters," he told her, squeezing her fingers gently. "Your unconditional love for them is one of the things I admire about you. I've never felt that way about anything or anyone. I'm not sure I have it in me."

"Then why are you suggesting I leave them behind?" She hated the catch in her voice and the tears that pricked the back of her eyes. The problem with loving her girls so darn much was that everything about them made her emotional. Or perhaps that was due to exhaustion or loneliness or the silly hope she'd allowed herself to have that Callum might not care about the tragedy that defined her life and her responsibilities as a mom.

"I'm not. I promise." He laced their fingers together, and the heat of his hand spread into all the cold, lonely places deep within her. "Of course I want to spend time with them. I just thought a night off would be good for you. Give you a little break."

"I don't need a break."

He traced tiny circles on the inside of her palm with his thumb. "Every mother I've ever known needs a break at some point. I'm not saying that because of how much I helped Marci growing up. You work full-time and dedicate every other waking minute to your daughters."

"They're my life."

He stared at her, and she found herself fidgeting under his perceptive gaze. "After Rick died," she said softly, "my parents pressured me to move back to Houston. When I refused, my mom told me I'd regret staying here on my own. She said if I didn't return home they wouldn't help me. I'd have to do everything on my own."

"I'm sure she was just angry and worried," he said.

"They haven't seen the twins since they were six months old."

"What about their first birthday?"

"I took them to the park on my own."

His thumb stopped moving.

"I don't understand," he told her. "These are their granddaughters."

Becky shrugged. "Maybe they'll come around eventually. It's not a big deal. The girls are too young to realize anything." She tugged her hand away from his when the waitress came to clear the plates. Luna's head drooped against her chest. "But I guess it's left me with something to prove. If I admit that I need time off from being a mom…" Her breath hitched, and she swallowed back the emotion that formed a ball in her throat. "That feels like failure."

Sasha gave a tiny cry, and Callum reached for her without hesitation. Becky tried and failed to stay unaffected by his easy way with the girls.

"You must know you're an amazing mother. Your girls are clearly happy and thriving."

She sniffed and busied herself loading the diaper bag while he managed to take out his wallet and then his credit card with one hand.

"I can take her," she offered, shifting Luna in her lap.

"All good." Callum waited until the waitress had taken his credit card to continue. "Tell me you know I wasn't trying to avoid being with Luna and Sasha."

"I know," she said with a nod. "I'm sensitive about them. About my status as a single mom."

"Your status is safe with me," he said in a tone that produced the desired result of making her laugh.

It had been so long since she'd laughed at anything but the antics of her toddlers. "I overreacted," she admitted. "Force of habit." She figured she didn't need to explain to him that at this point her life consisted of one spiral of exhaustion after another. It would be the height of foolishness not to want a night off, especially if it meant spending an evening alone with Callum.

"I don't have any babysitters I trust," she said honestly. "I guess I could ask one of the women from the pediatric center day care. The girls adore them." The waitress returned with Callum's card. He signed the slip and they both stood. "Would you like me to take Sasha?" she offered.

"I've got her," he said, snagging the diaper bag from the table and slinging it over his empty arm.

"Thank you," she said.

He gave her a slow half smile that she felt all the way to her toes. For a moment it was difficult to remember they were in a public place, each of them holding one of her daughters. The urge to lean in and brush her lips across his was almost too much to resist.

His grin widened as if he could read her mind and liked the path of her thoughts.

She spun on her heel and hurried out of the restaurant.

"You move quick for a woman holding a baby," he said lightly when they were on the sidewalk.

"I can do almost anything holding a baby." She cringed at how strange the comment sounded. "I mean—"

"I remember that from when my sisters were babies." He fell in step beside her as she started toward her car. "Stephanie was four when the triplets were born. All three of them loved being carried. We used to joke that for the first two years of their lives, their feet never touched the floor."

"My upper body is super strong," she said with a smile. "Although they're getting big enough that I won't be able to carry them both at the same time for long. Someone is going to have to learn to like walking since they're stuck with just me."

"They aren't stuck," Callum reminded her gently.

They'd reached the minivan. Becky hit a button on the key fob, and the side door slid open. She strapped the girls into their car seats, and the two of them immediately began babbling softly to each other.

"Spending time with you makes me feel like the lamest person in the world," she told Callum as she straightened from the car.

He blew out a disbelieving laugh. "I make you feel lame?"

"That didn't come out right." She pressed two fingers to her chest as her heart beat at a manic pace. "You make me realize how small my life is at the moment."

"Small and lame." He raised a brow. "The hits just keep on coming."

She shook her head as she pressed the button inside the car to close the side door. How could she explain the tumult of emotions racing through her? "We've had dinner twice now."

"Enjoyable both times," he said quickly.

"The first time, you had to hear about my late husband." She flicked a glance toward the car. "Tonight we covered all my insecurities about motherhood. Not exactly scintillating conversation on either count."

"It is to me." He took her hand and drew her forward a few steps so that they were standing a few paces away from the car door, out of the line of sight of the twins in their car seats. "I can't quite explain it, but everything about you fascinates me."

She laughed. "This isn't selling myself short, but

I might be the least fascinating person in Rambling Rose."

"You are brave, strong, independent, determined, loyal, loving."

"You make me sound better than I am." His words rolled around her brain, searching for a place to fit. She'd always thought of herself as a survivalist. She did what she needed to in the moment. Could she actually see herself the way Callum did? She loved the idea of it.

"That is who you are."

His voice rumbled over her, and she realized she'd swayed closer to him, lured by the promise of someone seeing her in the way Callum did.

The longing to kiss him that she'd felt in the restaurant pulsed through her again. Even in the dim glow of the streetlight, she could see the gold flecks in his dark eyes. They'd appeared solid brown at first glance but they were more distinct than that. Much like Callum, the nearer she got the more detail she could appreciate. There were so many facets to this man underneath the polished facade. She wanted to know them all.

She felt the hitch in his breath and then his mouth brushed over hers, light as a touch of a butterfly's wings. Awareness zinged along her skin like his touch was electric. Or maybe it was the energy inside her that had been waiting to be set free.

When he would have pulled back, Becky leaned in, unwilling to let the moment go so soon. Her enthusiasm was rewarded by Callum's soft groan of pleasure. He fitted his mouth to hers more thoroughly and his fingers gripped the back of her shirt like he was trying to root them both in place. Desire raced through her, a cresting wave she wanted to ride forever.

As lost as she was in his embrace, a soft squeak from inside the car had her jerking away. She peered in the window to see Luna and Sasha holding hands. It wasn't clear which one of them had made the noise, but they appeared content for the moment.

"I should go," she whispered, pressing her fingers to her kiss-swollen lips. It was a wonder she didn't feel a sizzle even now, like a drop of water on a hot pan. "The girls need to get to sleep. Thanks again for dinner."

"It was the highlight of my week," Callum said.

"Me, too," she told him, hoping her knees didn't give out. She didn't want the night to end but climbed into her car as Callum watched, her heart full and her body alive in the most intoxicating way.

Chapter Six

The next morning, Callum found his sister unloading supplies into a storage closet at the vet clinic. “Can you do me a favor?” he asked.

Stephanie looked over her shoulder. “As long as it doesn’t involve patching the drywall or installing flooring in the front lobby.”

“No manual labor,” he confirmed. “I need you to babysit.”

She turned. “That’s cute, Callum, but you’re a big boy now. I’ll make you a snack, but I don’t think you need a babysitter.”

“Funny, Steph.” He massaged a hand over the back of his neck. Asking for help of any kind didn’t come easy to him. But he needed this. “Would you babysit Becky’s twins for a night?”

His sister’s eyes lit up. “Are you serious? I’d love to get my hands on those babies.”

"Maybe take the enthusiasm down a notch. You sound a little scary right now."

"Do you want my help or not?" She gave him a playful nudge. "Those twins are adorable. I'm not scary, but I'm surprised Becky is willing to leave them for an evening. Obviously they go to day care, but she seems like the type of mom who'd have trouble taking any time for herself."

He sighed. "That's why I need your help," he admitted. "Luna and Sasha are adorable and sweet, but I'd like to treat Becky to a night out. She's worried about leaving them with a sitter."

"It's understandable," Stephanie said, her tone turning wistful in a way he didn't understand. "Being a mother is a big responsibility, especially on your own."

Callum studied his sister, trying to figure out where this contemplative mood had come from. He'd been in the role of big brother for so long that sometimes he forgot his younger sisters were adults with aspects of their lives he knew nothing about. "You'll find someone," he told her gently.

"I'm not looking for a man," she said, almost defiantly. "I don't need to fall in love to have a full life."

He held up his hands, palms out. "I understand that. I'm just saying I want to see you happy."

"Goes both ways. Becky makes you happy, doesn't she?"

How could he put into words all the things Becky made him feel? Excited. Nervous. Distracted. Enamored. Beside himself with desire. "We're friends," he said simply.

"Just because your marriage ended the way it did doesn't mean you're trash at relationships."

Callum chuckled. Leave it to Stephanie to cut right to the heart of his issue. Yes, he had a feeling he was garbage at commitment, to say the least. Too much responsibility on his shoulders so young in life had left him with a fierce streak of independence. He didn't like to be tied down by anything except his work because that was the only piece of his life he could truly control.

"I appreciate the vote of confidence."

"It's true."

"Maybe. But who knows how long I'll stay in Rambling Rose? All of our projects are on schedule. Once everything is up and running, it might be time for me to move on. I've been looking at a couple of locations around Texas—communities with potential."

"What about the potential for you to stick around?" Stephanie grabbed another box of supplies. "You can't keep hopping from one location to the next. We all need roots."

Sometimes those roots can feel like they're choking you, Callum thought, although he wouldn't say the words out loud. The topic of his role in the family and how that had impacted the man he'd become was a sensitive one.

He never wanted his sisters to feel as if he resented the role he'd played in their lives but he couldn't deny its effect on him.

"I'm happy with the life I have," he said, earning an eye roll from Stephanie.

"One of these days you're going to want more," she told him as if she were far older and wiser than her twenty-seven years. "For now, let's leave it that I'd be happy to babysit for Becky's girls. Most of my evenings are free so just let me know what night."

"Thanks." He pulled her close for a quick hug. "Steven texted that the new order of cabinets is almost ready. That should keep things on schedule."

"I never doubted either of you," she said.

After checking in with the on-site foreman, Callum drove over to the future site of The Shoppes at Rambling Rose, which was scheduled to open after the veterinary clinic, and then checked out progress at the spa. He thought about what could happen if he decided to make Rambling Rose his permanent home. His stomach pitched in response. A benefit to keeping his connections to the communities where he worked casual was he had no fear of being forced to put down roots or disappointing anyone when he couldn't. He was like a revitalization fairy godfather, swooping in to make changes, then moving on to the next big thing before anyone expected too much of him.

Callum wasn't sure if he had the capacity to change who he was now, even if he tried.

"Thank you so much for agreeing to stay with them." Becky offered Callum's sister a grateful smile. "They can be a handful."

"I'm used to multiple energy thanks to the triplets," Stephanie answered. Her shiny hair was pulled back into a loose bun and she wore a casual sweater and faded jeans, the epitome of effortless beauty. "And I love babies at this age." She grinned as Sasha started a game of peekaboo. Never wanting to relinquish the spotlight to her sister, Luna also began hiding her face behind her blanket, then popping back out. "The three of us are going to have a great evening." She met Becky's gaze, understanding darkening her blue eyes. "Don't worry. I'll text with updates and call if we need anything."

Becky gave a jerky nod. "I left instructions on the counter."

"We should go." Callum put a gentle hand on her elbow. "I'm not sure they'll hold the reservation if we're late."

Nervous energy fluttering in her chest, Becky kissed both girls goodbye. Often one or the other of them made a fuss when she tried to walk out of the day care center in the morning, but tonight they seemed more than ready to stay with Stephanie.

"Your sister is really good with kids," she told Callum as she shut the door behind them. Tonight he wore dark slacks and a white button-down shirt that seemed to accentuate his tanned complexion. His hair skimmed the collar, and the top button of the shirt was open. Becky had the almost uncontrollable urge to kiss that soft spot at the base of his neck.

"She was excited to babysit," he confirmed.

Becky scanned the street in front of her house. "Where's your truck?"

He grinned. "I thought we could take something a little sportier tonight since we don't have car seats to contend with."

He pointed to a sleek, two-seater Audi parked at the curb.

"How did I not notice that car?" Becky stifled a giggle. "It's so out of place in this neighborhood." She tugged on the sleeve of the dress she'd chosen for the evening, a floral-patterned wrap dress that just skimmed her knees.

Although she'd had it for a few years, she hadn't had

the opportunity to wear it since before her pregnancy. Slipping into it tonight, she was shocked to discover that it fit her differently from how it used to. She thought she'd lost her pregnancy weight, but the dress clung to her breasts and hips more tightly than she remembered. "Is this too casual for where we're going?"

"You look beautiful," he said as he took her hand. "Your skin is like ivory satin."

"Callum Fortune, are you a secret poet?" she asked with a grin.

"Just trying to live up to my reputation as a Renaissance man." He opened the door of the Audi for her, and she slid into the passenger side, unable to resist running her palm across the car's leather interior.

She'd never been in such a luxurious vehicle, and the reminder of how different their lives were had anxiety flitting through her like caffeine pumping in her veins.

"It's just a car," Callum said as he got in next to her. "It doesn't mean anything."

She barked out a laugh, then rolled her eyes at him. "Only a person who could afford a car like this would think that. You're rich."

He pulled away from the curb, shooting her a genuinely confused glance. "Is that a bad thing?"

"Would you believe I've never known any really rich people?" She scrunched up her nose. "Doctors around here make a good living, but not like your family."

"The car was a stupid idea," he muttered, and she instantly felt guilty.

"No. Of course not." She shook her head. "The car is fun." She placed a hand on his arm. "I just want you to understand that you don't need to try to impress me with your money or your connections or anything material. I like you, Callum. Who you are as a person means more than anything else. Even if you drove some kind of a beater car and didn't live in a huge mansion in a gated community, I'd want to spend time with you. I like you because of you."

They'd stopped at a red light just before turning onto the highway that led out of town. Callum looked toward her with so much intensity in his gaze, heat flamed her cheeks. "You're staring," she told him softly.

"You calling me out as a rich boy might have been the nicest thing anyone has ever said to me." He leaned over the console and quickly kissed her before the light turned green.

She laughed. "I meant it as a compliment. I know you work hard, and I'm not judging you for having money. But it isn't why I like you."

"I'm glad."

She blew out a breath and settled back against the seat as he drove. She was glad he hadn't been offended by what she'd told him. Saying the words out loud made her relax in a way she hadn't expected. There wasn't a true explanation for why the disparities in their backgrounds affected her. Becky had a feeling she was looking for any excuse as to why things couldn't work out between them.

She was falling for Callum, which gave him the power to hurt her. She normally kept her emotions on lockdown for the sake of her girls. There were certain things she didn't allow herself to feel—pity or regret for the life she'd lost when Rick died or bitterness at having to manage all the things on her own. Callum made her want to throw the shackles off her heart and claim a second chance at love.

Biting down on the inside of her cheek, Becky reminded herself that this couldn't be love. She'd known the man for just a week. He was handsome and kind. End of story. At least for her.

"This is why Rambling Rose needs more dining options," Callum said as the sun dipped below the horizon. "I don't want to have to drive almost an hour to take my girl out on a date."

His girl. Warmth bloomed inside her at the thought of being claimed by Callum. Could she trust what was happening between them? Was she even on the right page about it?

"A more upscale restaurant would be a nice addition to the community," she agreed. "Probably some of the people who live out by you would like that better."

He threw her a sidelong glance. "You make it sound as if we're the Texas version of *Downton Abbey*."

She groaned. "Do I sound like I have a chip on my shoulders? I don't mean to. My parents always made it really clear that I should know my place, so I guess that advice stuck."

"Know your place," he murmured. "What does that mean exactly?"

"Not to reach for things above my station."

"Seriously?"

"They meant it in a helpful way." She shook her head. "I think. When I say it out loud, it sounds terrible. I'd never want my girls to believe they shouldn't try for the moon. Whatever they want to accomplish, I'll support them, even if they fail."

"Everyone fails at something," Callum said, and his voice held a note of regret she didn't understand.

"What is your biggest failure?" she asked, curiosity and trepidation warring inside her.

His knuckles turned white as his fingers tightened on the steering wheel. He was silent so long Becky thought he might not answer. "Marriage," he said finally.

Becky tried to hide her gasp. "You were married?"

"And divorced after a year," he continued.

"What happened?" she blurted before thinking about it. Maybe he didn't want to share that part of himself with her. They'd had two dinners and a handful of lunches together and he hadn't mentioned having an ex-wife.

"I was a terrible husband." He pulled into the parking lot of a fancy-looking restaurant housed in a historic mansion on the outskirts of Austin.

"Callum."

He turned off the car, then faced her, regret shining in his eyes. "I shouldn't have brought this up tonight, Becky. I'm sorry. I've been wanting to tell you but now isn't the right time."

She reached for his hand. "I've talked to you about far too many details of my life. I'm glad you shared that bit of yourself with me. If it makes you uncomfortable, I understand. But I want to hear about it. I want to know you."

Lifting her hand to his mouth, he brushed a gentle kiss across her knuckles. "You really are amazing."

"Hardly." She laughed and dropped her gaze to her lap.

"Let's get our table and have a drink." He gave her a pleading look. "Then I promise I'll tell you anything you want to know about my past."

She tried not to let nerves settle over her as they entered the restaurant. It had a modern farmhouse vibe but still held true to the era of the house with rich textures and beautiful artwork. A stone fireplace dominated the far wall, and she wondered if she'd ever been in such a gorgeous establishment.

"What made you choose this place?" she asked as they approached the hostess's stand.

He shrugged. "It's been written up in several regional papers to rave reviews. Apparently, people come from all over to eat here. When I think about opening an upscale restaurant in Rambling Rose, I want to know what is already working in the area."

The hostess took his name and led them to a cozy table near the fireplace.

"So it's a date *and* a research trip?" Becky asked with a wink.

"Ninety-nine percent date," he assured her.

The waiter, an older gentleman with a shock of white hair, brought each of them a menu and explained the evening's specials, which included a scallop sashimi appetizer and Kobe beef tenderloin medallions with braised leeks for a main course. Becky was certain she'd never eaten anything as fancy as the dishes he described.

Callum ordered a bottle of wine, and she saw the waiter's eyes widen a fraction. When he left, she leaned in over the table. "What's so special about the wine you ordered?"

His thick brows drew together. "Nothing really. It's simply a good vintage."

"Does that translate as pricey?"

"Will you let me spoil you tonight?" he asked softly,

reaching across the table to lace their fingers together. "Please?"

The *please* got her.

"If you insist. We'll enjoy this evening and you can make me feel like a princess." She leaned closer to him. "Although I'll let you in on a little secret in case you haven't picked up on it. I always feel special with you."

His chest rose and fell as if her words made it difficult for him to catch his breath. She liked the idea of affecting him in that way. She didn't want to be the only one caught up in the spell of whatever was happening between them.

Chapter Seven

Callum was grateful that the wine steward approached their table at that moment. He'd been half tempted to tug Becky right out of her seat and into his lap. Or better yet to skip dinner altogether and find a nearby hotel where he could spend the next several hours making her feel special from head to toe.

The sommelier held up the bottle for his inspection and, at Callum's subtle nod, began to uncork it while praising the vintage and offering bland small talk about the wine industry. Callum was used to this routine in the restaurants he frequented, especially after ordering a five-hundred-dollar bottle. Of course, he wouldn't share the price with Becky. Part of him worried she'd be too nervous to actually take a drink if she knew how much it cost.

He hadn't been lying when he told her he wanted to

treat her this evening. If he'd been more on the ball, he would have chartered a helicopter and flown them to Houston or Dallas for a true five-star meal. Next time—if she gave him a next time.

As he took the cork from the sommelier, Callum felt a light pressure on his leg. He went to take the requisite sniff and ended up almost shoving the cork up his own nose when he realized it was Becky playing an innocent game of footsy with him under the table. Every nerve ending tensed and it took a herculean amount of effort to keep his features neutral.

One corner of her mouth curved up into a mischievous smile, but she kept her gaze trained on the wine steward.

"Perhaps the lovely lady would like a taste," Callum suggested as he handed the cork back to the man.

With an agreeable nod, the sommelier poured a finger of the deep burgundy liquid into a glass and gave it to Becky. She didn't bother to swirl the glass, and Callum noticed the man's mouth furrow into a disapproving scowl.

Instead, she took a dainty sip. "Tastes like red wine," she reported after a moment.

There was an indignant mew of distress from the sommelier. "It's not just ordinary wine," he explained, and Callum could tell the man was doing his best not to sound horrified. "That is a perfectly balanced vintage that's both bold and complex. It's like a symphony in your mouth."

"Which is a complicated way of saying 'great red wine,'" Callum explained, earning a slightly wider smile from Becky. What would it take to coax a full-fledged grin from her?

He desperately wanted to know.

"It's lovely," she told the sommelier, taking pity on the wine expert's obvious distress.

"I'm glad you're enjoying it," the man answered as he poured more wine into her glass. He filled Callum's glass as well and then left the table. The waiter returned to take their dinner orders, and then they were blessedly alone. Or as alone as they could be in a quiet corner of the restaurant.

"You distracted me," Callum accused playfully.

Becky held up her wineglass. "To distractions."

"You can distract me anytime," he told her as they clinked glasses, then frowned as he took a sip. "I'm missing something."

"What's that?"

"Your foot under the table."

She giggled, then flashed the exuberant grin he'd been waiting for all night. "I should probably apologize, except I'm not sorry. That man was far too serious for his own good."

"But you like the wine?"

"I understand very little about what makes it so special, but even I can tell that it is."

Callum opened his mouth to reply, then shut it again. He felt the exact same way about Becky. Yes, she was beautiful. He'd dated beautiful women before. Women who were ambitious and accomplished. But he couldn't remember ever having been so affected by any of them.

"Do you still want to know about my past?" he asked almost reluctantly.

"Of course."

He gave a gruff nod and took another drink. As much as he didn't want to speak about it, he knew they couldn't go further unless she understood his shortcomings. He liked and respected Becky, and was crazy attracted to her, but none of those things changed who he was on the inside. What he could and couldn't offer her. Best to have it all out now so she wouldn't hope for more.

"Doralee and I met at a bar in Nashville. It was a fast courtship, and we married within a couple of months."

"Like Rick and me," she murmured.

He hadn't realized the similarity in the time frame of their previous marriages. "I'm not sure I'd compare the two. I thought we were on the same page as far as the paths we wanted our lives to travel. Turns out we weren't even reading from the same playbook." He shook his head. "My business was starting to take off, and I had people coming to me about real estate deals in several smaller towns throughout Tennessee and the surrounding area. Steven and Dillon had joined me at that point, and I spent a lot of time working."

"You're dedicated."

"I should have been more dedicated to my marriage," he admitted, shifting in his seat. "She resented everything about Fortune Brothers Construction. In turn, I felt restricted, like she wanted to control me. The whole thing was a mess, and the entirety of it was my fault."

Becky inclined her head as she studied him, her gaze gentle. If she argued with him or offered false platitudes to assuage his guilt, Callum might lose his mind. He couldn't go back and fix the pain he'd caused his ex-wife, so the regret he carried with him like his own version of Sisyphus's boulder was all he had.

"Do you ever speak to her?" Becky asked, one slender finger circling the rim of her glass.

The breath he hadn't realized he was holding escaped his lips on a sudden hiss. "She called me this week, actually." Something flashed in Becky's dark eyes. He couldn't name the emotion, but it warmed him just the same.

"Just to catch up?" she asked, a little too evenly.

"To tell me she's engaged." He drained the rest of his wine, then waived away the server who moved to refill his glass. "She's been dating a guy since shortly after our divorce was finalized."

"How does that make you feel?"

"Like more of a failure than I already did."

"Callum, no."

"I'm joking." He gave what he hoped was a convincing laugh. "Sort of. I'm happy for her. She deserves a good man and a great life. I wish I could have been the one to give it to her. I'm sorry she had to go through our wreck of a marriage to find her happily-ever-after or whatever you want to call it."

"Sometimes it takes going through a difficult period to truly appreciate the happiness on the other side."

They were pretty words, but he didn't know if he could allow himself to trust them.

"Do you really believe that?"

The smile she gave him was filled with yearning. "I have to."

Right. Because this woman had been through something so much worse than the breakdown of a marriage.

Their food arrived, and he loved the way her eyes lit up at the sight of the mouthwatering dish the server set on the table in front of her. Becky had ordered some complicated chicken dish while he got steak.

She moaned in pleasure after her first bite. "I might

not know a lot about fancy wine, but this is the most amazing dinner I've ever had." She pointed her fork at Callum. "You should definitely take notes on this restaurant and recreate its goodness in Rambling Rose. Steal away the chef if you have to. I'll spend a month eating peanut butter sandwiches for every meal just to save money to go out to a place like this."

He wanted to assure her that she didn't have to worry about money because he'd take care of her, but he couldn't make that promise. Even if he could commit to it, he had a feeling he'd just offend her by offering. Even if they didn't say so out loud, most of the women Callum dated liked his wealth. The fact that Becky made a point of being genuinely not impressed felt refreshing.

"That's a ringing endorsement."

She nodded around another bite, then lifted up her hand to obstruct his view of her face. "Sorry," she said after a moment. "Eating quickly is a habit with me now. I can't remember the last time I ate at a leisurely pace."

"Have more wine," he suggested.

She flashed him a look of mock horror. "Are you trying to get me tipsy?"

"Not at all," he answered without hesitation. "But I do plan to kiss you tonight. A lot. And I want no question in either of our minds that we're both willing participants."

"I'm willing," she whispered, her eyes sparkling.

He smothered a groan. "When you look at me that way I want to skip dessert and ask for the check right now."

"When we're together," she said, leaning closer, "you make me want to be the dessert."

Color flooded her cheeks as she made the flirty statement, but the effect on him was the same as if she'd been a seasoned seductress.

As perfectly prepared as the meal was, Callum barely tasted it. He couldn't wait to be alone with Becky, even for a few moments.

"I'm so embarrassed," she murmured. "I don't say things like that."

"Then I'm not sure whether I'm more honored or turned on," he told her with a laugh.

They finished eating, the air around them charged with an electric current of desire. She left the table to call and check in with Stephanie as he paid the check. He found her just outside the restaurant's entrance, staring up at a clear night sky filled with stars.

"Everything okay?" he asked as he moved toward her.

"Yes," she reported with a relieved sigh. "Your sister said the girls went to bed without a fuss and have been sleeping soundly ever since." She dipped her chin, looking up at him through her lashes, and added, "She said to take our time."

"I intend to," he said, his voice rough even to his own ears. He took her hand and led her around the side of the building, then turned his back to the cool brick, drawing her closer. Need rushed through him as their lips met, and there was no holding back the flood of desire. She seemed as frenzied as he felt, opening for him as soon as he drew his tongue across the seam of her lips. The kiss deepened, need exploding through him like a wildfire.

Her body formed to his, soft where his was hard, and he spread his hands across her back, wanting more from her than she could possibly give out in the open, even sheltered as they were by the darkness and shadows.

He forced himself to bank his yearning, to slow the pace to where he could savor her. They kissed until he couldn't tell where he left off and she began. The flare of desire almost overwhelmed him with its intensity, his body hot and ready.

She broke away from the embrace when a horn sounded in a parking lot, glancing around in shock before offering a tentative smile. "I was afraid we were going to get caught making out like teenagers."

"Wouldn't have been the worst thing that's happened."

"But mortifying just the same." She straightened her dress. "I'm a mother of twins. Moms don't kiss like that."

He reached out and cupped her jaw, unable to stop himself from touching her. "Who told you that?"

She arched a brow. "Chapter three in *The New Mom Handbook*."

"There's a handbook?"

"I'm joking." She leaned into his touch, like a cat begging to be petted. He flicked the tip of her earlobe with his thumb, and she bit down on her lip. "We should go. I don't want to take advantage of your sister's generosity."

He wasn't ready for the night to end, but didn't want to push too far. This had been a big step for Becky, trusting her daughters with a babysitter and allowing herself a rare evening out.

"I've had the best time," he said as he took her hand.

"You really spoiled me," she told him. "I almost feel like a princess."

There was so much more he wanted to give her, to show her. If only she'd let him.

The thought pinged through his brain that maybe he should pump the brakes on their connection. Hell, he couldn't even commit to the restaurant idea, as strong as it was, because that would mean more time in Rambling Rose. His original plan had been to move on after the last of his initial slate of projects opened. That was his sweet spot as far as staying in one place. Enough time to make a difference in the community but not so long that he'd be tempted to stay.

Becky was a temptation he hadn't expected, and he had no clue what to do about it.

The next week was a blur for Becky. The pediatric center continued to be busy, and her days sped by in a whir of patient care and paperwork. Of course, that didn't count the moments she spent fantasizing about Callum.

She couldn't deny that her feelings had intensified since their special evening out. He was so much more than she'd expected him to be. Handsome as sin was hard enough to resist. Callum was the whole package—smart, successful, generous and kind.

As great as the fancy restaurant had been, she had just as much fun with him on casual nights at her house. He came over almost every evening after she got off work. They took turns grocery shopping and would cook together while the twins watched from the high chairs or played nearby. She would have thought he'd get bored with her daily routine, but he didn't seem to mind the monotony of life with toddlers.

After the girls went to bed, Becky and Callum would

spend hours each evening talking and then even more time kissing. She came alive in his embrace. It became more difficult each night to let him go. He seemed as reluctant to leave her as she was to watch him drive away through the flutter of curtains at her front window.

Which was how she found herself on an ordinary Tuesday night, standing in the open doorway of her small house trying to force her arms to unwind from around Callum's broad shoulders.

"I have to go," he said, then claimed her mouth with his.

"It's late," she agreed when they finally came up for air. "You should go."

It took another several minutes before she finally lowered her hands to her sides and backed up a step.

"I had an amazing time," he told her.

"We ate spaghetti with sauce from a jar and watched reruns," she pointed out with a laugh.

"It doesn't matter." He dropped a kiss on the tip of her nose. "With you, it's always amazing."

Stay, she wanted to tell him. Surely he would understand what that one word meant. She wanted more from Callum. As much as he could give her.

Right now she simply wanted him to stay.

But she didn't speak the word out loud.

Instead, she watched as he shoved his hands into the pockets of his jeans and backed away down her front walk.

"Good night, Becky," he called and then turned and jogged to his car. Almost as if he couldn't wait to get away.

She hoped he was moving quickly so that he wouldn't turn around and invite himself back into her house.

She slammed the front door shut like she might chase him down the street without the barrier between them. She moved to the window because it hurt her heart—not to mention the rest of her body—to know he was driving away. His taillights glowed red against the midnight darkness as he pulled away from the curb.

He'd driven only a few feet when his brake lights went on. Becky's breath hitched as the truck reversed back into its former spot against the curb in front of her house. For several long minutes nothing happened. No movement. No lights. No Callum.

Then the truck's interior lit up for a few seconds as he climbed out of the cab. He walked around the front of the vehicle and up her walk. Back to her house. To her.

Becky didn't give fear or doubt a chance to take hold in her brain. She dropped the curtain and rushed to the front door, throwing it open and dashing toward Callum. He grinned as she hurtled herself into his arms.

"I want you to stay," she whispered into his ear.

"Exactly what I hoped you'd say," he said as he carried her into the house.

Chapter Eight

As soon as Callum kicked the door shut behind them, Becky's doubts returned in full force. She wanted him more than she could have imagined, but her husband was the only man she'd ever been with in that way. And while she wasn't anywhere near over the hill, motherhood had changed her body.

She also had to deal with the issue of how much of her heart she could to give Callum. For her, sex meant more than just the physical act. Although she had no doubt he would be attentive and thoughtful, what if for him it was just a release? Scratching an itch between two people untethered to anyone else.

"Does it hurt?" he asked as he took a step away from her.

She blinked. "What?"

His mouth curved into that sexy hint of a smile that

never failed to drive her crazy. "You look like you're thinking way too hard. Typically, my brain hurts when I try that."

"You should *try* being less perceptive," she told him with an eye roll. "It's kind of annoying."

He chuckled, the low sound rippling across her already taut nerve endings. "Nothing has to happen tonight, Becky. You're in control."

Her breath caught in her throat. When was the last time she'd felt truly in control? Before tragedy had turned her into a widow and a single mother of two unborn babies. Since that moment, she'd been furiously treading water with the waves constantly lapping over her head.

"We can talk," he continued. "You can tell me to go."

"But I told you to stay," she reminded him.

He tucked a loose strand of hair behind her ear. "You're allowed to change your mind."

"I haven't," she blurted. "I'm just nervous. It's been a while and…" She shook her head.

"And…"

"Carrying twins pretty much wrecked my body," she said on a long exhale.

It was now, apparently, Callum's turn to blink. Poor guy. She had no doubt any man would struggle with a good response to that kind of statement. It had been stupid to put the silly doubt into words but…

"You're beautiful," he told her gently. His finger traced a path from the side of her jaw down her throat and along the edge of the neckline of the dress she wore. "Sometimes when you blush, it flushes all the way to your chest. I'm dying to know if I can make your whole body blush."

Her mouth went dry.

"I love how you're soft in all the places where I'm hard." He stepped closer, his warmth heating her like a fire on a cold winter night. "It's as if you're formed in the exact right way to fit me. If this is too soon, we don't have to—"

"I want to," she admitted, unable to offer any other response. She knew she had to stay in the moment. She had a feeling this was uncharted territory for both of them.

"Are you sure?" he asked, and she appreciated that he was giving her so many chances to decide. The feeling of being in control was a revelation in her current life where every day she felt strapped into an exhilarating and exhausting roller coaster with no safety harness.

She took his hand and led him through the quiet house to her bedroom. It had been the one space she'd changed after her husband's death, when sorrow had been her late-night companion. She'd thought her grief might engulf her, even knowing she carried a legacy of love inside her. Then she'd felt the first flutter of movement. A quiver of butterfly wings signaling the lives growing in her belly. At that moment she'd understood that she needed to make peace with her sorrow and try to find some measure of happiness again. For her babies.

She'd cleaned out the room, not just of Rick's belongings, but everything. She'd spent a portion of her meager savings to buy new furniture and hired a local handyman to repaint the walls from nondescript beige to a soft yellow. The color felt like hope, and now she realized she had been preparing for this new chapter in her life without even realizing it.

Moonlight slanted through the window, alighting on Callum's strong features. Slowly, she stepped closer and wound her arms around his neck. She didn't move deliberately because of fear. Somehow his allowing her to choose had chased away her doubts, at least for the moment. Instead, she wanted to enjoy each second they had together. Unwrap this experience like a precious gift.

He kissed her like he felt the same, molding his lips to hers until soft sounds of aching hunger escaped her throat. His hands moved along her back, over the dress's fine fabric, sending shivers along her skin. As good as his touch felt, it wasn't enough. She broke the kiss and began to unbutton his shirt, her fingers shaky with need.

"Let me," he told her as he took over. Within seconds he'd made quick work of the buttons and was shrugging out of the crisp fabric.

Becky did her best not to whimper. It had been no secret that Callum had an amazing body, his muscular physique evident even under his clothes. His bare chest and perfectly toned muscles made her forget her own name.

"Do you go to a tanning bed?" she asked, taking in all that golden skin and needing to regain some self-control.

He chuckled. "Uh, never."

She put her hands on her hips. "I just can't get over how naturally bronze you are."

"Do you want me to prove I have no tan lines?" He winked as he unhooked his belt.

"Yes, please," she whispered, and he laughed again.

"I think you need to catch up," he told her. "I'm feeling slightly underdressed at the moment."

"Don't let it bother you," she assured him. "It's working for me."

He arched a brow in response.

She hitched up the hem of her dress. The soft fabric pulled on over her head, no zipper or buttons to fuss with. But it also meant that in the disrobing, she'd bare her body to him without being able to see his split-second initial reaction. Becky couldn't decide if that was a blessing or a curse.

"Here goes everything," she whispered and lifted the dress up and off in one fluid movement. It fell to the floor in a whisper of sound, leaving her standing in front of Callum in her bra and panties. She didn't even own a matching set since motherhood had changed her breasts.

He didn't seem to mind. A shiver rippled through him as he stared at her. Her heart leaped in her chest at the intensity in his brown eyes.

His throat bobbed as he swallowed. "You take my breath away."

Confidence building in step with the desire pooling low in her belly, she reached behind her back and flicked open her bra. The straps dropped from her shoulders and then the lace fell to the floor.

Callum muttered a strained curse, his eyes going darker than she thought possible.

He closed the distance between them in two quick steps, claiming her mouth for a rough and ravishing kiss. She met his need with her own, thrilled when his big hands cradled her breasts, thumbs skimming over the sensitive peaks of her nipples.

Just as her knees gave way, he caught her and moved toward the bed, yanking back the covers and lowering her gently onto the sheets. They continued to kiss as he explored her body. It felt as if he was trying to memorize every curve and dip. She barely recognized herself in the way she responded, her desire greedy and sharp.

Becky was at her heart a people pleaser, always wanting to accommodate others without taking anything for herself. So the soft demands she spoke startled her, but Callum had no problem following every one. It was clear he wanted to learn how she liked to be touched. In the process, his inventive hands and mouth offered new insight into pleasure.

He was both gentle and demanding as he explored her. She easily opened for him as his fingers skimmed below the waistband of her panties, delving into her hot center in a way that made her arch into him. Blood roared in her ears, and pressure built inside her, more intense than she'd ever experienced. Her skin fairly crackled with the pleasure of the way he touched her.

She cried out his name when her release roared through her with all the force of a cannonball. Callum whispered sweet words into her ear as her body recovered, but still she wanted more.

"I need you," she said against his skin, delighted by the subtle tremor that threaded through him.

"The best three words I've ever heard." He kissed her swiftly, then climbed off the bed and reached for his discarded pants. He took a condom packet from the wallet, then turned to face her. Anticipation flooded her once again as he shucked out of his boxers, appearing not self-conscious in the least about standing naked in front of her.

Why should he? His body was perfection. He

sheathed himself as he returned to the bed, his weight giving her a feeling of safety.

"Every night," she said, leaning up to kiss the base of his throat, "I've watched you drive away, and a part of me has wanted to call you back."

He settled between her legs but didn't move to enter her. "Which part?"

"All of them, really." She offered a slow smile. "All of me."

With his elbows resting on either side of her, he cradled her face in his hands. "Those are the parts I want," he confirmed. "All of you."

"I'm yours," she whispered as he filled her in one sure thrust.

She'd been made for this moment, and it was everything and more. Her fingers trailed along the muscles of his shoulders and back, reveling in his strength and power. He continued to rain kisses along her face as they found a rhythm unique to the two of them. Time seemed to stand still as they remained suspended in this moment.

Her nerve endings shuddered when the pressure built again, different from what had happened to her minutes earlier. This time she and Callum climbed the high peak together, and then suddenly fireworks exploded throughout her body. She felt Callum go taut and he said her name like it was the most beautiful word he'd ever spoken.

"Amazing," he said into her hair moments later, dropping kisses like feathers on the top of her head.

She didn't know how to respond, what to say to explain how much this moment meant to her. She couldn't even admit it to herself, because she knew she loved this man. Not just because of great sex, although that was a bonus. She'd fallen for him for so many reasons, and being with him in this way had only served to crash through the last of her defenses.

Instead, she kissed him again, hoping to convey what she wanted him to know without giving away too much of herself. She let out a little groan of protest when he left her to go to the bathroom, only to return a few minutes later and gather her close.

"I'll be gone before morning," he promised, the comfort of his warm body making her blissfully drowsy. "But let me hold you awhile longer."

As an answer, she snuggled closer, falling asleep with his arms around her.

"Please don't say you're going to try to become a farmer now, too?"

Callum turned with a grin as Dillon and Steven walked into the abandoned feed house situated two blocks off the main drag of Rambling Rose's downtown.

He held out his hands, palms up. "Not exactly, although right now I don't think there's anything Fortune Brothers Construction can't accomplish in this town."

Dillon shook his head, a lock of sandy-blond hair falling across his forehead. "You shouldn't say that to anyone," his younger brother warned. "I've already heard rumblings about the locals not liking how much property we've bought in town. People think we're catering to the new millionaires—the gated community crowd."

"Not true," Steven argued before Callum could speak. "The pediatric center serves everyone, as will the vet clinic."

"What about the spa and the upscale shopping center and hotel?" Dillon kicked a toe at the dirty concrete floor. "Those aren't exactly meant for the average resident."

Callum stepped forward. "But they'll generate revenue and tax dollars that will help the town." He put a hand on Dillon's muscled shoulder. Dillon had always been the peacemaker of the family and the worrier within their business partnership, his cautious nature balancing the ambition that Callum and Steven shared.

"So if you aren't reopening the feed store," Dillon said, spinning in a slow circle to take in the dilapidated space, "why are we here?"

"Because I wanted the two of you to be the first to see the site of our next project."

Both of his brothers blinked.

"We're developing an upscale restaurant," he explained.

"In a feed store?" Dillon barked out a laugh. "I like the irony. Feed store as a restaurant, although it doesn't actually lend itself to upscale."

"You just need to see the vision," Callum assured his brother. He walked a few paces away from them and pointed to an open stretch of wall. "Imagine a long bar there, serving hand-mixed cocktails." He gestured to the far side of the space. "A kitchen with state-of-the-art equipment. We'll source local and regional ingredients along with the craft beer and liquor."

"My mouth is watering already," Steven said.

Dillon shook his head. "Do I need to point out that none of us has experience running a restaurant? We're contractors."

"But Ashley, Megan and Nicole do," Callum reminded him. "I talked to the three of them last night and they are interested in investing and heading up the design and menu."

"They want to come to Rambling Rose to run a restaurant?" Dillon scratched his chin.

"Their own restaurant," Callum clarified.

"The triplets are a force of nature." Steven shook his head. "You realize that, right?"

Callum smiled. "We've got plenty of room at Fame and Fortune." It might drive him crazy sometimes to balance all the intricacies of such a large family, but he and his siblings were undeniably tight. The thought of having the triplets in Texas felt right at a soul level.

Dillon paced halfway across the open space and then back again. "It has potential, but don't you think we've got enough on our plates?"

"If we don't seize the opportunity," Callum said, "someone else will. Ashley wants to target a late-spring opening. They can get things up and running plus work out any kinks before the summer tourist season swings into high gear."

Steven pulled his phone from his back pocket. "A guy over in Brenham emailed me about a barn that's being torn down. He's got almost a dozen pallets of reclaimed wood." He passed the device to Dillon, who then handed it to Callum.

"That would be perfect for the bar and an accent wall," Callum said, glancing from the photos on the phone to his brother. "I bet the girls would love it."

"I was thinking the same thing," Steven agreed.

Dillon had taken a few steps away, his back to them. Frustration pricked along Callum's spine. He didn't want to move forward without having both his brothers on board. The company was busier than ever since he'd moved operations to Rambling Rose. The pace of business would take all three of them working together in order for it to be a success. Failure wasn't an option.

If Dillon shot down the idea for their sisters to open a restaurant, Callum would respect that. He might be the company's founder, but it was a partnership now.

His younger brother spun around, meeting Callum's worried gaze with an unreadable expression. They stood like that for several seconds until Dillon gave a barely perceptible nod. "If we keep the pipes and ventilation ducts exposed, that will cut costs and make installation simpler. The concrete floor needs to be cleaned and polished, so insulation, electrical and plumbing are going to be the biggest hurdles, assuming there's no structural damage."

Callum and Steven exchanged a fist bump.

"What's that about?" Dillon demanded, eyes narrowed.

"I'm all about the big picture," Callum explained. "Steven goes right to design. You're the detail guy. If you're already working out the HVAC systems, that means you think the project is a go."

Dillon rolled his eyes. "Of course it's a go. What the triplets want, they get. Besides, once the 'big picture' guy is set on something, the rest of us make it happen. How do you think we ended up in this tiny speck of a town in the first place?"

"Not so tiny once we're through," Callum pointed out. "The Fortune brothers are putting Rambling Rose on the map."

"Does that mean you're going to stay?" Steven asked,

his tone casual. “After all the current projects are up and running?”

Callum shrugged, irritation making him twitch. Of course he wasn’t going to stay in Rambling Rose. He’d made certain that long-term ties weren’t part of the equation since the end of his marriage. He wouldn’t take the chance of hurting someone the way he had his ex-wife or opening himself to that kind of pain. But ever since his night with Becky, it felt like his priorities had been turned upside down.

He’d spent so long making his career the most important thing in his life because that kept him safe and in control. His growing feeling for Becky and her girls scared the hell out of him, and moving on would be the quickest way to keep them in check.

“I’m scheduled to drive over to a little town on the eastern edge of San Antonio next week,” he said by way of an answer. “It’s long past its heyday, but has great bones and easy access to the interstate. The place has potential.”

One of Steven’s thick brows lifted. “We were under the impression your relationship with Becky had potential, as well.”

Dillon cleared his throat. “Couldn’t help but notice your headlights coming down the driveway in the wee hours most nights. And a few early mornings.”

“Are you a vampire now?” Callum asked.

“Light sleeper,” Dillon said with a chuckle.

“You need to move into one of the guesthouses,” Callum suggested, not bothering to hide his annoyance.

“Who would have coffee ready for you in the morning?” Dillon shot back.

“Manny,” both Steven and Callum said at once, referring to the older caretaker who had come with the property. Manuel Salazar had worked at the ranch for decades. He had a gift with horses and happened to be a decent cook, as well. Callum and his siblings had come to rely on Manny to manage the property and their lives.

Dillon sniffed. "His coffee tastes like tar."

"But he serves it with the best huevos rancheros I've ever had," Steven countered.

"I won't argue that," Dillon admitted. "And no one better tell him I dissed his coffee. I've almost got him convinced to share his green chile recipe with me."

"Becky loves green chile," Callum murmured, remembering how excited she'd been when he'd brought a taco casserole to her house two nights earlier. He'd felt like a bit of a slouch admitting that an employee had actually done the cooking, but she hadn't seemed to care.

"Come on."

Callum stumbled a step as Steven brought him back to the present moment with a shove. "What?" he demanded.

"You like this woman," Steven said.

"Maybe even more than like," Dillon added, doing an annoying shimmy across the dirty floor.

"Shut up," Callum told both his brothers. "We're hanging out. She's nice. It's nothing more."

"Oh, look at that." Dillon pointed at him. "Your pants are on fire."

"Because you're a liar," Steven said helpfully.

"I get the reference." Callum felt a muscle start to tick in his jaw. "You both need to mind your own business."

"Our business is you," Steven said. "That's the way it works with family. Don't act surprised. Especially after you decided to buy a building for the express purpose of helping the triplets."

Callum blew out a breath, his annoyance disappearing. It would be great to have his younger sisters living in Rambling Rose.

"No more talk about my love life," he told them. "Let's discuss restaurant plans. I'm less likely to punch you that way."

Both his brothers laughed. "We'll let you off the hook," Dillon said.

Steven nudged him again. "For now."

Callum would take whatever kind of reprieve he could get.

Chapter Nine

"I'm not sure about this," Becky whispered, more to herself than anyone else.

"My sister's the best hairstylist in Rambling Rose," Sarah Martensen told Becky the following evening. "Brandi is an expert at color."

That vote of confidence did little to ease Becky's nerves, but she smiled. At this point, she sat in a stranger's basement hair studio, with the twins being entertained by Brandi's teenage daughter in the adjacent space. She'd wanted to update her look and remembered Sarah offering to babysit during the pediatric center's opening.

Becky had gotten to know Sarah's husband, Grant, well over the past couple of weeks. The building manager for the pediatric center, he was the kind, paternal type of man she would have wished her girls to have for a grandfather.

With few other options, she'd asked him for his wife's number and called Sarah to see if she would be willing to babysit while Becky got her hair cut and colored. She hadn't sported a real style since the girls had been born.

Sarah had immediately suggested that Becky make an appointment with Brandi, her younger sister, who'd recently opened a hair salon out of her home. It was a simple room in her basement but had all the essentials as far as equipment and supplies.

A benefit was that she'd been able to bring her daughters with her. Sarah had planned to watch them, but Brandi's sweet teenager, a senior at Rambling Rose High School, had captivated the twins.

"I'm going to make you so beautiful," Brandi promised with a wink, "that the handsome Fortune is going to fall at your feet."

"Brandi, hush," Sarah told her sister on a rush of breath.

Becky felt her eyes go wide. "How did you know I was doing this for Callum?"

Sarah shrugged, looking ten kinds of self-conscious. "Grant mentioned that the boy has been stopping by to visit you on the regular."

"He has business at the pediatric center," Becky protested weakly. It wasn't as if she and Callum were trying to keep their relationship—or whatever they'd call it—a secret. But it still felt odd to know people were discussing her personal business. The perils of small-town life, she supposed.

"My husband says Callum Fortune is quite taken with you." Sarah giggled like a schoolgirl. "To be honest, I don't know how you get any work done. I'd spend my days waiting for him."

"I love my job," Becky told them. She didn't bother to mention that she also loved Callum. Hair salon small talk was one thing. Revealing her biggest secret was quite another. "It's nice that he visits, but we're just having fun."

"A woman could have a lot of fun with a man like that." Brandi gave a throaty chuckle as she gestured for Becky to stand so she could move the salon chair in front of the sink attached to the wall. As Brandi turned on the water, Becky sat again, leaning back to rest her neck on the basin.

It felt strangely indulgent to have another person rinsing her hair. Brandi tugged at the thin strips of foil, then used a shampoo that smelled like lavender on Becky's hair. She closed her eyes and let out a blissful sigh.

Would Callum notice the change? In a way it didn't matter. She appreciated this small bit of pampering. It had been too long, she realized, since she'd taken care of herself. She hadn't even taken a vitamin since her jar of prenatal gummies had run out just after the girls were born. Luna and Sasha would continue to be her priority, but it was past time she started taking care of herself as well as them.

Not just with Callum as a motivator, but because she wanted her girls to see that joy and fun were an important part of life.

All too soon, Brandi turned off the water and tapped Becky's shoulder to indicate she could sit up.

"That was the most luxurious thing I've done in ages," Becky told the sisters, prompting them to share an incredulous look.

"Maybe Callum Fortune isn't as much fun as he

looks," Sarah said, both women dissolving into fits of laughter.

Color rushed to Becky's cheeks. "Not counting Callum," she muttered.

"Atta girl," Brandi said as she toweled off Becky's hair.

The next half hour rushed by in a blur of snipping scissors and small talk. Every few minutes, Sarah peeked out of the salon to confirm Brandi's daughter was still entertaining the girls. In this makeshift cocoon of feminine camaraderie, Becky suddenly felt connected to the Rambling Rose community in a way she hadn't since making her home in the small town.

Her status as a widow and single mother had defined her, and she'd allowed it to keep her from truly becoming close to people. A part of her expected everyone to judge her in the same way her parents had. Her mom and dad had never believed she could make a life for herself on her own. She'd wanted to prove them wrong, but in her quest for self-reliance, she'd cut herself off from making real friends in the process.

Brandi and Sarah were decades older than Becky, but the women made her feel like part of their tribe.

Becky was so lost in thought it took her a few seconds to really focus on her reflection in the mirror when Brandi finally spun her around to see her finished hair.

"It's gorgeous," she whispered, reaching up a careful hand to touch the soft strands. Instead of the one-dimensional brown she'd known her whole life, now her hair was subtly highlighted with strands of gold and auburn. The cut was layered around her face, but still hung over her shoulders in a way that looked both effortless and stylish. "You really are a genius with hair."

Brandi gave her a quick hug from behind. "Sweetie, my job is easy when I have someone as pretty as you in the chair." She undid the black smock covering Becky and gave her a hand mirror to inspect the back.

Becky swallowed down the emotion that welled up in her throat. She felt beautiful for the first time in ages, like she was still a woman and not just a mommy.

She paid Brandi, then walked out of the tidy hair salon room. The twins were curled into Brandi's daughter's lap, while the girl read them one of the board books Becky had brought over in the diaper bag.

"Mama," Luna called, scrambling up to toddle over to Becky.

She crouched down to hug her daughter, then glanced at Sasha, who studied her with a wary expression. "It's still Mommy, sweetheart," she said gently.

Sasha's features relaxed and she held up her arms. "Mama."

"Your girls are adorable," Sarah said as they walked up the stairs. "But I didn't get much of a chance to watch them."

"They're so sweet," Lilly, Brandi's daughter, murmured. "I hope I have twins someday."

"Shush your mouth," Brandi told her daughter in an exasperated tone. "I don't want you thinking about babies for another decade."

The girl groaned. "Duh, Mom. I'm just saying—"

"Don't say another word." At the top of the stairs, Brandi wrapped Lilly in a tight hug. "You're going to give me a heart attack otherwise."

Becky laughed at the obvious affection between mother and daughter. She hoped she'd have that kind of open relationship with her girls one day.

She said goodbye with a promise to call Sarah if she needed a babysitter and headed home. Callum had invited her and the twins to dinner at his family's ranch tonight. She felt both nervous and excited about being around the Fortune siblings en masse. While Callum made it easy to forget about the differences in their backgrounds, she wasn't certain things would be the same with the rest of the family. But she wanted to know the people who were important to him and see for herself how they interacted. The role he'd played as a caregiver in his family clearly had shaped the man he was today.

He seemed to believe he was a failure at commitment, yet somehow also remained a steadfast rock for his siblings. Who was the real Callum Fortune? The man who was attentive with her girls and so tender and sweet that Becky couldn't help but fall for him? Or the shrewd businessman who'd move onto the next challenge and town instead of putting down roots?

Becky had to figure out the puzzle of Callum before her heart was truly at risk.

"Stop pacing," Stephanie said, dipping a tortilla chip into the guacamole Manny had prepared before heading to his bunkhouse for the night. "You're like a nervous schoolboy."

Callum ran a hand through his hair as he stared out the window above the kitchen sink that offered a view of the long driveway leading away from the ranch. "I *am* nervous," he admitted. "It's weird. I've never really considered our family name or what it means to have money. I don't want Becky to think I'm some kind of rich snob living out here in this gated community."

Stephanie sniffed. "That's right. Women are so turned off by men with money."

He gave her a narrow-eyed glare over his shoulder. "You know what I mean."

"I do," she agreed after a moment. "I always hated girls fawning over my brothers because of our last name. And that was before we landed in Texas where the Fortunes are something of a dynasty."

"She doesn't care about any of that, which is refreshing."

"You really like her." Stephanie stepped closer.

"Is that such a surprise?" he demanded quietly. If his sister wanted to lecture him on getting involved with a single mother or a woman who'd experienced more than her share of tragedy, Callum would put up one hell of a fight.

"No," Stephanie answered without hesitation. "Becky seems great and her daughters are precious. I just can't figure out if this means you're planning to stay in Rambling Rose long term." She put a hand on his arm. "You convinced us to come to Texas, and now it looks like the triplets will be here, too. This town feels like home, Callum. But you've never been one to put down roots."

"Why does everyone keep harping on the future?" He blew out a long breath as dust whirled up at the edge of the horizon and Becky's minivan crested the hill and made its way toward the house. "She and I are enjoying the moments we have together. It doesn't matter to either of us what comes next."

When Stephanie didn't respond, he turned to find her staring at him, arms crossed over her chest and one foot tapping on the floor in apparent exasperation. "You know nothing, Callum Fortune."

He rolled his eyes. "Just be nice tonight. Make her feel welcome."

"You say that as if I'm normally a social ogre. Remember, brother, I'm a proud rescue animal mom. Between the dogs, the cats and the bunny, those twins are going to love me."

With a chuckle of assent, Callum moved past his sister toward the front door. The property was perfect for him and his siblings. It allowed them to be close but still have their own space. He wouldn't have traded it for another home in the area and hoped Becky wasn't overwhelmed by its size.

He jogged down the steps and came around the front of her vehicle just as she climbed out. The afternoon was clear, with only a few puffy clouds floating along the wide expanse of Texas sky. The temperature hovered in the low fifties, cool enough for long sleeves, but still comfortable. He couldn't wait to take the twins to the barn and see their reaction to the horses.

"Wow." He stopped in his tracks as Becky turned to face him.

She tugged self-consciously on the ends of her hair, which had been transformed since the last time he'd seen her. Her chestnut hair now gleamed with gold highlights that gave it a cohesively warm look.

"I got my hair done," she said as if he needed clarification.

"You look beautiful."

"You tell me that every time we're together," she said with a laugh.

"It's always true." He closed the distance between

them and kissed her, threading his fingers through her soft locks. "I like the new do."

"Thanks." She grinned up at him. "It was time for a change."

The style might be a subtle update but the shift in Becky's confidence felt massive. Of course, he liked her no matter what, but was thrilled to see the light in her eyes that made him know she liked her new look.

"Do you two like Mommy's hair?" He took a step toward the open door of the minivan and Luna and Sasha. His chest pinched as both girls kicked and squirmed at the sight of him.

"Cawl," Sasha shouted in her high-pitched voice.

"Up," Luna demanded.

"They're so excited to see you." Becky leaned into the minivan to unstrap the girls. She wore a simple yellow sweater and a pair of snug jeans tucked into cowboy boots.

"The feeling is mutual," he assured her, ignoring the fast thumping of his heart as his sister's words played on repeat in his head. Was he considering staying in Rambling Rose? He couldn't think about the future without sweaty palms and a nagging feeling that he was bound to mess things up with Becky. That's what he did.

He might want to commit, but he knew there was something broken inside him that prevented him from giving himself fully. Too deep of an independent streak perhaps or he lacked the gene for commitment. Either way, he didn't want to consider the idea that he could hurt or disappoint Becky and her daughters. They meant too much to him.

"Are you okay?" Becky asked softly.

He squeezed shut his eyes for a quick moment, then

grinned at her. "Sorry," he said automatically. "It's been a long week with the finishing touches on the Paws and Claws clinic and the triplets' constant barrage of texts and calls with ideas for the restaurant."

"If you want to reschedule dinner…" She bit down on her lower lip, and he cursed himself for the doubt that flashed in her dark eyes.

"Not at all." He lifted his arms, gratified when Sasha reached for him. "I've been looking forward to showing the three of you my home."

Becky took Luna from her car seat, then hit the button on the vehicle's interior to shut the side door. "It's really great." She cleared her throat. "I actually don't think I've ever been in a house this big."

"The footprint makes it seem larger than it is," he assured her, earning a laugh.

"I don't care that you're rich," she told him, going up on her toes to kiss his cheek. "I like you despite the gobs of money, not because of it."

"I wouldn't describe it as *gobs*," he said, looping his free arm around her shoulder.

"Massive piles?" she suggested playfully.

"You're funny."

She giggled. "I try."

"What would you like to see first? The house or the barn?"

"I think the twins would love to visit the animals, if that's possible."

"Anything is possible for you." He dropped another kiss on the top of her head and led the way to the barn that sat adjacent to the main house.

His sister was waiting inside the wide row of stalls that connected to a spacious arena. The previous owner had been a show jumping enthusiast, and although the arena went largely unused by the Fortunes, Callum appreciated having it available. Unbidden, an image of Sasha and Luna a few years from now popped into his brain. They had the same dark hair as their mother and wore matching riding costumes as they trotted ponies around the arena.

He felt a muscle tick in his jaw as he forced away the mental picture. By the time the girls were old enough for riding, he'd be a distant memory to them and their mother.

"I hope you don't mind me crashing your date," Stephanie said, shooting him a curious glance. "I couldn't pass up the opportunity to get my hands on these little cuties."

"It's nice to see you again," Becky said as Luna waved. Sasha, always the more cautious twin, snuggled against the soft fabric of his chambray shirt, but smiled shyly when his sister tickled her leg.

Luna was happy for Stephanie to hold her, and the look of delight on his sister's face gave him a bit of a start. He knew Stephanie liked babies and young children, but the mix of happiness and yearning in her blue gaze as Becky's daughter relaxed into her arms seemed oddly intense. Stephanie wasn't dating anyone seriously, at least as far as Callum knew, but she certainly looked like a woman ready to become a mother.

"Your hair is so great," Stephanie told Becky. "I need a reference for your stylist."

"She's a local," Becky explained quickly, "who works out of her house. I'm not sure she'd be—"

"Perfect." Stephanie grinned. "I'd love to give her a call."

At the sound of a soft whinny, Luna squealed and

Sasha sat upright, her eyes widening. "Do you hear the horsey?" Callum asked.

"That's Buttercup," Stephanie told the girls and Becky. "He likes visitors." She reached into the front pocket of her jeans and pulled out a handful of baby carrots. "And treats."

They walked forward to where the sleek bay had popped his head over the wall of the stall.

"Sweet boy," Becky murmured. "Isn't he a beauty, girls?"

She stepped forward and held out her hand, palm out. The horse snuffled and rubbed against it. The twins watched in obvious awe as their mother loved on the large animal.

"Do you want to pet him?" Stephanie asked Luna gently. "He loves little girls."

"Uh-huh," Luna murmured, spellbound.

Callum stayed back with Sasha, who seemed less willing to investigate the big horse close up. She watched with fascination as Stephanie helped her sister reach out a hand to touch the animal's soft nose.

Buttercup blew out a contended breath, reveling in the attention. Stephanie placed a carrot in Luna's chubby hand and uncurled the girl's fingers so that the horse could snuffle it up.

"I've never seen her look so happy," Becky said with a wide grin.

"She's horse crazy already." Stephanie dropped a gentle kiss on top of the girl's head, then turned to Callum and Sasha. "What about you, sweet girl? Do you want to give Buttercup a treat?"

Sasha looked less confident than her sister but nodded nonetheless and reached for Stephanie.

"I'll trade you," Callum said with a laugh as he and his sister switched twins.

Becky pulled out her phone and snapped photos of the girls taking turns petting and giving carrots to all the horses housed in the barn. When they'd visited with each of them, Stephanie introduced them to her personal menagerie, which included two cats, Violet and Daisy, plus two dogs, Mack and Tallulah, not to mention a bunny named Orville who charmed both her daughters.

By the time they were finished, the girls were sticky, sweaty and covered with a fine coat of dust. Becky beamed from ear to ear, and Callum's heart felt full to bursting.

The rest of the evening was just as perfect. He'd purchased two high chairs in town, which seemed to make Becky inordinately grateful. She slayed him with her low expectations. If he had his choice, he'd give her anything in his power. Except the one thing that deep inside he feared she wanted the most—his heart.

It was getting more difficult by the moment to ignore his inability to commit to making Rambling Rose his permanent home.

Once again, he focused on the present. They ate the chicken fajitas Manny had prepared, and Becky seemed to be entertained by Steven and Dillon. His brothers flirted with her and the twins, and it was obvious she was both delighted and embarrassed by their attention.

They stayed later than the girls' normal bedtime, and Luna and Sasha had already dozed off by the time they loaded them into the car seats. "I'll see you tomorrow," he told Becky as he kissed her under the sliver of moonlight.

She shivered when a breeze kicked up, and he pulled her closer.

"I'm working tomorrow," she told him.

"It's Sunday. You don't work on Sundays." He wasn't fazed at having her schedule memorized. The moments he spent with Becky, even on her lunch break, were always the best of his day.

She laughed. "I know, but one of the other nurses needed the day off for her son's birthday. The girls like going to the day care center, and it shouldn't be busy."

"How about lunch?" he asked.

"You don't have to—"

"Please." He brushed his mouth over hers. "Let me see you again."

"You see me all the time."

"I can't get enough."

She bit down on her lower lip. "That makes me happy."

"You make me happy."

"Lunch tomorrow," she promised. "I should be able to take a break around noon. Does that work?"

"I look forward to it." He smoothed his hands over her cheeks. How could she be so precious to him after such a short time? There was no explaining the deep connection he felt, but no denying it, either. He'd take her to lunch, to dinner. Hell, he'd drive her to the gas station to fill up her minivan if that's what she needed from him.

He watched her drive away, then turned to walk back up the porch steps. Funny how one evening with Becky and her girls had made his big house finally feel like a home.

Chapter Ten

As she and Callum drove toward the pediatric center the following afternoon, Becky stole glances at her fingers entwined with Callum's larger, tanned hand, her heart hammering in her chest. They'd had lunch at the diner in town and then Callum had taken her to see the feed and grain building he'd just bought with a plan for his younger sisters to convert into a restaurant.

More Fortunes were coming to Rambling Rose, causing nerves to bubble up inside her. She wanted to meet Callum's younger sisters, both because he talked so fondly of the triplets and also due to her curiosity about the bond of adult multiples. Would her girls always be as close as they seemed now? She hoped so, and from what Callum had told her, Ashley, Nicole and Megan might provide great insight.

But each time her ties with the Fortune family deepened, she worried about what that would mean when and if Callum decided to leave Rambling Rose.

Although her love for him seemed so sure and strong, she still had no idea how he felt about her. Certainly she knew he cared for her and her daughters. But that was different from being in love. She thought about broaching the subject even though the doubtful part of her heart worried about what answer she might get.

"Looks like trouble at the center," Callum said, his tone laced with concern.

She looked up from their joined hands to the pediatric center's entrance. Two police cars, lights flashing, were parked in front of the building.

Becky's first thought went to her daughters, although she knew Luna and Sasha were safe in the building's secure day care center.

"Will you drop me off in front?" Adrenaline pumped through her.

As soon as Callum pulled to a stop, she bolted from the truck, flashing her employee badge to the officer who stood just inside the sliding doors when it looked like he might stop her.

Grant Martensen stood near the information desk with another officer. Shannon Goering, the young admissions attendant, stood next to him, wiping at her cheeks.

"What's going on?" Becky's instinct was to rush to check on her girls, but she forced a deep breath. Nothing good would come of her panicking. She placed a hand on the woman's arm, wanting to offer comfort for whatever was so upsetting.

"I didn't know," Shannon said miserably, shaking her head. "She wanted to leave the baby and we learned about the Safe Haven law in training. If I thought the mom might be a danger to herself, I would have tried to keep her here."

Becky looked from Shannon to the thin-lipped police officer to Grant.

"The baby's with Dr. Green," the older man said. "He can give you the details."

Relief and worry battled inside Becky as she headed toward the primary care wing. Relief that the crisis was limited to a single child, but concern about the details of that baby's situation. Parker Green leaned against the high counter of the nurse's station as she entered, holding a phone to his ear. He gave her a swift nod and crooked a finger, beckoning her forward.

"Tell me about the baby," she said when he put down the phone, her eyes darting to the exam room with the closed door.

"He's stable." Parker massaged a hand along the back of his neck. "Vitals are good and no signs of neglect."

"How old?" She was already moving past him. "What's the story?"

"Becky, wait." He placed a gentle hand on her shoulder. "It's the little guy from the ribbon cutting."

She blinked, trying to follow his words. There had been no patients at the opening ceremony except…

"The woman in labor," she said, absently rubbing her arms. "Laurel?"

The young doctor nodded, lines of tension bracketing his mouth. "She left a note tucked into the blanket she'd wrapped the baby in. She said he's better off here for a while and she'll be back as soon as she can."

"Where is she now?" Becky's heart broke for a mother who felt so desperate to relinquish her baby.

Thanks to Callum watching the twins, Becky had been the one to stay with Laurel. The woman had been a heartbreaking mix of strength and fragility. She'd seemed terrified about becoming a mother but determined to take care of her baby.

Becky had empathized with her plight on so many levels. It was exactly how she'd felt the moment her water broke with Luna and Sasha. As much as she'd tried to prepare during her pregnancy, panic had fluttered through her chest like a bird caught without shelter in a rainstorm. She hadn't known how she would handle the reality of motherhood, but she had managed due to a deep sense of devotion to her babies.

She didn't for one instant doubt Laurel's love, but Becky also understood that there were so many factors that went into successful parenting. If Laurel was experiencing some form of postpartum depression and had no support system, it could force her into an act of desperation.

Like giving up her child.

"The authorities are reaching out to the hospital where she delivered the baby," Parker said, as if reading her mind. "The law provides for anonymity, but they want to make sure she's not a danger to herself. Shannon said Laurel seemed to be coherent, but the note mentions the history of the Fortune's Foundling Hospital. It's as if she believes she was leaving the baby at a modern-day orphanage."

A sick feeling spread through Becky's stomach, but she forced herself to focus on what she could do to help. "Can I see the baby?"

"Of course," Parker answered immediately. His phone rang at the same moment. "I've got to take this.

I'm trying to coordinate a plan with the Department of Human Services."

Foster care. Becky drew in a sharp breath at the thought of the tiny infant going to a stranger. Then she reminded herself there were amazing families involved in the foster care system in Texas. If Laurel felt she needed to relinquish her baby, she must have had a good reason, and the welfare of the child was critical at this stage.

She pushed open the exam room door, surprised to find the space empty other than a portable bassinet situated at one end. Her rational side understood. The child's arrival on a low-staffed Sunday afternoon had thrown the pediatric center into crisis mode.

But the mother in her roared in silent disapproval. This baby had been abandoned. He needed someone with him. On instinct, she dimmed the lights, knowing that a baby born only a few weeks ago needed the calmest environment she could provide.

A soft coo from the bassinet had her hurrying forward. She paused long enough to wash her hands in the exam room's small utility sink. One of the other nurses had swaddled him in a hospital blanket and placed a tiny blue cap on his head. He looked like a squirming burrito.

"Hello, big guy," Becky said gently, reaching out to stroke a finger across the boy's cheek.

He immediately turned toward the touch, his rooting reflex kicking in, and she realized he was hungry.

The door to the exam room opened, and Sharla entered, holding a bottle. "Poor little dude." She frowned. "He doesn't have any idea what's going on."

"I'll feed him," Becky offered immediately. "There

has to be some explanation. I talked to the mom during her labor. She seemed overwhelmed, but it was clear she loved her baby even then."

"Who knows," the other woman murmured, handing the bottle to Becky. "My hormones got all out of whack after Thomas was born. It took months of me crying on the bathroom floor before my husband insisted I talk to the doctor. She helped me, but this munchkin's mom was totally alone. Maybe she didn't have anyone to tell her she'd be okay."

"I wish I would have been here when she came in today." Becky lifted the baby into her arms, then took a seat on the bench meant for family members waiting with a young patient. "Maybe I could have helped. Did the note give any details about his care?"

Sharla shook her head. "We don't even know if he was breast- or bottle-fed. All we can do now is try to keep him healthy and hope they track down the mom or find an amazing foster care placement for him."

The baby sucked greedily from the bottle, his tiny fingers grasped on to the front of Becky's scrub shirt. "Does he have a name?" she whispered, tears pricking the back of her eyes at his vulnerability and resilience.

"There wasn't anything in the note about a name." Sharla sighed. "We know Laurel is the mom, so he started out as Baby L. I'm calling him Linus on account of the blue blanket he was wrapped in when he got there."

Becky fingered the soft white fabric that swaddled him now. "Where is that blanket?"

"We got him a fresh one. Figured the blue one might be in need of a good washing."

"Don't do that. It probably smells familiar."

"Do you think she'll come back?" Sharla asked softly. "His mama?"

"I hope so, but more than anything I hope she's okay." Becky maneuvered baby Linus onto her shoulder and gently patted his back until he let out a robust burp. "He's eating like a champ."

The door to the room opened again, and Callum peeked in. "Parker filled me in on the situation," he said gravely.

"You can keep the two of them company," Sharla told him, moving toward the door. "I need to check on another patient."

Callum washed his hands without being asked, then came to sit next to Becky.

"Can you take him for a minute?" she asked. Now that it was just her and Parker, she was having trouble holding back tears.

"Sure." Parker easily transferred the baby to his arms, then took the half-full bottle and offered it to Linus.

"I don't understand how this happened," Becky whispered, wiping at her eyes. "I know Laurel loves him."

Parker's mouth thinned. "She obviously felt like she couldn't care for him the way he needed."

"She should have asked for help."

"That's not easy for some people," Callum reminded her.

Becky knew that all too well. Sometimes it felt like she'd muscled through those first few months of mothering twins on willpower alone. Like Sharla, she'd cried almost every day from sheer exhaustion, but hadn't wanted to admit to anyone how she was struggling for fear they'd judge her or deem her unfit to care for her girls. Looking back, she understood all three of them would have been better off if she'd asked for help.

Even now, she struggled to reach out even though the friends she had in the Rambling Rose community seemed happy to rally around her.

"What's going to happen to him?" Callum asked as the baby finished the bottle. Becky was amazed at how naturally he handled the infant. He'd told her how much responsibility he'd taken on with his younger sisters. Obviously, those skills were deeply ingrained in him. He didn't miss a beat with burping Linus, even thinking to pull a towel off the counter to flip over his shoulder.

Becky glanced down at her own shoulder and cringed at the wet spot of spit-up. She'd never been great at remembering a burp cloth. "Do you mind sitting with him for a few minutes while I get an update from Dr. Green?" She used the edge of her sleeve to dab at the corner of one eye. "I'd also like to take a look at the note Laurel left. I'm hoping something helps me make sense of this whole thing."

She took a step toward the door without waiting for an answer, shock making her feel fragile.

"Becky." At the sound of her name in his deep voice, she stilled.

He came up behind her and pressed a kiss to the top of her head. "It's not your fault."

How did he know what she was thinking?

Drawing in a steadying breath, she turned and glanced down at Linus in Callum's strong arms. The baby had fallen back asleep, lulled by a full stomach and the feeling of security he no doubt had being held by Callum.

"What if I had done more?" she asked, realizing she

sounded as miserable as she felt. "I could have offered to go along with her in the ambulance…"

"You had the twins with you that day," Callum pointed out gently. "I have mad babysitting skills and an insanely trustworthy face, but I doubt you would have just left them with me indefinitely."

"Mad skills," she repeated with a soft laugh. "In so many areas."

When he wrapped his free arm around her, she rested her head against his chest, the steady beat of his heart calming her slightly.

"I could have followed up with her," she said against his shirtfront. "I've thought about her so many times since that day. I saw a lot of myself in Laurel and her situation. What if I'd intervened and given her the support she needed to not give up on herself?"

"You still could," he told her. "There's no telling what will happen next. Hopefully, they find her quickly and get her the help she obviously needs. If that happens, Laurel and Linus will benefit from any support we can give them. Until then, this little guy is most important."

"You're smart, ridiculously handsome and have mad skills as a baby whisperer. Remind me again why you haven't been scooped up by some lucky lady?"

She meant the question as a joke to lighten the mood but knew she'd miscalculated when his body went rigid.

"I'm a bad bet in the commitment department," he said without emotion, taking a step away from her, his gaze shuttered.

She wanted to argue. To tell him that he just needed to believe in himself and to find a woman willing to take a chance on love with him. She could be that woman if he'd let her.

But Callum was right. Linus had to be the priority at the moment, the way Luna and Sasha were always first in Becky's heart and mind. If Laurel couldn't give her baby what he needed, Becky would make sure the community stepped in to help until the situation could be resolved.

"I think you're the perfect bet," she murmured, then quickly left the room, not wanting to gauge his response to her comment.

Dr. Green—or Parker, as he'd told her on multiple occasions to call him—was still at the nurses' station. He ended another call as she approached.

"How is he?"

"He just took down two ounces like a champ." She gave what she hoped was a reassuring smile. "We're going to take care of him."

"That boy will need our care." Parker spoke absently, almost more to himself than her. "It could be a rough road for such an innocent baby."

Becky couldn't allow herself to consider that possibility. She needed to stay focused on resolving the situation. "Any leads on tracking down Laurel?"

Parker's jaw tightened. "She relinquished the baby," he said quietly.

"Temporarily," Becky clarified. "Her note specified that. It's what she told Shannon, as well. She needed a temporary reprieve."

"I understand. But the point of the law is to offer a safe option for the baby that also protects the parent who can't care for him."

"Temporarily," Becky repeated, enunciating each

syllable. "You were here when she came in the first time, Parker. You know as well as I do that she loves her baby. I don't know what Laurel is going through at the moment, but she needs our help and support as much as Linus does."

"Unless the hospital in San Antonio doesn't believe she's a threat to herself, the authorities won't aid in the search for her," he explained, his voice tight. "That isn't how it works when someone voluntarily gives up a child."

"She left him at what she believed was a decades-old orphanage." Becky threw up her hands. "She's confused and she could even be suffering from postpartum depression. We can't just abandon her."

Parker drew in a deep breath, closing his eyes for a moment as if he were deep in concentration. He returned his strained gaze to hers. "We're on the same side, Becky. I want to find and help Laurel and reunite her with Linus if that's what's best for the child."

She opened her mouth to argue that of course being with the mother was best, but she'd worked in pediatrics long enough to know that wasn't always the case. Still, nothing could shake her belief that Laurel would be a good mother if given the chance and the support she needed.

"Where does that leave us?" She pressed a trembling hand to her chest and forced herself to ask the question that had been burning a hole in her gut for the past few minutes. "What happens to Linus now?"

"I've talked to a half-dozen people from social services already." Parker looked past her toward the exam room where she'd left the baby with Callum. "He'll need to be placed with a foster family, and we'll make sure it's someone who will give him the right kind of care." He thumped a hand on the top of the counter, clearly frustrated at not being able to come up with an easy fix for the situation. "Let's go take another look at Baby L."

"We're calling him Linus." Becky fell in step with him. "Callum is with him now."

Parker gave her a funny look. "I wouldn't have expected Callum Fortune to be so comfortable with a baby."

"He took care of his triplet sisters when he was younger." Becky couldn't help the pride that swelled in her tone. "He's really great with kids."

She opened the exam room door to find Callum just finishing up a diaper change for the baby.

"He does diaper duty, too," Parker murmured behind her, chuckling softly. "This one might be a keeper, Beck."

Tension gathered between her shoulder blades at the way Parker's teasing words made her heart leap. She should know better than to allow herself to daydream about the future, but with Callum she couldn't help it. In the weeks and months after her husband's death, Becky had resigned herself to a life with Luna and Sasha as her only focus. She had to be both mom and dad for them, and she'd become accustomed to the loneliness that sometimes found her in the rare quiet moments.

Callum filled that void, but she had to keep reminding herself their relationship was only temporary. He knew how to make her feel special and was a natural with her girls, but when his work in Rambling Rose was finished, he'd move on. If she wasn't careful, he'd take her heart with him when he left.

"All systems are a go for this little trouper," Callum reported, cradling Linus in his arms once again. "What's the plan?"

Parker shook his head. "Social services can't arrange a foster placement until tomorrow morning, so I think he's going to be a guest of the pediatric center tonight."

"I could take him home," Callum said.

Becky felt her mouth drop open, shocked at his willingness to step in. By the way color tinged his cheeks, she had a feeling he was just as surprised at his offer.

"I know I'm probably not the first choice to be responsible for a baby," he clarified, his tone almost self-deprecating in its casualness. "But we might as well take advantage of all that training I had with my younger siblings."

"Callum would take good care of him," she told Parker, hoping Callum knew how much his actions meant to her. Linus was a precious boy but not a child with whom Callum had a personal connection. It was just the kind of man he was to take on a virtual stranger's baby because it was the right thing to do.

"I'm sure you're right," Parker said, giving Callum a tight smile. "Unfortunately, that's flaunting protocol a bit too flagrantly, even for a small-town medical center." He stepped closer to peer down at the sleeping baby. "It's not ideal, but baby Linus will be spending the night with us. I'll make sure the nurses on duty take good care of him."

"Then I'll stay." Callum's hold on the baby tightened ever so slightly. "If it's okay with you? That way we'll know someone is with him at all times."

Parker appeared marginally affronted by that. "You

can stay if you'd like, but rest assured my staff does an exemplary job of caring for our patients."

"I have full confidence in your staff," Callum said, his gaze darting to Becky. "I'll still stay."

"Your choice." The men shared a silent look that Becky couldn't interpret but somehow eased the tension crackling between them. It was as if they'd come to an understanding, and Becky felt her heart go soft at the sight of these two strong men bonding over the care of an abandoned infant.

"I'll have our largest room made up with a bed for you," Parker said before leaving them alone again. "Thanks, Callum. We all appreciate it."

As the door shut behind the doctor, Becky checked her watch, then let out a frustrated sigh. "I have a short shift today because the day care center closes early on Sunday." She offered a wan smile. "I'd rather not bring the girls to see him since he seems to have settled in so peacefully. The last thing this baby needs is more unfamiliar stimulation at this point."

"It's fine." Callum pressed a swift kiss to her mouth. "I'm going to text my brothers and Stephanie and let them know I won't be home tonight. The nurses will take care of both Linus and me tonight."

"I know," she said softly. "It's an amazing thing you're doing."

He chuckled. "I'm sleeping on a hospital bed for the night. Not quite hero material."

"You are to me," she blurted, then felt her cheeks heat as a look of panic passed over his face. "I'll check in later," she said quickly, careful not to meet his gaze. The emotions churning inside her from the baby's plight were making her speak without thinking. She'd been careful not to push Callum more on his future plans. She had to believe that his willingness to become involved with Linus meant he was ready to commit to Rambling Rose. He cared about this town, and she hoped he cared about her, as well.

Chapter Eleven

Callum woke the next morning to the sound of his sister's soft singing and the smell of fresh coffee. Stephanie stood in front of the bassinet, blocking his view of the sleeping infant.

He scrubbed a hand over his eyes and they focused on Becky entering the room. She walked over to him and gently swept her fingers along his jaw, then kissed the top of his head. Her touch was comforting in a way that pricked along his nerve endings. Last night had made him far too vulnerable, more than he'd expected or felt equipped to handle.

He'd told her yesterday he wasn't a hero. He'd simply gone with his natural instinct to protect little Linus, whose young life had changed irreparably in an instant. Coupled with his need to ease the tension he saw in Becky, he'd had no choice but to get involved.

It wasn't the man he knew himself to be, and his greatest fear at this point was that she would expect from him something he wasn't capable of giving.

"Why aren't you in the bed?" Becky frowned as he stretched his neck and sat up straighter in the chair where he'd spent most of the night.

"I was afraid of falling asleep too deeply and not hearing him," he admitted. "What time is it?"

"Almost seven." Becky handed him a cup of coffee. "Stephanie and I arrived at the same time. You look like you could use this."

"Intravenously," he said with a laugh.

"Did Linus wake a lot?" Stephanie asked over her shoulder as she leaned down to pick up the baby.

"Every three hours like clockwork," Callum said, marveling at the care with which his sister held the small baby. Once again, he was struck by the maternal side he hadn't realized was part of Stephanie's makeup. "Bottle, diaper change and some deep conversations about life. The little man and I covered all the bases."

He took Becky's hand, brushing a kiss across her knuckles. "Where are the twins? I thought it was your day off so they wouldn't be coming to day care."

"A friend is watching them." At his raised brow, she added, "It's Sarah, the building manager's wife. She's really good with them, and I wanted to check in on you and Linus."

"I took a personal day," Stephanie said, finally turning toward them. "I couldn't stay away."

"Since when has your biological clock been ticking like a gong?" Callum asked his sister.

"She cares about Linus and Laurel." Becky pushed a

brown paper bag toward him with more force than was necessary. "She's got a big heart."

"Yeah," Stephanie agreed, her eyes narrowing. "Listen to your girlfriend, Callum. She's obviously the brains between the two of you."

He tried to hide the agitation that rose to the surface at Stephanie referring to Becky as his girlfriend. Of course she was his girlfriend. What else would he call a woman with whom he spent almost every night?

But something about the word gave their relationship a gravity that made his flight instinct kick into high gear. Or maybe it was just his lack of sleep. Either way, he busied himself with opening the bag and pulling out a foil-wrapped burrito.

"It's from the food truck out near Mariana's," Becky told him, her voice unusually light. "Best breakfast in town."

Callum wasn't familiar with Mariana's but didn't ask, unsure how to handle the strange current of tension running between them. If Stephanie noticed the awkwardness, she didn't mention it, all of her attention focused on the baby.

The door opened and Parker walked in, his gaze tracking between the three of them. "Then you've heard the news," he said to Becky and Callum before turning to Stephanie. "You're doing a wonderful thing."

"Holding a baby?" Callum scoffed in the way of big brothers everywhere. "She's not that impressive. Wait until she deals with her first blowout diaper."

"There'll be plenty of time for that," Parker said. "As soon as the social worker gets here, we'll finalize the paperwork."

Callum finally glanced up at Becky, who looked as confused as him. "What paperwork?" he asked.

"I haven't told them," Stephanie said, biting down on her lower lip.

"What's going on?" Callum rose from the chair, placing the coffee and breakfast on the counter. He didn't like the way Dr. Green was looking at his sister, like they shared some kind of secret.

"It's not really my news to tell," Parker said carefully. "I'll give you all some time. Stephanie, come to my office when you're ready and we'll go over a few items."

"Ready for what?" Callum demanded as the doctor closed the door behind him.

"Hush," Stephanie whispered when the baby stirred in her arms. "You're going to wake him."

"I should go, too." Becky took a step toward the door, but Callum instinctively reached out and enclosed her thin wrist with his fingers. He might bristle about putting a label on what was between them, but that didn't change the fact that he wanted her at his side.

"You're overreacting for nothing," Stephanie said, then transferred her gaze from Callum to Linus. "I've been approved as this sweetheart's foster mom."

Callum felt his mouth drop open. He looked to Becky, who seemed as bewildered as him. "Since last night?" He shook his head. "That's impossible. It takes—"

"Months," Stephanie finished. "I put in my application right when we moved. I've gotten background checks, gone through interviews." She looked up at him and cringed. "I even did a home visit that weekend in November when you, Steven and Dillon went camping."

"I don't understand." Callum prided himself on knowing every intricacy of his siblings' lives, especially Stephanie and the triplets. They'd always been close. How could she have undertaken something so monumental without telling him about it? "Do Mom and Dad know?"

"I called them this morning," his sister answered, her tone thick with emotion. How had their parents reacted to the news?

He ran a hand through his hair, fatigue and frustration threatening to engulf him. "You shouldn't have done this without running it by the family first."

Stephanie's shoulders went rigid. She carefully placed Linus into the bassinet, then took the few steps across the room to stand in front of Callum. At the same time, he felt Becky shift closer and was profoundly grateful for her sweet protectiveness, even if it was unnecessary.

As one of eight kids, Callum was well versed in sibling squabbles. He loved his family beyond measure and knew they could disagree and still maintain their closeness. But he'd never seen a fire like the one that glowed in his sister's eyes at the moment.

"I'm an adult," Stephanie said, her hands on her hips, her voice like a laser cutting through him. "Don't forget, I'm only a few years younger than you. So as much as I appreciate the big-brother-knows-all routine, you don't know everything about me. I make decisions for my life based on what is right for me." She tapped her chest with two fingers. "I'm going to be that baby's foster mom, and I will care for him like he's my own as long as he needs me."

"This will change everything," he said, although he wasn't sure whether he spoke the words for her benefit or his own. "Paws and Claws is about to open. You'll be busy with that. There's so much going on. Fostering Linus is going to—"

"Give my life more meaning," she interrupted, a gentle catch in her voice. "It will make me happy and challenge me in ways I probably can't imagine." Stephanie laughed softly. "I know what I'm getting into, Callum. You might not be ready to settle down and build a life and home in Rambling Rose, but I am."

Becky let out a startled gasp next to him, but he couldn't take his eyes off his sister. It was like seeing her for the first time, or at least seeing her in a different light. Only a few years separated them in age, but he'd taken on a protective role toward her as much as he'd had with the triplets. Now they'd all grown up.

Ashley, Megan and Nicole were going to open their restaurant in Rambling Rose, linking three more members of his family to this community. And Stephanie was becoming a foster parent to a sweet, innocent baby who needed her. Linus would be living under their roof until his future was settled. Was that odd pain in his gut the uneasy feeling of his siblings passing him by?

He'd thought he knew what he wanted from life, but now questions and doubts swirled through him like a cold gust of wind. He didn't know how to buffer his heart from the potential damage other than to close it off.

All he could control was his reaction to the present moment, and right now he understood he needed to change his attitude. He might not understand Stephanie's reasons for choosing this path, but his only job was to support her on it.

"I'm sorry," he said gently. "Blame it on sleep deprivation or—"

"Your typical high-handedness," she added, but one side of her mouth curved into a smile.

"That, too," he admitted. "You will be the most amazing foster parent. All of us, and especially Linus, are lucky you made that decision." He ran a hand through his hair. "It's one of the most selfless things I can imagine, and I'm actually in awe of you right now."

Stephanie sniffled and dabbed at the corner of her eye. "It's about time."

"It really is a gift you're giving baby Linus," Becky added. "If there's anything I can do to help you with the transition, please let me know."

For the first time since she'd revealed her plans, Stephanie looked the tiniest bit panicked. "I'll take you up on that," she told Becky. "I have the best of intentions, but very little experience with infants. And virtually no supplies."

Becky wrapped his sister in a quick hug. "That I can take care of for you."

He could see Stephanie relax and understood that response. Becky's generous spirit and quiet confidence had that effect on him, as well, easing any of the sharp edges of his life and allowing him to enjoy the small moments that meant the most.

"I'd appreciate it so much." Stephanie offered Becky a wide smile. "I'm trying to appear like I know what I'm doing, but inside I'm terrified."

If Callum hadn't felt like a jerk before, that admission sealed the deal. His sister needed his support, not judgment or doubt.

"You'll do great," Becky assured Stephanie. "While you meet with Parker and the social worker, I'll head home and gather up supplies. I didn't find out the sex of the twins during the pregnancy, so I still have tons of neutral baby clothes. I'll meet you at the ranch and get Linus settled in with you."

Stephanie nodded. "Thank you. I just realized I don't even have a car seat for him." She shook her head. "What kind of foster parent doesn't have a car seat?"

"The kind who wanted to meet her tiny charge right away." Becky squeezed Stephanie's arms, then took a step toward the door. "We keep a couple of infant seats stored in the utility closet next to the day care center in case patients need them."

"I'll go get it," Callum offered, needing to feel useful in some way. "Then I'll call Steven and Dillon to explain what's going on." He flashed a wry smile at his sister. "I can at least save you from having to deal with them the way you did me."

"It's probably good that your initial reaction was so lame." Stephanie winked. "Now you'll feel guilty about it for weeks and will happily do diaper duty or late-night feedings to make it up to me. Right?"

He wrapped her in a tight hug. "Whatever it takes, li'l sister."

Becky tried to focus on the twins' happy babbling from the back seat as she drove toward the ranch and not on the disappointed beating of her own heart.

All those silly fantasies she'd had of Callum had evaporated like dew on the grass in the morning sun. Listening to him speak to his sister about losing her freedom made Becky know that he wasn't thinking of staying. At least not now.

She had no idea how he felt about her and her girls. Sure, he liked spending time with them. And the way he touched her body in the quiet hours of night made her feel cherished. But was it all just a temporary arrangement for him?

The Fortunes were doing so much for Rambling Rose. She hated to think that he could easily move on after all the work they'd put into revitalizing the town. She'd heard rumblings that some of the locals weren't happy with all the changes. People were afraid that their community was falling prey to a sort of cowboy gentrification, and that longtime residents would be pushed aside for businesses that catered to the wealthy people moving into areas like the Rambling Rose Estates.

She knew that wasn't the intent of Callum or his brothers. They wanted to add to the community, but if his plan didn't include staying long-term, how much would Callum care about his impact?

And what about the impact he'd already had on her heart, she thought as she pulled up to the gatehouse at the entrance of the gated subdivision.

She offered a smile to the uniformed attendant, who frowned in response, giving her dusty minivan a dismissive once-over.

Acid seeped into Becky's veins. Callum and his family had never made her feel like less because of their differences in social and financial status. The man staring at her now, with his cropped cut and ice-blue gaze, managed to do just that without saying a word. The older gentleman who'd been working the first night she'd come to the ranch was nowhere in sight.

"I'm visiting the Fortunes," she said, forcing a cheerful tone.

"You aren't on the list," he said flatly.

"It's been a whirlwind kind of morning." Becky

hitched a thumb toward the cargo area of her vehicle. "I'm bringing supplies for Stephanie and her new baby. Maybe you heard about the baby relinquished at the pediatric center yesterday? The Fortunes have stepped in to care for him, and I'm helping with that."

She drew in a breath and tried to calm her beating heart. Nerves made her babble, and the way this man looked at her as if she were dirt on the bottom of his boot gave her a feeling of indignity she didn't appreciate.

Sasha began to whimper from the back seat, as if she could sense her mama's tension and wanted to offer her own kind of toddler empathy. Unfortunately, the last thing Becky needed was a meltdown on top of everything else.

"I'm Callum Fortune's girlfriend," she said, changing tactic. "He's expecting me."

"Not on the list," the man repeated. He pointed to a few open parking spaces. "You can turn around over there."

Becky almost did what he told her. That was how she was raised. Listen to authority. Don't make waves. Know your place.

This surly man was a literal gatekeeper. She was tempted to drive home and ask Callum to come and pick up the baby supplies from her house. It would be much easier that way.

If motherhood had taught her one lesson, though, it was that she possessed enough strength that she didn't have to take the easy way out. She understood how to win a battle of wills. If this dude thought he had anything on a pair of grumpy toddlers, he was sorely mistaken.

"I'm not leaving," she said, moving her sunglasses to the top of her head so she could return the gatekeeper's glare. "You can choose to trust me or you can call Callum." When the guy opened his mouth to argue, she held up a hand. "But just so we're clear, he's going to be very angry that you doubted me."

The guard's already pinched mouth thinned even further. After several long moments of staring at the clipboard in his hands, he thrust it at her. "Write down your name, address and phone number. If there are any questions, we'll know how to contact you."

"Okay," she answered and scrawled the information with trembling fingers. It had worked. She'd held her ground and gotten her way. Forcing herself not to cheer or break out in song, she returned the clipboard to him. "You made the right decision today. Thank you."

He gave a brief nod, then went into the gatehouse and hit the button to open the wrought-iron gate.

Becky drove through with a wide grin on her face. "Did you see how Mommy stood up to the rude man?" she asked her daughters, glancing at each of them in the rearview mirror. Sasha stared at her solemnly, binky shoved in her mouth, while Luna stared out the window at the rolling hills. "You girls are going to understand your worth a lot earlier than I did. I'm going to make sure you know that you deserve to be treated well all the time. No exceptions."

She blew out a shaky breath, adrenaline pumping through her at the small stand she'd taken. "We will respect authority, but also know that we should be respected, as well. I'm going to become a strong woman so I can raise strong women." She laughed at the depth of conversation she was having with her daughters.

They couldn't understand the meaning of her message but she continued to speak about their value as she drove down the winding drive that led to the Fortune ranch, needing to say the words out loud for herself as much as for them.

Callum and Steven walked down the porch steps as she pulled to a stop in front of the large house.

"How are Stephanie and Linus?" she asked as she came around the front of the car.

Steven grimaced. "Who knew our sister had the heart of a drill sergeant? She's been barking orders in a weird singsong voice since they got here."

"I don't think she wants the baby to realize that he's being cared for by a foster mom dictator," Callum added with a snort.

The brothers shared a pained look that made Becky stifle a giggle. The combined handsomeness of the two of them almost took her breath away. She knew they were stepbrothers, but the similar way they held themselves showed their family connection. She glanced up as the front door opened and the third of the Rambling Rose Fortune men appeared.

She knew from Callum that Dillon was his full-blood brother. He had sandy-blond hair and was more thickly muscled than the other two, but his features resembled Callum's. She'd met their father only on that one occasion, but both boys looked like David Fortune. She could only imagine the string of broken hearts they'd left in their collective wake and hoped to never be among that group.

"Linus is a lucky boy," Becky said, wanting to show solidarity with Stephanie.

Callum laughed softly. "Good answer."

"She sent us out here to unload the haul," Dillon told her.

Becky hit the button on the key fob to unlatch the back cargo door and then opened the side door to reveal the twins. Both girls looked with wide-eyed curiosity at the trio of handsome men staring at them.

The Fortune brothers could even dazzle ladies still in diapers. Impressive.

Luna clapped her hands as her gaze fell on Callum. "Cawl," she shouted happily.

Sasha pulled her binky from her mouth and squealed his name, as well.

"Nice fan club," Steven told Callum and then followed Dillon to the back of the vehicle.

Becky leaned in to unfasten the girls' car seats, but Callum quickly grabbed her from behind, pulling her close and reaching around to plant a gentle kiss on her throat. "Hi," he whispered against her hair.

"Your brothers will see," she protested, wiggling out of his grasp.

"I'm pretty sure they know I kiss you." He chuckled at his own joke, but released her. "Did you have any problems at the gate?"

She stilled. "Why do you ask?" She threw the questioning glance over her shoulder.

"The new guy is a real piece of work," Dillon said, reappearing with a bouncer seat. "He actually made me show him my driver's license the other night. As if I don't live here."

"I didn't have any trouble," Becky lied. It was easier to let them believe she'd made it through without incident.

"He probably took one look at you," Steven told her

as he hefted a big box of clothes, "and thought he better not mess with a boss mom."

Color rose to her cheeks. "That's me," she confirmed with a grin.

As she spoke to his brothers, Callum had reached around her to get the twins. He lifted Luna out of her car seat and handed her to Becky, then undid Sasha's car seat strap and straightened with the girl in his arms.

"Do you think Stephanie's up for visitors?" she asked, pausing at the base of the porch steps. "If you think she'd rather get settled in peace, I can come back another time."

"I know she'd love to see you," Callum told her with a smile. "She's already started a list of baby care questions for you. I think she's hoping you'll be her expert resource."

"Anything I can do to help." Becky followed him up the steps and he paused to let her enter the house before him.

"I really appreciate—"

When his words cut off, Becky glanced up at him.

"I appreciate you," he said, the intensity of his tone sending shivers down her spine.

She drew in a breath. Maybe she hadn't misinterpreted how he felt. Maybe her heart was safe with Callum after all. Could she dare to believe that?

Chapter Twelve

Callum sat in his truck, finger hovering above the send button on his phone. It was nearly midnight, and he should be home and in bed. The problem was he didn't want to be in his bed, not without the woman whose house he'd been parked outside for the past fifteen minutes.

He'd driven to Becky's on a whim, without a plan for what to do once he arrived. If he texted her, would it look like a booty call? He didn't mean it that way and certainly wanted to avoid giving her that message. Not that holding Becky in his arms wasn't as damn near close to perfection as he could imagine.

But after the unexpected events of the last twenty-four hours, he craved something more. The comfort he found in her arms.

Linus's arrival and the thought of the baby's mother

out there in the world, so desperate that giving up her son felt like the best option, had rocked him to his core. Despite the unrest in his early years from his parents' contentious divorce, Callum had always known love growing up. Marci had come into their lives and immediately taken him and Dillon into her heart.

Even when her health suffered during those years of trying to conceive again and after the triplets' birth, she'd never wavered in her maternal devotion. He'd had two parents who loved him and a gaggle of siblings who made him crazy but also helped him to never feel truly alone.

The baby his sister had taken on had been abandoned in the world. At least for now. He knew Stephanie would do everything in her power to love and protect little Linus. His sister had shown a depth of spirit and service that humbled Callum. He couldn't force himself to commit to staying in Rambling Rose long-term because of the risk of being hurt, or causing pain to someone who loved him, the way he had with Doralee.

He'd never thought of himself as a coward. He'd established his company and grown the business to the point where he could cherry-pick the most appealing projects. His brothers had found a place with him, and he'd naively assumed that his success as a real estate developer and contractor was enough for a fulfilling life.

A couple of hours ago he'd understood how far he truly had to go, and it had terrified him.

A part of him had wanted to cut and run. He'd gotten in his car after an hour of restless tossing and turning, not sure whether to head out of town or just drive until exhaustion sent him home again. Almost unaware of where he was going, he'd ended up at Becky's.

He startled as his phone vibrated now, the tone alerting him to an incoming message.

Are you going to sit in your truck all night or come in?

A text from Becky.

He glanced through his windshield toward the house to see Becky standing at the family room window, the lamp behind her bathing her in light.

His fingers trembled as he typed in a two-letter response.

In.

He climbed out of the truck and headed for the front door, heart pounding.

Becky met him at the door, her honey-colored eyes unreadable. She wore a thin cotton nightgown with two kittens curled together on the front and the words *snooze squad* scrawled beneath them. He must have it bad when he found kittens sexy as hell.

"I know it's late," he said, offering an apologetic smile. "If I woke you I'm—"

His words were cut off when she launched herself at him, wrapping her arms around his neck as she fused her mouth to his.

He lifted her off the ground as he stepped into the house, kicking the door shut behind him. She seemed as frenzied with need as he felt, like she couldn't get enough of him. Her tongue delved into his mouth, and he groaned out loud, almost stumbling at the power of the desire pulsing through him.

Instead of moving toward the bedroom, he detoured into the nearby family room and lowered her to the couch. "I need you so badly," he whispered, shocked by the intensity of his own voice.

"Yes," she answered, smoothing her soft hands across his face. "Please, Callum."

It was as if he'd devolved into some kind of inexperienced schoolboy overwhelmed at the possibility of a night with his biggest crush.

In such a short time, Becky had come to mean so much to him. He still couldn't allow himself to acknowledge the depth of his feelings in his heart or mind, but his body seemed to have no such constraints.

It took only a few seconds to pull the sweatshirt he wore over his head and unfasten the button on his jeans. He paused then because Becky had sat up on the sofa and taken off her nightgown. She sat before him in only a pair of lacy blue panties, the perfection of her body making his mouth go dry.

"You never cease to blow me away with your beauty."

"You should close the curtains," she told him with a slight smile. "Before you give my neighbors a glimpse of a full Fortune moon."

He yanked the ends of the linen drapes together, then kicked off his shoes and pushed his jeans and boxers down over his hips. He grabbed his wallet from his pocket before stepping out of them, taking out the condom packet as he turned back to her.

"It goes both ways," she said as he moved toward her. "The way you look takes my breath away." She bit down on her full lower lip. "And the way you look at me makes me want you more than I thought was possible."

He closed the distance between them and lowered himself over her, taking her mouth in a kiss that he hoped communicated everything he wasn't able to say out loud. As the kisses deepened, he moved his hand down her body, loving the feel of her soft skin and the way she arched into his touch. He cupped one full breast in his palm, skimming his thumb over the sensitive peak.

She moaned, and he caught the sweet sound in his mouth. Then he moved lower, snagging the waistband of her panties with his fingers. Trailing kisses down her throat and chest, he continued to move lower, pushing the scrap of cotton over her hips and lower until she was completely naked under him.

He gently spread her legs and pressed a kiss to the most intimate part of her. She gasped and reflexively stiffened, but he murmured words of encouragement and praise, feeling like he'd won some kind of lottery when she relaxed again.

"Let me have all of you," he told her, glancing up to meet her desire-hazed gaze.

She gave a shaky nod, and he turned all of his attention to pleasing her. With his tongue and lips and fingers he explored her, gratified at the sensual noises she made.

Soon her whispered words became a chorus of *yes* and *please* and his name. When the release broke over her, it was almost his undoing. Her body seemed to come apart with pleasure.

He plucked up the condom packet he'd dropped to the floor, ripped it open with his teeth and then sheathed himself. As he positioned himself above her, she gave him a smile that just about melted his heart. This was how he wanted to make her feel all the time—languid and blissfully content.

She reached for him, opening again and taking the length of him as if they'd been made to fit together. They moved as one and he lost track of where she started and he began. As pressure built inside him, he tried to tamp it down. His needs didn't matter until she was fully satisfied.

Her nails skimmed lightly across his back, sending quivers of need swirling through him. He lost track of time and place, lost in the moment and the joy of sharing it with Becky.

When she finally cried out his name and her body clenched around him, his breath caught in his throat. The release roared through him like a runaway train, pounding euphoria through every cell in his body.

He'd never experienced something so intense, and the force of it caught him off guard. His body tightened for several long seconds as he was suspended in a maelstrom of emotion. As the shockwaves subsided, he lowered his head, nuzzling the side of her neck.

She smelled of citrus and woman, a combination that he would forever associate with Becky.

He almost laughed at the thought that he'd never be able to smell the scent of lemons without thinking of this moment.

She pushed her fingers into his hair, and he lifted his head to drop a kiss on her forehead. "Sorry I ruined your good night's sleep."

She flashed a slow smile. "I'll forgive you this time."

Her eyes darkened. "What brought you here tonight, Callum?"

"I wanted you." He didn't dare try to express to her all the emotions tumbling through him. The level of need he felt. At this point, it was easier if she believed their physical connection had led him to her. Anything more would reveal too much.

She continued to smile but for an instant he would have sworn a shadow passed over her gaze. "I'm glad," she answered, although he got the feeling she wanted to say more.

He didn't want the moment to end but forced himself to get up, grabbing his boxers from the floor. "I'll be right back," he told her, hoping he was imagining the awkwardness suddenly radiating between them.

It took him only a few minutes in the bathroom, and he figured she might have moved to her bedroom in the meantime. Instead, he saw the glow of a light coming from the kitchen.

As he entered the room, Becky gave him a tight smile. "Thanks again for stopping by." She held out his jeans and T-shirt, which she'd folded into a neat pile along with his socks and shoes. "You'll probably want to get dressed before heading out."

"Um…" He frowned but took the clothes from her. "Yeah. Is everything okay?"

"Fine." Another stiff smile. "I have an early day tomorrow, though, so I should get to sleep."

"Sure." He realized he sounded like an idiot with all of his one-word responses, but her actions left him rattled. They'd just shared mind-blowing intimacy, the best of his life. Now she was basically kicking him out.

What the hell?

Instead of arguing or asking for an explanation, he quickly donned his clothes and shoved his feet into the boots. As far as she knew, he'd gotten what he came for and if he wasn't willing to reveal the depth of his feelings for her, he didn't deserve any more.

She stood leaning against the cabinets on the far side of the room, her expression guarded. The adorable kittens on the front of her nightgown seemed to taunt him. They had a place here, and he had a big pile of nothing.

Because he had nothing to offer. And apparently Becky knew it.

"Thanks again for…" What exactly should he say?

Her chest rose and fell on a quick inhalation of breath.

"Everything," he finished softly.

The smile that curved her lips looked forced, but he didn't ask about it. Not when his own emotions felt too jumbled and unsure.

"I'll talk to you tomorrow," she told him as she walked him to the front door. "Or I guess I should say later today."

He sighed. "I'm sorry I woke you tonight." He had to offer something.

"You didn't. I got up to check on the girls and saw your truck out the window. I'm glad I saw you." She shook her head and huffed out a faint laugh. "Otherwise, you could still be sitting at the curb."

Why did he feel like he was being kicked there now?

She gave him a quick kiss after opening the front door. "Good night, Callum."

He said good-night and a moment later stood alone in the darkness of an empty January night.

* * *

"I'm the one who's sleep deprived," Stephanie told Callum later that week as they stood in the front lobby of the veterinary clinic. "Why are you so grumpy?"

"I'm not grumpy," he answered through clenched teeth, earning a laugh from his sister.

When he didn't respond, she sucked in a quick breath. "Tell me there's not another delay for the clinic." She gestured to the men carrying in the new cabinets for installation. "You and Steven managed to avoid one potential disaster. My nerves can't take another one at this point, not with the opening coming up so quickly."

He pulled out his phone and glanced at it for what felt like the hundredth time that morning, then lifted his gaze to Stephanie's. "Everything's on track. The crew will be putting in some long hours, but the facility is going to open on time and be fully functioning." He flicked another look at the annoyingly dark phone screen and then added, "It's all good."

"Something isn't right with you." Stephanie reached out a finger and tapped it on the edge of his phone case. "Are you angry about Linus?"

Callum blinked. "What are you talking about?"

"I get that you had your fill of kids underfoot when we were growing up." She flashed a weak smile. "Even though he's still tiny, it's kind of shocking how much stuff comes along with having a baby. The peacefulness of the house has been disrupted, and I'd understand if you resent the intrusion."

"I don't," he told her, shocked and a bit chagrinned that he'd given off that impression. "Linus is adorable and I meant it when I said you're doing an amazing thing for that baby."

"Yes," she agreed slowly. "But I'm beginning to wonder about Laurel returning. No one has heard from her." Stephanie crossed her arms over her chest. "Of course I'm happy to keep him for as long as needed, but I guess I thought it would be a short-term placement. What if his mama doesn't return to claim him?"

Callum looped an arm around his sister's shoulder. "Then he'll be lucky he's got you as a foster mom. I'm sorry I made you question whether I'm okay with having Linus in the house. Make no mistake, Stephanie. He's where he needs to be, and I support you 100 percent." He squeezed her arm. "The baby routine is an adjustment for all us, but I wouldn't have it any other way." He frowned. "I like babies. Hell, I helped take care of the triplets for years. And Becky's girls love me. Why do people think I'm antibaby?"

She patted a hand against his chest. "That's funny. No one believes that, but you've made it pretty clear that domesticity isn't your cup of tea at this point. I don't necessarily agree with that and would offer Becky and the twins up as evidence to the contrary, but—"

"Do you think that's why she's avoiding me?" he blurted.

Stephanie took a step away from him, inclining her head. "I didn't realize she was, but it certainly explains your mood."

"My mood is fine," he growled.

"Uh-huh. Tell me more about being ghosted."

He ran a hand through his hair, glancing around to make sure no one could overhear them. From Callum's experience, construction workers liked to gossip as much as a posse of teenage girls. The last thing he needed was to be the topic of conversation for his crew.

"I wouldn't call it ghosting. We had lunch once this week and I took her and the girls to dinner last night. She's not ignoring me completely, but there's a distance between us, even when we're together. I can't figure out why or what's causing it."

His sister frowned. "When did it start?"

"After Linus arrived at the pediatric center," he said after thinking on it for a few seconds. "But that doesn't make sense. Becky has a clear attachment to his welfare. I think she bonded with Laurel on that first day."

"Becky has been an amazing support for me," Stephanie said with a nod. "She checks in several times a day and answers every tiny question I have right away. Since he started going to the day care at the center at the beginning of the week, she's made a point of stopping by and sends me updates on how he's doing. I don't get any strange vibes from her."

"Then what could it be?" Callum shook his head, frustrated that he couldn't figure this out. Part of why he was so successful in the renovation business was his love of solving complex problems. With a historic building or old property in need of revitalization, there were always unique challenges that didn't present themselves with new construction. He thrived on managing those kinds of issues. The fact that he couldn't seem to decipher the actions of one woman made him want to shout in frustration.

The toe of Stephanie's boot tapped on the newly installed floor. "Have you been an idiot?"

"What kind of question is that?"

"A valid one based on your defensive tone."

He shook his head. "I don't know. I don't think so. I like her. She likes me. Her girls like me."

"Are you sure *like* is the *L* word you're looking for at the moment?"

"Stop." He held up a hand. "It's been a few weeks. You know what a bad bet I am, Stephanie. We can't rush into anything when I don't even know if I'm staying in Rambling Rose."

She shook her head. "That's your past talking, Callum. Not your future. You know Dad always says it only took him a moment to know Mom was the one. If he'd let his divorce from your mother define him, our family wouldn't be what it is today."

Callum swallowed. How could he explain to the sister who looked up to him that their father was a better man in so many ways?

"Maybe she's just changed her mind about things," he forced himself to say. "I know she was wary of getting involved in the first place because of the twins. They're her priority and I respect that. It could be as simple as Becky not wanting her life complicated."

"You sound pathetic," his sister told him.

He rolled his eyes. "Not at all helpful."

"Could be the kind of help you need is a swift kick in the pants."

"Forget I mentioned anything."

"I want you to be happy," Stephanie said, her tone gentler. "Tell me if there's anything I can do. Maybe I could talk to Becky for you?"

"No." He shook his head. "This isn't junior high where I need you to pass her a note and have her check the box whether or not she likes me."

"I hated those notes," his sister murmured. "So much pressure."

"Yeah." Feeling pressured was exactly his problem at the moment. But he didn't want to push Becky until he felt certain about what he could offer her. If only he could work out the puzzle of his heart, maybe everything else would fall into place.

Chapter Thirteen

Becky sat in front of the computer at the nurses' station entering stats on a recent patient when she felt someone watching her. She looked up to find Sharla and Kristen staring at her from the other side of the counter.

"I didn't eat the last doughnut," she lied without hesitation, wiping a finger across her bottom lip in case any leftover crumbs might give her away.

"We're not here about doughnuts," Sharla said, crossing her arms over her ample chest.

Kristen nodded in agreement. "We just saw Callum Fortune walking out of the building looking like someone stole his new puppy."

"He doesn't have a puppy," Becky muttered, refocusing on the computer.

"What's going on with the two of you?" Sharla demanded. "Don't tell us you're going to waste your chance with a man who is hot, rich and clearly way into you."

Dragging in a slow breath, Becky pushed back from the desk and stood. "I'm not telling you anything. There's nothing to tell."

"We haven't seen the two of you together as much lately," Kristen pointed out, none too helpfully.

"Things are busy around here," Becky countered. "As you'd know if you stopped trying to pump me for information."

Sharla arched a superbly penciled brow. "Defensive much?"

Becky set her jaw and returned the other woman's steely stare. "I'm not…" She paused, concentrating on the air that seemed caught in her lungs like a moth in a spider's web. "I don't know what's going on." She glanced around to make sure no one could overhear their conversation. "I did a really stupid thing."

"You're pregnant again," Sharla guessed, her eyes widening.

"No." Becky shook her head. "I fell in love with him."

Kristen reached out a hand and squeezed Becky's trembling hand. "Oh, honey. You're only human."

Becky laughed. "Right?" she agreed. "The problem is I don't know how he feels about me. I'm not even certain he's planning to stay in Rambling Rose long term. What if I give him my heart and he breaks it?"

Sharla started to answer, then snapped her mouth shut when one of the exam rooms opened and Parker walked out. "We're just waiting on a lab report and then they'll need a follow-up appointment." He approached the desk. "Everything okay here?" he asked, concern in his tone.

"Peachy keen, Dr. Green," Kristen answered.

He must have heard something in her voice that made him wary because he stopped in his tracks and immediately pulled his phone out of the pocket of his white lab coat. "Look at that. I need to return this call. I'm going to just… I need to go my office." He flashed a tight smile. "And close the door."

"We'll hold down the fort out here," Sharla told him.

"I'm going to go check on the family waiting for labs," Kristen said, then pointed a finger at Becky. "Whatever Sharla tells you, that's what you're going to do. No questions asked."

Becky gave a small shake of her head. "I don't know about—"

"No questions," the redheaded nurse repeated.

"Okay," Becky whispered, watching Kristen disappear into the exam room.

Sharla propped her elbows on the desk and leaned in. "Have you told him you love him?"

"Of course not."

"Do you think you might want to start there?"

"What if it freaks him out and he breaks up with me?"

"What if he feels the same way and doesn't know how to tell you because you're acting so strange?"

"I'm not acting…" She clasped a hand over her mouth when a sob tried to break free. "It wasn't supposed to happen like this," she said, more to herself than Sharla. "I already had my love story. Rick was the love of my life. If I tell Callum I love him, am I being disloyal to my late husband? Am I a terrible person?"

"For wanting to be truly happy again after overcoming a tragedy no one should have to face?" Sharla offered a tender smile. "Of course not. You're a good person, Beck, and an amazing mother. I didn't know your late husband, but I can only imagine he'd be proud of the life you'd made for your girls. You deserve happiness."

"Thank you," Becky whispered. She hadn't realized how badly she needed someone to give her that permission until her friend did. "I don't just want to blurt out the words while we're taking turns feeding the twins. I know Callum cares about the girls and they will always be my priority, but I'd like to do something special for him." She shrugged. "Romantic gestures aren't exactly my forte. Any ideas?"

"Oh, girl." Sharla swiped at her eyes, then grinned like the cat that ate the canary. "I've got you covered on romance."

"You need to come with us."

Callum turned from where he was meeting with the foreman at The Shoppes to find Steven and Dillon striding toward him.

"What happened? Is it Linus? Stephanie?" He threw up his hands. "What's going on?"

"Bro, chill. Everything's fine." Dillon gave him a strange look. "You're wound as tight as a top."

"We've got a lot of work going on," he told his brother, gesturing to several dozen pallets of lumber lined against the far wall. "In case you haven't noticed."

"I've noticed," Dillon told him. "And we've got it all covered."

"At least for the next twenty-four hours," Steven added with a smug smile.

"You two aren't making any sense." Callum narrowed his eyes. "Are you drunk?"

"Give us a couple of minutes, Dan," Steven told the older foreman when he chuckled at Callum's accusatory question.

"Sure thing, bosses." The wiry man with a shaggy beard walked toward the space where the electricians were roughing in recessed lighting.

"Seriously, you need to loosen up." Dillon walked behind Callum and half guided, half pushed him toward the door.

"You still haven't explained what's going on," Callum said through clenched teeth. His patience was at an all-time low. He hadn't seen Becky since he'd stopped by the pediatric center yesterday, and she'd done little more than give him a swift kiss before turning her attention back to whatever she was doing on her large desktop monitor.

Not that he expected her to drop her work for him, but he missed her. He missed the closeness they'd had and hated the tension he couldn't quite put his finger on that seemed to pulse between them.

He'd texted her earlier in the morning, but hadn't received a response. And no, he told himself, he definitely wasn't compulsively checking his phone in case he'd missed the tone or vibration of an incoming message.

"Do you trust me?" Dillon asked as he continued to herd him like a farm animal.

"Normally, yes." Callum shrugged off his brother's grasp but continued walking to the building's entrance. "Right now I trust you about as far as I can throw you."

He pointed a finger at Steven, who stood holding open the front door.

"You'll be sorry you doubted us in about ten seconds," his brother warned with a Cheshire cat smile. "What do you think of that Corvette over there?" He gestured toward a vintage sports car parked in the shopping mall's empty lot.

"It's a beauty." Callum squinted at the cherry-red vehicle, shading his eyes from the bright winter sunlight. "Did you buy a..." His voice trailed off as Becky appeared from the driver's side. Her hair tumbled over her shoulders and she offered a tentative wave.

"Waiting for the apology," Steven said with a nudge.

"What's going on?" Callum whispered. "Why is she here?"

"Your girlfriend has more appreciation for romance in her pinkie finger," Dillon said, thrusting a duffel bag into Callum's arms, "than you do in your entire lunkheaded body."

"Becky arranged an overnight getaway for the two of you," Steven explained. "We're covering you for the next twenty-four hours. A smart man would stop asking questions, mute his phone and go kiss the beautiful woman waiting for him."

Callum's mind might be spinning in a thousand different directions, but he wasn't a total idiot. "You two are the greatest brothers in the history of the world. If you tell Wiley I said that, I'll deny it. But thank you."

"Have fun," Steven told him with a grin.

"Don't do anything I wouldn't do," Dillon added.

When Callum shot him a look, his younger brother laughed. "I'm giving you a wide berth of options."

"I think I can handle it," he murmured, flipping his

phone to silent mode. He slung the duffel over his shoulder and headed toward Becky.

She watched him approach, looking almost as wary as she did excited. "I hope you don't mind a little kidnapping," she said.

He cupped her cheeks between his palms and kissed her by way of an answer, ignoring the cheers and wolf whistles from his brothers.

"Are you sure about this?" he asked when they finally broke apart several minutes later. He smoothed the pads of his thumbs over her cheeks. "What about the girls?"

"Sarah and Grant are staying with them for the night," she answered, and he couldn't help but hear the catch in her voice.

"You don't have to leave them," he assured her. "I don't need a getaway, Becky. Any time we have together is special."

"I want this night," she said, her gaze sure and steady as she looked into his eyes. "If you do?"

"More than anything," he said and kissed her again.

They climbed into the car, and Becky pulled out onto the road that led to the highway.

"New ride?" Callum asked, grinning as she giggled at the Corvette's rapid acceleration.

"It's Grant's weekend car," she explained. "He inherited it from an uncle who lived in Florida. I guess he and Sarah don't drive it much around Rambling Rose, but he thought it would be more of a statement than picking you up in the minivan. I know it's not as fancy as the Audi, but—"

"You could pick me up on a bicycle, and I'd be happy."

"This is way more fun than a bike ride," she said with a wink.

He laughed. "That's true. Can I ask where we're headed?"

"Austin. We have reservations for dinner at a farm-to-table restaurant that has great reviews, and then a room at the Driskill. Your sister recommended the hotel, and the photos online look amazing."

"Everything about this is amazing," he told her without reservation.

After the doubts and worry that had been weighing on Callum's mind the past few days, being swept away for a romantic night in the city was the last thing he would have expected. Excitement zipped through him. He and Becky talked and laughed as she drove, and a heavy weight slowly lifted off his chest, replaced with an almost giddy lightness.

He could imagine how much it took for her to leave Sasha and Luna for the night, even with friends she trusted. It humbled him that she'd made that choice in order to spend more time with him.

The day was clear with the winter sun shining down on them like a bright omen. They arrived in Austin in the late afternoon and checked into the hotel located in the heart of downtown. Becky seemed enchanted by the Driskill's opulent lobby and the old-world charm of the decor. She insisted on giving her credit card to the front desk, and while Callum appreciated the gesture, he hoped he could convince her to allow him to pay for both dinner and the room. Just the fact that she'd arranged this evening meant the world to him.

He carried his duffel and her overnight bag to the room and watched with delight as Becky marveled over every understated but luxurious detail of the hotel. He liked seeing the world through her eyes. Despite all she'd been through, Becky still seemed able to appreciate the small joys.

"Oh, my gosh."

He was taking in the view from the room's wide window when she rushed out of the bathroom.

"There are three shower heads in one shower. I've only seen that on fancy home improvement shows."

Tenderness radiated through his heart and he pressed two fingers to his chest, unable to identify the feeling. Unwilling was more like it. He understood on some level that if he acknowledged the depth of his emotions toward this woman, they would change him in ways he couldn't handle at the moment.

So Callum did what he seemed to do best where Becky was concerned. He shoved down all the unfathomable feelings and concentrated on what was simple.

His need for her.

"We have some time before the dinner reservation." He made a show of looking at his watch as he walked toward her. "Just enough time by my calculations."

She bit down on her lower lip, sending a wave of lust rushing through him. "Enough time for what?"

"For the best shower of your life."

Her eyes went even darker. "You sound pretty confident about that."

"One thing I'm not lacking—" he nipped at the edge of her mouth "—is confidence in my ability to please you."

"That makes two of us," she said and led him into the hotel room's oversize bathroom.

* * *

"Can you zip me?" Becky asked, walking out of the bathroom later that evening.

Callum gave her an exaggerated ogle. "If I say no, can we get naked again and order room service for dinner?"

She rolled her eyes. "We've been naked pretty much since arriving in Austin," she reminded him.

"Best trip ever," he agreed.

The look in his dark eyes made her heart flutter. She never wanted that feeling to end, and somehow she knew with Callum it would last forever. Or at least as long as they had together. They'd had a magical afternoon, first in the shower and then moving to the bed. Part of her wanted to take him up on his half-joking offer. To spend the entire night wrapped in his arms.

But she gave a playful shake of her head and turned her back to him. "I've never been to Austin. We're hitting the town before we hit the sheets again."

"Whatever you want," he whispered, placing a gentle kiss on her exposed back before zipping up the dress. "You look beautiful tonight."

Becky drew in a deep breath as she glanced in the mirror that hung above the hotel room's cherry dresser. She felt beautiful. She'd bought the dress she wore, a silk sheath in a gorgeous blue, just before she found out she was pregnant. Only a few weeks prior to the accident that had claimed her husband's life.

When she went to pack for the trip early this morning, she'd found it shoved in the back of her closet, tags still intact.

Tears had pricked her eyes at the memory of those

dark days after Rick's death. She'd been desperate and overwhelmed, unsure of how she was supposed to manage her world without him. At that time, she hadn't even been able to imagine a moment when she'd feel as happy as she did right now.

Things weren't settled between her and Callum. She hadn't yet told him the three little words that could change everything. *I love you.* She wanted to wait for the right moment, but the longer she put it off the more significance the declaration seemed to take on in her mind and heart.

Still, the past few hours had bolstered her confidence. Callum seemed relaxed in a way that felt like a positive sign for the future. She couldn't imagine that he wouldn't return her feelings. Even if he wasn't ready to say the words back to her, she knew in her heart that he cared. Every thoughtful touch, every intense look made her know that she mattered to him.

As long as they were both willing to work at it, she believed they could overcome the pain of their individual pasts to build a shared future that would last a lifetime.

Chapter Fourteen

As they walked back to the Driskill later that night, Becky felt like she was floating on air, her feet barely touching the sidewalk.

"This night has been wonderful." They held hands, and his thumb grazing the pulse on her wrist made shivers track along her spine. "Austin is such a great city." She glanced up to the historic buildings they passed on their way to the hotel. "I can't believe how much of Texas I haven't seen when I've lived here all my life."

"Your parents didn't take you on many vacations?"

She shrugged, the mix of bitterness and affection she always felt when thinking of her parents settling over her like a blanket. At the moment, affection for them won out. It was difficult to feel anything but happy with her heart so full.

"My parents are simple people. They didn't feel like

they needed to travel, and money was always tight. My grandma and grandpa lived down on the coast, so I spent most summers with them. Even though I didn't go anywhere special, I never felt the lack of it growing up. I loved spending long days exploring the woods near their house and taking trips to the beach. Those memories are part of why we moved to Rambling Rose. I didn't want to raise my family in the city. Wide-open spaces are important."

"What about after you were married?" he asked quietly.

They were almost to the hotel, and she paused to enjoy the lights of the city. One day when they were older, she'd bring the girls here for a long weekend. They'd go to the zoo and the children's museum. She wanted to give them every experience she could so they'd understand life was an adventure. Hope burned in her like a flame that she and Callum might share that adventure.

It was strange to be thinking of that after he'd asked a question about her late husband. She wanted to believe Rick would be happy for her finding love again. He was that kind of man, and she knew he'd approve of Callum.

She glanced up at Callum, then straight ahead again. It was too difficult to share these deeply personal parts of herself while looking into his dark eyes. "Rick didn't talk about it, but he supported his mom financially from the time he graduated high school. His parents had divorced and his mom was an alcoholic, in and out of rehab. They weren't exactly close, but he loved her and wanted to take care of her." She took comfort in the steady pressure of Callum's hand holding hers.

"She was diagnosed with ovarian cancer after two

years of sobriety. Rick and I had just gotten married. We decided to postpone the honeymoon so that he could be with her through the surgery and treatments."

"He sounds like a wonderful son."

"He was a good man," she agreed. "His mom didn't have much in the way of health insurance, so there were a lot of doctor and hospital bills. We took care of as many of them as we could, but that meant there wasn't much money left over." That period ran through her mind like a movie. It had been stressful on Rick and on their marriage, but she would have never argued with his need to take care of his mother. "I guess my whole point is I haven't had a lot of opportunity for traveling."

"You can change that," he told her, lifting his free hand to tuck a lock of hair behind her ear.

"Oh, yes." She laughed. "One-year-old twins are really portable. There will be time for adventures. And I plan to take the girls on as many of them as I can manage."

With you at my side, she added silently. She should just say the words. Put them out there so that he knew how she felt.

But something held her back.

Callum wrapped his arms around her and pulled her close. "The more I learn about you, Becky, the more impressed I am at what a spectacular person you are."

"Anyone would do the same in my situation," she said automatically.

"I don't know about that." He kissed the top of her head. "I think you're special."

"Thanks," she whispered.

"Your late husband was a lucky man."

"I was the lucky one," she corrected, then pulled away to look at him. "I still am."

His jaw tensed for a split second before he flashed a smile. "We should get back to the hotel. It's late, and I have plans for you."

"For us." She lifted a hand to his face, smoothing her fingers over his stubbled jaw. "We're in this together."

"Together," he repeated softly.

Now, she told herself. *Tell him now.*

Her breath hitched and her mouth went dry. Why was saying she loved him so darn difficult? Was she truly so afraid of his reaction, or could it have more to do with the feeling of being disloyal to her late husband?

That thought made her stomach clench. She took Callum's hand and continued toward the hotel, hoping her sudden silence didn't tip him off to her emotions.

As difficult as it was to express how she felt, Becky had no trouble telling him everything she wanted to say with her body. Every time they came together, she learned more about both Callum and herself. And when she drifted off to sleep in his warm embrace, Becky couldn't help but believe everything would work out for the best.

The next morning, Becky and Callum checked out of the hotel and then walked to a popular breakfast spot a few blocks away. After filling up on omelets and stuffed French toast, they headed for a path near Lady Bird Lake. The temperatures hovered in the high fifties with low clouds on the horizon that meant they might be driving back to Rambling Rose in the rain.

A mother jogging behind a double stroller on the trail made her miss her girls. As lovely as the evening had been, she couldn't wait to get home and hug her babies. Sarah had FaceTimed her earlier, and the twins had smiled and blown kisses, bringing happy tears to Becky's eyes.

She felt refreshed but also anxious. She'd promised herself that before they left Austin to return to Rambling Rose, she'd talk to him about their future together.

"I hate for our getaway to end," Callum said with a charming grin. "I appreciate all the work you put into making last night special. It's going to be hard to top that as far as romance goes." He leaned in closer. "But I've got a few tricks up my sleeve."

She stopped walking and turned to fully face him. "I love you," she blurted.

He blinked and then blinked some more.

Becky opened her mouth, an apology ready to slip from her tongue. But no. She wasn't sorry. Even though Callum looked at her as if she'd just sprouted a second head, she didn't regret telling him how she felt. Maybe she could have done it with a bit more eloquence, but already she felt less nervous than she'd been since she'd decided she had to tell him.

"It's okay if you can't say it back to me." She offered what she hoped passed for an encouraging smile. "I don't want to rush things, but I needed to share that. You're an amazing man and these past few weeks have made me happier than I've been in a long time. I want it to continue. I want us to continue." The anxiety that had melted away for a moment began to reform, congealing in her belly like curdled milk. Something was wrong with Callum, and she couldn't bear to consider the reason for his reaction.

He continued to stare at her, then turned on his heel

and stalked several steps away. His shoulders went rigid with tension as he raked a stiff hand through his hair.

Something was very wrong.

"Callum." She moved toward him, reaching out a hand.

The moment she touched him, he recoiled, spinning to face her again.

"I'm leaving, Becky."

"Excuse me?" Her mind reeled. "I get it. We're both leaving this morning but—"

"Rambling Rose." He shook his head as if trying to shake his thoughts into some order. "Not for a while, at least not until the first round of projects opens. But after that…" He gave her an apologetic shrug. "I have to go."

"Why?" She breathed out the word on a ragged puff of air. "You love it in Rambling Rose." *I thought you loved me*, her heart screamed.

"I'm sorry," he said, sounding as miserable as she felt. "My business takes me all over the place. It's how things have always been."

"But they don't have to continue that way," she insisted. It wasn't like Becky to push. Normally she accepted whatever someone told her as fact and didn't argue or put up a fight. Her love for Callum made her a fighter. "I don't care if you travel. We can find a way to make it work. You and me together, Callum. I want—"

"That's just it." He started walking toward the street that led to the hotel, and she fell in step beside him, trying to make sense of what he was saying. "This isn't only about you and me. You have the girls to consider."

"They love you, too." As soon as the words were out of her mouth, she realized they were wrong. For a man clearly terrified of commitment, hearing that a pair of toddler twins cared about him might send him running even faster in the opposite direction.

"I don't want to hurt the girls or you."

"You already are," she told him, forcing herself to be honest. "I think you're hurting yourself the most. By believing the worst or that you're incapable of commitment or whatever bogus line you're telling yourself in your head and your heart. You're hurting all of us."

His step faltered as he glanced down on her, a pain so raw etched across his features it took her breath away. They'd come to the hotel's entrance, and she watched as couples, families and the hotel's efficient valet staff moved about. She thought she might have finally gotten through to Callum. Made it past whatever defenses he'd erected to avoid risking his heart.

But instead of uttering the words she longed to hear, he opened his mouth, then closed it again, shaking his head. "I'll get the car from the valet. I can drive home if you want."

"Sure," she whispered. *Home.* The word ricocheted around her mind like a bullet tearing through flesh. Callum had come to mean so much to her. He'd made her lonely little house feel like a home. But it had all been an illusion. No wonder she hadn't been able to express her feelings before now. Apparently, she should have trusted her preservation instincts.

Now she wanted to run and hide.

Instead, she wiped the emotion from her features and thanked the valet who opened the Corvette's passenger door for her. Everything about the past twenty-four hours seemed to mock her. The time she'd taken to set it up. Borrowing the car and making reservations.

The fact that she thought last night was a turning point in their relationship.

Turning it all to hell.

Callum climbed in behind the wheel and pulled out onto the downtown street. "Becky, I know—"

"You don't know anything," she said, working to keep her heartache in check. "I'm done talking for a while, Callum. I just want to go home and see my girls."

He gave a sharp nod, and a strained silence fell between them. Becky closed her eyes and let the sound of the engine lull her to sleep. As broken and rejected as she felt, somehow her body knew she needed a respite from the pain. It felt like only minutes passed, but the next time she opened her eyes they were pulling off the highway toward Rambling Rose.

"I guess I owe you an apology for keeping you awake most of last night," Callum said, flashing a sheepish smile. "You needed some extra sleep."

"I'm a single mother," she answered stonily, swiping a finger across the side of her mouth in case she'd drooled during her nap. "I always need sleep."

His smile faded. "I handled things badly this morning. I'm sorry. It's a huge honor to hear your feelings for me. I wish I could be the man to deserve your love."

"Seriously?" She took a deep breath. "Are you really going to give me the line about how 'it isn't you, it's me'? You're a good man, Callum. Everyone except you seems to realize it."

"I don't think I'm a bad guy," he said slowly as he pulled to a stop in the parking lot at The Shoppes, where the Fortune brothers had their modular office. "But I know I can't give you what you need."

Becky unbuckled her seat belt. "*Can't* and *won't* are two different things."

His eyes widened slightly.

She still wasn't ready to play nice when so much was on the line. She'd loved and lost once before. The tragedy and sorrow of her husband's accident had brought her to her knees, literally and figuratively. It had taken a long time for her to manage to get up on her feet again. As much as her heart hurt, she wouldn't let herself fall back down again.

"I'm sorry," he repeated. "This doesn't mean things have to end between us right now. I'm leaving tomorrow on a scouting trip to San Antonio for a couple of days but when I get back—"

"San Antonio?" She turned to face him. "So you already have a plan for where you're moving next?"

"Not exactly a plan, but Fortune Brothers Construction has a few irons in the fire."

She swallowed against the bile rising in her throat. He'd known all this time he was leaving. She shouldn't be surprised. Callum hadn't made promises to her. Yet how could she have misread the situation so completely?

"It would be better if we ended this now," she managed, not bothering to worry that a tiny sob slipped out along with the words. She dabbed at the corners of her eyes. "I need to think about the future for myself and my girls. If you aren't going to be a part of it, there's no point in continuing."

"I care about you, Becky."

"It's not enough." Before he could answer, she got out of the car and slammed shut the passenger door. She was too close to losing it to continue this conversation. Besides, what was left to say?

She couldn't stand for him to try to convince her they could continue until he finally left Rambling Rose. Her daughters already had a special connection with him. A few more months would only make it harder when he left for good. Not to mention what it would do to Becky.

A clean break now was the right decision even though her heart screamed in protest.

He got out of the car as she walked around the front.

"Things don't have to end this way," he said, moving to stand in front of her.

She forced herself to look up at him. "Things don't have to end at all, but you're too afraid of being hurt to commit to anything." She drew in a ragged breath. "You're too much of coward to even try."

He seemed to freeze at her words, and she elbowed her way past him and into the car. With shaking fingers, she gripped the steering wheel with one hand and the gearshift in the other. She put the car into Drive and roared out of the parking lot, leaving a cloud of dust and Callum Fortune behind.

Chapter Fifteen

Callum threw himself into work for the next several days, refusing to discuss Becky or their breakup with Stephanie or either of his brothers.

He told himself the situation was his personal business, but in truth he didn't want or need his siblings to point out how he'd behaved like an idiot. Not when he was handling that so effectively on his own.

How could he have been so happy and then ruin it on purpose? He barely understood why he'd made the choice to tell her he planned to leave Rambling Rose.

Up until that instant, he hadn't decided anything for certain. Hell, he hadn't actually scheduled a visit to potential investment properties near San Antonio, although he needed to come up with a plan for where his company could do the most good.

Too bad that the thought of leaving held no appeal.

He'd dropped that little bomb in the aftermath of those three tiny words she'd shared with him. Any man would be lucky to be loved by a woman like Becky. Callum knew that without a doubt.

Unfortunately, he also believed that eventually—whether he meant to or not—he'd hurt her. His short-lived marriage had taught him that he simply didn't have the capacity for love a man needed to keep a woman happy. He was a man who needed independence. He'd already given everything he could and had nothing left.

Becky might want to believe he was worthy of her, but Callum knew better. He rolled his shoulders as he stared at his computer monitor, trying to shrug off some of the tension that had rooted there like one of the ranch's decades-old oak trees.

Whenever he wasn't on-site, he was, like today, at his desk in the Fortune Brothers Construction office near The Shoppes. There were so many aspects of the business to manage, especially now that the triplets had jumped headfirst into designing the restaurant. Ashley, Megan and Nicole were planning to visit Rambling Rose at the end of the month, and Callum wanted to make their trip a productive one. The breadth of projects they'd taken on in this town were the most expansive of his career.

He'd also never felt so connected to a place as he did to this small town. His father had worried about them moving to Texas and the possible influence of the extended Fortune family. The kidnapping that had occurred at last year's wedding of Callum's uncle Gerald had shaken David, making him wary of deepening his branch's ties to the rest of the Fortunes. Callum hadn't given it much thought. Before now, the locations he'd chosen for his projects had been based solely on the historic value and financial prospects.

Rambling Rose was proving to be different, and not just because of Becky. Maybe it was the history the Fortune family played in the town. It still gave Callum goose bumps to think about the pediatric center, their first major project, being built on the site of the Fortune's Foundling Hospital. Linus also had a link to that piece of history, given that his mother had purposely left him at the site of the former Fortune orphanage.

If he didn't know better, he'd swear he could feel the spirit of this community trickling into him, changing who he was at a cellular level. It was a ridiculous thought, of course, brought on by the lack of sleep and missing Becky.

A million times since that drive home from Austin, he'd wanted to call her. He hated how they'd left things, what she must think of him. He hated that he couldn't be the man she wanted.

"Is this an okay time for a break?"

A smile broke over his face as his stepmom walked into the office. For the first time since Becky drove away in her red Corvette, he took a full breath. Marci wore beige slacks and a cashmere sweater, not a hair out of place as she grinned at him.

"This is the best surprise I could imagine," he told her, standing and walking around the desk to wrap her in a tight hug.

Marci smelled like lilacs and vanilla, two scents he'd always associate with home. "Stephanie said she didn't need help," his stepmom explained, placing a quick kiss on his cheek. "But that baby is such a cute little guy. I couldn't resist an opportunity to love on him."

"We're all so proud of her. Everyone is still holding out hope that Linus's mother returns, but there's no better place for him than with Stephanie."

Marci's smile turned wistful. "You were such troupers when the triplets were born. I know you took on the lion's share of the responsibility for them when I needed help."

"It wasn't a big deal." He didn't like discussing that time with anyone in his family because the lingering resentment he harbored made him feel like a jerk. He loved the triplets and the rest of his family. It had been his choice to step up when Marci needed help. No one had forced him. He'd simply done what he had to for his family.

"All that responsibility took a toll on you," she said softly.

There was no point bothering to deny it. Not with his perceptive stepmom. "Would you like to see some of the projects we're working on?" he asked instead. "We can start right here at The Shoppes."

She studied him for a moment, clearly understanding a distraction when one was shoved at her. "I'd love that."

Callum breathed a sigh of relief as he led her from the office. "Have you seen Steven and Dillon?"

"Not yet. I flew into Houston last night and drove over to Rambling Rose this morning. I called Stephanie on my way into town and met her at the pediatric center so that I could visit Linus at day care. Then I came here."

"Steven had a meeting about the hotel, but then he was due back here so we could go over some paint samples with the designer. Dillon is probably at the spa or the vet clinic."

"It feels like you're so busy," Marci said, and he heard the pride in her voice. "I can't believe how much you've taken on in such a short time."

"I like to be busy." Callum laughed softly. "But we both know Fortune Brothers Construction wouldn't be half as successful without Steven and Dillon in the mix. The three of us together bring the magic."

"You've always had a soft spot for your brothers and sisters." Marci reached across the console and patted his arm. "I can't help but worry about what that's cost you."

They walked from the modular office toward the entrance of The Shoppes at Rambling Rose. The building had housed an old five-and-dime, but they'd taken it nearly down to the studs to rebuild it into an upscale set of shops that ultimately would include fashion, jewelry and a designer home accessory store. Their neighbors in Rambling Rose Estates seemed especially excited about this upcoming addition to the community, although Dillon still worried locals weren't totally on board with the plan.

He didn't give much credence to that. Every one of his projects had received a bit of pushback in the initial stages. He believed beyond a doubt they were improving this town for everyone, and Callum hoped that as the longtime residents began to patronize the new businesses they'd realize the changes benefited everyone.

"I have a great life that's even better because of how close we all are. Although it's going to be interesting when the triplets arrive. I'm not sure Rambling Rose has ever seen anything like the three of them on a mission."

"If anyone can help ease the transition for the girls, it's you." Marci stopped and shook her head. "I'm sorry,

Callum. That's the problem. We all assume you'll help with whatever someone in the family needs."

"I will," he answered without hesitation.

"But you shouldn't have to," she told him gently. "It's past time we allow you to put your life first. The family you create for yourself with your own—"

"No." He held up a hand. "I tried going down that path and failed. I'm not going to have a family of my own. My independence means too much to me."

"You and Doralee weren't a good match. That doesn't mean you have to give up on love completely. What about that nurse and her adorable twins from the ribbon-cutting ceremony? Stephanie told me you've been spending a lot of time with her."

"Stephanie shares too much," he said and started walking toward the building again. He waved to a few guys on the crew as Marci caught up to him.

"Don't get snippy. Your sister wouldn't have to keep me apprised of what's going on in your life if you'd tell me yourself."

"Becky and I are over," he said simply. "She doesn't want to waste time on a guy who's a bad bet for the future."

"You are not a bad bet," his stepmom insisted, sounding affronted that he'd dare utter those words.

"I love you," he said, giving her shoulder a quick squeeze. "But I'm not ready to talk about it."

"I'm here when you are," she answered.

Steven caught sight of them at that moment and strode over with a wide grin, catching Marci in a big bear hug.

The pain in Callum's chest eased slightly as he spent the rest of the workday with his brothers and stepmom.

After a quick tour of the progress on The Shoppes, they caught up with Dillon at the planned spa location. Like the devoted mother she was, Marci oohed and aahed at all the improvements they were making in town.

They took her to lunch at the Mexican restaurant where he'd eaten with Becky and the girls, and then they headed toward the old feed and grain building that would be the triplets' restaurant.

"The three of them have been able to talk about little else since you put the wheels in motion on this project," Marci confided as she spun in a slow circle to take in the space. "It's really exciting."

"We're staging a Texas takeover," Dillon said with a laugh.

Marci arched a brow. "You're a few decades behind the curve on that. Fortunes have been making their mark in Texas forever, it seems."

"But this place is ours," Steven clarified. "I know the Fortunes have longstanding ties here as well, and maybe that's why Rambling Rose feels like home."

Callum's chest ached at his brother's words. A significant part of why the town felt like home to him was Becky. Even though not speaking to her over the past few days had been horrible, he could still feel their connection. She might hate him at the moment, but just knowing she was nearby gave him some comfort.

Of course, it also motivated him to ensure the current slate of projects stayed on schedule so there'd be nothing to prevent him from moving on. Surely some other man would swoop in and capture Becky's heart. Though it might actually kill Callum to see her with someone else.

"You look so sad," Marci told him quietly as Dillon

and Steve launched into a discussion about how many treatment rooms they'd need.

"I wish Dad wanted to spend more time in Texas," he told his stepmom when her perceptive gaze landed on him. Let Marci think his inner turmoil centered on that and not Becky.

"He worries about all of you and wants you to be safe."

"We are."

"I know." She offered a gentle smile. "He'll come around. He was so proud of you at the opening of the pediatric center, and he's excited to see the vet clinic, especially since Stephanie will be working there." Marci checked her watch. "Which reminds me, she's picking up Linus in a few minutes and I promised I'd be at the ranch when they arrived."

"We can head back to the office to get your car."

They said goodbye to Dillon and Steven, both of whom would be joining them for a big family dinner at the house later. If Becky hadn't ended things, she and her girls would have been invited, too. He knew Marci would have been thrilled to have three babies to love on.

He didn't mention it, but he missed Becky more than he could say. How many times would he have to remind himself the breakup was for the best before he believed it?

Becky drove out to the ranch the following afternoon, her stomach fluttering with nerves.

To her surprise, the surly young man who'd given her so much trouble when she'd approached the gate the last time waved her through with a smile on this occasion.

She should feel vindicated, but it had been difficult

to muster any kind of happiness ever since she'd said goodbye to Callum.

Stephanie had texted and asked her to visit baby Linus. Callum's sister hadn't directly referenced the breakup, but she'd made a point in the text of telling Becky that Callum wouldn't be home.

Maybe Becky should have said no. Cutting off ties with anyone named Fortune was probably best. But she wanted to see the baby and considered Stephanie a friend. She hadn't just lost a boyfriend when she ended things with Callum. The Fortunes had made her feel so welcome, and she'd soaked up their generosity and friendship like she was a sponge left out in the rain.

"Cawl," Luna shouted as they pulled up to the house. How had she remembered?

Sasha popped the binky out of her mouth. "Cawl."

Blinking away tears, Becky unbuckled her seat belt and turned to face her daughters. "Callum's not here right now, but we're going to see baby Linus and Miss Stephanie."

"Gog," Sasha whispered.

"Yes." Becky smiled at her sweet girl. "I'm sure we'll get to see the animals, too."

She got the girls out of the minivan and carried them toward the front door. Before she could knock, it opened to reveal Marci Fortune, Callum's elegant stepmother.

"Hi," Becky breathed, her hold on the twins tightening.

"Hello, Becky." Marci gave her a disarmingly friendly smile. "It's nice to see you again. Please come in. May I hold one of your sweet girls?"

"Sure."

As soon as Marci held out her hands, Luna reached

for her. Sasha rested her head on Becky's shoulder, watching her sister as she sucked on her beloved binky.

"Stephanie didn't mention you were visiting," Becky said, then blushed at the thought that Marci must know about her breakup with Callum. He'd told her that Marci was protective of her children, even as adults, and wondered what the older woman thought.

Probably that Becky was the biggest idiot alive to reject her handsome, wealthy, charming stepson.

"My daughter appreciates all the help you've given her with the baby," Marci said as she led Becky through the house toward the wing that Stephanie occupied. "She tells me you've been invaluable sharing your expertise and offering support."

"It's a wonderful thing she's doing with Linus," Becky answered honestly. "Obviously she had a great role model because her maternal instincts are spot-on." She cleared her throat, then added, "I'm still holding out hope that Laurel returns to claim her baby. We talked a bit that first day she came to the pediatric center. Who knows how much she remembers of the things she told me, but it was clear she had a lot of love to give. I don't know what happened to push her to the point of relinquishing Linus."

"Becoming a mother isn't always as easy as people want you to believe," Marci said with a sigh. "I struggled with my health, both physical and mental, after the triplets. Even before when we were trying for more children." Her eyes gleamed with unshed tears. "I'm sure Callum shared with you how much responsibility he took on during that time."

"I know he loves you and his sisters very much."

"That's kind of you to say, but it took a toll on him. I

didn't realize how large of one until recently. He cares about you, Becky. You and your girls." She bounced Luna gently in her arms.

Becky nodded. "But he's planning to leave Rambling Rose. My life is here, and I can't have someone become close to the girls who isn't going to be a part of their lives long-term. It's not fair to them."

"I understand." Marci reached out to stroke a finger across Sasha's cheek. "They're precious. My hope would be that he changes his mind and you give him another chance."

Becky closed her eyes as she considered that possibility. Would she give him another chance? She almost laughed at the absurdity of the question. Callum could have a thousand chances if that's what it took.

"Mom." Stephanie appeared in the doorway, the baby wrapped in a blue blanket and cradled in her arms. "Stop hogging Becky. I want her to see Linus before he falls asleep again."

"I think he's gotten bigger already," Becky exclaimed as she walked to her friend, and Stephanie beamed in response. "Hey, buddy."

Her girls babbled at little Linus and they all headed for the sitting room Stephanie had set up with a play mat, bounce seat and motorized swing.

They visited while her girls played with the baby's toys, largely entertained by Marci. Stephanie had a list of questions about the infant's care and specific milestones that Becky was happy to answer.

Neither Stephanie nor her mom brought up Callum again, which was both a relief and a disappointment. She wasn't sure she could handle talking about him, but wanted so badly to ask how he was doing.

Was he as miserable as she?

After almost an hour of wakefulness, Linus fell asleep in Stephanie's arms. She transferred him to her mother and walked Becky and the twins to the front door.

"Thanks for coming over," she said. "I hope it wasn't too weird with how things stand between you and Callum."

"Actually, it wasn't," Becky said, surprised to find the statement to be true. She buckled Sasha and Luna into their car seats and then turned to Stephanie. "Even though things ended with your brother, I hope we can still be friends."

"Me, too," Stephanie said. "You might be the first real friend I've made in Rambling Rose. At least the only one who doesn't think I'm crazy for becoming a foster parent."

"They must not realize how big of a heart you have."

Stephanie leaned forward and gave Becky a hug. "Thank you," she whispered, then added, "I'm sorry my brother's a big dummy."

A laugh popped out of Becky's mouth. "He's a good man," she corrected. "He just needs to realize it."

After another squeeze, Stephanie released her and Becky climbed into the minivan and headed home. The sun had started to set across the western sky, leaving trails of pink and orange in its wake. A glance in the rearview mirror showed that her girls were staring out at the beauty of the sky, and their wide-eyed wonder made Becky smile.

She didn't know if it was possible that she and Callum might get another chance, but the conversation with his sister had given her a bit of hope.

Hope that turned to dust in her throat as she approached the entrance gatehouse. A large silver truck, which she immediately recognized as Callum's, pulled through the gate.

Becky's heart hammered in her chest as their gazes met. Then she realized he wasn't alone. In the passenger seat sat a beautiful blonde. It was difficult to get a good look at the woman as she drove past, but Becky could tell she was young and strikingly gorgeous.

Swallowing hard, she turned her attention back to the road and tried not to cry. The moment was over in seconds, but the meaning of it lashed her like the sting of a whip.

Callum had moved on. His sister and stepmom might claim he still cared about Becky, but how much could she have meant to him if he was already on a date and bringing the woman home?

Becky hadn't realized it was possible for her heart to break any more until it splintered into a million pieces.

Chapter Sixteen

"I thought you were going to try to get home early last night."

"Good morning to you, too," Callum told his step-mom as she walked into the kitchen early the next morning. He'd expected to be gone by the time anyone else in the family woke, but should have known Marci wouldn't let him off the hook so easily.

"Good morning," she said with a smile. She joined him at the counter. He handed her a mug from the cabinet and then watched as she filled it with the coffee he'd just brewed. "Did I misunderstand the plan?"

Frustration wove its way through his veins like a needle and thread. He'd planned to return home before Becky left, hoping he'd get a chance to talk to her. He missed her so badly it felt like he'd lost part of his heart without her in his life. "I got sidetracked by a neighbor's daughter. She's home from college for the weekend and her car broke down in town. I helped her get it to the mechanic, then gave her a ride home." He rolled his shoulders. "Becky was just pulling through the main gate when I drove in."

"She's lovely, Callum. Not just her looks, either, although she's quite pretty."

"Beautiful," he countered softly.

Marci inclined her head. "Beautiful. Yes. But I got a sense of her kindness and strength yesterday. Her daughters adore her and she patiently answers every one of Stephanie's questions and seems so interested in Linus's welfare, even after a full day at work. I could tell she's a truly good person."

"Is this supposed to make me feel better?" He pushed out a laugh to soften the question when his tone came out harsher than he'd meant it. "I know I messed up with a one-in-a-million woman. But there's nothing—"

"You can fight for her," his stepmother interrupted.

"I've texted to check in with her every day since she ended things. She never replies."

"Your generation and those infernal devices." Marci sniffed. "You don't win a woman back with a text. Be bold, Callum. Give her a reason to try again."

"I'm afraid I don't have one," he admitted, pressing the heels of his palms to his closed eyes. "I'm not willing to risk my heart. She was right about me."

"What makes you think that?" Marci asked. "Your divorce?"

He dropped his hands to his sides and forced himself to meet his stepmother's concerned gaze. "I failed at marriage once, and it about killed me to hurt Doralee that way."

"She wasn't right for you from the start."

Both he and Marci turned as Stephanie joined them in the kitchen, a sleeping Linus cradled in her arms.

"I'm not sure I can take being double-teamed by the two of you," he told his sister.

Stephanie rolled her eyes. "Be an awesome brother and pour me a cup of coffee. This little guy was up more than normal last night. I'm dragging right now."

"I'll take him," Marci offered, setting down her coffee. "While you talk some sense into your brother." She smiled when Callum narrowed his eyes. "I'm stepping back so you don't feel like we're ganging up on you. But know I agree with everything Stephanie says."

His sister handed the baby to Marci, then faced Callum. "You're an idiot," she said simply.

Callum snorted. "What happened to the family rule of no name-calling in front of Mom?"

"It's not exactly how I would have put it," Marci admitted, "but she has a point."

"You know it, too." Stephanie accepted the cup of coffee he offered, sighing as she took a long drink. "You love Becky Averill and her daughters and you want to make a life with them." She pointed a finger toward him. "In Rambling Rose."

He shook his head. "I don't—"

"This is your home," Stephanie interrupted. "And Becky is your person. Stop trying to deny it."

"She broke up with me," he pointed out, his heart twisting painfully in his chest.

"From what I gather, you left her no choice." She leaned in closer. "I tried to get her to talk bad about you last night. I really did. And she wouldn't do it. She loves you and if you'd just get out of your own way, you could have the life we all know you want."

Marci joined her daughter. "I told you I'd agree with everything she said. We all know how much you sacrificed for this family and how the divorce made you question things. But you're a family man at heart, Callum. You always have been."

He opened his mouth to argue, then paused and drew in a deep breath instead. He'd spent a lot of years convincing himself he didn't want the responsibility of that kind of commitment.

Now he couldn't imagine his life without Becky and the girls in it. He hadn't expected his life to take this turn, but his sister was right, as usual. He'd be an idiot not to risk his heart when he had this chance at real happiness. And yet…

"I can't compete with her late husband," he said quietly, finally voicing his greatest fear when it came to Becky. "From all accounts, he was damn near a saint. The perfect husband who would have been a perfect father."

"Callum." Stephanie squeezed his arm. "I promise you that Becky isn't looking for perfect. Her girls don't need that, either. They just need someone to love them."

"I do," he whispered. "I will if she'll let me." Allowing himself to acknowledge that undeniable fact lifted the weight that had been crushing his chest.

His stepmom and sister shared a smile. "Then don't you think it's time you shared that with Becky?"

He gave them each a quick hug, dropped a kiss on the top of baby Linus's downy head and quickly headed for his truck.

Becky would be at work by now, so he drove straight

to the pediatric center, trying to work out a plan in his mind for how to win her back.

The best he could think of past his racing heart and sweaty palms was throwing himself to his knees and begging her for another chance.

Surely something better would present itself in the moment, but either way Callum wasn't going to let anything stop him.

He rushed through the lobby and down the hall that housed the primary care wing.

Becky's friend Sharla sat at the nurses' station, giving him a look that could freeze the sun as he approached.

"I need to speak with Becky," he said, forcing a calm tone.

"She's not here."

He glanced around as if he could will her to appear. "When will she be back?"

"Dunno."

Okay, this wasn't going the way he'd planned, but if his bid for another chance with Becky needed to include groveling to her coworker, he'd do that.

"I've been an idiot," he told the surly medical assistant. He figured if his sister had been willing to tell him that out loud, most people in Becky's life must agree.

"Go on," Sharla said slowly, proving him right.

"She's the best thing that ever happened to me, and I'm sorry I hurt her."

"You hurt her badly."

He sucked in a breath. "I want to make it up to her and the twins. I can't lose them. They're my world."

The woman studied him for several long moments

before nodding. "I actually believe you… But she still isn't here."

He sighed. Damn. "When will she be back?"

"Two days." Sharla tapped a finger against her chin. "Maybe three. If she doesn't decide—"

"Decide what?" Callum's mind reeled. "Where did she go? She left Rambling Rose? That's impossible. This is her home."

"Slow down, cowboy." Sharla stood and placed her palms on the desk. "I believe you love our Becky, but that doesn't mean I'm convinced you're what's best for her. Especially after she saw you bringing home another woman."

Callum felt his mouth go slack. "What woma—" He muttered a curse. "Last night when I passed her at the gatehouse? I wasn't on a date or bringing anyone home. I'd wanted to get to the ranch before Becky left, but I had to give my neighbor's daughter a lift home when her car broke down in town."

Sharla's pink-glossed lips formed a small O.

"Please don't tell me Becky left town thinking I was already dating someone else."

"I won't tell you." Sharla made a face. "Which doesn't make it any less of a fact."

"I have to talk to her."

A patient came out of one of the exam rooms with Parker, who lifted a questioning brow in Callum's direction.

"I might have fibbed about her return date," Sharla said quickly. "I need to get back to work, but she went to see her parents in Houston. She's planning on coming home tomorrow night. Talk to her then and you better make it good. Becky deserves the best you've got, Mr. Fortune."

"She deserves the best of everything," he agreed. He just hoped he could convince her a second chance was best for both of them.

Becky blinked away tears as she watched her mother place a kiss on Sasha's chubby cheek. The quieter twin sat in her mom's lap while Luna grinned and banged a wooden spoon on the colorful xylophone that had been Becky's as a child.

"I can't believe you saved all these toys," she told her mom.

Ann Averill shrugged. "They were your favorites, so I figured if you had kids one day they'd like them, too."

"The girls are in heaven."

It wasn't just the twins, either. A sense of peace had descended over Becky as she'd relaxed in her childhood home. Despite how they'd acted toward her in the past, she wished she hadn't waited so long to reach out.

A twinge of sorrow pinched her chest as memories of the weeks after Rick's death filled her mind. She'd been overwhelmed by grief, which had quickly morphed into anger when her parents tried to convince her to move home to Houston.

She'd felt their lack of confidence that she could make it on her own in Rambling Rose like a slap in the face. Her pain had made her even more determined to manage life on her own without asking for help. They'd never been a particularly close family, and the rift had seemed to widen on its own until it had been easier not to speak to them at all than to listen to her mother's subtle digs or her father's outright condemnation.

Spending time with the Fortunes had reminded her of the importance of family. Her relationship with her parents might not be perfect, but she wanted her daughters to know their grandma and grandpa.

"They look like your grandmother," her mom said, her gaze wistful as she snuggled Sasha and smiled at Luna. "I thought the same about you when you were a baby."

Becky nodded. "And they have Rick's smile," she whispered.

"You're a good mom, Beck." Becky glanced up to where her father stood in the doorway, a spatula in hand. Her dad grilled all year round and had started prepping the steaks almost as soon as Becky and the twins had arrived that morning.

Tom Averill was a gruff man, quiet and solid, and he'd always communicated his affection through action rather than words. Some of the best memories Becky had from her childhood were of her father flipping pancakes while Becky watched Saturday morning cartoons at the kitchen counter.

"Thanks, Dad." Becky managed the words without crying, which she knew would embarrass her stoic father.

He gave a curt nod and disappeared again.

"He's proud of you," her mother said. "We both are."

"Really?" Becky laughed. "I had the impression you thought I was in over my head."

"Perhaps at the time of Rick's death," her mother admitted. "We were so worried about you recovering from that kind of tragedy. Then when you found out you were carrying twins…" Ann shook her head. "I didn't believe in you as much as I should. You're much stronger than either your father or I realized."

"You raised me," Becky said softly, "so you can take some of the credit."

Her mother chuckled. "No. You get it all." Her expression sobered. "I still worry about you and wish you'd move home. The girls need—"

"Rambling Rose is our home, Mom." Becky smiled and clapped along with Luna's enthusiastic banging. "We're part of the community." Her breath hitched as she realized how true that statement was. She owed a large debt to Callum for helping her finally muster the courage to come out of her shell. Because of the way she was raised, she'd thought of asking for help as a weakness.

Rick had been equally independent and their relationship had been the two of them against the world. It worked until his death, and then she was lost at sea with not even a paddle to aid her in getting to dry land.

From the first moment Callum had volunteered to watch the twins while she helped Laurel, he'd made it easy to lean on him. She'd gotten close to the people at work in a way she hadn't before and begun to expand her circle of friends, enriching both her life and the twins'.

Would she have been willing to make that happen without Callum's innate support? Hard to say, but Becky would remain forever grateful to him.

Her feelings about Callum must have shown on her face because her mother's expression became suddenly assessing.

"Have you met someone new?" Ann asked as she smoothed a hand over Sasha's back.

"I went on a few dates with a guy, but it didn't work out."

"Why?"

"We wanted different things, I guess." Becky picked an invisible piece of lint from her pant leg. "He's not sure if he's going to stay in Rambling Rose long-term, and my life is there."

"Is it?" Her mother sounded more curious than judgmental. "You're a nurse, Beck. You can have a career anywhere. The girls are so young that a move wouldn't really impact them. There's something about how you look right now that makes me think this man was special to you."

Becky drew in a sharp breath, and her mother sighed. "We might not have the closest relationship," Ann said, "but I'm still your mom. I know you, sweetheart."

"I can't leave my home," Becky said, her voice cracking on the last word. She cleared her throat. "Rick and I chose Rambling Rose. Even if I wanted to relocate, I don't know how I could. It would feel like I was being disloyal to his memory. Like I was moving on."

"No," her mother answered immediately. "That isn't true."

Sasha climbed off her grandma's lap, as if sensing Becky's distress, and toddled toward her, Luna quickly following suit.

Becky opened her arms and cradled her twins. "People tell me that," she said to Ann. "They tell me it's okay to move on. But I don't want to *move on*. Rick will always be a part of me. He's a part of our beautiful daughters. His death made me who I am today."

"I understand." Her mother nodded. "Which is why I don't believe you have to stay in Rambling Rose. It's fine if you want to. I'm not trying to convince you to leave. But if you meet someone who makes you and the girls happy, that's important. Rick would want you to be happy again. You can honor him by living life to the fullest."

Was she doing the opposite now? Yes, she felt a connection to Rambling Rose. The town was her home. But it didn't compare with how happy she'd been with Callum. She didn't know if he'd even consider the option of Becky and the girls going with him when he left. But she knew his fear of staying in one place wasn't about her. They could make a life together wherever the work took him if that's what he needed. She understood his fear about settling down, but she could show him that the home they both craved wasn't simply a matter of four walls. It was in their connection to each other. Had she given up too easily? Had her doubts and fears about what she had to offer led her to make the biggest mistake of her life?

Callum's heart beat double time as he drove past the park on the edge of town and saw Becky's minivan parked in the gravel lot.

Sharla had texted him that Becky was definitely coming to work the following morning so his plan had been to talk to her after her shift tomorrow night.

He could still do that, he thought, as nerves thrummed through his veins. Chances were she'd gotten back recently and probably wanted some time to decompress after the visit with her parents.

Excuses. He had a million of them.

None could mask the fact that he was afraid Becky wouldn't give him a second chance. That he'd put his heart on the line and have it well and truly broken. His ex-wife hadn't been the only one hurt when their marriage ended. It had taken a while for Callum to admit it, but he still carried the scars from his divorce.

He'd been a less than perfect husband and didn't want to ever fail in that way again. But now he realized if he continued to guard his heart so tightly that there wasn't room for anyone inside it, he might protect himself from pain but he'd also prevent himself from finding true happiness.

The kind he knew he'd have with Becky.

Before he changed his mind, Callum pulled into the parking lot and stopped next to her vehicle, refusing to waste one more minute on doubt and regret. It was close to sundown, but the air was calm and the lingering scent of an earlier rain shower made everything earthy and fresh.

He passed a few people walking dogs or jogging on the path as he walked toward the bench overlooking a small pond where he knew he'd find Becky and the girls.

His hand strayed to the side pocket of his cargo pants and the outline of the black velvet box he'd carried around with him since that morning.

She seemed lost in thought as he approached, her lips moving as if she were talking to her daughters or maybe to her late husband. She'd shared that this was the place she felt closest to Rick, and suddenly Callum felt like an interloper, intruding in a moment where he didn't belong.

Then Luna, who was leaning forward in the double stroller, spotted him.

"Cawl," she cried, then shoved a piece of oat cereal into her mouth and lifted her arms toward him.

Sasha pulled the binky out of her mouth to call out to him as well, and Becky met his gaze with a gasp.

"I hope you don't mind company," he said as he got closer.

"No," she whispered and offered a tentative smile.

The girls bounced and clapped and reached for him, like two little baby birds in the nest. "Is it okay if I pick them up?"

"Of course." Her fingers clasped and released the hem of her faded sweatshirt over and over. Apparently, he wasn't the only one with a case of nerves.

He unbuckled the girls, lifted them into his arms and then sat next to Becky on the bench.

"I heard you went to visit your parents," he said as Sasha snuggled into him and Luna patted his cheek. He'd missed not only Becky this week, but her girls, as well. His heart stammered at the thought of getting another chance to be in their lives, hopefully on a permanent basis.

"Just for a night," she confirmed, then frowned. "How did you hear?"

"I stopped by the pediatric center yesterday."

"Oh."

"To see you."

"I gathered that," she said with a slight smile.

"You haven't returned my texts."

Her gaze softened. "I thought a clean break between us would be easier."

"Right," he muttered. "And now here I am intruding on your evening walk."

"It's okay, Callum. I'm glad to see you."

Hope had never played a huge role in his life, but now he grabbed on to the kernel of it, holding it close to his heart like a lifeline. "Were you visiting with Rick?" he forced himself to ask.

"I know it seems silly, but yes. I wanted to talk to him after being with my parents and this is the spot where I come for that."

"Is anything the matter with your folks?"

She shook her head. "It had been too long since I've seen them. I want the twins to know their family." She reached out a hand and squeezed his arm. "The Fortunes have inspired me, actually. It's great how close all of you are, even when you live halfway across the country from each other."

"Family is a gift." He kissed the top of Sasha's head. "Until they drive you crazy."

"Yeah." She laughed and lifted Luna from his arms. "It was good to see the girls with their grandparents. Hard to tell if we'll be able to put everything in the past behind us, but I'm glad I made the effort. My mom actually had some great advice about my future."

A momentary flicker of panic gripped his gut. "Tell me you aren't moving away from Rambling Rose."

"No plans for that at the moment." She adjusted her hold on Luna. "Although Mom doesn't understand my devotion to this town, and what she said made a lot of sense."

"It's your home," he argued, not wanting Becky to compromise her commitment for anyone. "Rambling Rose is the place you and Rick chose to build a life. Of course you're dedicated to this town."

She studied him for a moment. "Believe it or not," she said, "she wasn't judging me. That's what I'd always thought about my parents. I think they're glad that I'm happy here, but they also want me to know I could make a home anywhere. Rick will always be with me."

"And with your girls. His love is a part of all three of you."

"Exactly." She swiped at her cheek. "You understand."

"I hope *you* understand that I'd never try to take his place." Callum swallowed. Hard. "But I love you, Becky. I should have told you before now, and I'm sorry I hurt you. You were right to call me a coward. You make me want to be brave. I'd do anything for another chance. I promise I won't mess it up again."

"I love you, too," she whispered. "I never want you to think that this town—that anyplace—is more important to me than you."

He lifted a finger to her lips. "It's your home, and it's my home, too. I want to build a life here with you." He hugged Sasha closer. "With the girls. They will never forget their father, but it would be my great honor to raise them and be as much of a dad as I can be."

"Do you mean that?" She sniffed and the tenderness in her gaze made his heart melt all over again. "I know you've had enough of a burden with taking care of little ones and that—"

"It would never be a burden," he corrected. "Being a part of the twins' lives would be the best thing that I could imagine."

He fished in his pocket for the velvet box. "In fact…"

Becky's dark eyes widened.

"I hope you'll excuse me if I don't get down on one knee," he said with a chuckle. "Sasha seems to have fallen asleep on my shoulder and I don't want to disturb her."

"No knee necessary," she whispered.

"Becky Averill." He flipped open the box to reveal the ring he'd chosen at the jeweler's that morning. It was a round diamond set in a platinum band with two smaller stones flanking the one in the center. "Would you be my wife? I promise to never give up on our love and to spend the rest of my life making you happy."

Luna cooed out her approval of the ring as she grabbed at it. Becky held her daughter out of reach, then met Callum's gaze. "Yes," she told him and it felt like a symphony swelled in his chest.

"There's something else." He set the box on the bench and reached in his opposite pocket, taking out a small velvet pouch and handing it to Becky. "I got these for the girls."

She pulled out the two gold bracelets he'd also chosen at the jewelers. "I love you, Becky," he repeated. "And I love your daughters. This is my way of telling you that my heart belongs to all three of you." He shook his head. "You're crying. Don't cry."

"They're happy tears," she promised, her voice catching on the last word. "But you better put that ring onto my finger now. I'm not sure I can wait any longer."

"Then let's not wait," he said, plucking the ring from the box and slipping it onto her left hand. "I want us to be a family."

She leaned in and brushed a kiss across his lips. "Don't you know we already are?"

For the first time in forever, Callum felt truly at home. He knew in his heart that the joy of this moment would last forever.

Epilogue

"I like seeing you smile."

Becky turned toward Callum as he parked the truck in front of the Paws and Claws Animal Clinic, so much happiness filling her heart she could almost feel it beating against her rib cage. It was another Texas blue-sky day, the brightness of the sunshine reflecting the glow in her heart.

"You make me smile, Mr. Fortune," she told him.

"For the rest of our lives, Mrs. Fortune," he answered.

She glanced down at her left hand and the eternity band that had joined the engagement ring on her finger.

It had been a little less than a week since Callum proposed, and they'd driven to the county courthouse with the twins earlier that morning to exchange their wedding vows.

Some people might question a whirlwind courtship and wedding, but Becky didn't worry any longer about raising eyebrows. The moment Callum had sat down on the park bench with her, any doubts and fears she'd had fled like night shadows chased away by the light of dawn.

She'd felt her late husband's spirit surrounding them, a quiet whisper of approval that she could move forward and truly love again.

They were a family and had both wanted to make it official as soon as possible. With Callum's busy schedule, her dedication to the pediatric center and the continuing saga of baby Linus's future, a simple ceremony felt right.

Callum's stepmom got them to agree to celebrate with a larger reception once their lives calmed down a bit, although Becky wondered if that would ever happen. She didn't care. Becoming Callum's wife, even with no fanfare, fulfilled her in ways she couldn't have imagined.

They'd driven straight to the vet clinic so they could attend the afternoon's grand opening celebration and would begin the process of moving Becky and the girls to the ranch later that night.

As Becky opened the passenger door, Marci and David greeted her. Her new mother-in-law enveloped her in a tight hug, whispering words of congratulations into her ear.

"Welcome to the family," David told her when it was his turn for a hug.

"It makes me so happy to be a Fortune," she said, and the older man kissed both of her cheeks.

"I'm a grandma," Marci murmured as Callum put Luna into her arms.

"Gigi," the girl said with a toothy grin, staring into Marci's eyes.

"That's perfect," the older woman said, blinking back tears. "I'm your Gigi."

"And you can call me Papa." David held out his hands for Sasha, who automatically reached for him. Once again, the Fortune charm had worked its magic on Becky's cautious daughter.

"Papa," Sasha repeated.

"Uh-oh." Callum shut the door and placed an arm around Becky's shoulders, pulling her close. "I have a feeling our girls are going to be spoiled rotten by their Gigi and Papa."

"Nothing rotten about spoiling our granddaughters." Marci looked between Becky and Callum. "You've made us so very happy."

Becky nodded, unable to speak around the emotion clogging her throat. The sense of contentment she felt at being a part of the Fortune family almost overwhelmed her.

Callum squeezed her arm. "Let's go check out the new vet clinic. I'm sure the rest of the family will be champing at the bit to give you a proper welcome."

"It feels like they already have," Becky told him. The triplets had arrived yesterday and they'd had a big family dinner at the ranch. It amazed her how warm and gracious every member of Callum's family seemed to be. They made her feel as if she belonged with them, and she knew that whatever life brought, she could handle it surrounded by that depth of love.

As much as Becky loved Rambling Rose, she'd found

her true home with Callum. Gratitude bubbled up inside her along with an abiding joy. Tragedy had marked her but not defined the whole of who she was.

She linked her arm with her husband's as they headed toward the new building, thrilled to walk toward their future together.

* * * * *

MILLS & BOON

Coming next month

HER TWIN BABY SECRET
Therese Beharrie

He laughed. Gave in to the urge to tuck her hair behind her ear as he'd seen her do earlier.

She exhaled. 'What are you doing, Benjamin?'

He dropped his hand, looked at her face. 'I don't know.'

'You do know.'

'No, I don't.' He smiled. Almost as soon as he did, it vanished. 'Except for right now. Right now, I'm contemplating how to get you to kiss me again. I'd say it's an appropriate response to how incredible you look.' He shook his head. 'I was staring earlier because I didn't have anything to say. You're so beautiful. And this dress is...and your hair, your face...' He shook his head again. Offered her a wry, possibly apologetic smile. 'I'm sorry. I think the last couple days have officially caught up with me.'

Her expression was unreadable, but she said, 'It's been a rough couple of days.'

'Yeah.'

'Because of me.' She paused. 'I'm sorry.'

'You don't have to apologise. You already have, at least.'

'Right.' She leaned back against her door, which he realised only now she hadn't moved away from. 'This hasn't been easy for me either.'

'I know.'

'A large part of it is because you get on my nerves. A lot,' she added when he frowned.

'That seems uncalled for considering I just gave you a bunch of compliments.'

'You want acknowledgement for that?'

'A thank you would nice,' he muttered.

'You're right.'

'Sorry—could you say that again?' He patted his pocket, looking for his phone. 'I want to record it for posterity.'

'This, for example, is extremely annoying. But at the same time, I can't stop thinking about the kiss we had the other day.'

He stilled.

'Which gets on my nerves, too. An interesting conundrum. Am I annoyed because I'm attracted to you? Am I annoyed because you annoy me but I'm still attracted to you?' She exhaled. It sounded frustrated. 'I don't have answers, but I keep asking these questions. Then, of course, you do something decent, like pretend to be my boyfriend even though you have no reason or incentive to. You stand up for me in front of my brother, which I found disturbingly hot. In the same breath, you act stupidly, and tell your mother—your *mother*—that I'm your girlfriend. Which, tonight, we have to rectify.'

She shook her head.

'Honestly, Benjamin, these last few days have been the most frustratingly complicated of my life, and I'm an entrepreneur with a crappy family. And I'm *pregnant,* about to become a single mother. Complicated is the air I breathe. But you make things…' She trailed off with a little laugh. 'And still, I want to kiss you, too.'

Continue reading
HER TWIN BABY SECRET
Therese Beharrie

Available next month
www.millsandboon.co.uk

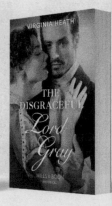